Paul Scott was born in London in 1920 and educated at Winchmore Hill Collegiate School. He served in the army from 1940 to 1946, mainly in India and Malaya. After demobilization he worked for a publishing company for four years before joining a firm of literary agents. In 1960 he resigned his directorship with the agency in order to concentrate on his own writing. He reviewed books for *The Times*, *The Guardian*, the *Daily Telegraph* and *Country Life* and devoted himself to the writing of thirteen distinguished novels including his famous *The Raj Quartet*.

In 1963 Paul Scott was elected a Fellow of the Royal Society of Literature and in 1972 he was the winner of the *Yorkshire Post* Fiction Award for *The Towers of Silence*, the third novel in *The Raj Quartet*. In 1977, *Staying On* won the Booker Prize. He went to the University of Tulsa, Oklahoma, as a visiting Lecturer in 1976.

Several of his novels were adapted for radio and television, in particular *Staying On* and *The Raj Quartet*, which was turned into a highly acclaimed television series under the title *The Jewel in the Crown*.

Paul Scott died in 1978.

By Paul Scott in Pan Books

The Raj Quartet

The Jewel in the Crown
The Day of the Scorpion
The Towers of Silence
A Division of the Spoils

Paul Scott

The Towers of Silence

Pan Books
in association with Heinemann

First published in Great Britain 1971 by
William Heinemann Ltd
This edition published 1988 by Pan Books Ltd,
Cavaye Place, London SW10 9PG
in association with William Heinemann Ltd
9 8 7 6 5 4 3 2 1
© Paul Scott 1971
ISBN 0 330 30996 1
Printed and bound in Great Britain by
Richard Clay Ltd, Bungay, Suffolk

This book is sold subject to the condition that it
shall not, by way of trade or otherwise, be lent, re-sold,
hired out, or otherwise circulated without the publisher's prior
consent in any form of binding or cover other than that in which
it is published and without a similar condition including this
condition being imposed on the subsequent purchaser

To Penny
With All my Love

Contents

PART ONE

The Unknown Indian

1

In September 1939, when the war had just begun, Miss Batchelor retired from her post as superintendent of the Protestant mission schools in the city of Ranpur.

Her elevation to superintendent had come towards the end of her career in the early part of 1938. At the time she knew it was a sop but tackled the job with her characteristic application to every trivial detail, which meant that her successor, a Miss Jolley, would have her work cut out untangling some of the confusion Miss Batchelor usually managed to leave behind, like clues to the direction taken by the cheery and indefatigable leader of a paper chase whose ultimate destination was not clear to anybody, including herself.

Miss Batchelor, christened Barbara (Barbie for short), knew she had many shortcomings, most of which were due to two besetting sins. She seldom stopped talking and was inclined to act without thinking. She had often prayed to be blessed with a more cautious and tranquil nature but had always done so by falling enthusiastically on her knees and speaking to God aloud, which may have accounted for the fact that these prayers were never answered. Her attempts to reform without intercession were also unsuccessful. When she held her tongue people asked rather anxiously about her health – not without cause because the stress of keeping quiet gave her headaches; and the headaches were not helped by the worry of work piling up if she put any of it off to think about it first. So in the end she was content to bear the burden of her own nature in the belief that God had known best what was right for her. Secretly she was rather proud of her voice. It carried.

Barbie was a believer in the good will and good sense of

established authority. If the mission had told her that her furrow was not ploughed, that she was good for a few years yet, she would have squared her shoulders, spat on her palms and pressed, on, grateful to be made use of. But the mission said no such thing and she outwardly accepted the situation with her usual bustling equanimity. Inwardly she accepted it with mingled relief and apprehension.

'I shall be glad to slow down,' she said. People smiled. They could not imagine Barbie except at top speed. In putting her out to grass the mission, which always looked after its own, would have provided her with temporary accommodation in Ranpur and helped to establish her eventually in Darjeeling or Naini Tal where they had twilight bungalows. They would have given her an assisted passage home, but the war made that difficult and in any case Barbie said she didn't want it. She had not been in England for thirty years.

It seemed that Barbie wanted nothing except her pension and her freedom to go where and do what she liked. She let it be known that she had plans. She said she did not intend to be idle in retirement. She would find a pied-à-terre and devote herself to some kind of voluntary work. She had saved. She was perfectly content, perfectly happy. She would always be available should the mission need her help or advice. They had only to ask and she would come, at the double.

The facts were that she had no plans and no clear idea where to go or what to do. She would have liked to be of use to someone or something but could not visualize whom or what. On the whole it did not matter much so long as being useful left her with a certain amount of time to devote to a personal problem.

Barbie had what her mother would have called a secret sorrow. She had been a fairly competent teacher, especially of small children, because they brought out her maternal instincts, and she had often been rewarded by proofs of her capacity to earn affection and esteem from pupils and their parents. But to Barbie the teaching of reading, writing and arithmetic had never been as important as the teaching of Christianity.

For almost as long as she could remember she had believed in God, in Christ the Redeemer and in the existence of Heaven. They were very real to her. The fate of unbelievers was equally real, particularly the fate of those who were unbelievers through no fault of their own. This was why when both her parents were dead she had given up her job at a Church school in South London, joined the mission and come to India.

To bring even one Hindu or Muslim child to God struck her as a very satisfactory thing to do and she imagined that in the mission it would be open to her to do this for scores, possibly hundreds. Once in India she was disappointed to find that all the emphasis was upon the mission's educational function, that the mission gates were ajar to let Indian children in to learn things that would be useful to them but not wide open in a way that encouraged teachers to go out and bring the children in, as into a fold.

Initially disturbed by this secular attitude and by the discipline imposed inside the mission to discourage its members from excessive displays of zeal, she soon accepted them as sensible measures taken by those who knew best and who were anxious to preserve and hold what had been won rather than risk losing it all in trying too hard to gain more. She discovered that the missions were not popular with the civil administration or with the military authorities and had not been since the mutiny of 1857, which people said started because the Indian sepoys believed they were to be forcibly converted, having first been polluted by the introduction of cartridges greased with pig fat. Moreover, the authorities, both civil and military, seemed to take considerable trouble to enable Hindus to go on being Hindus and Muslims to be Muslims by giving them every opportunity to practise their rites and hold their festivals and by giving official recognition to the communal differences between them.

'Well, one step at a time,' Barbie told herself and settled to the business of teaching Eurasian children

11

whose parents were Christians already, the children of converts and the children of Hindu and Muslim parents who were anxious for their sons, and occasionally daughters, to get a good grounding in the English they had to know if they wanted to get on, but very few of whom would ever be baptized.

Over the years she became inured to this system. The Bishop Barnard schools, named after one of the founders of the mission to which she belonged, had expanded considerably between the wars and in the principal cities become distinguished and proud of an academic reputation that attracted Indian girls and boys whose parents were advanced enough to want to educate them to the standard required for entrance to government colleges and Indian universities. As reputation and supply of pupils increased so did the demand for teachers with the right kind of qualifications. Year by year the religious basis of instruction was chipped away and women like Barbie kept in junior posts or elevated to administrative positions in which neither their missionary ambitions (what was left of them) nor their lack of academic stature could do much harm. With the appointment of Barbie's successor, Miss Jolley, even that preserve of the old guard was infiltrated. Miss Jolley was young, she had letters after her name and her file disclosed her religion as nonconformist, not C of E which in Barbie's day had been a primary requirement.

But it was not in all this that Barbie's secret sorrow lay. It lay in the fact that in recent years she had felt her faith loosening its grip. She believed in God as firmly as ever but she no longer felt that He believed in her or listened to her. She felt cut off from Him as she would if she had spent her life doing something of which He disapproved. This puzzled her because she didn't think He could disapprove. He could be better pleased, but that was another matter entirely and one for which neither she nor the mission was exclusively responsible. One did what one could and it should not be necessary to be a saint or a martyr to feel His presence. She no longer felt it. She

12

could not help blaming the mission just a bit for this and she thought there might be a chance of regaining the joyful sense of contact now that she was retiring. She would not hurt anyone by explaining this but her cheerful expression was not entirely due to her habit of keeping one; although that came into it too because she secretly feared a lonely old age.

The address in the advertisement for a single woman to share accommodation with another, which appeared in the *Ranpur Gazette* a week or two before Barbie's retirement, sounded attractive: Mrs Mabel Layton, Rose Cottage, Club Road, Pankot.

She had never been to Pankot. It was the hill station where most official Ranpur people spent the hot weather and to which a few of them eventually retired. Since Ranpur was the place in which she chanced to be when her career petered out the idea of retiring to Pankot herself appealed to her. She wrote to Mrs Layton at once, giving an account of herself, mentioning the sum she could afford and suggesting that if she took the short holiday she had been thinking of spending in Darjeeling – seeing old missionary acquaintances – in Pankot instead, they could meet and come to a decision.

She assumed that Mrs Layton was a widow and that the advertisement implied means as small as her own. The name of the house, seeming diminutive, rather bore that out. Barbie had long since lost the immediately tell-tale signs of a poverty-stricken lower-middle-class English background and could stand her own in any company as what, in her earlier life, had been called a gentlewoman, but she had remained a little fearful of women born in superior walks of life, expecially if they had money to support their position.

Mabel Layton's reply was encouragingly simple and friendly.

'Dear Miss Batchelor, I have had a number of answers to my advertisement but I imagine from your own that we could get on well together. Unless you have changed your

13

mind, in which case please write and tell me, I shall do nothing further about the accommodation available until you have had a chance to see it. If you come to Pankot on holiday perhaps you would like to spend it here at Rose Cottage. Smith's Hotel – a tiny branch of the one you will know of in Ranpur – is rather crowded nowadays and a bit expensive. With regard to a permanent arrangement, should we decide to make one, the sum you say you can afford is ten rupees a month higher than I intended asking, and should expect. Rose Cottage is a very old bungalow, one of the oldest in Pankot. Its main attraction is the garden. It is a little inconveniently situated but after your arduous work in the missions I fancy you don't especially wish to be at the hub of things. If you decide to come up just write or telegraph the time of your arrival and I will get my old servant Aziz to meet you and help you with your bags. As you probably know the train leaves Ranpur daily at midnight and reaches Pankot about 8 A.M.'

The kindly tone of this letter offset Barbie's first impression on receiving it. The envelope was lined and the writing paper thick. The address and telephone number were printed; in fact engraved. A smoothing motion of Barbie's fingers confirmed this. She felt alarmed, uncertain that she could live up to such things. But having read the letter she felt only pleasure and gratitude. Out of a number of applicants Mabel Layton had selected her and was actually prepared to keep the vacancy open until she could go to Pankot and see Rose Cottage for herself. This meant, Barbie thought, that although Mabel Layton needed someone to help with expenses the need was not so desperate that she could not afford to wait for the right person. She seemed to be a woman who liked to keep up standards, in important matters such as her choice of friends and in minor ones like the kind of paper used when writing to them.

Barbie sat down to reply.

'Dear Mrs Layton, Thank you for your letter and for your very kind suggestion that I should spend my holiday

14

at Rose Cottage. I accept most gratefully. I hand over officially to my successor here on 30 September. She is very capable and my duties are already negligible. Therefore I can plan to leave without delay. I should be able to come up on the train that reaches Pankot on the morning of 2 October. As soon as I have made the booking I shall write to you again or telegraph. Meanwhile I can begin my packing at once. I hope you will not mind if I bring with me rather more luggage than might be expected of someone coming to Pankot on vacation. Conditions here do not easily permit of other people's stuff lying around for long, so I am anxious to leave behind as little as I can even if it means bringing things with me which I do not actually need for a holiday and should have to bring back with me if we do not come to a permanent arrangement. Fortunately I have always travelled fairly light. A long experience of postings from one station to another has taught . . .'

At this point Barbie realized she had set off on a tack that could well have the effect of boring poor Mrs Layton to tears.

But her luggage was a priority. She had wanted to make this clear. The importance of luggage was often overlooked. Barbie had never overlooked it but since hearing officially from mission headquarters in Calcutta that her retirement 'need not be postponed' her luggage had been perhaps overmuch on her mind. At the end of her career the tide of affairs which had involved her was on the ebb, leaving her revealed. And what was revealed did not amount to a great deal, which meant that every bit counted. There was, to begin with, herself, but apart from herself there was only her luggage and of that there was little enough although rather a lot in comparison: bedroll, camp equipment, clothes, linen, many unread books, papers, photograph albums, letters, mementoes of travel, presents from past pupils, a framed and very special picture, a few ornaments and one piece of furniture. This latter was a writing-table and was the only item that still remained from the stuff she had originally brought out from England. It had legs that folded in and so was portable. Someone once told her that it was late Georgian or early Victorian and had probably belonged to a general for use in writing orders and compaign dispatches under canvas. She was very fond of it, kept it polished and the tooled leather surface stuck down at the corner where it tended to come away. It rather annoyed her to see Miss Jolley using it as if it were mission property and not Barbie's private possession; but so far she had not felt quite up to warning her that when she went the table went with her.

Mrs Layton could not possibly be interested in such things but it was important to Barbie to establish their existence as inseparable from her own and therefore to be taken into account in any plan to welcome her in Pankot. The luggage by itself, with the exception of the table, was merely luggage she knew, but without it she did not seem to have a shadow.

However, commonsense prevailed. She crumpled the letter, began again, determined to put herself into the recipient's place as she had been taught by her earliest mission instructor in the field, and record no more than was necessary to convey the prosaic details of her acceptance of Mabel Layton's invitation and of her intended time of arrival.

This accomplished she sealed the letter and called Thomas Aquinas. Thomas Aquinas was not her personal servant. He went with the superintendent's bungalow. He tip-toed everywhere but banged doors so loudly that sometimes you jumped out of your skin. He also suffered from chronic catarrh and sniffed perpetually. He was called Thomas Aquinas because the Catholics had got him first. She gave him the letter and told him to post it at the Elphinstone Fountain post office and not in the collection box on the Koti Bazaar road which she thought untrustworthy. She did not want the letter delayed. She hoped, as she watched Thomas take it, that she had struck the right note in it.

'Always remember,' she had been told, 'that a letter

16

never smiles. You may smile as you write it but the recipient will see nothing but the words.'

The time was 1914, the man Mr Cleghorn, the place Muzzafirabad. Mr Cleghorn was handing her back the draft of her request to mission headquarters for a special discount on another half-dozen *First Steps in Bible Reading*, a limp-bound book illustrated by line drawings which the children earned marks for colouring – good marks for delicate tints, poorer marks for bold ones. A little Hindu girl once gave Jesus a bright blue complexion because that was the colour of Krishna's face in the picture her parents had at home.

Barbie sighed, got up from the writing-table, opened the almirah and got out a suitcase. At Muzzafirabad she had succeeded a younger, brilliant, indeed heroic woman, and was conscious of her shortcomings even then. Among them was the tendency to make a ruling without first thinking out its consequences. After the Krishna episode she had taken away the blue crayons. And then the children had no way of colouring the sky.

2

When she arrived in Pankot at twelve minutes past 8 A.M. on 2 October, Mrs Layton's old servant Aziz was waiting at the station looking from one alighting European woman and another to the snapshot she had sent with her second letter as insurance against not being recognized immediately and being left until only she and some strange old man occupied the platform and there could be little doubt that each was waiting for the other. She had wished to appear efficient and thoughtful. She had also always had a horror of being stranded. She had just managed to restrain herself from sending two different snapshots by separate posts, realizing in time that these might both irritate Mrs Layton and confuse the servant.

'Perhaps he would like to keep it,' she said when Mrs

17

Layton offered the snapshot back, complimenting her on the foresight which had eased Aziz of some of the burden of his responsibility. 'He was so good with the bags and so helpful about the trunk.'

The trunk, a metal one, was full of relics of her work in the mission schools. It had been her intention to leave it and the writing-table in Ranpur and to send for them later, if she were staying in Pankot. Thomas Aquinas had misunderstood and had the trunk loaded on to the van which preceded Barbie to the station. When she got there the van had gone and trunk, suitcases and cardboard boxes were already crammed into the coupé which Thomas Aquinas stood guard over. She was less worried about arriving in Pankot with the trunk than about leaving the writing-table behind now unaccompanied. There and then she wrote a note to Miss Jolley telling her what had happened and confirming that she would send for the writing-table at the first opportunity. She gave the note to Thomas, with a further five rupees to add to the fifty she had already given him as parting baksheesh.

Mrs Layton's servant, Aziz, had two tongas waiting in the concourse of Pankot station. Seeing the trunk he declared it too heavy for a tonga, took charge of it and left it in the ticket office for delivery by some mysterious agency he assured her he could command. He loaded one tonga with Barbie and her small hand baggage and the other with her suitcase, bedroll, cardboard boxes of odds and ends, and himself. He sat in the passenger seat gripping on to this paraphernalia and indicated that his tonga would lead the way.

On the old two-wheeled horse tongas you rode with your back to horse and driver and watched the ground unravel beneath the footboard, back towards the place you had come from. Driving like this from the station, Barbie had an impression mainly of the rock face which brought the railway to a halt, then of a narrow metalled road with broad strips of kuttcha on either side, steep banks of rocky earth and overhanging trees. The road curved uphill, this way, that way. There was nothing much to see but after the plains the air at this altitude struck her as sweet and welcoming. In a while she felt the strain put on the horse and tonga slacken, as if a crest had been reached. The tonga stopped. Twisting round to discover the reason she found the other tonga also halted and Aziz getting down.

'Memsahib,' he called, rather fiercely. 'Pankot.'

He spread one arm towards the panorama revealed on this side of the miniature mountain pass. She got down to see it better and stood for quite a minute before saying aloud, 'Praise God!'

Down in Ranpur after the rains, in places where there were grass and trees, the green nature of these things re-asserted itself. Through so much of the year they showed dusty, parched and brown. But in the plains, after the wet, there was never any green like this. Here, all looked like rich and private pasture. Flocks of blackfaced sheep and long-haired goats, herded by sturdy skull-capped peasants, tinkled down a slope, making for the road down which the tongas would also go: a long straight road that led directly into the valley formed by three hills – on the crest of one of which Barbie was standing. The valley itself was under a thin blanket of morning mist. At its centre was a township: the bazaar, a triangular pattern of wooden buildings whose upper storeys, decorated in Indian hill-style with verandahs and ornamental roofs, were clearly visible above the vapour. Beyond the bazaar one hill rose to the left and another much more steeply to the right. She could tell it was to the right that the British had chosen to build. She could see the roofs of many bungalows and buildings, a golf-course and the spire of a church. On this side of the town she could make out the random pattern of army installations.

The crests of the hills were forested. Apart from the receding clunk of the sheep and goat bells there was a holy silence.

'Rose Cottage *kiddher hai*?' she asked Aziz.

Again making the gesture with his fully extended right

19

arm he answered in English, 'There. On the other side of the big hill.'

She looked in that direction and saw how beyond the hill more distant ranges marched towards a mountainous horizon. Was that snow or sunlight on the farthest peak? She sighed, content to have seen such a vision of beauty even if it was not to be her luck to live out her days in constant sight of it.

Looking away from the panorama he had presented, as if it were in his gift, she found him watching her. She nodded her thanks and made her way back to the tonga with a forthright manly stride.

It was on the long haul up the hill from the bazaar, going past the golf-course and the club, that she felt quite suddenly that she had passed Aziz's test. 'Memsahib, Pankot,' he had said. Like a command. And she had looked and said, Praise God. Even if Aziz hadn't heard, or had heard and hadn't understood, the praise on her face must have been unmistakable.

The snapshot she told Mrs Layton Aziz might like to keep (and which she discovered later he had put in a little silver frame) probably still exists, may even be on display along with other items of iconography on the rough walls of a hut in the Pankot hills, in the distant mountain village Aziz came from. If so one wonders what his descendants make of it, if with the snapshot they have inherited knowledge of the white woman of whom it is a likeness: Baba Bachlev, who had much *saman*(luggage) and much *batchit* (talk), a holy woman from the missions who came to stay at the house with the garden full of roses.

This snapshot (of which she had several copies because it was her favourite) showed the canal network of lines on her parchment skin. The iron-grey hair, cropped almost as short as a man's but softened by attractive natural waves, gave an idea of sacrificial fortitude rather than of sexual ambivalence. Her costume, severely tailored, and made of hard-wearing cloth, did not disguise the rounded shape of her unclaimed breast.

She wore dresses but favoured coats and skirts. With them she wore cream silk blouses or one of plain white cotton. Always about her neck hung the thinnest of gold chains with a pendant cross, also gold. A present of eau-de-cologne on her birthday gave her twelve months of lasting pleasure as did Christmas gifts of fine lawn handkerchiefs on which to sprinkle it. With these annual endowments the voluptuous side of her nature was satisfied. Like everything else she owned, cologne and handkerchiefs were cherished, but the cologne, although eked out, was in daily use so that she was always pleasant to be near. She washed mightily and sang in her tub: not hymns, but old songs of the Music Hall era about love on a shoestring. Such songs had been her father's favourites.

'My father loved life,' she told Mabel Layton during the period accepted by both of them as probationary. 'I never heard him complain. But then there wasn't any reason to. I mean he only had himself to blame, poor man. He gambled and drank. Champagne tastes and beer income, according to my mother. People said he could have been a clever lawyer but he never qualified. He didn't have the education and could never have afforded to, but he worked for a firm of solicitors in High Holborn and they thought highly of him. Well, they must have done because they had so many little things to overlook. Not, heaven forbid, that he was ever dishonest. But he was erratic and a great spendthrift.'

She wanted to be sure that Mabel Layton knew the Batchelors had been very small lower-middle-class beer. In Rose Cottage there were photographs of Laytons, and of Mabel's first husband and his family (it turned out she had been married and widowed twice) and all of them looked distinguished and well off, very pukka, the kind of people who belonged to the ruling class in India: the *raj*. Mabel, it was true, had let herself go, but in the manner that only people of her upbringing seemed capable of doing without losing prestige and an air of authority.

Barbie's first view of her was of an elderly shapeless woman wearing muddy grey slacks, an orange cotton blouse whose sleeves and collar had been ripped out to afford more freedom and expose more to the sun the brown, freckled and wrinkled arms, neck and shoulders. An ancient straw hat with a frayed brim shaded her face. She had seemed unwillingly distracted from the job she was doing: grubbing out weeds from one of the rose beds, a task she performed without gloves, kneeling on the grass on an old rubber hot-water bottle stuffed (as Barbie discovered later) with discarded much-darned cotton stockings. She did not look up until Barbie, obeying Aziz's gesture of permission and invitation, approached to within a few feet of her and cast shadow on the busy work-roughened hands.

She was in the garden every day of the year, she said. The mali usually did only the heaviest work of digging and keeping the grass cut, and even then under Mrs Layton's supervision. In the wet season she would go gum-booted and sou'-westered and macintoshed in search of a job that needed doing. The heavier downpours would drive her into the verandahs, but these were vivid with shrubs and creepers: azaleas, bougainvillaea and wistaria – and flowers such as geranium and nasturtium. All needed constant attention.

Seeing the garden at Rose Cottage Barbie realized she had always longed for one. She was ashamed of her ignorance of the names and natures of plants.

Built in the old Anglo-Indian style, Rose Cottage was a large rectangular structure with cream stucco walls and colonnaded verandahs at front, back and sides. There were two main bedrooms and a third which was called the little spare. There were a dining-room and a living-room. Central to the rooms was a square entrance hall which had been panelled in the 'twenties by its former owner. On the panelling Mabel had hung a variety of brass and copper trays. On either side of the doorway into the sitting-room stood a rosewood table with a crystal bowl of flowers – usually roses, as on the day of Barbie's arrival. These could be cut from the bushes almost continually from February to November.

Barbie's bedroom was to the right of the hall and Mrs Layton's to the left. Both had windows on to the front verandah and french doors on to the verandahs at the sides. Barbie's room connected to the little spare through a shared bathroom. Mabel Layton had a bathroom of her own. Her bedroom connected to the dining-room which, like the living-room, had views on to the back verandah. Dining- and living-room also interconnected. In all but the cold weather these doors were left open to give extra air. Behind the dining-room lay the kitchen and storeroom. Here Aziz had a bed made up. The general servants' quarters were reached by a path from the kitchen but were screened from the garden by a hedge.

Mabel Layton said she hoped Barbie would not mind being looked after mainly by Aziz. She had never cared for personal maids and in recent years had done without one entirely. Aziz, she said, was as competent to look after a wardrobe as any woman. The mali's wife came into the house to collect soiled household and personal linen and could attend to Barbie if that was what she preferred. Barbie said she was used to being looked after by male servants and had every confidence in Aziz. It seemed that Aziz cooked too. After her first meal, lunch, she no longer wondered why Mrs Layton, who appeared far better off than Barbie had expected, depended so much on him. The food was simple but exquisitely prepared and served.

'So long as I have Aziz and a mali to do the rough work in the garden,' Mabel Layton said, 'I don't much care to be bothered about servants. I leave Aziz to hire and fire whom he will. That way we get along perfectly. And he's been with me since my second husband died, which makes it twenty-two years next month. I'm not sure how old he is but James took him on in Ranpur the month before he was ill and Aziz seemed quite elderly then.'

Barbie's holiday was originally agreed as one of three weeks' duration. During the first few days there were quite a number of casual visitors and Barbie assumed that she was being submitted by Mabel Layton to the test of selected friends' approval.

23

She made a careful note of names and apprehended that they were in all probability names with which any woman who deserved to live at Rose Cottage should have been familiar. Mrs Paynton, Mrs Fosdick, Mrs Trehearne: these were the most formidable. Their husbands were probably all generals or colonels at least. Mabel Layton was herself what Anglo-Indian society called Army: Army by her first husband, Civil by her second and Army again by her second husband's son, her stepson, no less a person than the commanding officer of the 1st Pankot Rifles which Barbie had heard enough about to know was a very distinguished regiment indeed, particularly in the eyes of Pankot people. She was spared a meeting with Colonel Layton and his wife and the two daughters who had just returned from school in England, because they were all down in Ranpur. She was sure that the younger Mrs Layton would also be formidable, the daughters hard and self assured.

In fact she was puzzled why a woman like Mabel Layton should advertise accommodation and go to the length of vetting such an unlikely candidate as a retired teacher from the missions. She decided she could cope with the situation best by just being herself. Mabel Layton had really little of the burra mem in her at all although obviously she was one. But with the other women who called in for coffee Barbie felt exposed to a curiosity that was not wholly friendly.

She admitted to having an indifferent head for bridge but no prejudice against gambling, in spite of the fact that her father lost more on the horses than he could afford from his wages as a solicitor's managing clerk which meant that her mother had had to earn money herself by taking in dressmaking.

'We lived in Camberwell,' Barbie explained, 'and it was a great treat going with her to big houses in Forest Hill and Dulwich. I helped her with the pins. She had an absolute horror of putting them in her mouth because of a story she'd heard of someone swallowing one and dying in agony. So I used to hold the pincushion. I called it the

24

porcupine. It was filled with sand and absolutely bristled and was really awfully heavy, but it was covered in splendid purple velvet with seed-pearl edging and I used to stand there like a little altar boy, holding it up as high and as long as I possibly could. I can tell you it was tough on the arms but worth it because I was positively enchanted, I mean by watching my mother turn a length of silk or satin into a dress fit for a queen. I only hated it when she was doing mourning because then we both had to wear black and the houses we visited always smelt of stale flowers. And of course we knew we'd have to wait ages to be paid. Weddings were the big things. We got all sorts of perks.'

After such expositions a little silence used to fall, like a minuscule drop of water from the roof of an underground cave into a pool a long way below, where it made more noise than the scale of the actual situation seemed to merit. And the situation was worsened by Mabel Layton remaining immobile and expressionless as though what she always appeared willing to listen to when she and Barbie were alone, even if slow or reluctant to comment on it, bored her when it was told in front of her friends. It was left to the visitors to respond, which they did in those little silences and in then recalling, as though suddenly reattuned to the realities of life, other obligations and appointments that took them away wearing airs of concentration. There was, after all, a war begun in Europe. At any moment the Empire might be at stake.

'Come on, Batchelor,' Barbie said on a morning she decided there could be no future for her in Pankot at Rose Cottage, 'chin up.' She went to her room because Mabel had gone back into the garden. She sat at the borrowed mahogany desk to write yet another letter on the beautiful engraved paper, supplies of which had been placed in a wooden rack for her convenience. There were as well supplies of the matching purple-lined envelopes with stamps fixed at the inland rate, a mark of hospitality that amounted to graciousness but suggested a limitation of it, there having been but twelve; a generous but perhaps significant calculation of four letters a week for three weeks being enough to meet the requirements of any reasonable visitor.

But there were now only four stamped envelopes left which meant she had used two weeks' supply in one. She was a prodigious letter writer. She believed in keeping up. She once estimated that she wrote upwards of a dozen for every one she received, but the proportion had since changed to her further disadvantage.

'I know,' she said, murmuring aloud, the morning having become unusually still, pregnant with the possibility of her immediate eviction, 'that my own addiction to pen and paper is a form of indulgence. It's also of course a form of praise, I mean praise for the fascination and diversity of life which if you notice it yourself is always nice to bring to someone else's attention. I have written eight letters which means that there are now eight people who know things they didn't know, for instance how beautiful Pankot is and that I have hopes of living here. They know that a Miss Jolley has taken over my job. They know that I am happy and comfortable and looking forward to taking things easy. They know about the ridiculous mistake made by Thomas Aquinas and about Aziz and how helpful he was, and that the trunk is still at the station. They do not know that I am slightly worried about the trunk and the table because it is as unfair to share one's fears as it is right to share one's hopes. I shall share my hopes now with someone else.'

But when she had a sheet of writing paper squared up on the blotter and her Waterman fountain pen poised (it was one that was filled through a rubber top on the ink bottle into which the pen was inserted and pumped with a motion whose faint indelicacy was a constant source of slight embarrassment to her) she was aware of being about to project her thoughts not to one of the many people to whom she was in the habit of writing but into that deep that darkness was once said to be upon.

And suddenly she felt what she had felt once or twice before in Ranpur, the presence of a curious emanation, of a sickness, a kind of nausea that was not hers but someone else's; and sat stock still as she might if there were something dangerous in the room whose attention it would be foolhardy to attract. On the earlier occasions she had attributed the emanation to some quality of atmosphere in the Ranpur bangalow and so it surprised her to encounter it again. She felt instinctively that if the sickness touched her she would faint. And then she might come to with Mabel Layton standing over her telling her that Aziz had found her unconscious clutching a piece of paper on which she had written, 'Dear . . .' and no more.

'And that of course would be the end,' she said aloud in a normal conversational tone so that the emanation could observe that she was not bothered by it. 'Mrs Layton would quite ignore my assurance that there was nothing wrong with *me* and that there was no need to send for a doctor. I'd be off out of here and popped into a hospital bed as quick as winking. But I'm not ill. There's illness in the room but it isn't *my* illness.'

She gripped the edges of the desk and hoped she wasn't due to become a visionary. 'At my age! I mean how awfully disagreeable, not to say inconvenient.' She gripped the edges so hard that her palms hurt. Cautiously she removed her hands and was relieved to find nothing scored in the flesh that bore any resemblance to the stigmata.

'Whatever it is or whoever you are who isn't feeling up to par,' she said, having lost her fear of the emanation, 'I'm awfully sorry but there's nothing I can do for you, so please go away. Preferably in search of the Lord.'

She waited and felt the room return to normal.

'I've seen it off,' she thought. And at once thought of the person she should write to. She recovered her fountain pen, inscribed the date, 9 October, 1939, and wrote 'Dear Edwina,' and then found herself stuck for words, a rare event but an effect that Edwina Crane had always had on her. Edwina was the woman Barbie succeeded at Muzzafirabad and to Barbie she remained the heroine of a quarter of a century ago when alone, with the children cowering behind her in the schoolroom, she stood valiantly in the open doorway, at the height of serious civil disturbances, facing a gang of crazed and angry Muslims who had come to burn the mission down, and told them to be off; which they were (so the story went) in a subdued and silly-looking bunch, whereupon Miss Crane, leaving the door open because it was very hot, returned to the dais and continued the lesson as if she had just said no to an undeserving case of begging; a lesson that no doubt centred upon the picture she was reputed to have put to such brilliant use as an aid to teaching the English language that Barbie had never dared attempt emulation but had introduced instead *First Steps in Bible Reading* and taught from this, almost literally in the shadow of the picture which hung on the wall behind the dais.

This picture, of which she had a miniature copy among the relics in her trunk, a coloured engraving showing Queen Victoria receiving tribute from representatives of her Indian empire, had originally aroused in Barbie a faint dislike which she had prayed to be purged of because she guessed it was not the picture but Miss Crane for whom the dislike was felt, and at that time she had not even met the woman. Edwina had gone from Muzzafirabad before Barbie arrived to take her place. But spiritually she was very much still there, in the picture behind Barbie and in the minds of the little boys and girls who faced her, challenging her to do half as well for them. And Mr Cleghorn had a tendency to make comparisons between Barbie's methods and Miss Crane's.

Miss Crane, she was told, had been presented with a large gilt-framed replica of the picture as a memorial of her Muzzafirabad appointment and heroic stand, which even the civil and military authorities had applauded. When Barbie was posted away south scarcely a year after taking the appointment up she was given a miniature of the same picture, as if it would do her good to have a permanent reminder of her lesser merits. Possibly her expression when receiving it had stayed in Mr Cleghorn's mind and penetrated the mists of mildness in which he

28

normally existed to the clearer brighter region where his deeper conscience lay, because he wrote to her in Madras: 'You had a difficult, perhaps impossible task. It was one Miss Crane envisaged for herself, which is why she asked to be sent elsewhere. She hated to be a heroine. She said the children had stopped giving her their attention, their eyes being on the doorway, anticipating the reappearance of the mob, for her to quell once more with that look, that flow of words. Perhaps I should have explained this to you. Your successor will have a comparatively easy task. The children have lost the sharpness of their adulation of Miss Crane in the process of comparing Miss Crane with Miss Batchelor. And so young Miss Smithers stands a chance of being compared with no one, but of being accepted for what she is. Life will be duller, but we can all get on with the work we are supposed to be doing.'

'I was the guinea-pig,' Barbie thought, with her pen still poised and the letter to Edwina still not advanced beyond the salutation. 'I suppose I resented it, but it was a revelation to know that Edwina had taken her work so seriously that she would not stay in Muzzafirabad. I suppose up until then I'd assumed that she grabbed promotion as her right and went off consciously trailing clouds of glory for me to step on at my peril. The truth was quite otherwise. When I met her at last her modesty was an inspiration to me. She hated being reminded. She has buried herself in her work since and has sought out the most difficult and unpopular, indeed dangerous posts. God is truly with her.'

She wrote: 'It seems ages since we were in touch,' and continued in the rather flat and mundane style that often seemed to impose itself, like a bridle on her thoughts, when writing to Edwina, just as when meeting her every couple of years or so at major mission conferences an uncharacteristic inarticulacy dammed the free flow of her speech. At their last meeting, in 1938, she could have sworn that momentarily Edwina had not recognized her and that when she did their shared recollection of Muzzafirabad

29

was felt by Edwina to be a greater impediment than ever to conversation.

Now, before sealing the letter, she checked her address book and the last issue of the mission's quarterly magazine to make sure she had not overlooked a note about a new appointment. She had not; her address book was correct. She inscribed the envelope: Miss Edwina Crane, Superintendent's Bungalow, The Bishop Barnard Protestant Schools Mission, Mayapore.

Aziz announced lunch.

She went into the living-room prepared to find more guests, casual callers-in whose real purpose was to sum up and later advise Mabel Layton whether her prospective p.g. was up to snuff. But Mabel was alone, presiding over the tray – a decanter of sherry and two glasses. No one had come to lunch. This seemed especially significant as though a point of no return had been reached.

When the meal was over she and Mabel parted, ostensibly to sleep; and for a while Barbie tried. She stretched herself full-length on the bed with her arms at her sides and her eyes shut, counting the tufts of an imaginary dandelion clock which she blew at rhythmically, puffing out her lips in the manner of someone happily dozing. She often recommended it to friends as an association of ideas more effective than counting sheep; but this afternoon the dandelion clock she had conjured was a tough proposition. Not a tuft stirred. Try (she told it), try to be more co-operative; waft, waft, waft away, as I huff and puff. She replaced the obstinate dandelion with the image of a yellow rose. She stopped blowing and took in slow methodical lungsful of air and scent and then sat up to guard against being overcome by something inexpressible which seemed to be connected with the whole of her life in India.

The house was soundless and the world outside the window was full of bones.

She left her room and went out to the back verandah.

'Oh, you're up too, Mrs Layton,' she said in her best elocutionary voice. 'I do admire your industry. And how worthwhile it is.'

She gazed at the potted shrubs on the balustrade and at the garden with its immaculately cut lawn in which oval and rectangular beds of roses were set to provide infinite pleasure to the eye, rest to the mind and balm to the soul. Beyond the lawn and the bordering shrubs where the garden ended the land fell away, and rose again several miles distant in pine-capped hills from which scented breezes always seemed to whisper. And more distant yet were the higher hills and the celestial range of mountain peaks.

She looked at Mabel Layton again but Mrs Layton was still working at a pot of cuttings. Barbie was upset by this unexpected and total disregard. Dejected, she sat on one of the three wicker chairs that were set round the verandah table, kept an eye open and a smile ready for the moment when Mrs Layton abandoned her work and came to join her. She examined her conscience but found no special cause for blame in her behaviour that morning. On the other hand it wasn't Mrs Layton's fault if she found her an unsuitable companion. In her oddly withdrawn way Mrs Layton had been meticulous about arrangements for her guest's comfort. But clearly in Mrs Layton's view theirs were not complementary temperaments. She had probably never had a paying-guest in her life and was bound to find it difficult to open her lovely home to a stranger. It must be companionship, not money, Mrs Layton needed and she probably already regretted putting the advertisement in the paper. She may since have heard of someone more likely to fit in – an old army friend for instance – but felt in honour bound to stand by her suggestion that Barbie should spend her holiday in Pankot. Perhaps – and Barbie felt a sympathetic twinge of understanding – Mrs Layton was steeling herself to say that there could be no permanent arrangement. Barbie was not sure whether to be glad or sorry. When she and Mrs Layton were alone they seemed to get on together well enough and she was already in love with the bungalow and garden, its views of the outside world, and ready to love it more, aware that in coming here she had been afforded a glimpse of something life had denied her but which she was not unfitted for, having prayed for it once in a different form: tranquillity of mind and nature. That, perhaps, she would never achieve but there was a sense of tranquillity here, of serenity, which someone like herself might enter and be touched by, lightly if not deeply.

And watching Mabel Layton busy with the plant pots she had the feeling that Mabel had not entered it yet herself, not fully, but was trying to and finding it difficult to do so alone. 'We could have helped each other,' Barbie thought, 'but I'm a disappointment to her. I'm simply not her kind of person. She must know I'm here on the verandah but is pretending not to and hardening her heart to tell me the room will not be vacant after all.'

She stared hard at Mrs Layton's back, attempting telepathic persuasion to make her turn round and come out with it so that they would both know where they stood and the uncertainty could be ended. She saw Mabel hesitate. The busy probing fingers were suddenly still. For a few seconds it seemed that the fingers and arms stiffened to support weight. Then one hand was removed from the plant pot and placed on her chest near the base of the throat, and for a while she seemed to look at the garden as if struck by an idea about it.

Barbie got to her feet, moved forward a bit, and thought that Mabel wasn't looking at the garden at all. Her eyes were open but on her face was an expression of the most profound resignation Barbie had ever seen.

'Mrs Layton? Are you all right?'

Barbie spoke distinctly and calmly but her object of letting Mrs Layton know that assistance was at hand if needed was not achieved. The other woman stayed in that position of remarkable stillness and slowly it was borne in on Barbie that whatever else was the matter with Mabel Layton that caused her to stand as if waiting for some kind of pain to go away, she was deaf. She hadn't heard Barbie come out and hadn't heard her speak.

'Mrs Layton?'

The other woman glanced round.

'Are you all right?' Barbie repeated, going nearer, involuntarily putting out her hand as if to take Mabel's arm.

'Oh – ' Mabel said; then removed her hand from her breast and touched Barbie's arm: a reversal of roles. 'Couldn't you sleep? I don't blame you. It's such a lovely afternoon.'

She hadn't heard or understood the question. But she hadn't been startled. The touch was scarcely more than a sketch of one and she was now busy again with the earth in the pot of cuttings, tamping it down.

'Actually,' she said, talking to Barbie via the plant pot, 'I seldom have forty winks after lunch so don't feel you have to if you find if difficult. I don't suppose you're used to it either.'

She moved on to the next pot and did something expert with a pruning knife. 'I ought to have done these this morning,' she said, 'but we were interrupted again. I suppose it's wrong of me to worry but there aren't usually quite so many visitors. I expect you've realized they mostly come to satisfy their curiosity. We get the Ranpur papers up here and everyone saw my advertisement. What worries me a bit is that after a while when they've got used to the idea there'll be days when nobody comes at all and then you'd think it rather dull I dare say. You're used to lots of people around you, I imagine, and I expect you enjoy it. I'm not and don't particularly. I'd say I've become something of a recluse but of course that's not possible in India, for *us*. Even when we're alone we're on show, aren't we, representing something? That's why I can't stop people turning up. They come to make sure I'm still here and that we're all representing it together. But I go out as little as possible, in company I mean. I wonder if you'll be happy here?'

'Yes, I see. I quite understand,' Barbie murmured.

'What?'

'I said I quite understand.'

Mabel had stopped potting and was staring at Barbie who under the weight of that resigned expression began to

33

feel that she understood nothing. Her smile of assumed cheerfulness made her mouth as awkward to bear as something God had added to her in a fit of creative absent-mindedness.

'Oh, no,' Mabel said, 'I don't think you do. I meant that if you decide to stay I want you to feel that Rose Cottage is your home as well as mine and that you could have as many friends here as you care to make and go out as often as you wish, without bothering about me or whether I joined in or not. I know it's selfish of me to ask someone as gregarious as I believe you are to live here. On the other hand it would be disastrous to share the place with someone as selfish as myself and – ' she paused, made a gesture drawing attention to the garden, the bungalow, the whole complex at whose heart this notion of serenity lay, 'I think it could do with sharing, but only by someone who appreciates it. I got the feeling from your letter that you were the kind of person who would. I still think so, but I'd hate you to think it had to be appreciated in my way and no one else's. I'd hate you to feel cut off.'

She glanced at the garden. 'It often strikes me as something the gods once loved but forgot should die young and that there's only me left to love it. I'm not here forever and I'm not sure I love it enough.'

Barbie said, speaking loudly to make sure she was heard and understood, 'I'd love to stay, Mrs Layton. Actually I shall be glad to slow down and live a quieter life. It's what I hoped for. To have some time to myself.'

Mabel looked at her. She felt the look penetrate, right down to the core of her secret sorrow, and then withdraw, back into its own.

'I'm so glad,' Mabel said, returning her attention to the plant. 'Please ring the bell and ask Aziz to give us an early tea if you'd like it. I think I should. It won't be long before we find it chilly enough to have tea indoors and that always depresses me a bit. And you'd better remind him about your trunk. He's getting a bit forgetful, poor dear. And do send for anything else you've left behind in Ranpur.'

'My writing-table,' Barbie cried; but Mabel merely nodded. She probably hadn't heard. Barbie turned, pressed the bell on the board of switches, some of which lit the verandah and some the floodlights in the garden (these presently were to be robbed of their bulbs to conserve electricity as part of Pankot's war effort). Mabel continued to deal with the pots of cuttings and when Aziz came she left it to Barbie to tell him they would both like tea brought out now instead of at four o'clock. He gave her a sideways nod, accepting that it had become her place to give some of the orders.

'Oh, Lord,' she prayed that night, her knees punished through the thin cotton of her nightgown by the thick woven coarse rush mat at her bedside, 'thank You for Your many blessings and for bringing me to Rose Cottage. Help me to serve and, if it is Your will, bring light to the darkness that lies on the soul of Mabel Layton.'

She prayed for longer than usual, hoping for a revival of that lost sense of contact. But it did not revive. She could feel the prayers falling flat, little rejects from a devotional machine she had once worked to perfection. The prayers hardened in the upper air, once so warm, now so frosty, and tinkled down. But she pressed on, head bowed, in the hailstorm.

3

In a woman with a less well-authenticated Anglo-Indian background than Mabel Layton's what was accepted as eccentricity would probably have been seen as hostility to what Anglo-India stood for, but Mabel's background was impeccable, she criticized no one and seldom expressed any opinion let alone a hostile one. Her absorption in garden and bungalow, her habit of taking solitary walks, her refusal even of invitations it was generally considered obligatory to accept, her complete detachment from Pankot's public life, were attributed to the personal idiosyncrasy of someone who had lost two husbands in the cause of service to the empire, one by rifle fire on the Kyber, the other by amoebic infection; and having thus distinguished herself retired from the field of duty to leave room for others. Her withdrawal was accepted with feelings that lay somewhere between respect and regret; which meant that they were fixed at a point of faint disapproval, therefore seldom expressed, but when they were, an idea would somehow be conveyed of Mrs Layton's isolation having a meaningful connexion with an earlier golden age which everyone knew had gone but over whose memory she stood guardian, stony-faced and uncompromising; a bleak point of reference, as it were a marker-buoy above a sunken ship full of treasure that could never be salvaged; a reminder and a warning to shipping still afloat in waters that got more treacherous every year.

This sense of danger, of the sea-level rising, swamping the plains, threatening the hills, this sense of imminent inundation, was one to which people were now not unaccustomed and although the outbreak of war in Europe had momentarily suggested the sudden erection of a rocky headland upon which to stand fast, the headland was far away, in England, and India was very close and all about. And as the war in Europe began to enter its disagreeable phases it looked as though the headland had been either a mirage or a last despairing lurch of all those things to which value had been attached and upon which the eye, looking west from Pankot, had been kept loyally fixed through all the years in which the encouraging sensation of being looked at loyally in return was steadily diminished until to the sense of living in expectation of inundation had been added the suspicion that this inundation would scarcely be remarked or, if it were, not regretted when it happened.

The slight disapproval which counterbalanced the respect in which old Mabel Layton was held could probably have been traced to the haunting belief that in spite of everything she was among those people who would not regret the flood. Her whole demeanour was, in fact, that of someone who already saw the waters all around her, had found her boat and did not want it rocked.

A few months after Miss Batchelor's arrival, in answer to the advertisement for a single woman to share, an interesting situation had arisen. In retrospect it looked as if Mabel Layton had anticipated it and for some unintelligible but perhaps typical reason taken steps to protect herself.

This situation was the one arising in regard to accommodation in Pankot for Mildred Layton, the wife of Mabel's stepson, Lt-Colonel John Layton and his two grown-up daughters Sarah and Susan whom he brought up to the hill station at the beginning of the hot weather in 1940 and established in the only place now available: a rather poky grace and favour bungalow in the lines of the Pankot Rifles regimental depot, opposite the mess. The bungalow they had occupied for a few weeks in the late summer of 1939 before going down to Ranpur in September had since been appropriated by Area Headquarters as a chummery mess and Colonel Layton failed to persuade the accommodations officer to give it back.

Having settled his family in what comfort he could he returned to Ranpur where the battalion he commanded, the 1st Pankot Rifles, was under orders for abroad. The 1st Pankots sailed for the Middle East a few weeks later, and in Pankot Mildred Layton settled down as a grass-widow in the grace and favour bungalow with her daughters who had got back to India from school in England only in July of the previous year.

Before 1939, the year of family reunion, the Laytons had not been on station for many years but they were Ranpur and Pankot people. The parents had been married in Pankot and both girls born there. It took no time at all for the Laytons' friends to fit them mentally into Rose Cottage and find that the arithmetic worked. Sarah and Susan could share the second large bedroom currently occupied by Miss Batchelor, Mabel could stay in the room she had and Mildred sleep in the little spare.

37

Although there were three bedrooms in the grace and favour bungalow down in the Pankot Rifles lines, they were small and the whole place had an atmosphere of barracks: PWD furniture, a view at the front of the rear of the mess and at the back of a bare brick wall hiding the servants' quarters. The garden was bleak – weedy grass and no flowers – and one's peace indoors and out interrupted by parade-ground noises. A military wife and her daughters would be expected to pig in there without complaint if it was the best that could be done for them, but its discomforts and inconvenience (the wrong side of the bazaar and twenty minutes' tonga ride to the club), the enchanting prettiness of young Susan around whom Pankot males were already gathering, and the quiet but obvious efficiency of the elder daughter, Sarah, hardened the conviction that Rose Cottage was their proper and rightful place.

Mildred Layton refused to be drawn on the subject but when a question was put to her in any one of several oblique ways whose meaning was simply: Did Mabel discuss her plan to take a paying-guest with Colonel Layton? she left little doubt that the answer was no, and that the first she and John knew about it was down in Ranpur when they saw the advertisement.

Nevertheless relations between Mildred and Mabel Layton seemed perfectly amiable. No abnormal strain was apparent to the inner circle of Pankot women who were in the habit of dropping in to make sure Mabel was still there and representing what had to be represented. Mildred and her two girls were frequent droppers-in at Rose Cottage themselves. In fact for the first few weeks after her arrival from Ranpur Mildred made free of Rose Cottage as if it were a logical extension of her life, which it was, being only a few minutes' drive from the club; and her right, which it also was, because when Mabel died Colonel Layton would inherit the property along with what was believed to be a considerable amount of money.

The girls made free of it to a slightly lesser extent; Sarah more often than Susan who tended to be occupied appeasing as many as she could of the young subalterns who made demands on her time and company, swimming, riding and playing tennis. In the elder sister's case, visitors noted, making free was not quite the phrase to use. Sarah was less volatile than Susan, far less off-handedly possessive than her mother. She seemed very fond of the place, particularly of the garden, and much more communicative with Mabel (whom she and her sister called Aunt). She was also more patient with Miss Batchelor who chattered at her as she chattered at everybody but was given attentive replies to her comments and questions.

Sarah was a quiet girl. According to her mother she suffered badly with her periods, as badly as Mildred had suffered before having her. Mrs Paynton, Mrs Fosdick and Mrs Trehearne, the three women who could claim some intimacy with Rose Cottage's silent chatelaine, observed this well-mannered and presumably sometimes stoic behaviour of Sarah's with sympathy and approval. Colonel Layton's elder daughter was an unassuming and intelligent girl with a face a bit too bony to be called pretty, and obviously took her obligations seriously. Her quietness suggested to them that the perplexity of her English years was still upon her. She probably had some strange ideas because life at home was no longer what it had been, but there was backbone there. The other girl was as clear and uncomplicated as daylight by comparison. England had not touched her except to give her a necessary scraping to detach the barnacles gathered while becalmed in the sea of Anglo-Indian childhood; a ruinous experience if not corrected by schooling in England: all privilege and no responsibility. But here now was young Susan, sharp-keeled from home, clean and eager. It heartened one just to look at her. She seemed to know it, and that could be dangerous, but presently she would settle and the gravity of Anglo-Indian life would touch her pretty face soon enough.

The flush would disappear. The enchanting laugh would give way to the kind that reflected the gratitude felt for anything that still exercised one's sense of humour and kept it from atrophying. The years would play havoc with that rosy skin, tauten the mobile mouth, expose the sinewy structure of the neck that turned so attractively as she looked about her, endlessly responsive to the stimulus of surroundings which woke her adult perceptions as well as her childhood memories.

In the garden of Rose Cottage Susan's gaiety was especially flowerlike. Her bewitching quality was heightened for the other women by their sad awareness that her bloom must fade as their own had done. But not yet. And before then she would be plucked and carried off. She seldom came to the bungalow unaccompanied by young men. If she did she was attended by them later and quickly spirited away, alone or with Sarah who played the chaperone role of sensible elder sister.

With all this Mabel seemed perfectly compliant, although it was apparent that she was not keen on Susan's black Labrador puppy, Panther, who threatened havoc among the rose beds but came at Susan's call and learned the hard way that the garden was not his. This disciplining of the dog (until in going into the garden, heel-tracking Susan's progress in an awkward splay-footed progress of his own, he looked conscious of special dispensation) was – apart from Sarah's more tentative approach to the act of being in Rose Cottage – the one acknowledgement Mildred and Susan publicly made of enjoying little more than a dispensation themselves. The use of a pet as a symbol of that acknowledgement was a guide to the dissatisfaction felt with the arrangements that kept them from living there. The mock-severe tone of Susan's and Mildred's voices and the impatience of the gestures Susan used to admonish the dog, instructing him to be quiet, lie down, come here, stop slobbering, keep his paws off the table, behave properly, were clearly not intended to correct him but to advertise and simultaneously relieve an exasperation with something other than the dog's exuberance.

While Mabel raised no objection to this invasion of her home, allowed it to develop unhindered until scarcely a day went by without a coming and going on the front verandah,

40

a settling in chairs on the back, a persistent tinkling of the telephone, she did not become involved; so it emphasized her detachment, even strengthened it, enlarged its scope. There was now more for her to be detached from. Caught up in the midst of these unusual activities she assumed a protective colouring and merged into the backgrounds of normality which the activities created.

If it was Mildred's intention to force the issue, this capacity Mabel had for creating an illusion of not being in possession of anything anyone could want to take from her or force her to share was an effective deterrent; far more effective than Miss Batchelor's physical presence.

Demonstrably Miss Batchelor had what presumably Mildred desired, but to judge from her reactions she was increasingly self-conscious of the fact, daily more embarrassingly aware of enjoying what she had comparatively no right to, and obviously torn between the conflicting beliefs that she should either make herself pleasant, or scarce.

Whichever course the poor woman adopted the effect on Mildred was the same. Outwardly her attitude towards the missionary was one of unchanging indifference and Miss Batchelor could not disguise from visitors that she was frightened of her. Her inconsequential conversation began to be accompanied by nervous gestures: hand to throat, hand rubbing hand, hand clutching elbow. She jumped up and down fetching things, providing comforts, answering the telephone. Such energy hinted at an over-loading even of her remarkable power-house. At any moment a fissure might appear in her structural organiza-tion and she would then collapse in fragments and a little cloud of dust; from the sight of which phenomenon Mildred Layton would surely turn, as if this sort of thing were an everyday occurrence and only vaguely to be regretted in the brief instant it would take for her atten-tion to be given to some other evidence of the oddity of Anglo-Indian life.

In company Mabel made no effort to protect Miss Batchelor from Mildred's presence. It became doubtful that the missionary woman could survive and it was not at all clear whether Mabel cared one way or the other. It was just possible that the reappearance of her stepson's wife and her two grand step-children, their proximity, their needs, their standing, would remind her of her own duty to the station.

For there was – let there be no doubt of it – a distinction, a virtue attaching to Mildred Layton which set her apart and gave her a weight quite independent of her actual rank. In that, she was not above Nicky Paynton whose husband commanded a battalion of the Ranpurs, or above Clara Fosdick whose late husband had been a civil surgeon and whose sister was married to a judge of the High Court in Ranpur. She was junior in rank to Maisie Trehearne, the wife of the Colonel-Commandant of the Pankot Rifles depot and junior, naturally, to the wife of whatever officer occupied Flagstaff House.

The special virtue of Mildred Layton was not to be found in the place she enjoyed in the formal hierarchy nor even in the fact that her father, General Muir, had been general officer commanding in Ranpur in the 'twenties, and that she and her sisters had lived at Flagstaff House in Ranpur and Pankot as girls. The virtue was not to be found either in her being the wife of a man whose father (Mabel's second husband) had a distinguished career in the Civil, was still remembered in the Pankot hills and whose portrait hung in the chamber of Government House in Ranpur where the council sat and where before his death of amoebic infection in 1917 he had distinguished himself further.

Her position as John Layton's wife brought one closer to the secret of her virtue but it was a virtue that could have escaped them both, settled on other shoulders. All her history of eminent connexion counted once the virtue became attached to her, but the virtue itself was the gift of a condition, the visible source of which was down there in the valley in that random pattern of army installations which Barbie had seen from the miniature mountain pass; its actual centre a low, ugly, rambling brick and timber building: the Pankot Rifles mess.

This building, like a temple, was only an arbitrary enclosure but it was a place in which the particular spirit of Pankot was symbolically concentrated. No more nor less than any other station whose history was inseparable from the history of a regiment, Pankot's pride and prejudice and lore were deeply rooted in its famous Rifles. The gentle roll of the hills, the tender green, the ethereal mists: these were deceptive. There was not a village as far as the eye could see and in the rugged terrain beyond that marched towards a mountainous horizon which was not steeped in Pankot's regimental tradition.

In the ordinary smoke of morning and evening fires the ghostly smoke of old campaigns was mingled. There was always an opacity. Clean and hard and clear as the sunshine struck it seemed to strike gun-metal. On a hot still day the snapped branch of a forest pine resounded like a sniper's shot. A sudden flurry of birds led the eye away from them to the dead suspect ground from which they had risen. There was an air of irrelevancy in husbandry.

The mind could never quite free itself from the hard condition imposed by the military connexion. This condition could be mocked but it lay deeper than a joke about the honour of the regiment ever probed. From the curious quality of flatness of their eyes a stranger arriving in Pankot and warned to look out for it might have told which men among several in civilian clothes were Pankot Rifles officers. In uniform this guardedness of eye was even more noticeable; a visible sign of a man's awareness that his virtue instantaneously commanded a recognition which he found onerous to bear but proper to receive. It could be and was accorded by senior officers to juniors of the same regiment but in that case the recognition of virtue was mutual. The real subtlety of the virtue lay in the recognition it commanded in Pankot from any officer however senior of whatever regiment or arm. There was a scale in the condition of life in Pankot in which a Pankot Rifles subaltern, on station, pegged higher than a general who had been less ambitious in his choice of regiment.

And there was a scale within the scale, and here was the secret of Mildred Layton's virtue. The men's virtue fell upon their women and the scale within the scale gave precedence by battalion as well as by rank. A subaltern of the 1st Pankots was a fuller embodiment of virtue than a subaltern of the 4/5th whose cool weather station was in distant Mayapore. Ranging outward and upward through a host of permutations of regimental and non-regimental employment the logical peak of attainment was reached in the supreme active regimental command, the command of the 1st Battalion. An extra glow warmed the peak if the distinction was achieved by an officer whose parent battalion it was – as was the case with John Layton – but no Pankot Rifles officer would willingly accept an appointment however attractive if he had reason to suppose that the command of the 1st was an alternative within his grasp; even though to have held it once did not enable him to bear the special virtue subsequently. It passed like a crown, itself perpetual, the heads it adorned coming and going. Trehearne had held it, a 4/5th man, now red-tabbed and banded, a full colonel; in effect father of the regiment; but the crown was presently John Layton's on whose head it glinted in a middle eastern sun; and his wife Mildred, in the scale of this condition, had more virtue than Mrs Trehearne who took precedence over her in every other way.

Through the 1st Battalion of its Rifles Pankot especially judged itself, felt itself judged, gave hostages to its fortune, sent emissaries into the world. At this level an element of sentiment was allowable but it was a sentiment supported by the condition which only one thing could shake and weaken: the disclosure of a fault in the rock, disaffection, disloyalty. Everything else was forgivable: incompetence, failure, defeat, even cowardice which was a private affair, a personal and not a corporate failure.

So there was Mildred Layton, a still handsome woman whose face quite properly showed not a tremor of the concern she would feel for her husband away on active service in North Africa, and no change as she looked at

44

and through her stepmother-in-law's talkative and intimidated companion in that expression of constantly and perfectly controlled dedication to her duty to withstand the countless irritations to which English women in India were naturally subjected.

If the men's eyes were flat the women's – to judge from Mildred's – were slightly hooded as though belonging to the weaker sex they were entitled to this extra protection; and the mouths, again to judge by hers, being less allowably firmed than a man's, were permitted a faint curve down at the corners which could be mistaken for displeasure, in the way that Mildred's languid posture when seated could be mistaken for *ennui* (closer observation of her as she was standing or walking suggested that she had probably achieved this economy of movement as a result of a long experience of the need a person in her position had to get through the day with the least trouble to herself).

But in the matter of Rose Cottage her distinction got her nowhere. The elder Mrs Layton remained impervious to it and something of that imperviousness seemed slowly to rub off on to Barbara Batchelor. It was imagined that the missionary must have asked Mabel outright whether she should go and had been asked to stay put and thereafter had girded her loins to the task of staying. The basis of her efforts to make herself pleasant changed, but too gradually for the day and circumstances of the substitution of security for insecurity to be determined.

Subtly she became endowed with some of the attributes of a co-hostess, a member of the family. She enlisted Aziz's aid in fetching and carrying, at first covertly and then openly because he had a habit of coming out and asking her what it was she had asked him to do for the guests. She assumed responsibility for the dog by making a friend of him, throwing his ball in an invisible but clearly demarcated zone within whose bounds he could do no damage, saw him fed and took him for walks when his mistress Susan abandoned him for more adventurous pursuits.

Her attitude to the girls became that of an aunt who knew her nieces had heard her discussed unfavourably but could not help showing her interest in them and some of her affection. Indeed she seemed to acquire something of the thick skin such a woman had to cultivate if her feelings were not to be constantly hurt by inattention to her questions, opinions, and fund of boring anecdotes.

And within a month or two the visits began to thin out as though the holidays were over and more serious affairs demanded attention. The poky grace and favour bungalow showed signs of being grudgingly settled in. It was (Mildred seemed to suggest) rather more convenient for Susan's followers, more convenient for herself whose duties were much bound up in the life of the regiment, for instance in helping Maisie Trehearne keep a matriarchal eye on the wartime crop of young men lucky enough to have got their emergency commissions into it. While suggesting this Mildred's expression did not change from the one which inspired fear in Miss Batchelor. It did not need to because it was an expression for all occasions, the expression of a person who could not allow herself to doubt that she was right, would always do what was right and therefore had nothing to explain even when not done right by, except to people who did not understand this and to such people an explanation was never owing.

But expression or not Mildred could not remove from people's minds the notion that she had suffered a defeat. The question was whether she was hurt by it. Later when a certain weakness began to reveal itself in that apparently indomitable armour it seemed likely that she had been hurt more deeply than she may have admitted even to herself.

There was something especially unpalatable about a family quarrel because it could undermine the foundations of a larger and essential solidarity. There was no known quarrel between Mabel and Mildred but family feeling had not been conspicuously shown. Blood had not proved thicker than water. 'Mabel's been like she is as long as I've known her,' Mildred once commented. 'According to

46

John she was like that when he got back from the first war, quite different from the way he remembered her when he was a subaltern. He believes she never got over his father's death.'

This was the only remark she ever made that had any bearing on her stepmother-in-law's refusal to get rid of the Batchelor woman but it confirmed the impression that Mabel and Mildred had never hit it off and it was natural to wonder why, even if Mabel was not a person with whom it was easy to associate the idea of a close relationship.

It was odd that Mabel should squander upon a retired missionary what Mildred had a positive right to and would grace in a way that the Batchelor woman never could. And by depriving Mildred of this right she deprived her of another: trust. It was as if in Mabel's eyes Mildred could not be trusted; which was thought ridiculous at the time and just as ridiculous later even when the weakness began to show.

This weakness, so admirably and typically controlled, had to be put down to a particular cause, a blow courageously sustained – the news in 1941 that the 1st Pankots had been severely mauled in North Africa and Colonel Layton with the remnants of his command taken prisoner by the Italians (an especial wound to pride).

For a week or two after receiving the news Mildred Layton acted with a fortitude she never afterwards lost but which in this initial phase was found exemplary. None of her husband's fellow officers, killed or imprisoned, had wives living in Pankot but she wrote to all these women offering sympathy and any help that was needed. On horseback and accompanied by the depot adjutant, Kevin Coley, she visited the nearby villages to talk to the wives and widows of the 1st Battalion's VCOs, NCOs and sepoys. Any who came in from outlying districts for confirmation or interpretation of the news, for help and advice, assurances about pay allotments, and who expressed a wish to see her, she talked to in the lines, in the adjutant's verandah; and once or twice – receiving deputations – in the compound of the grace and favour bungalow.

'It's sad,' she said to her old acquaintance, the newly arrived occupant of Flagstaff House, Isobel Rankin, 'they think John will still be able to look after their men in prison-camp but of course the men will be separated from their officers and I have to tell these women what the position is. Then they ask me to write to the Italian general to make sure that John's allowed to visit them and I have to tell them it's highly unlikely he'll be allowed to but that if he is he'll need no reminder from me, and that seems to satisfy them.'

Thus Mildred conveyed to the new Area Commander and his wife, Dick and Isobel Rankin whose paths she and John had crossed in Lahore, New Delhi and Rawalpindi and with whom they were on Christian name terms, that it did not really satisfy her.

The station concurred. As if the disaster befallen the 1st Pankots weren't bad enough, in prison-camp the other ranks would be deprived of their inalienable right to the comradeship, the guidance and unstinted moral support of their officers and the officers of the privilege of giving them. It was a hazard of war but for a regiment like the Pankots situated in a valley from whose surrounding hills its soldiers were traditionally recruited it struck at the foundation of the trust between officers and men.

Was it the act of trying to reaffirm that trust which exhausted Mildred or reaction to the blow she had personally received? Or, in going among the villagers on horseback had she suddenly become conscious of acting out a charade which neither she nor the women she comforted believed in for a minute?

As often as not it is the sense of the unbearable comedy of life that lights those fires which can only be damped down by compulsive drinking. Whatever the cause in Mildred's case the idea of her fortitude as exemplary did not survive the discreet but unmistakable evidence that she was starting on the Carew's gin too early in the day and arriving for bridge, for committees, for morning-coffee, for lunch, with that look and air of being less sensitive than anyone else to the crosscurrents of feeling and opinion in the room she entered. Her natural languor, to which everyone was accustomed and which she had worn lightly, like a protective cloak, seemed a degree heavier and her gestures more studied as if they demanded a shade more effort than was usual. At first her expression remained stable, what it had always been, but presently, although still unchanging, it began to lose definition, as though the face which it controlled was gradually slackening.

By then Mildred Layton's drinking habit was too well established in people's minds for it to give rise to much comment; and it was indulged with such style that nothing about her was diminished by it. In a curious way it sharpened her distinction. In her, drink released none of the vulgar or embarrassing traits disguised by soberness in people of softer grain; it gave extra keenness to those edges in her personality that made her a woman no one in her right mind would want to cross. One approached her with the same discretion she displayed in her own behaviour but did so perhaps slightly more aware of the need.

No longer exemplary, aided by drink which it was known she could not afford, there were occasions when her fortitude was felt by those who knew her well to be a fortitude shown not just for her own benefit but for theirs as well, so that the drinking was for them too; a resistance to pressures they were too conscious of not to acknowledge as collective and likely to increase. In the guarded eyes, the faint upcurve of the downward curving mouth, there was the authority of the old order and an intelligence that could calculate odds accurately, interpret them as indications that the game that had never been a game was very likely up.

So Mildred drank; compulsively and systematically: two or more up on everyone when drinking in a fairly hard-drinking community officially began and more than that when a session ended. One became so used to it that really it became part of the manner which with the impeccable background and irreproachable behaviour had always promoted and still promoted the image of her utter reliability. Even the little matter of mounting bridge debts could be seen in a certain light as the exception that proved the rule of her soundness. Her forgetfulness was annoying and embarrassing but whichever way her luck was running, win or lose (it was mostly lose), one could not help feeling that she saw debts due only in the context of larger and more important issues; and then in speaking gently to Sarah (the one sure way of getting paid) one was bound to understand that in that grander context even so sacred a thing as a card debt was enclosed in an aura of irrelevance.

And after all it was not a question of honour alone but of money, and for money Mildred clearly had an upper- class contempt which meant that her attitude to it was one of complaint at not having enough but of this being no excuse for not spending it. Unpaid bills at local stores and overdue mail order accounts at the Army and Navy were not her personal fault. She had standards to maintain and two girls as well as herself to dress, especially Susan who had a perfectly proper streak of what her looks and figure excused – extravagance. With both girls now enlisted in the WAC(1), working as clerks at Area Headquarters with Carol and Christine Beames, the civil surgeon's daughters, spending much of the working week in uniform, the number of new dresses Susan needed was reduced to what Mildred described as less unmanageable proportions, but unlike Sarah, who tended to stay in uniform, Susan changed immediately she got home; which was quite early quite often. There was not a great deal for a girl to do at the daftar if she thought it not her job to look for work and stupid to look busy if she weren't; and in Susan's case working in Dick Rankin's office had doubled her number of escorts. It was her obligation to look fresh and pretty and Mildred's obligation to help her do so.

How often, people wondered, did old Mabel Layton come to the rescue? How many times were bills (which Sarah had helpfully taken it upon her shoulders to see

50

settled before they became an embarrassment) paid with cheques supported at the bank by money Mildred had off her absent husband's step-mother? A half-colonel's pay did not support the style of life to which Mildred was accustomed and which she kept up rather better than anyone else. It was not expected to in peace time. It was ironic to think that so much of the *raj's* elegance which provoked the Indian temper had always been supported by private incomes. From the Viceroy down the difference between his pay and allowances and necessary expenses meant that a man was usually out of pocket administering or defending the empire. One was used to debt, to cutting down, to the sense of imminent shabbiness in approaching retirement. After a year or two of war the shabbiness was rather closer than that. It seemed to settle like a layer of dust, clouding certain issues, such as the reason for being in India at all. Anything that proved durable and resistant to the dust and retained the bright gleam of a stubbornly clear conviction was precious because it stood out, a challenge to dark and perhaps superior forces, and this meant that if you went down you would be pretty sure what it was you went down defending.

Mildred stood out. Almost disdainfully. The virtue that attached to her as Colonel Layton's wife was crystallized by the other virtues of her family connexion with the station. One had (as Barbie had done) only to wander in the churchyard of St John's and see the names Layton and Muir on headstones to realize that in those lichened-over advertisements for souls there was an explanation of Mildred, even a reference to the habit she had acquired in the slightly drunken tilt which age and subsidence had given them but not yet given her.

Nor would they. She would not rest there, one felt, would not want to. Her languor was not that of someone superiorly regretting the passing of the golden age. The illumination of Mildred Layton made by the stones aslant in the hummocky grass was one of contrast; contrast in deductions and expectations from identical premises and identical investment. Mildred's enemy was history not an early death in exile, but neither end was the kind that could have been or could be assumed, and the evidence of cessation which a clear look into the future might reveal did not countermand her duty to the existing order of things if she continued to believe in it.

And there in the picture one might have had of her going to her not-so-secret hoard (the bottle in the al-mirah to save her the boredom of sending Mahmoud to the drinks cupboard, the flask in her handbag to guard against the tedium of finding herself held up in a dry corner at the wrong hour) the question of her belief was posed and perhaps only ambiguously answered; but the picture is much the same as the one presented by Barbie on her knees in the hailstorm (the sole kind of tempest that the devotional machine now seemed capable of conjuring). If Mildred had been a religious woman she might have prayed for John, for the remnants of his battalion, for the wives and widows among whom she had graciously gone offering the solace no woman could give to others or herself. At the turn of the year (1941–42) she could have prayed for the bodies and souls of those who faced, were to fall before or extricate themselves from the destructive tide of the extraordinary and beastly little Japanese: among them, quite unknown to her, her future son-in-law Teddie Bingham who in the early months of 1942 enters the page as it were in the margin, a dim figure limping at the head of a decimated company of the Muzzafirabad Guides across the grain of the hills of upper Burma towards India, temporary safety, Susan's arms, a moment of truth and fiery obli-vion. Depressing as Teddie's contribution sounds one can be sure he would have had a generally cheerful idea about it.

. But Mildred was not a praying woman; and the drink suggests that had she been she would have prayed like Barbie not for particular favours but for a general one; the favour of being disabused of a growing and irritating belief (which drink soothed) that she had been aban-doned to cope alone with the problems of a way of life which was under attack from every quarter but in which she had no honourable course but to continue.

4

In the old days both the military and civil authorities of the province had spent half the year in Ranpur and half in Pankot which meant that between April and October the hill station had enjoyed the formality of an official season, with the Governor and his wife at the summer residence and the general officer commanding and his wife at Flagstaff House.

The last full official season had been that of summer 1939. It ended on 1 October when the Governor went back down to Ranpur preceded or followed by his staff, clerks, files, lorry and train loads of baggage; one day before Barbie arrived by the opposite route with her own encumbrances.

A few weeks later like governors of other provinces in which the Congress Party had taken office after the elections of 1937 he was accepting the resignations of every member of the ministry, headed by Mr Mohammed Ali Kasim, a prominent Muslim of the Congress Party which many English people suspected of being the party of the Hindus in spite of its claim to represent the whole of India.

After accepting these resignations, unconstitutionally forced on the provincial ministers by a party whose leaders had no central duty to the limited Indian electorate and an apparent antipathy towards assisting the British to preserve democracy and show Hitler what was what, the Governor assumed governor's control, as he was entitled to do under the safeguard clause in the Act of 1935 by which attempts had been made to go some way to meet the Indians' insistent demands for self-government; and thereafter ruled the province directly, in the old pre-reform style, from Government House in Ranpur.

In Pankot in 1940 there was half a season. Flagstaff House was open, indeed had never been shut because on the declaration of war the general officer commanding in Ranpur, then situated in Pankot for the summer, elected to stay put, but the Governor and his wife did not manage to come up until May, and in June they had to return suddenly to Ranpur. One of the effects of the Congress ministry's term of office from 1937 to 1939 had been to reduce the scale of the annual removal of the majority of the secretariat to the hills, and although on reassuming autocratic control the Governor would have liked to reinstate this traditional move in full he would have found it difficult to house more than a skeleton of his civil service because by now the army had infiltrated into the complex of buildings where the civil departments once enjoyed the cooler air for six months of the year.

Frustrated in his attempt to direct from Pankot a secretariat largely left behind down in Ranpur and denied his simple need to lead a peaceful life by new viceregal attempts to come to terms with unco-operative Indian leaders after the fall of France, the Governor, choleric and savage, stormed back to Ranpur en route for Simla and, as he put it, further fruitless talks with the Viceroy who would have further fruitless talks with bloody Gandhi and bloody Jinnah in a further fruitless pursuit of the bloody Pax Britannica, when all that was needed to scare the Indians into toeing the line and getting on with the war was a regiment or two of British infantry and a Brigadier as spunky as old Brigadier-General Dyer who had mown down hundreds of bloody browns in Amritsar in 1919. No one cared to remind him that the Lt-Governor of the Punjab who had stood by Dyer both at the time and in the years of Dyer's subsequent disgrace had only this year been shot dead in London by an Indian in delayed retribution, in Caxton Hall of all places. It was felt in any case that the Governor did not need reminding. He was a man of the old school – actually a bit of an embarrassment – the kind who if he could not have peace preferred a row and might even welcome being shot at now or twenty years later. His lady followed him, as pale as he was scarlet, and as talkative as he was taciturn between outbursts of bad temper, leaving Pankot bereft of the two people who most graced its official public occasions.

In 1941 when the choleric Governor's term of office ended and he was succeeded by a new Governor, Sir George Malcolm, there was scarcely a season in Pankot at all (other than the tentative one provided by the energetic new GOC's wife, Isobel Rankin, at Flagstaff House). The Rankins made their presence felt, but in the right sort of way. Malcolm, it was said, was an example of the rather alarming kind of person whom the war was throwing up, people with an immense and exhausting capacity for work and an impatience with any tradition which, like the annual movement of an entire administration from Ranpur to Pankot and back again, put the slightest strain on an overworked executive.

'Sir George will settle down,' people said; and there were hopes of a full season in 1942; but at the turn of the year the war that had seemed so far off was suddenly on India's doorstep. Malaya went first, to the Japanese, then Singapore. Burma followed. With these stunning losses the hope of anything ever being quite the same again faded quietly away into the background. And as if things weren't bad enough with the enemy at the gate there was an increasingly troublesome enemy inside it: Indian leaders who screamed that defeat in Malaya and Burma was a forerunner to defeat in India, that the British had shown themselves incompetent to defend what it was their duty to defend but which wouldn't need defending at all if they weren't there, inciting the Japanese who had no quarrel with the Indians themselves.

The political situation sizzled dangerously from the March of 1942 throughout the summer and finally exploded in August with a violence that set people talking about a new mutiny.

Forseeable as it had been to anyone with an ounce of commonsense and regrettable as it was it was not actually unwelcome. It cleared the air. The policy of placating the

Indians and getting on with the war at the same time had failed as it was bound to. Now the question of further Indian advances to self-government could be firmly shelved for the duration. It was felt to be a pity that it had not been shelved at the beginning when Indian politicians proved that there was hardly a man with statesman-like qualities among them.

After the absurd *débâcle* of 1939 when the Indian Congress Party threw away all the political advantages it had won, by resigning provincial responsibility on points of principle (failure of the Viceroy to consult it before declaring His Majesty's Indian empire at war with Germany, refusal to co-operate in a war with whose aims it pretended to be in sympathy but said should have included immediate freedom to Indians to do as they liked) the more troublesome firebrands (that man Subhas Chandra Bose for instance) were popped neatly into clink under the Defence of India rules, but it was felt that the Viceroy should have made a broader sweep.

The Viceroy in question was Linlithgow; described in Pankot as an odd chap, sound but tactless and as usual not quite the thing because he didn't know enough about the country. Viceroys seldom did and few had the panache of Curzòn who had tried to make not knowing a virtue in itself. The Congress-wallahs had put one over on Linlithgow by adopting this policy of official approval of the war against Hitler but disapproval of the means by which they were to be allowed to co-operate in it; and only those who stood up in the market place and opened their mouths too wide found themselves silenced by imprisonment.

If the Congress-wallahs had had any political cunning as well as political stubbornness they would have stayed in office in the provinces as the few Muslim League ministers had done, co-operated so far as was necessary in the war effort, expanded their political experience and power and, simultaneously, their grip on the administration, so that when the war was over their claim to speak and act for the majority of Indians and their right to advance steadily to self-government inside the Common-wealth would have been difficult to refute.

But they had thrown their opportunity away and one began to wonder whether in doing so they hadn't set their cause back to a point where independence would seem as far away on a post-war horizon as it had been on a pre-war one. There were sensible men among them, the ex-chief minister in Ranpur, M. A. Kasim (known popularly as M.A.K.) was an example, but they were all either under Gandhi's saintly spell or too weak-kneed to exorcize it, and the saintly spell of Mr Gandhi had finally been exposed for what it was: a cover for the political machina-tions of an ambitious but naïve Indian lawyer whose successes had gone to his head.

His demand now that the British should quit India, should leave her to 'God or to anarchy' sounded fine, courageous, desperate and inspired, but it meant that they should leave India to the Japanese who were already on the Chindwin but with whom Gandhi obviously expected to make a political bargain. Unless you were stupid you did not make bargains with the Japanese but war. Even the liberal American Jew, Roosevelt, had been forced to understand this and it was entirely to placate Roosevelt that Churchill (who knew a thing or two, including the fact that the Americans' only interest in India was that the sub-continent should remain a stable threat in the rear to Japanese ambitions in the Pacific) had sent out that Fabian old maid, Stafford Cripps, to do what Churchill knew couldn't be done: put pepper into Indian civilians and politicians by offering them what they'd been offered before, but which a pinko-red like Cripps, unused to office, would see as new, generous, advantageous, a Left-Wing invention. The farce of this particular confrontation between an English pinko-red and grasping Indian leaders had not been lost on the English community. Its total and inevitable failure had been a smack in the eye to Cripps who went home eating crow as well as his bloody veget-ables. Given a chance to show that a modern British socialist could achieve what the old-fashioned Right had never achieved, unity among Indians and political co-operation between Indians and English, he had also been hoist with the responsibility of office; a responsibility which meant, quite simply, having to make things work.

And he couldn't of course make them work because Indian politicians always wanted more if offered anything. Not understanding this he returned to Whitehall with that smile like a brass plate on a coffin and a conviction that while someone had been unco-operative it was not clear who. Once he had gone the Quit India compaign gathered momentum; which was also funny because it made Cripps look as if he had invented it; and early in August the Congress Party officially adopted the resolution calling for the British to leave or take the consequences. For once the government in New Delhi seemed to have been prepared. Within a few hours prominent Congressmen all over the country were detained under the Defence of India rules in an operation of arrest that gathered them in from Gandhi all the way down through the scale to members of local sub-committees in the towns and cities. Even the moderate ex-chief minister Mohamed Ali Kasim was reported arrested.

The country held its breath and then with a fierceness not equalled in living memory the leaderless mobs rose and for three weeks the administration was virtually at a standstill.

5

From the Ranpur Gazette: 15 August 1942

ENGLISH WOMEN ATTACKED

It has just been officially disclosed that on the afternoon and evening of 9 August two Englishwomen were victims of violent attacks in the Mayapore district of this province.

In the first case which occurred in the rural area of Tanpur no arrests have yet been made. In the second which took place in the town of Mayapore six Hindu youths are being held. It is understood that a charge is likely to be made under section 375 Indian Penal Code. The prompt action of the Mayapore police in apprehending the suspects within an hour or two of this disgraceful attack will be applauded. The arresting party was under the personal command of the District Superintendent of Police.

In a statement issued to the press DSP said, 'It is not in the public interest to reveal the name of the girl at this time. She worked on a voluntary basis at the Mayapore General Hospital. Her family is one that distinguished itself in service to India. According to her statement she was attacked by about six Indian males who stopped her on her way home at night from the place where she also did voluntary and charitable work for sick and dying people of the scheduled castes. She was dragged from her bicycle into the derelict site known as the Bibighar Gardens where she was criminally used.'

DSP confirmed that among the men arrested was one with whom she was acquainted in the course of her work at the poor people's dispensary.

The earlier incident in Tanpur took place in broad daylight. Miss Edwina Crane, Superintendent of the Protestant Mission schools in Mayapore district, was attacked by a large mob who obstructed the passage of her motor-car en route from Dibrapur back to her headquarters in Mayapore. Accompanying her was the teacher in charge at the Dibrapur mission, Mr D.R. Chaudhuri. He had left the school to give his superintendent protection from gangs of badmashes rumoured to be roaming the countryside following news of the arrest of Mr Gandhi and other Congress Party leaders.

Mr J. Poulson, assistant commissioner in Mayapore, said he left Mayapore in a police truck at approximately 3.45 P.M. on 9 August to investigate reports that telephone lines had been cut between Dibrapur and Mayapore and

59

that troublemakers were gathering in rural areas. He stated: 'At Candgarh we found the local police locked in their own kotwali and having released them pressed on in pursuit of the mob who had terrorized them. It was raining. A few miles short of Tanpur we saw first a burnt-out motor-car and then a hundred yards beyond, Miss Crane, sitting on the roadside guarding the body of Mr Chaudhuri who had been clubbed to death. She was soaked to the skin. In attempting to save Mr Chaudhuri from the mob, which had apparently objected to an Indian driving with an Englishwoman, Miss Crane had been struck several times. When she recovered consciousness she found Chaudhuri dead and the mob gone.'

Miss Crane is presently in the General Hospital in Mayapore where her condition although improved still gives some cause for anxiety. Although Ranpur remains quiet, Dibrapur and Mayapore have been the scene of serious riots and in Dibrapur Congress flags have been run up on the court house and the magistrate's private residence. Troops are reported on the way to Dibrapur in anticipation of a request for aid from the civil power. The senior military officer in Mayapore is Brigadier A. V. Reid, DSO, MC.

The rapidity with which the whole situation has deteriorated so soon after the Congress Committee's endorsement of Mr Gandhi's Quit India resolution in Bombay on 8 August, suggests that plans had been laid well beforehand for these acts of insurrection. The scale on which civil disobedience has been offered in this and other provinces, the reports constantly being received of riots, wanton destruction, burning and looting, hardly support the opinion expressed in some quarters that these are 'spontaneous demonstrations of anger by the people at the unjust imprisonment of their leaders'.

The authorities showed foresight in arresting members of Congress within a few hours of the committee passing the resolution. It behoves us all to be equally on our guard. And it is to be hoped that those who are guilty of these vicious and outrageous attacks on two innocent

Englishwomen and the murder of the Indian school-teacher will quickly be brought to justice.

This confirmation of rumours there had been in Pankot of attacks on Englishwomen down in the plains produced a full house at the club-meeting. People arrived with their copies of the *Ranpur Gazette* opened and folded at the page on which the report appeared, on the off-chance that someone had not read it. 'I see you've all got your tickets,' one member said. But it was no laughing matter.

The purpose of the meeting, announced several days earlier, was to discuss arrangements to protect lives and property in the event of riots occurring in Pankot. So unlikely had this seemed that provision had been made for only half the number of people who came. The meeting was delayed for a quarter of an hour while more chairs were brought into the main lounge. Eventually it got under way with an address by Colonel Trehearne in his capacity as senior member of the cantonment board. His voice, although musical, lacked power. 'Can't hear!' someone at the back shouted. He was shushed. Older hands knew from experience that Trehearne's contribution to any public gathering bore the same relationship to what followed as an overture did to an opera. If you came in after he had sat down you'd missed nothing.

He was succeeded by two civil officers from district headquarters down in Nansera: Bill Craig, assistant to the deputy commissioner, who assured the meeting that the district was so far unaffected by the disturbances in the plains and expected to remain so; and Ian MacIntosh of the Indian police who confirmed Craig's report and opinion and added that three men from Ranpur, on whom the CID had kept an eye, had just been arrested for disturbing the peace by attempting to harangue the inhabitants of a nearby village. Mr MacIntosh added that he used the word 'attempting' advisedly because the villagers had simply laughed at the men and might have stoned them if a truck-load of constables had not intervened and taken them off to a place of safety: gaol.

The atmosphere in the club which had been rather tense at the start as a result of the reports in the *Ranpur Gazette* now reverted to near-normal. The groundswell of indignation, of determination to stand no nonsense, of fear, of sad annoyance that things should have come to this pass, was checked by the counter-pressure of communal good-humour; hilarity, almost.

At this point an Indian officer from General Rankin's staff, Major Chatab Singh, known affectionately as Chatty (which he was) got on his feet and explained in broad outline civil and military plans to keep control in Pankot and Nansera (which was ten miles down the road, on the way to Ranpur), should the unthinkable actually happen. There were to be collection points for residents who desired to seek refuge from riots and attacks on European property and installations; for example women living on their own, or with children, and women whose husbands were off-station or likely to be in the event of serious disturbances in the area. One such centre would be the club itself. Chatty said he appreciated that these would henceforth be known as funk-holes but hoped that would not put people off using them if the need arose.

He spoke with humour and precision. His handsome wife, who headed the small Indian section of military wives, made precise notes. People laughed at his jokes, which were not too clever. Had they been so the suspicion might have arisen that Chatty harboured bitter thoughts inside that neatly turbanned head.

After a short pause for question and answer Isobel Rankin got up and announced that after refreshments the heads of the various women's committees were to meet in the card room. These women were co-opted to form the special Pankot women's emergency committee. She said she hoped this would turn out to be both its inaugural and closing session. She refered to the notice in the *Ranpur Gazette* and to the rumours of such attacks which had been current in the last few days, grossly exaggerated in regard to the number of women said to have been hurt.

She did not (she said) wish to play down the seriousness

62

of what had apparently happened in Mayapore but warned against the effects of what she called excessive reaction. Before she left the platform she asked whether Mrs Smalley was present and finding that she was (she could not have been in doubt) invited her to act as secretary to the emergency committee. Mrs Smalley was already secretary to three permanent committees.

'I'm sorry to throw another job at you but you're the obvious choice,' Mrs Rankin said.

'Oh, that's all right,' little Mrs Smalley said, sitting down and, small as she was, promptly disappearing. People smiled. Mrs Smalley would have been piqued if the general's lady had given the job to someone else. She was a glutton for work.

Most stations had their Smalleys; a number of stations had at some time or another had these Smalleys. Because they looked nondescript and unambitious they provoked no envy and hardly any suspicion. In Pankot, where they had been since the end of 1941, they arrived at parties harmoniously together and then put distance between them as if to distribute their humdrum selves in as many parts of the room as possible. Leaving, they did so arm-in-arm, giving an impression that by playing their separate parts in a communal endeavour something integral to their private lives and mutual affection had been maintained.

The Smalleys were slight bores but very useful people: Major Smalley with his expertise in routine A & Q matters at Area Headquarters and little Lucy Smalley with her knowledge of shorthand and patient way with paper: The perfect dogsbody for any committee. Socially they were thought dull but it was always just as well to have some obvious dullness around. The sight of Lucy and Tusker standing arm-in-arm in the porch when a cocktail party was over, looking into the night for the tonga that had once again failed to stay or return for them, brought out the Samaritan instinct in gaier and better-organized guests because this constant breaking-down of arrangements they made for their personal convenience seemed

63

to emphasize the willing efficiency they showed in affairs that affected the community as a whole. The Smalleys always managed to get a lift home.

They lived in Smith's Hotel. They had a suite: a small dark living-room and a smaller darker bedroom. Tusker declared himself perfectly happy with this accommodation (he received a special pay allowance for living out) and while Lucy was often heard to say she wished they could find a little bungalow of their own where they could more easily entertain their friends to dinner, Pankot was happy with the arrangement too. Cocktail parties were one thing, dinners another. The experience of being sat next to either Smalley at an official function – he in the dress uniform he insisted on wearing in spite of the wartime dispensation from such formality and which was tight round the shoulders, and she in her crimson taffeta gown (familiar enough after a while for her to be seen as a struggling little point of patient modest reference in a restless and sometimes greedy world) had helped Pankot to form the sensible opinion that the Smalleys were ideally placed where they were. In fact it became almost disagreeable to imagine them outside the context of Smith's; they went well with the napery and the potted palms; and, residing in an hotel bedroom, they were interestingly endowed with the attributes of perpetual honeymooners even after ten years of childless marriage. In this light their arm-in-armness was not only agreeable to see but satisfactorily explained.

When Lucy Smalley took her place in the card room, notebook and pencil neatly balanced on her neatly arranged legs, she added the final touch to a picture of the female hierarchy to which it can be assumed she aspired – in her shy but persistent way and irrespective of which station she was on – to belong. Her timid glances were more penetrating than they seemed. Content to appear mediocre and dull she looked for opportunities to offer opinions that struck people as just clever enough to confirm them in their own opinion that while she was dull she was not too dull, and mediocre in the right sort of dutiful and helpful way.

Six card tables had been placed together so that the committee could do its work in comfort. Around them sat Isobel Rankin, Maisie Trehearne, Mildred Layton, Nicky Paynton, Clara Fosdick and Clarissa Peplow, the wife of the Reverend Arthur Peplow, incumbent of St John's and chaplain to the station. Lucy Smalley sat a foot away from one end facing Isobel Rankin who had her elbows on the table at the other. Apart from Isobel's choice of seat no special order of precedence had been observed. The omission was probably deliberate. An equality of a kind had been established.

The meeting was informal. Isobel had made a draft agenda and out of general chat she formulated every so often a minute for Lucy to record.

The quietest member was Maisie Trehearne. She was tall, slender and stately in the way that a woman given to private preoccupation can be if she has the figure for it. What Maisie Trehearne's preoccupations were no one knew. There may have been another explanation for the impression she gave of having more important things to think about than the matter under discussion.

There were people who said that her mind was as blank as her pale patrician face was comparatively and unfairly unlined; but she never fumbled if asked to comment on a view just given. She seldom smiled. But she was seldom upset either. The only thing known about Maisie Trehearne's emotional life was that she had a fondness for animals and a horror of cruelty to them. But she expressed both the fondness and the horror in much the same tones as those in which she spoke on other subjects.

No one had ever uncovered in her the steel core which a military career in India normally required and which was presumably responsible for keeping her so upright even when sitting down. Perhaps the uprightness was due to an uncomfortable corset, but she looked too composed for that. Composure was Maisie Trehearne's main characteristic. Were it not for the war her husband would have been coming up for retirement but she conveyed neither pleasure nor disappointment at the postponement of – as in her case it curiously but suitably was – Cheltenham.

Of the other women only Clarissa Peplow had any kind of physical affinity with Maisie. Clarissa was also pale although she was plump with it. She was stately but in her case the stateliness was that of someone conscious of the dignity of Christ's church militant. Lucy Smalley excepted, Clarissa Peplow was the least important woman in the room; unimportant in temporal terms. Her clear-blue eyes proclaimed circumstances in which other terms prevailed.

Opposite her sat the widowed Clara Fosdick, whose sister was married to Mr Justice Spendlove of the High Court in Ranpur. Clara was big-boned and well-fleshed. She had a resonant contralto voice which enabled her to argue convincingly even when it was obvious that she had reached an opinion through a process of emotional reasoning, not logical deduction. She got on well with young men. She conformed in many ways to a young man's idea of the perfect mother. She struck them as affectionate, even-tempered, good-humoured, restful, tough when necessary but blessed with a considerable capacity for understanding and forgiveness in that part of her which at her age and with her build could properly be called a bosom. It came as no surprise to such young men to learn from her friend Nicky Paynton that Mrs Fosdick had lost her only child, a boy, at the age of five, when he died of typhoid in the Punjab.

Mrs Paynton, the most talkative woman at the table and with whom Clara Fosdick shared a bungalow, was wiry, tight-wound, energetic. Her husband Benny Paynton, the commanding officer of the 1st Ranpurs, was on active service in the Arakan. She had two boys at school in Wiltshire whom she had not seen since her and Bunny's spell of home leave in 1938. She had seen little of her husband too. Only in the frequency with which she introduced the subject of the absent Bunny and the far-away children could one detect how seldom she was not thinking about them. But the references were all light-hearted, in keeping with the discipline the station expected such a woman to impose on herself. She was referring to Bunny now and to the report in the *Ranpur Gazette* which had named a Brigadier Reid as commander of the troops in Mayapore where the attacks on the two English women had taken place.

'I shan't tell Bunny Alec Reid's got a brigade. We never knew him well but always thought him a bit of a duffer. I thought he was still in Rawalpindi which was where we last saw him. You remember Alec and Meg Reid don't you, Mildred?'

'Vaguely.'

'Meg Reid was a bit of a wet blanket too. I can't think why they've given Alec a brigade. He's been behind a desk for years. If I write and tell Benny Alec Reid's got a brigade he'll probably blow his top.'

'Shall we get back to the agenda?' Isobel Rankin said.

She tapped her sheet of paper with a pencil. One noticed her knuckles. They looked hard. Her finger-nails were bright red. No languor about Isobel Rankin. She allowed some gossip at a friendly meeting such as this but kept it checked and did not contribute to it. She got things moving in the direction she desired. The slightest gesture – an index-finger adjustment of her reading spectacles on the bridge of her nose – was dynamic.

Concentration of energy distinguished her from the other women at the table, even from Nicky Paynton whose vitality, potentially as great, seemed by comparison to lack purpose. But then Isobel Rankin could not afford to relax as her colleagues could. She bore the burden of command. It could have fallen on several of the other women – on Mildred, on Nicky, on Maisie – and they would have borne it just as capably. The question of which of them sat at the head of the table as the GOC's wife had been settled by their choice of husbands. With a long war and any luck Bunny Paynton could end up not merely with a brigade but with a division, and Mildred's husband would probably have had a brigade by now if his wartime promotional expectations had not been brought to a grinding halt in North Africa.

But these were military roles. Dick Rankin would never get an active command. He was a military administrator and young and well-connected enough to anticipate capping his career with military appointments at government level.

An air of power more far-reaching than that of the Army alone emanated from Isobel. She was preparing for the world where things were arranged and matters of consequence decided. A certain secretiveness, dressed as discretion, already hinted at a familiarity with what went on behind the scenes.

Outside the inner circle of her friends she was of course much misunderstood. Those who thought themselves not as well-used by her as they deserved interpreted her flashes of wit and natural hardness of tone as evidence of malice and her impatience in argument as a sign of mental inflexibility. She was neither a stupid nor a malicious person and was in fact quick to detect stupidity and malice in others. And she was far from being the hidebound stickler for rules which she may have appeared in the eyes of people who, puzzled by the brusque manner she adopted towards the time-wasters, the ignorant and the prejudiced, decided that they had erred socially.

But today, Clarissa and Lucy apart, she was among friends and had she after adjusting her spectacles announced her personal creed instead of the next subject – the special arrangements for Indian mothers and children who came into defended areas for protection from riots, rape and arson – she would have found a measure of agreement, because in her there resided in a highly developed form the animus of declining but still responsible imperialism.

She had an astringent affection for the people and the country in which she had spent so many years of her life, and no personal prejudice against Indians as Indians. As with members of her own race she allowed her instincts to guide her when it came to separating those Indians with whom she was happy to associate from those with whom she officially had to deal or whom she could ignore. She counted quite a number of Indian men and women among her friends but these, like her English friends, were people she felt could be relied upon to preserve for India's sake everything the English and the Indians had done together which could be reckoned of lasting value. She was under no misapprehension about the mistakes made in the past and still being made by her own people in India but if she had been asked to say in what way India had most benefited from the British connexion, what it was that could be offered in extenuation of fault, error, even of wickedness, she would have been perfectly clear that it was the example so often given of personal trustworthiness: a virtue that flowed from courage, honesty, loyalty and commonsense in what was to her a single definition of good. She did not see how a person or a country could survive without it.

She was convinced that most of the things that offered some assurance of India surviving on her own resources in the post-war world would reflect the example of personal trustworthiness set by her countrymen in the past. She was in two minds about the benefit that might be had if the connexion with England were much prolonged. She accepted the fact that at home her own people had often been indifferent to Indian affairs and that this indifference sprang from ignorance. But in the old days when the code by which she lived had been widely upheld in England this indifference to India had not mattered much, because those who came out to shoulder the responsibility could rely to a great extent on moral support at home. But of recent years, in England, she knew that these values had been eroded and she thought that this mattered a great deal because govern India as one might from Viceregal House, Government House, the commissioner's bungalow, the district officer's court and a military headquarters, the fount of government had always been and still was in the mother country and the moral climate there was bound to influence the climate in which the imperial possession was ruled.

In judging moral climate she took little account of factors usually selected to show evidence of decline. She was a tolerant woman in many of the matters that woke intolerance in others. She held the view that it was a bad thing for society to remain static, a desirable thing for it to be on the move and to divide its rewards more fairly and distribute its opportunities more equitably. She did not feel that there was a conflict between her idea of the way society should change and her conviction that certain principles should be inimical to change. She was aware however of there being that sort of conflict in other people's minds. She was unsympathetic both to the prejudices of stubborn traditionalism and to the anarchic influence of those who often set about destroying it. She believed that through the business of attempting to divest old authorities of power the notion could become current that authority of any kind was suspect. To Isobel Rankin a world without authority was meaningless. There would be no chain of trust if there were no chain of command. She feared that in such a climate there could be a demission of authority in India by her own people that it would be possible only to describe as dishonourable, if by demission one implied as one should a full discharge of every obligation.

She was intent on discharging one such obligation now.

'The problem with mothers and children is that the mothers look after their own to the detriment of community discipline. What we want is a strong-willed woman who's good with kids and can keep them occupied while the mothers do their bit for the community.'

'It's difficult with Indian mothers,' Clara Fosdick said.

'We have to conceive of a hypothetical case, a state of siege lasting say a week,' Isobel went on. 'The teachers at the regimental schools can cope with the boys but I'm thinking of the girls. Mildred, what about that ex-mission teacher your step mother-in-law has living with her?'

'Barbara Batchelor,' Clarissa Peplow said before Mildred had the chance, presupposing the inclination, to reply. 'I think Barbara would be an excellent choice.'

'But she'd never leave Mabel,' Clara Fosdick pointed out. 'And Mabel wouldn't budge from Rose Cottage if the hordes of Ghengiz Khan were galloping down from the hills.'

'She might have to,' Isobel said. 'Mildred? Any comment? Would Miss Batchelor be capable of controlling a gang of Indian boys and girls?'

'Presumably she's made the attempt in the past. I should think if Clarissa were in charge of her she might be of some use.'

'I want someone capable of running her own show,' Isobel put in. 'Could you take it on, Mrs Peplow?'

'It's more Barbara's line.'

Lighting a cigarette Nicky Paynton said, 'Clara's absolutely right though. She'd never leave Mabel. They'd die together on the verandah of Rose Cottage. Aziz too.'

Lucy Smalley coughed.

'What is it Mrs Smalley?' Isobel recognized the request to speak.

'I'm sure Mrs Fosdick and Mrs Paynton are right and that it would be difficult to prise Miss Batchelor away from Rose Cottage so long as Mrs Layton senior elected to stay there. But there's another reason why I don't think she would be, well, much good at the moment.'

'What reason?'

'She's in a terrible state this morning because the woman who was attacked in Mayapore district is a friend of hers. I mean the mission teacher, the one whose name was given. Miss Crane.'

She had the whole attention of the meeting. One of the advantages of having Mrs Smalley on committees was her more intimate knowledge of the affairs of the lower deck. Isobel turned to Mildred.

'Really? A close friend?'

'My dear Isobel, don't ask me. I know absolutely nothing about Miss Batchelor's connexions.'

Isobel looked back at Mrs Smalley and raised her chin inviting further information.

'I wouldn't have known myself,' Lucy said, 'if I hadn't

71

met her in the bazaar a couple of days ago. She was quite worried then because of the reports of things being bad in Mayapore. I didn't pay much attention, well, she does tend to go on. You don't actually need to listen to every word, do you? But when I read the Gazette this morning and saw the name of this woman I remembered Miss Batchelor had been telling me about a mission friend of hers called Crane in Mayapore who'd been a heroine in what sounded like the dark ages. So I rang her after breakfast. She'd just read the report too and was hardly coherent. She seemed to think I was someone else, ringing up with *news* of her friend. So I don't think she'd be much good looking after the children if we have riots in Pankot. From the way she was talking you'd have thought her friend was the other poor girl, whoever she is, who's been criminally assaulted.'

'Raped,' Isobel snapped. Lucy Smalley blushed. 'And her name is Miss Manners. Her uncle was governor in Ranpur back in the late 'twenties or early 'thirties. They've been trying to keep her name secret but it's leaked out as it was bound to. Did you know Sir Henry Manners, Mildred?'

'We were in Peshawar and Lahore while he was in office. He was rather pro-Indian wasn't he? I mean politically.'

'Nicky?'

'We were off-station too.'

'Dicky says he had a good reputation,' Isobel said. 'His widow is still alive in Rawalpindi, I gather, but nothing's known about the girl. It could be a sticky case, from what I hear.'

Isobel did not say what she had heard. She tapped the agenda again.

'Right,' she said, 'we obviously rule out Miss Batchelor, and I'm not keen on making Chatty Singh's wife responsible for *everything* to do with the Indian community. She'll be over-worked as it is. What about the librarian, Mrs Stewart?'

* * *

'My dear, my poor Edwina (Barbie wrote), I was so shocked to read in the *Ranpur Gazette* about your truly terrible experience. For an age I wandered about distracted, wanting to help but not knowing how. Mayapore is so far away and even so, what could I do? My good kind friend here, Mabel, coming in and seeing me in this restless state, this state of great, of overwhelming anxiety, and learning the reason, said at once well if you can get through you must ring and find out how she is and leave a message. Practical woman! I followed her advice. It took an age. But I got the Mayapore exchange at last and then the hospital and spoke to a Sister Luke who said that you were quite comfortable, past the crisis, that she would give you my love and of course any letter I cared to send. Past the crisis! I dared not ask of what. Sister Luke seemed to think I would know, though Heaven knows how. Once again it is Mabel who lifts the veil from my uncertainty with her suggestion that after that shock and exposure, waiting, waiting in the rain, you must have been struck down with fever, perhaps pneumonia. My poor Edwina. You must, now on the mend, take care, take care.

'All this was yesterday. I delayed writing to you until today in order to get some sense into my thoughts. The point is that presently when you are better the Mission I am sure will want you to take sick leave to get your strength up properly again. Please take that sensible course. God knows how long these terrible disturbances will last – we aren't troubled by them in this lovely peaceful old station – but we can only hope and pray that they will end soon before more lives are lost. It is they, *they*, poor people who will suffer in the end.

'Well now when you are better, when you are ready, there is a room for you here. It is Mabel's suggestion. But it would be so very wonderful to have you, for as long as you are able to spare before buckling to work again as I know you will but must not too soon. I shall say no more for the moment. But let it sink in as an idea. Pankot is a beautiful place. I've been happy here as you know from

73

my previous letters. You can be sure of the friendliest welcome but all the privacy and seclusion you wish, or otherwise. It quickly got round that I knew you and people have been so kind in their inquiries. Today in the bazaar I was stopped many times and asked for news of you. All those of whom I have written before ask especially for their good wishes to be conveyed to you. The Reverend Arthur and Clarissa Peplow, Mr Maybrick who plays the organ at St John's, Mabel of course and sweet Sarah. I have not seen Susan for a day or two. One feels dreadfully for these young girls, I mean in view of the terrible reports about that other poor woman in Mayapore. Her name was not given in the *Gazette* but we had rumours in advance and now it is freely said by people here who seem to know that her name is Manners, the niece of a one-time governor of the province. Poor girl, poor girl. You probably know her for it seems she was much involved with charitable work among the untouchables and lived with an Indian lady, a friend of her aunt who is now a widow in Rawalpindi and who must be suffering. One is so puzzled. One senses a mystery, an imponderable – I mean in regard to those who are hurt like yourself, Edwina. Your life too has been so utterly devoted to *them*. I shall write again very very soon. Meanwhile my love and prayers. May God protect you, through Jesus. Sincere, sincere good wishes, Barbie.'

Miss Crane, Miss Manners; Miss Manners, Miss Crane. At times there was a tendency to confuse them; to forget momentarily which of the two victims it was Miss Batchelor knew until a few seconds' thought made the missionary connexion; and then a different kind of confusion arose because there being nothing to identify Miss Crane the shortest way to her was through the familiar face and figure of her friend Miss Batchelor. At any given second a fleeting glimpse might therefore be had, as Barbie strode downhill to the bazaar, of the Crane woman doing that very thing for no particular reason unless it were to snatch the observer's thoughts and concentrate them upon a special issue: the safety of women.

There would now enter into the pine-scented and gun-metal air a stiff breeze of the kind that cooled without actually being felt to blow and in Miss Batchelor's, Miss Crane's, wake all kinds of horrors coupled and multiplied and gave her the look of a woman in danger who did not know it, walking in broad daylight, inviting attack, creating conditions in which an attack could take place.

Met face on she had the surprised happy appearance of someone who a few minutes ago had survived assault. It was irritating to find that she had no information; none, that was, that stood the test of sifting from the mine-tip of her inconsequential chatter.

'I am reminded,' she said, 'of Miss Sherwood, Amritsar, 1919. She was a school superintendent too. I never met her, she wasn't Bishop Barnard, but Edwina met her I'm almost certain. She had such a pretty Christian name. Marcella. Perhaps we missionaries are singled out because they see us as agents of the dark, although actually of light. She narrowly escaped with her life. A Hindu woman rescued her, in that awful place, that little lane we sealed off afterwards and made people *crawl* down, on their bellies, in the dust and dirt, to punish them. I sometimes think none of that has been forgiven.'

The word forgiven seemed wrong in present circumstances and the introduction of yet another name, Miss Sherwood, an unnecessary complication. Miss Sherwood was not Miss Crane, neither was Miss Batchelor who after all was merely herself and in no danger except from passing traffic. What she had survived was being in wartime Pankot but not quite of it, three years of comparative obscurity now interrupted by her brief prominence as a friend of the less interesting of the two Mayapore victims.

She was a familiar enough figure though, recognizable from a distance, the length of the bazaar say, whose busy road she had a habit of crossing and recrossing or walking down the middle of at full tilt, narrowly avoiding tongas, bicycles and military trucks; intent on performing innumerable and apparently urgent tasks at bank, post office and shops, in the shortest possible time; shortest in her judgment. The actual economy of method was open to doubt, but presumably old Mabel Layton was satisfied with it. Bit by bit Miss Batchelor had taken over the running of Mabel's household. If Mabel had been looking for someone who would make her withdrawal easier she could not have done better than choose this retired missionary; obviously the kind of person who cried out to be used, like a cow with a full udder moaning for the herdsman to lead her to the pail.

But her yield in information was low and the suspicion arose that she knew Miss Crane less well than had at first been generally assumed from her manner. If the affair of the attacked missionary had not been so serious Miss Batchelor's association with it might have introduced a note of comedy; but it was undoubtedly serious and there were questions it would have been nice to have answers to. For instance was there any significance in the fact that the burnt-out motor-car was one hundred yards away from the dead teacher's body? Had he jumped clear and run back along the road to Dibrapur, attempted to save his own skin, before being caught by the mob? And why after he was dead did she stay with the body and not attempt to seek refuge in the next village? Would she recognize any of the men who had hit her?

Satisfying though it would be to have questions like these settled, the picture of old Miss Crane sitting by a dead body in the road in the pouring rain was of less intense interest than the picture of the other victim, the girl who was criminally assaulted, Miss Manners, whom no one in Pankot knew, of whom no one had ever heard even if the name Manners was familiar to people whose connexion with the province extended back ten or fifteen years. That the late Governor Sir Henry still had a widow living in Rawalpindi was a surprise to most people; that he had a niece in Mayapore living with an Indian woman (so the reports had it) was a greater surprise.

Apparently her other name was Daphne which for those who still remembered snippets of classical mythology produced the image of a girl running from the embrace of the sun god Apollo, her limbs and streaming hair already delineating the arboreal form in which her chastity would be preserved, enshrined forever; forever green. For her, then, the god could pluck no more than leaves. But this image could not be sustained and the other unknown Daphne stumbled on from antique laurel-dappled sunlight into a plain domestic darkness, dressed in her anonymity, and something simple, white, to suit her imagined frailty, her beauty and vulnerability; now half-sitting, half-lying on a couch in a shaded room with her eyes closed and one hand, inverted, against her aching forehead, speechless in the presence of friends who smiled when they were with her but otherwise looked grim.

And the violence done to her was not over yet. In due course she would have to leave the darkened room, go half-blinded by sunlight (or soaked by rain) to the ordeal of courtroom evidence unless she could be spared that which was not likely, so deeply had the democratic process undermined personal privilege. No closed doors for Miss Manners. The press would make sure of that. And the arrested men would not lack clever Bengali lawyers who would plead without fee, anxious for the publicity and the opportunity to sling mud, to impugn the morals of an English girl. It would be a high court case with a full gallery and the police out in force in the city to discourage the inevitable demonstrations on behalf of the accused. The judge would probably be an Indian. It was hoped so. The sentences of transportation for life to a penal settlement would come better from Mr Justice Chitteranjan than from Clara Fosdick's brother-in-law, Billy Spendlove. And then, only then, might poor Miss Manners fade back into the oblivion from which she had been cruelly dragged.

But her name would be written on the tablets.

The riots spread to Ranpur. Several lorry-loads of British and Indian troops left Pankot, ostensibly on convoy

77

exercises but in fact bound for an encampment outside the city. In Ranpur the city police fired to disperse mobs. The military assisted them on two occasions. An attempt to sabotage the railway between Ranpur and Pankot was discovered in time. The night train up and the day train down now went under armed guard. For several hours the telephone connexion was cut. When it was repaired reports came in thick and fast. The *Ranpur Gazette* offices had their windows broken. A mob had penetrated the civil lines with the intention of surrounding Government House. This mob carried banners demanding the release of 'the innocent victims of the Bibighar', meaning the boys arrested for the rape. Scurrilous pamphlets appeared accusing the Mayapore police of torturing and defiling these six Hindu youths by whipping them and forcing them to eat beef. Factories were at a standstill and so was public transport. Life was reported quiet in Ranpur cantonment but there was a sense there undoubtedly of calm before storm. Things were said to be very bad farther afield, particularly in Mayapore and Dibrapur.

Politically in Ranpur it was a difficult time; in Pankot peaceful and, climatically speaking, marvellous: clear skies by day, refreshing rain by night, the perfect combination and a rare one even in the old station which was protected from the streaming and steamy monotony of the southwest monsoon by the very hills that made Ranpur so wet and humid. As Isobel Rankin said – at least the weather was pro-British.

There was bridge at Rose Cottage: the first session for some time. Mildred said she was tired of the club where the Pankot emergency committees had been meeting. Through the open french window came the velvet smell of roses and the marquee smell of cut grass. At midday Aziz brought drinks out to the verandah and cards were abandoned. Mabel was still in the garden cutting flowers for the house. Miss Batchelor was out shopping in the bazaar. Mildred Layton, Maisie Trehearne, Clara Fosdick and Nicky Paynton had the place to themselves.

Presently the girls were due with some of the boys; and there was to be curry lunch down at the club.

But into this idyll, this scene reminiscent of more pacific times, Barbie erupted unexpectedly accompanied by the spectres of broken bloody victims and the Reverend Arthur Peplow's wife, blue-eyed Clarissa, whose expression was one of constant challenge to the devil, an uncomfortable attribute but useful so long as it did not get out of hand which it had never been known to. Her presence was a kind of corrective to over-optimism, at the same time calming. She had a still clear voice and used it tellingly like a gift harnessed for professional purposes.

'Of course,' Miss Batchelor was saying, 'we weren't at all bound by such things at the Bishop Barnard. Oh, hello. Hello. I was telling Clarissa, that it was teaching first last all the time, well practically speaking, that is especially after the Great War. Miss Jolley is nonconformist which hides a multitude of sins. In my day and Edwina's day it had to be C of E. It's in my trunk or should be. I'll go and look and bring it out and then everyone can see. If I can find it. In spite of one's resolution to be neat and tidy, as my father used to say a human being's no better than a magpie.'

She went indoors. The silence that followed was explicit. Mildred broke it, beating Clarissa perhaps by the shortest head.

'What treat have we in store?' she inquired.

She had her elbows on the arms of the wicker chair and her glass at chest level, held there by the fingers of both droop-wristed hands, and like this seemed to define the limit of her contribution to public interest in Miss Batchelor as the friend of a victim of the riots. Her indifference to her as the sharer of Mabel's kingdom was unchanged. Clarissa, who sat upright on a stool with her feet together and her handbag on her knees, directed her Christian gaze at Mildred but finding no fault unless it were in the large glass of gin and lemon summoned her still clear voice and said, 'It's some kind of picture I gather. One that has to do with her friend.'

79

'How *is* her friend?' Nicky Paynton asked.

'The question that concerns me more,' Clarissa answered, 'is how is *she*? She has just been acting very strangely on Club Road.'

Walking without due care; a danger to herself, indeed to others, up the long stretch from Church Road which tongas bowled down or strained up, which no one *ever* walked or if they did walked with accidents in mind, keeping well into the bank on the golf-course side and facing the oncoming horses, bicycles and vehicles; not – like Barbara – on the left-hand side and certainly not in the middle, stopping, starting, drawing her own or an invisible companion's attention to some aspect of the Pankot scene which she must have seen hundreds of times before. And talking. Not in a loud voice. But quite definitely talking. To herself.

'I felt,' Clarissa said when she had described this curious and dangerous behaviour, 'that she imagined herself in the company of her friend, Miss Crane. I made my tonga stop and pick her up and directly she got in she said how kind it was of Mabel to let her invite Miss Crane to Rose Cottage when she is better. And then she started talking about a picture and insisted that I come in to see it.'

One after the other, Clarissa last, heads or eyes were turned towards the garden where Mabel stood motionless except for her hands and arms cutting roses. In the heavy air the click of the secateurs was clearly audible. The sound had a slightly enervating effect but suddenly there were other sounds, voices indoors, all but one of them male. A dog barked and Panther appeared scuffling blackly on to the verandah to greet the company one by one with a sniff of curiosity and a wag of tribute before gallivanting back to the french window, barking and skittering backwards as Susan came out ahead of four affable looking subalterns. Nigel you know, she said, this is Bob, Derek, Tommy. My mother, Mrs Trehearne, Mrs Paynton, Mrs Fosdick oh and Mrs Peplow, hello, no Panther come here.

'I expect there's some cold beer,' Mildred said. 'One of

you ring and Nigel we could do with refills, you'll find the trolley indoors. No, don't bother, Aziz has forestalled you, but tell him to bring the beer and if you don't mind making yourselves useful get me another of these and anyone else who wants one. Susan you're looking hot. There's some nimbo on the trolley, go and say hello to your Aunt Mabel first while one of the boys gets you a glass only stop Panther going mad for god's sake. Is Sarah coming or joining us at the club?'

'She said she'd join us at the club and may be late. Come on, Panther, come on old boy. Oh don't be silly. It's all right.' She grasped the dog by its stout leather collar and took it down steps it remembered as the scene of chastisement, and just then Barbie reappeared.

'I've found it!' she announced. The men made way for her and each other. She held the framed picture – measuring twelve inches by eight – and was cleaning the glass with the sleeve of her jacket, gripping the cuff with her fingers to make a firm rubbing surface. 'Isn't it extraordinary when you see something you haven't actually looked at for a while how familiar it is. The way the old man holds the alms bowl and the other leans on his staff. If you'd asked me to draw it from memory I couldn't have but one look at it now and one thinks of course! that's how they stood, that's how the artist drew them and left them, caught them in mid-gesture so that the gestures are always being made and you never think of them as getting tired.'

She gave the picture to Mrs Peplow and now stood to one side and a pace behind, both hands behind her back, legs apart (tightening her skirt at the calves) her head tilted, looking down over Clarissa's shoulder.

'You have to imagine it much larger, on the schoolroom wall behind the desk and all the children gathered round just as the people are gathered round the Queen, and Edwina standing with a pointer, not that I ever saw her give a lesson because she'd left Muzzafirabad before I got there but Mr Cleghorn gave me a demonstration and wanted me to try it but as I said, no, no, one must plough

81

one's own furrow. I can see him now, copying Edwina. Here is the Queen. The Queen is sitting on her throne. The uniform of the Sahib is scarlet. The sky here is blue. Who are these people in the sky? They are angels. They blow on golden trumpets. They protect the Queen. The Queen protects the people. The people bring presents to the Queen. The Prince carries a jewel on a velvet cushion. The Jewel is India. She will place the Jewel in her Crown.'

'Yes, I see,' Clarissa said. She was holding the picture like a looking-glass. 'Most admirable. To teach English *and* loyalty. Thank you for showing it to me.'

She handed the picture back. Miss Batchelor caught hold of it, strode across and thrust it at Mildred who had her refilled glass in both hands so that a young man with freckles and dark red hair gallantly reached out and took the picture and held it where Mrs Layton's glance might fall upon it, which fleetingly it did.

'Do pass it round,' Miss Batchelor said. 'It's a copy of a picture my friend Edwina Crane used years and years ago. The children adored it. Pictures are so important when instructing the young. But one has to be careful. Edwina once told me she had a very grave suspicion that in the end the children confused her with Victoria! Isn't that amusing? You must admit the artist got everything in, Mrs Fosdick. Disraeli's there, the one with the scroll and the smug expression. Generals, admirals, statesmen, princes, paupers, babus, banyas, warriors, villagers, women, children. And old Victoria in the middle of it sitting on a throne under a canopy in the open air of all things, really quite absurd but allegorical of course, she never came to India. She looks quite startled, don't you agree, Mrs Trehearne? But I think that's the effect of the reduction in scale. The print on the schoolroom wall was ten times as big and in that I remember – thank you, Mrs Paynton – she looked terribly wise and kind and understanding.'

Receiving the picture back from Mrs Paynton via a young man with a fair moustache she looked at it again herself. 'It always seemed to me to be a picture about love rather than loyalty. Perhaps they amount to the same thing. What do you think?'

She looked at the moustached young man whose mouth was puckered in concentration. He was pulling his left ear-lobe.

'Have you got transport?' Mildred asked one of the men, who said yes they had. 'Then directly you've downed your beers we ought to be getting along to the club.'

There were movements of departure. Two of the men went into the garden to rescue Susan.

'Oh, are you all going?' Miss Batchelor asked in her carrying schoolroom voice. 'Let me just say I do appreciate everyone being so kind, so solicitous for Edwina.'

She hammered a nail into the wall above the old campaigner's writing-table and hung the picture. Aziz approved. He would pause in his work to consider it, stand like one of the children of Muzzafirabad grown old but still possessed. She had told him about her friend Miss Crane, that she was in hospital in distant Mayapore hurt trying to save someone who was attacked and killed, and might when better stay for a week or two in the little spare. He nodded his understanding in the Indian way. In Aziz this was a gesture of great economy. He had the dignity of the people from the higher hills who walked shrouded in blankets and secrecy and made excursions into Pankot, involved in mysterious errands whose object escaped her since they came and went empty-handed as if merely to look and reassure themselves that nothing was happening in the valley of which they disapproved.

Mabel, in her solitary walks, went in their direction but nowadays went less often. On her own walks the other way downhill Barbie had become used to feeling like a dove sent out to check the level of the flood. After three years the darkness still lay on Mabel's soul and Barbie felt a bit discouraged. But since the incident on the road from Dibrapur the nature of her outings seemed to have changed and the familiar route had become unfamiliar. She anticipated revelation.

In her mind she too guarded the body. It lay near the milestone half way up (or down) Club Road. Passing the milestone made her light-headed; almost there was a sense of levitation. Edwina'a act of guarding the body had been one of startling simplicity and purity which possibly only a woman like Edwina could have had the occasion to perform and in performing it sum up the meaning of her life in India. From the schoolroom door at Muzzafirabad to the place on the road from Dibrapur was a distance measurable in miles, in years, but between the occasions there was no distance. Right from the beginning Edwina had been close to God and therefore to herself. Not teaching but loving. From her plain face, her manner, you might not have guessed this. Only from her actions. And in this most recent action, this guarding of the dead Indian's body, it seemed to Barbie that Edwina had achieved her apotheosis.

Oh how I long, Barbie said, standing still suddenly, having passed the milestone and accepted the sad fact that there was no body there for her to guard, how I long for an apotheosis of my own, nothing spectacular, mind, nothing in the least grandiose nor even just grand but, like Edwina's, quiet with a still centre to it that exemplifies not my release from earthly life although it might do that too but from its muddiness and uncertainty, its rather desperate habit of always proving that there are two sides to every question; my release from that into the tranquillity of knowing my work has been acceptable, good and useful perhaps, perhaps not, but performed in love, with love, and humility of course, indeed, humility, and singularity, wholeness of purpose. That is the most important thing of all.

But not knowing what kind of apotheosis this could be she walked on in the direction of the bazaar to settle the accounts at Jalal-ud-din's and Gulab Singh Sahib's, and buy more stamps to write more letters to Edwina who did not reply. No news she said to Sarah who inquired, being also at Jalal-ud-din's querying a bill upon which was writ large the rising cost of living in her father's continuing absence, no news is good news. She hoped for both their sakes that this was so.

She was in love with Sarah Layton and with Susan but more with Sarah who seemed to need it more. She was in love with Pankot and her life there and her duty to Mabel and the wind in winter. She was afraid to be in love with Mr Maybrick who played the organ at St John's and was widowed and retired from Tea, because he was to begin with a man and to go on with a man with a temper and an air of self-enclosure who did not normally invite proofs of attachment even of Barbie's kind, which did not extend to flesh. In any case he had large hands with more hair on the wrists than on his head and when he played the organ his hands looked extraordinarily vivid and enterprising. He lived alone except for his Assamese houseboy in a tiny and very untidy bungalow not far from the rectory-bungalow on the same tree-shaded road. In his bungalow there were many photographs of his dead wife and in most of them she had her hand above her eyes to keep the sun out, a fact which always made Barbie feel outdoors when really in.

On her way back from the bazaar she looked in at St John's to collect his album of Handel which was falling to pieces and which she had volunteered to repair. Mr Maybrick was at practice. She could hear the organ as she approached the church door. Bach. Toccata and fugue.

She sat in a pew and listened. She imagined Mr Maybrick's red face and bald head reflected in the mirror above the keyboards. The mirror was a framed picture. Who is this? This is the Planter. The face of the Planter is reddened by the sun. Here is his Lady. She shades her eyes from the light. She is of the North and ails in the climate. But keeps going. What is the Planter doing? He is showing the coolies how to pick only the tender leaves. As he shows them God sings through his fingers. The leaves are green. When they are dried they will be brown. The music will be preserved in caddies. The Planter and the

85

coolies between them will bring Tea to the Pots of the Nation.

She thought: I shall bring Edwina to St John's to hear Mr Maybrick at practice and on Sundays to hear Arthur Peplow's sermon. And afterwards we shall return to Rose Cottage. And I shall be large again and shapely with intent, so close to Edwina that God will remember and no longer mark me absent from the roll.

The attitude of the old Queen inclining her body, extending her two hands, was then suddenly an image of Edwina on the road from Dibrapur holding her hands protectively above the body of the Indian. Flames from the burning motor-car were reflected in the sky where the angelic light pierced bulgy monsoon clouds.

In this image she had a surrogate for God, a half-way house of intercession, capable perhaps of boosting the weak signals from the rush mat and transmitting them through the crackling overloaded ether which her direct prayers could not penetrate. She knelt with her body upright, facing the writing-table and the picture that pointed the reality of a Christian act, the palms of her hands turned to receive whatever was offered. She exposed her chest well below the gold pendant cross to give the metal room to act as a lightning conductor and sometimes felt it warmed by the reflected light from the burning vehicle; which was a promising beginning. Otherwise everything remained as it had been.

Once a week she visited the club subscription library for Mabel, seldom for herself who found what Mr Cleghorn had called the book of life sufficiently entertaining and puzzling to keep her occupied without recourse to the print and paper of imaginary or refurbished adventure.

Lost between the shelves among which she and Edwina would wander she heard a voice say, 'I'm told the whole trouble is she was infatuated with the Indian. She'd have done anything to save him.' She recognized the voice of little Mrs Smalley, the station gossip, and then Clarissa's saying, 'You can't know that.' To which Lucy Smalley replied, 'It's what people in Mayapore are saying, according to Tusker, and they have been in a position to judge. They say she was always out with him, holding his hand in public places. And now she's threatening to say the most dreadful things against the authorities if the men they've arrested are charged and tried, because *he's* one of them. The police officer who made the arrests is almost out of his mind.'

Barbie emerged armed with a volume of Emerson still open at the page with her thumb on the line, 'Man is explicable by nothing less than all his history,' which a moment ago had caused her to catch her breath. She cried out, 'Of whom are you talking?'

Not, it seemed, of Edwina, but – Lucy Smalley explained, recovered quickly from the nasty shock of Barbie emerging and bearing down like a Fury – of 'the Manners girl', the other victim. 'You didn't think we were talking about your friend, surely?'

Barbie took Emerson home with her. She had not meant to but he was in her hand as she arrived at Mrs Stewart's desk and was marked out to her with a rise of Mrs Stewart's eyebrows because Mrs Stewart, a widow from Madras with a literary turn of mind, was more used to receiving from Barbie her interpretations of Mabel's standing order for something light, which generally turned out to be so easy on the mind and lap that Mabel nodded off over it in her wing chair having pronounced it earlier 'just right'.

Presented with Emerson's essays Mabel said, 'Oh, I read those as a girl, I don't think I could bother again.'

'I'll take it back tomorrow,' Barbie promised. 'It was a mistake, or rather absent-mindedness, my attention was taken as it can be all too easily. Well, you know, you know. I *am* sorry.'

But Mabel merely smiled and touched Barbie's arm as she did from time to time as if to make up for all the occasions when she might have failed to let Barbie know she was appreciated.

Barbie sat at the writing-table, opened the rejected book. 'If the whole of history is one man,' she read, 'it is all to be explained from individual experience. There is a relation between the hours of our life and the centuries of time.' She closed the book abruptly and made herself busy in the room, opening drawers and rearranging their contents.

Not taking Emerson back she returned to him daily like a sparrow easily frightened from a promising scattering of crumbs by the slightest noise, with a nagging sense of having more duties than intelligence. It was pretty plain she was not cut out for the philosophical life but through Emerson it impinged on her own like the shadow of a hunched bird of prey patiently observing below it the ritual of survival. The bird should have been an angel.

She began to feel what she believed Emerson wanted her to feel: that in her own experience lay an explanation not only of history but of the lives of other living people, therefore an explanation of the things that had happened to Edwina and to Miss Manners of whom she had only the vaguest picture, the one that had been commonly shared in Pankot of a reclining figure, in white, in a darkened room. But now it had changed. The girl's hand was no longer pressed inverted against her forehead but held by another which was brown like the dead teacher's. The picture shimmered, became fluid. Colours and patterns ran. When Barbie sat at her desk and gazed at the actual picture she was no longer sure of what she saw: Edwina guarding the body; Mabel kneeling to grub out weeds or inclining to gather roses; or herself, Barbie, surrounded by the children she had presumed to bring to God; or Miss Manners in some kind of unacceptable relationship with a man of another race whom she was intent on saving.

From this there emerged a figure, the figure of an unknown Indian: dead in one aspect, alive in another. And after a while it occurred to her that the unknown Indian was what her life in India had been about. The notion alarmed her. She had not thought of it before in those terms and did not know what to do about it now that she had. She could not very well look for him because she did not know where to do that. Aziz for instance seemed content even in his alternative persona of a man from the hills with a blanket and a secret. He did not strike her as being in distress of any kind.

But the dead man in the vicinity of the milestone had moved. Overnight there had been a rearrangement of his limbs as if while it was dark he had sat up. And howled. The hills were hunted by jackals. People would not have noticed. But she thought that she would henceforth be able to distinguish the man's cry from the cries of the animals.

She began another letter to Edwina.

'4 September. Why don't you write Edwina? I need your letter,' then tore it up and began another sensibly.

'Some people from Mayapore have been here. I didn't meet them but a woman called Smalley who lives at the little Smith's Hotel where these people stayed for a couple of days told Clarissa Peplow that according to these visitors whose name I think was Patterson or Pattison you were reported well on the mend and about to be discharged. How thankful this news has made me. I have not rung the hospital again because of the expense and the delay in getting through and then getting only the briefest official answer to the question. But I have written several times. I hope my letters all arrived. The posts have been badly delayed, indeed disrupted. If you are already discharged no doubt the hospital will send this note round to your bungalow. I shall mark the envelope please forward and shall probably send a separate note to you at home. How glad you will be to be there. I hope, hope that you are truly recovered, Edwina.

'Is there a possibility of your making the journey to Pankot? The invitation still stands. Mabel has asked me to emphasize this and also to say that we should keep you free from the prying and the curious. I do trust that you are not too disagreeably involved with the aftermath of that awful business. It is said officially that the country is returning to normal and that now surely is the time for magnanimity. But one hears the unhappiest accounts and most unpleasant remarks. I am, my dear Edwina, a bit concerned for you as a result of something Clarissa said, echoing Lucy Smalley and presumably these Patterson Pattison people. It would be monstrous if after all you have been through you were in the least criticized for stating that you could not either describe or recognize individuals among that wicked mob. It must have been a nightmare and after a nightmare the details are often mercifully forgotten. Only those with vengeful natures would wish to see you drag some detail back into the light, one upon which they could then proceed to act over-righteously perhaps and in all likelihood unjustly. No doubt you feel as I do that God will punish and perhaps has already punished. As Clarissa says, some of the men who hurt you and killed the teacher may since have been killed themselves in the rioting. Divine retribution!'

Here Barbie's pen hesitated as if of its own accord and she could not continue. Divine retribution was all very well. It did not help the unknown Indian who seemed this morning to be crying out harder but still soundlessly, begging for justice and not alleviation. She found it difficult to distinguish between the teacher who died in the attack on Edwina and the Indian who was supposed to have had Miss Manners infatuated with him. Lucy Smalley's opinion was that the Indian boy Miss Manners thought she was in love with must have been some kind of hypnotist. But perhaps love was a form of hypnosis anyway. Had not Barbie been mesmerized herself years and years ago?

My life, she thought, has become extraordinarily complicated. There is more than one of me and one, I'm not sure which, has a serious duty to perform. 'It seems perfectly dreadful (she wrote suddenly, allowing the Waterman pen its now free-flowing head) how within the space of a few weeks poor Daphne Manners has become "that Manners girl".' And she continued for a page or two becoming while she did so a projection of that poor misused creature who it was said was not frail and pretty after all but rather large and ungainly and in need of spectacles, so that the sympathetic transference of Barbie to Daphne and back again was easier to make than it would have been had the idea of Miss Manners as frail, ethereal and beautiful in victim's white turned out to be accurate.

Instead here she was according to reports from people who had been in a position to know, in a rather grubby dress to suit the circumstances arising from her extraordinary behaviour, throwing up blinds, peering shortsightedly and threatening to create a scene, standing in shafts of sunlight which were alive with particles of dust. Barbie understood this image better than the other.

Miss Manners said the men arrested were the wrong men. Barbie wondered how that could be but was impressed by the reported strenuousness of Miss Manners's insistence which everyone else seemed to feel outraged by, just as they were ready to be outraged by Edwina's insistence that she had no contribution to make to the identification of a few men in a large crowd. In those circumstances they all looked alike anyway in their murky dhotis and Gandhi caps and filthy turbans. And the smell. Suffering, sweating, stinking, violent humanity. It was the background against which you had to visualize Jesus working. People did not remember this important thing about His presence. Edwina did. Did Miss Manners? Or was she only intent on confusing the police to save her lover? Apparently she kept changing her story. According to the Pattersons she had threatened to say that if the six youths who included her lover were charged and tried for rape she would stand up and say that the men who assaulted her could just as easily have been British soldiers with their faces blacked.

In that threat, that outburst, which had scandalized her countrymen, Barbie detected what she thought of as the girl's despair and was sorry for her. She would have liked to take Miss Manners in her arms and comfort her. She was not convinced though that Miss Manners was telling the whole truth so she was also sorry for the police officer who had arrested the men and was convinced of their guilt. It was said by the Patterson Pattisons that the police officer had warned Miss Manners about her association with this particular Indian who was handsome if you liked that sort of thing and educated, so he claimed, in England but certainly beyond his real station, and had already been questioned over something to do with political affiliations. On the face of it, Barbie saw, the Indian was as likely to be guilty as not, leading Miss Manners on, laughing at her behind her back as Lucy Smalley suggested, and planning to attack her in the dark on the way home from one of her errands of mercy, in the company of five of his westernized friends, student-types, who came at her from behind, dragged her off her bicycle into the Bibighar Gardens, covered her head with her own raincape, raped her and left her to stagger home in pain, in torment, totally disorientated.

If they covered her head how could she see who they were? When did they cover her head? Only after she had a glimpse (as apparently she began to say), a good enough glimpse of them to be able to insist that they were dirty peasant-types not well-groomed European-style dressed boys of the kind arrested? And there had been some confusion about her bicycle. Had it been found by the police in the ditch outside the Indian boy's house? At first this was what had been said but it had been denied later by the police officer himself. The most damning thing of all had not been denied though. When arrested the Indian boy had been bathing his face which was scratched and bruised. He would not say how; had never said, had refused utterly to talk. The others denied any complicity, any connexion with his English girl friend, pretended they had spent the whole evening drinking hooch in a hut near the Bibighar Gardens where the attack had taken place. They had been arrested in the hut.

Now they were disposed of, all of them, to gaol, without trial, as political detenus. And Miss Manners seemed to have won. But what had she won except disgrace among her own people? And her Indian boy-friend; what had he got away with?

Barbie did not even know his name. She began to have dreams about him, but in these dreams he was the Indian Edwina had tried to save. In this dream his eyes were blinded by cataracts. He had a powerful muscular throat which was exposed because his head was lifted and his mouth wide open in a continuous soundless scream.

6

It was the element of scornful rejection implicit in every violent challenge to authority which hurt most deeply and blighted the tendrils of affection which entwined and supported the crumbling pillars of the edifice. Upon faces already drawn from the strain of conveying self-confidence and from the slight but persistent malaise suffered by constitutions imperfectly designed to withstand the climate, there would fall – during these periods of pressure – shadows of brooding melancholy, even when the face was expressing scorn or indifference, amusement, wrath; whatever it was that was being felt or assumed. In the cries of shock and outrage with which news of victims was heard and passed on, in the calls for condign punishment of culprits, a plaintive note managed to be struck which corresponded to the melancholy shadow; a note of awareness that the victims must have been people in whom the impulse to show as well as feel affection in the performance of their duty had been stronger than was usual, even than was wise, so that the fates of these people were seen through all the tangle of misfortune and circumstance as sacrificial.

But in the aftermath, as the status quo was re-established, these original victims were replaced by the figures of those who had tried to avenge them and become victims themselves; and then that melancholy shadow was burnt away by fires of irony which, lighting faces, gave them the glowing look of belonging to people who found themselves existing on a plane somewhere between that of the martyr and the bully.

The irony lay in the fact that the new victims were sacrifices offered by one's own side as a placatory measure in restoring order and regaining Indian confidence. It had happened before, it would happen again, but that did not make it any more palatable when it was happening now. As early as the beginning of September when the jails were crammed and the country and administration nearly back to normal it was said that Brigadier Reid, openly accused by the Indians of having used excessive force in putting down the riots, was not receiving the kind of support from above which he had the right to expect. At the end of the month he was reported posted to another command.

Nicky Paynton said, 'It seems to me Alec Reid did damned well. The civil always expect us to be on tap to pull their chestnuts out of the fire but when we do they start complaining that we've burnt *their* fingers.' She was stating what was generally felt to be true. In Reid's case community sympathy for him was strong because although he had used his British battalion in Mayapore he commanded as well a battalion of the Pankots (the 4/5th) and one of the Ranpurs. But this sympathy had been deepened by the news that at the height of the riots in Mayapore his wife died of cancer in Rawalpindi. It was also known that his only son had been captured by the Japanese in Burma earlier in the year, news which could hardly have made Meg Reid's last months any easier for her or Alec Reid to bear. But, called by the civil power to give military aid, he had done so, so far as one could tell, resolutely and effectively. If a larger than average number of Indians was killed or wounded in Mayapore and Dibrapur that was because the riots in those two towns were worse than in any other town in the country and because the civil power had dithered, had been unwilling to call the army in until the situation had got completely out of hand.

It was quite obvious to Army people that the civil

authority in Mayapore lacked nous. Apart from the almost criminal negligence shown by the long postponement of a request for troops, the revolting affair of the rape of Miss Manners had been allowed to disintegrate in the most scandalous way. The only people who had come out well of the troubles in Mayapore, in Pankot opinion, were the brigade commander and the District Superintendent of Police who had arrested the suspects in the rape case within an hour or so of the assault. And now, like Brigadier Reid, this officer was said to be in bad official odour.

What was needed of course was some first-hand information and for that one had to wait for people like the Pattersons to arrive from Mayapore. They had been interesting on the subject of Miss Manners but, being civilians, a poor source of intelligence in the matter of the alleged excessive use of force. The first man to arrive in Pankot from Mayapore, a junior officer of a British regiment fairly recently out from home, found himself much in demand. But his mind seemed to be on other things. In regard to the rape, for instance, he said, 'Really, one began to suspect there hadn't been one.' He described the military action taken in aid of the civil power 'like something out of Gilbert and Sullivan mixed up with the last act of Hamlet.' The discovery that this young man had been an actor in civilian life and was in Pankot en route for a sinecure in welfare and entertainment in Delhi was made early enough to put his views into proper perspective. He was vulgarly handsome. Probably a chorus boy, Mrs Fosdick suggested.

After the theatrical lieutenant had gone there arrived as many as a dozen men and women who had been in Mayapore at the time of the riots. They said that the number of dead in Mayapore, considered uncomfortably high by the authorities, was accounted for chiefly by people drowned in the river when scattering in panic at the sound of rifle fire and the sight of troops on both sides of the Mandir Gate bridge. In Dibrapur it had been a different matter. There the rebels had used home-made bombs and landmines. They got what they asked for. Brigadier Reid nearly lost a whole rifle company when it was cut off by a blown bridge; and when you thought of that, and that the company was part of a brigade he was trying to get ready to fight the Japanese and stop them invading India, you had to agree it was inhuman to start crucifying him for showing a bit of sand. In Reid there was obviously more sand than the desk-wallahs thought it right for a British officer to show these days. They were getting ready to dish him. The command of the brigade was Alec Reid's first real job of soldiering for more than ten years. If it hadn't been for the *débâcle* in Malaya and Burma he'd probably have ended his career fretting at a desk. He'd now been given command of a brigade that was almost ready to go back into the field but it was rumoured that GHQ thought it better to promote him to a job he'd quickly prove he couldn't do than send him meekly back to a staff appointment because the civil in Mayapore had kicked up a stink about him.

There was a rather sordid little joke going round among Mayapore Indians that if you spelt Reid backwards it came out sounding like Dyer who shot down all those unarmed people in the Jallianwallah Bagh in Amritsar in 1919. It never took long for people to home in like vultures on the reputation of a perfectly decent and competent officer. The only comfort to be had from the business was that if Reid did prove himself just too old to command a brigade of more seasoned troops his fate would be better than old Dyer's. He'd likely get a general's hat and even if there was nowhere else to hang it except on a peg in an air-conditioned office the pay while it lasted and the pension when it ended would be some compensation.

The first of the officers who gained Pankot's full atten-tion was the adjutant of the battalion of the British regiment that had been brigaded for training with a battalion of the Ranpurs and the Mayapore Battalion of the Pankots under Reid. This officer was on short local leave. His knowledge of India was infinitesimal but he was a regular soldier and gave a fascinating account of the action in aid of the civil power in Mayapore at the Mandir Gate bridge, following which an unfortunately large number of women and children had died in the river. He knew the departed theatrical lieutenant, of course, but surprised everybody by describing him as a first-rate platoon commander who had won the MM as a lance-corporal at Dunkirk. He claimed to be the originator of the famous comment about that retreat: The noise! The people! To men the adjutant confided that he thought young X was probably as queer as a coot but that if so he had the courage of an Amazon. He was among those who had led a detachment of British soldiers in aid of the civil. He had behaved well but perhaps the experience of firing on unarmed civilians had 'turned him'. The adjutant remembered finding him vomiting in his quarters when going to ask why he hadn't reported to the daftar on his return from aid duty in the city. 'My dear fellow,' the actor-soldier had said, 'I'm being sick because in a properly organized production the extras never actually get killed. The little thing today was wildly under-rehearsed.'

The next arrival was an even more promising source of information. This was Ewart Mackay, the brigade major whom Reid's successor had replaced with a man of his own choice. Mackay was in Pankot for a couple of days. He had broken his journey to his regimental depot in Muzzafirabad in the North West Frontier province, where he anticipated being offered the command of the battalion of the Muzzafirabad Guides that was now being brought back up to strength after limping out of Burma.

Initially he seemed more interested in standing drinking at the men's bar in the club than in answering questions about Mayapore which he deflected with frosty blasts of his Carew's gin and icechunk-cooled breath and chilling stares of a keen blue eye. His sandy pranged moustache was kept airborne by constant manipulation of his restless fingers.

But after he had put down what one member swore were twelve burra pegs in the course of two hours he became brisker, informative, and introduced a speculative element into the hitherto clear-cut argument that Reid had been badly treated.

Apparently Ewart Mackay had quite a good opinion of White, the Deputy Commissioner in Mayapore. He said, 'We all knew the Brig's son was a POW with the Japs and we knew his wife was in hospital up in 'Pindi. But I was the only one who knew she was dying of cancer and I didn't know that until quite late in the day. I think if the DC had known he and the Brig would have got on better because he would have made allowances. As it was I often had to pour oil especially during the time the Brig was pressing him to call the troops out and the DC was digging his heels in and saying the civil police could cope. It's nonsense to say excessive force was used but it could be that if we'd used troops say a day earlier the result wouldn't have been so bad. I think the DC would have called for troops the day before if the Brig had given him more confidence about how they'd be used. Old Alec Reid's a bit of a fire-eater you know. And nowadays the civil distrust us if we look anxious to have a crack. I suppose if your wife is dying and you're stuck in a place like Mayapore· with all hell let loose you'd want to get stuck in, but it's never a good thing for the man at the top to be under an emotional strain. All the same old Alec Reid's had a shabby deal. Giving him that other brigade was only a face-saver for him and the army. He won't be keeping it. I know the man who's been told he'll be getting it. Reid will be back in Delhi by Christmas.'

And Miss Manners? No, he had not had the pleasure of meeting Miss Manners. He pronounced her name in mock Scottish as it were with a deliberate skirl of the pipes and a whirl of the kilt. Since that unfortunate affair he had of course learned quite a bit about her. No, she wasn't particularly attractive according to reports. Big and gawky he understood. She was staying in one of the oldest houses in Mayapore, a place called the Macgregor House built by a Scottish nabob in the early nineteenth century but now the property of an Indian woman. Lady Chatterjee, one of the Indians with whom the DC and his wife played bridge. Miss Manners was quite new to India. Although born in the country she had been taken home by her parents while still an infant. She lost both parents before the war and her brother had been killed. She'd driven ambulances throughout the blitz in London but been invalided out. Her closest surviving relative, her aunt, old Lady Manners, widow of ex-Governor Sir Henry, arranged for her to join her in Rawalpindi. There she met Lady Chatterjee. Sir Henry Manners and Sir Nello Chatterjee, a Bengali industrialist, had been old friends and after their deaths their widows had kept the friendship up. Lady Chatterjee was a Rajput, Chatterjee being her second husband. Her first was a prince who broke his neck playing polo. Chatterjee was knighted for founding and financing the Mayapore technical college which produced young Indian engineers, not unemployable art graduates. Lady Chatterjee was considered okay.

Major Mackay had met Lady Chatterjee once in the course of his social duties. Miss Manners may have been at the same function but he didn't recall seeing her. The fact was she was probably otherwise occupied. After coming to stay with Lady Chatterjee and do voluntary work at the general hospital she had become friendly with this Indian journalist fellow who was among the six young men the District Superintendent of Police arrested for raping her.

Mackay was offered another drink. He accepted and said nothing more until it reached him. After a couple of swallows he reflighted his moustache and said, 'Curious business altogether. And it made life extra difficult because it gave the troublemakers something special to shout about. I expect you heard the tales that got around that the police tortured the boys and defiled them by making them eat beef to get them to confess, which they never did. A lot of our own people felt that if the tales were true they only got what they deserved. I don't expect they were handled any too gently. Some of these Indian inspectors and sub-inspectors can be pretty ruthless but the rabble were accusing the DSP himself. It got so bad the DC ordered an Indian magistrate to question each one of them but none of them complained of ill-treatment. They might have been scared to. Anyway it made no difference. The crowds were still screaming blue murder. I never cared much for the DSP, he wasn't my kind of chap, but the Brig liked him and considering the crowds were out to get him if they could he acted pretty coolly. I saw him once in the thick of it on horseback rallying a squad of police that looked as if it had had enough. If there'd been one rioter with a shotgun he'd have been a dead man. As it was a bloody great stone missed him by inches. Still, guts don't count if you fail in another direction. He never made the rape charges stick and I don't suppose his department will let him forget it. But that's life. Bring home the bacon and you're forgiven a lot. Don't, and you're sunk.'

One of the other men said, 'From what we hear that wasn't his fault but the girl's. She sounds round the bend to me.'

Mackay glanced at the man, emptied his glass, put it on the counter and ordered another round.

'You think so?' he said.

'Don't you?'

'I just think she was in love. Not round the bend. Not infatuated. Not intimidated. In love.'

'With the journalist fellow?'

'That's right.'

'Even after he and his friends raped her?'

'Forget the friends. The trouble about this case is that nobody's ever been able to forget the friends or start from the simple proposition that Miss Manners was in love and still is with the Kumar chap. And that the Kumar chap was and still is in love with her.'

'Was that his name?'

'There were six names but I think Kumar was the lad in question. Hari Kumar.'

'Harry?'

'H,a,r,i. He was brought up in England. He went to school at Chillingborough.'

'Good God.'

'Quite so. Interesting, isn't it?'

'Well what the hell was he doing working in a place like Mayapore on a local rag?'

'They tell me his father died bankrupt in England before the war and he came back penniless to the only relative he had, an aunt who lived in Mayapore. She was a widow and lived on the charity of her dead husband's orthodox Hindu family. Young Kumar must have had a tough time adjusting himself to *that*. It could be he failed to adjust himself. The police had an eye on him. He was politically suspect. That's the other red herring.'

'Red herring?'

'It introduces complications. It makes it hard to concentrate on the proposition that he and Miss Manners were in love.'

'What's the other red herring?'

'The friends. The police had files on them too. I think you have to forget the politics, the friends, even the rape, and concentrate on this one proposition. They were in love.'

'What do you mean, forget the rape?'

Mackay's glass was empty. He put it on the counter. A man in the group ordered refills.

'I mean forget it because it's irrelevant.'

The word irrelevant came out slightly blurred and Major Mackay lost something of his grip on his audience. But with his next sentence he regained and hardened it.

'She's pregnant, you know. She's gone back to R'l'Pindi pregnant. People say she'll get an abortion. Myself, I doubt it. I concentrate on the proposition that she and Kumar were in love, still are, he in clink and she pregnant in R'l'Pindi. Having what she thinks is his child. Thinks, hopes or knows. You can't tell. Perhaps she can't either except in the way women think they can. The old intuition.'

A man with a red face and sparse hair, a civilian, asked, 'What's your theory, Major Mackay?'

'Well yes I have a theory. Glad you asked. My theory's

101

this. If you love and marriage isn't on or isn't easy sooner or later you get round to poking, to put it crudely. My theory is Miss Manners and this Kumar fellow poked in the Bibighar either that night for the first time or that night for the umpteenth but that that night whatever teenth time it was these so-called friends of his who'd not only guessed he was poking her but had found out where, were all lined up waiting for the show to begin and when it was over jumped on him, sat on him and then –

Major Mackay made an arm.

'Then why didn't Miss Manners say so?'

'Say what? That she and Mr Kumar had been making love at night in a derelict garden doing no harm to anyone when up come these friends of his and say, okay Hari, move over?'

'Why not? From all accounts she's not the easily embarrassed type. And if what you suggest is true and she and this journalist fellow had made a clean breast of it that part of it might have been kept dark and the other fellows just charged and sentenced.'

'And do you think any of them would have let Kumar get away with that? They'd have implicated him like a shot. They'd have said it was Kumar's idea, to share her.'

'Well wasn't it? The police thought so.'

'Which is where you come back to my proposition. If it had been like that I don't care what kind of act he put up she'd have known and she'd have stopped being in love with him. If you stick to my proposition that they were in love, are in love, everything's as clear as daylight. These so-called friends of his jumped him and beat him up. She may not have seen who they were. If not he told her afterwards and told her what they'd threatened, that they'd accuse him of arranging it if there was any trouble. Well, she wasn't a bloody fool. Everybody in Mayapore knew she'd been going out with him. Neither of them was popular as a result. He wouldn't have stood a chance however much she swore his innocence. So they cooked up a story that they hadn't seen each other for days and they damned well stuck to it, right though. What she hadn't reckoned with was finding when she got home that Lady Chatterjee had already reported her missing to the DSP. It was the night the balloon was expected to go up and she hadn't come home at the usual time. She wasn't at the club or at any of old Lady C's friends and the woman was pretty worried. And when she got home there wasn't any disguising what had happened. Her clothes were torn and she was in a state. Lady C had a woman doctor from the Purdah hospital up to the house in a brace of shakes. Maybe Miss Manners panicked. But she said she'd been assaulted by a gang of men and that was the situation the DSP found when he called at the house. He had no time for Hari Kumar. He'd had his eye on him. He'd warned Miss Manners about associating with a fellow like that. So young Kumar's the first chap the DSP thinks of. He hares off to the Bibighar, finds Kumar's pals drinking in a hut not far away, arrests them and hares off to Kumar's house and finds him bathing cuts and bruises on his face, the sort a fellow might get if he attacked a girl who fought back. What other evidence did he need? He jumped to the conclusion most people would. And he was right in my opinion except in this one case, the case of Mr Kumar who never did explain how his face got like that and just went on insisting as she did that they hadn't seen each other since the night they visited a temple.'

'What about the others?'

'Oh they played dumb too. They pretended they'd spent the whole evening drinking in the hut. They never changed their story but if Hari Kumar had split on them they'd have taken him with them. There was a pretty odd thing happened about her bicycle. The one she was supposed to be dragged off. First the police said it was found outside Kumar's house and then the DSP said no that was wrong it had been in the Bibighar Gardens near the scene of the rape and put in the police truck that went to get Kumar, and a sub-inspector who came on the scene late thought one of the constables had found it in the ditch outside the house and put that down in a report. Indians said the DSP planted the bike himself and then realized it looked too bloody obvious. My own theory is that these other five took the bike from the Gardens and stuck it outside Kumar's place and that the DSP didn't find Kumar's or any of their fingerprints on it because they'd wiped it clean, and guessed they'd been trying to incriminate him alone. It's just the sort of crazy thing boys like that would do, forgetting that if Kumar was incriminated they wouldn't stand a chance themselves.'

'But that would mean this police chap withheld vital evidence.'

'Messy evidence. Rigged evidence. Without Kumar's prints on the handlebars or the saddle the sort of evidence he didn't want. He wanted Kumar. A jury would have been very wary about the girl's bike being found outside Kumar's house even if wiped clean of fingerprints. I don't think he was very interested in the other fellows. Whenever people talked to him about the case Kumar's was the only name he ever mentioned. I think he disliked the chap because of the kind of boy he is. First-rate British public-school education, but black as your hat and going out with an English girl, and politically unreliable.'

'Was he politically unreliable?'

'A young educated Indian? It's likely, isn't it? On the other hand the paper he worked for was Indian-owned but pro-British. Not that that means anything. The police must have had enough on all six for the civil to decide to lock them up without trial as political detenus when the rape charge couldn't be got to stick, but everyone knows that locking them up like that was nothing more than a face-saver. She wasn't able to stop that. But by God she stopped the charges and she stopped the trial. The assistant commissioner was scared stiff about what she might come out with. They hadn't a hope in hell of bringing the beggars into court with Miss Manners as the only witness for the prosecution ready to swear blind that the fellows who raped her were peasants, and saying God knows what else. You have to admire her. Well. You do if you accept my proposition that Kumar had her but didn't rape her and that they're both bloody well in love.'

'Did the DSP know her well?'

'In a place like that everybody knows everybody as likely as not. If you mean was he sweet on her himself I can't answer. He wasn't married and plain as they say she was she'd have been a good catch for a man like him, but he struck me as a pretty cold fish. Thought of nothing but his job, I'd say. Not a sociable character. Abstemious. Never heard him make a joke. Old Reid liked him though, but then Reid always admired a man for his guts first. Anything else came a poor second. Well, there it is. That's my theory. Who else is thirsty?'

No one was. The theory was peculiarly unacceptable. An hour later when the bar had been closed for some time Major Mackay was lifted off his stool by three servants and carried through to the room he occupied, undressed and tucked into bed. He smiled in his sleep. With that, the troubles could be said to have come to a happy end.

Barbie got up from the rush mat, buttoned the high-necked nightgown and shivered. It was cold enough now to have the electric fire on in the bedroom but she had asked Aziz not to switch it on as he did Mabel's an hour before bedtime. She climbed chilled into bed, turned the lamp off and lay for a while blowing dandelion clocks, each one as useless as the last. The grey-white tufts wafted away almost before her breath reached them, leaving her to hold a limp sappy stalk. And tonight the alternative, smelling roses, didn't work either. They were of a scentless variety and on the turn, bulbous seed-boxes with a few overblown petals so precariously attached she hardly dared to touch them. She counted sheep but they were stubborn and the gate too high.

She counted children. They submitted to her calculations with expressions of ill-concealed dislike of such regimentation. She called the roll and crossed names out with a blue crayon. When all the names were crossed out one child remained uncalled: the little Indian girl to whom the blue crayon had belonged. She could not remember the little girl's name. The little girl couldn't remember it either and accused her silently of depriving her both of name and crayon. The little girl would not go away until her name was called. It was an impasse. We are stuck with each other, Barbie said, which is absurd because you have Krishna and I have Jesus. We are separately catered for. Let's shake hands and call it a day. But the little girl had her hands behind her back and kept them there.

Hold it higher, her mother said, so she held the porcupine higher and counted pins going into the place where the neck and shoulders had to be altered. Altared. Her mother was sticking the pins in too deep. Little beads of blood appeared like drops of red sweat on the white satin. The bride continued to smile like the Spartan boy with the stolen fox under his shirt. Observe, her mother said, the advantages of a strict upbringing in a family of rank.

Her father was singing one of his funny songs. I've seen a deal of gaiety throughout my noisy life. Barbie sang it to her mother. Stop that vulgarity, her mother said. So she sang alone under her breath but found she had forgotten everything except the first line. The stairs were always dark and smelt of damp and gas jets and old linoleum. The paper on the walls was brown and patchy. She sang the first line of the vulgar song over and over going up the stairs but still under her breath because the stairs frightened her. She counted the stairs but there had only ever been twenty of them including the landing floor. Twenty stairs were not enough to send her to sleep.

She switched on the lamp. Slowly she was in India again and as she returned to India she became homesick, ridiculously, unaccountably, inexpressibly homesick. The old chaukidar would be asleep on the front porch huddled in his blanket like a tired shepherd. She felt disturbed and then, hearing the weird calling of the jackal packs, lost in an immense area of experience, the whole area that separated her from childhood and young womanhood. She thought of it as an area because the separation seemed to be in space, not in time.

She sat up wrapped in her own arms. The light from the bedside lamp did not reach the farther walls but the glass that protected the picture gleamed faintly. Behind the glass there was nothing. The picture had gone out.

She thought: I have gone out, Thou hast gone out, He she or it has gone out.

She reached for Emerson who had not gone out but had been renewed and renewed to Mrs Stewart's perplexity.

'Each new law and political movement has meaning for you,' Barbie read and was convinced that this might be so because Emerson told her. 'Stand before each of its tablets and say, "Here is one of my coverings. Under this fantastic, or odious, or graceful mask did my Proteus nature hide itself." This remedies the defect of our too great nearness to ourselves.'

She put Emerson aside and picked up her pocket dictionary. Proteus. Changing or inconstant person or thing. Amoeba. Kinds of bacteria. She laid aside the dictionary and recovered Emerson from the bed-cover. She had lost the place but with Emerson that never seemed to matter.

'The world exists for the education of each man. There is no age or state of society, or mode of action in history, to which there is not somewhat corresponding in his life. Everything tends in a most wonderful manner to abbreviate itself and yield its own virtue to him. He should see that he can live all history in his own person. He must sit at home with might and main, and not suffer himself to be bullied by kings or empires, but know that he is greater than all the geography and all the governments of the world . . .'

Suddenly she was aware of the intense stillness of Rose Cottage. Intense stillness and a faint odour as of something singed. She put Emerson away, got out of bed, put on her slippers and her long blue dressing-gown. She wondered whether Mabel had remembered to turn her fire off, whether something was in danger of scorching or bursting into flames.

She left her door open so that she could see her way across the hall. There was a slit of light under Mabel's door. She hesitated. The smell had gone. She went to the

107

door and tapped very gently. She got no answer. She tapped again and said, Mabel. She would have gone back to bed because she realized how silly it was to expect a deaf person to hear and she did not want to open the door and frighten her. But potential alarm was exerting its hollow fascination. She opened Mabel's door until she had a gap wide enough to admit her head and one shoulder.

Mabel was asleep propped on the pillows. The light was still on. Mabel's head had fallen to one side and her reading glasses were low down on her nose and looked as if they might come adrift and get broken and cause damage to her eyes and face. A book was open on her lap. The hand that had held it lay inert.

The fire was off. Barbie went to the bedside. She took the book away, placed it on the table with its tasselled marker between the pages at which it had been open. Next, she very carefully removed the dangerous spectacles, returned them to the leather case. She settled the pillows, drew the sheet and blankets farther up. She wanted to cover Mabel's hands but decided not to in case she woke her up. She seemed to have disturbed her slightly as it was. A sigh came. And then a sound in the back of the throat almost like something being said.

Barbie looked down at her friend. Very briefly she had a ridiculous idea that she didn't like her. At the same time she knew that she loved her. And she knew that Mabel was fond of her in spite of not appearing to be fond of anyone much. It was a curious relationship, like one between two people who hadn't yet met but who would love each other when they did. Mabel had come closer to meeting her than she had come to meeting Mabel. After three years Barbie still knew almost nothing about her friend but even if one discounted facts not taken in because of deafness Mabel must now know almost everything about Barbie because Barbie had told her over and over. Telling Mabel things was part of the job of looking after her, almost more important than doing things to absolve her from household cares and responsibilities. Without the actuality of Barbie's voice incessantly saying things Barbie thought that Mabel would not have appreciated so much the silence in which she seemed to exist. The only thing Barbie had never told her about was her secret sorrow. When she looked at Mabel as she was doing now she believed Mabel knew about it anyway and had known from the beginning.

She thought: In a way my secret sorrow is Mabel. I don't know how much of me gets through. I'm rather like a wave dashing against a rock, the sounds I make are just like that. There is Mabel, there is the rock, there is God. They are the same to all intents and purposes.

Mabel stirred but did not wake. How old she looked in bed, immensely old. Barbie put out her hand to switch off the lamp. The old woman made that noise in her throat again as if disturbed by the shadow of Barbie's arm. She made it again. She was muttering but the sound came from her throat because her lips were too far gone in the drug of each day's little death to come together properly. She muttered for several seconds then paused and then said something which caused Barbie to stand alert and undecided with her finger and thumb on the little ebony key-switch of the old-fashioned brass table-lamp, willing the echo of the sound to pause too before continuing on its flight into a state of being beyond recall. She caught the rhythm back first and then the vowel sounds, then the consonants. A name, a woman's name, Gillian Waller.

She watched Mabel's face but could not tell anything from it. There was no more muttering. Mabel had reached wherever she had been going. Beyond Gillian Waller she had found the dark of dreamless sleep.

TRAGIC DEATH OF ENGLISH MISSIONARY

Ranpur, 29 October 1942

The death is reported in Mayapore two days ago of Miss Edwina Crane, superintendent of the district's Protestant Mission schools who was roughly handled by a mob during the August riots and narrowly escaped with her life when another teacher, Mr D. R. Chuaudhuri, was murdered.

Police have so far been unable to apprehend their attackers.

At an inquest held yesterday in Mayapore a statement obtained from Miss Crane's servant was submitted by the police. According to this man his mistress sent him to the bazaar at 3.45 P.M. to collect a package from the chemist. Since her return from hospital he had frequently gone on such errands. On this occasion however the chemist said he knew nothing of a prescription for Miss Crane. The servant then returned home.

Reaching there he smelt burning and saw smoke. A shed in the compound was a mass of flames and servants from neighbouring houses were attempting to extinguish it. One of these men called out that Miss Crane was in the shed.

The police submitted a statement from this other man. Shortly before 4 P.M. he had seen a woman in a white saree in the compound of the mission superintendent's bungalow. Thinking it was someone who had no business there he challenged her. She motioned him to go away. He observed that the woman in the white saree was Miss Crane. Neither he nor her own servant had ever seen her adopt this mode of dress. He watched her go into the shed and then returned to his work. Shortly afterwards he smelt smoke and noticed that the shed was on fire.

The police also submitted a note found in Miss Crane's study addressed to the Coroner. An official in Miss Crane's Mission confirmed that it was in her handwriting. The note which was not read out at the inquest was accepted by the police as satisfactory evidence of Miss Crane's determination to take her own life.

Dr Jayaprakash, consultant physician at the Begum Mumtez Zaidkhan Purdah hospital and health officer to the mission schools stated that he had attended Miss Crane for some years. Normally in excellent health she had not regained it since the attack on her in August. After her discharge from hospital he precribed tonics and advised her to take a holiday. On his last visit about a week before her tragic death she told him she had decided to retire from the mission.

A verdict of suicide while the balance of the mind was disturbed was recorded.

A touching note was struck when Miss Crane's servant who seemed to confuse the proceedings with a legal case asked whether 'Madam was to be released and restored to him.' A colleague of the late Miss Crane at the Mission who led the weeping man from court told your reporter that this man, Joseph, had served Miss Crane since he was a kitchen boy at the mission in Muzzafirabad (NWFP) where Miss Crane taught before the Great War. 'She was a heroine to him. She stood alone at the door of the school guarding the children and faced up to a gang of armed hooligans who threatened to burn the school down.'

The funeral took place later in the day. Waiting outside the cemetery were groups of Indian women, mothers of some of the children who attend the mission schools. After the funeral rites were over your reporter noted that these women entered the cemetery and placed flowers on the grave.

She went into the bathroom and locked the door and the other door that led to the verandah and the door that led into the little spare. She got down on her knees on the cold floor and clasped her hands on the rim of the smooth white porcelain hand-basin, then groped for her damp flannel and stuffed it into her mouth so as not to disturb the house. She reached up and turned the tap on full. The water splashed into the bowl, down the pipe and out into the open runnel that carried it away. She sank lower until her body was almost touching her thighs and let herself sob aloud.

Edwina had sinned. But that was not why Barbie wept. The question of what would happen to Edwina's soul was beyond her power to calculate. It would be settled in limbo which to Barbie was a bleak and incomprehensible but real place chilled by God's breath and darkened by the Devil's brow; barren neutral territory where the dead waited, trembling and naked, incapable of further action to support a claim to either kingdom. To kill oneself was wicked. Her father had killed himself with drink walking with a skinful under the hooves and wheels of a horsedrawn carriage on the Thames Embankment. Her widowed mother had killed herself not with work as people said but with a combination of heartless love and heartless pride better known as keeping up appearances. Their deaths were small sins in comparison with Edwina's terrible act of self-destruction but in their private little despairs of which the drinking and the pride had been evidence she had long since learned to see a glimmer of the devil's face; thoughtful, chin in hand, offering recompense, suggesting anodynes that were not that at all but addictive means of excitation of the ill he did.

Barbie's Devil was not a demon but a fallen angel and his Hell no place of fire and brimstone but an image of lost heaven. There was no soul lonelier than he. His passion for souls was as great as God's but all he had to offer was his own despair. He offered it as boundlessly as God offered love. He *was* despair as surely as God was love.

And that was why she wept. Blinded by her tears, still kneeling, she reached out, entering that moment that should have brought her to the centre of the sublime mystery but did not because there was no mystery. She was an old woman like Edwina and the dead body was the one Edwina guarded – her life in India come to nothing.

She wept because the gesture that had seemed sublime revealed an Edwina who was dumb with despair not purified by love. Revelation of Edwina's despair uncovered her own, showed its depth, its immensity. For herself she could have borne the knowledge, would have to bear it. For Edwina it must have been a cruel thing. Edwina had always seemed so strong and sure in God, in God's purpose, so richly endowed that just to be near her was to share her gift and feel one's doubts turn sour for want of nourishment.

And yet Edwina must have felt it too, the ever-increasing tenuousness of the connexion, the separation in space as God inexplicably turned His face from humble service He no longer found acceptable but was too kind actually to refuse.

She rose painfully from her knees and soaked the

flannel under the running tap, carried it sopping to her face and repeated the process until her face was chilled and only her eyeballs felt hot. Edwina's faith had been of a higher order than her own, she had no doubt, and as a consequence her despair had been great enough to disturb the balance of her mind. But the disturbance could not be offered in mitigation because it was, itself, the work of the Devil. She looked in the mirror that hung above the basin. On the opposite wall there was another mirror. She was multiplied back and front. Frontwards she was Barbie, approaching herself, and backwards another self retreating through one diminishing image after another into some kind of shocking infinity.

She felt her skin freeze and harden as warmth went out of her blood. The bathroom was suddenly rank with the nausea, fetid and foul, but there was in its foulness a sense of exquisite patience and desire. She clutched her abdomen and her throat, leant over the bowl and was sick. She reteched and gasped. The tap was still on and the running water carried the horror away. Now she supported herself gripping the procelain basin. She let the water run until the whiteness sparkled again. Her whole body felt clammy. Slowly its warmth returned.

She rinsed her mouth over and over and then turned the tap off. When the last gurgle had died away there was a silence such as might follow a sigh.

'Poor creature,' she said. She shut her eyes. 'I know who you are and I know you are still here. Please go.'

She waited, then caught her breath at the sound of a slow ungainly winged departure as of a heavy carrion bird that had difficulty in overcoming the pull of gravity. She waited for a few minutes and then fastidiously washed her face and hands, but – still dissatisfied – unlocked the door to her bedroom, collected clean clothes, returned and dropped each discarded article into the dhobi basket until she stood naked. Redressed and cologned she went back to her room and tidied her hair.

Beauty is in the eye of the beholder, her mother had said but she had not said who might behold.

PART TWO

A Question of Loyalty

Notices in the Times of India, May 1943

Births
> MANNERS. On 7 May at Srinagar. To Daphne, a daughter, Parvati.

Deaths
> MANNERS. On 7 May, at Srinagar, Daphne, daughter of the late Mr & Mrs George Manners, beloved niece of Ethel and the late Sir Henry Manners.

Forthcoming Marriages
> CAPTAIN E. A. D. BINGHAM AND MISS SUSAN LAYTON
> The engagement is announced between Captain Edward Arthur David Bingham, Muzzafirabad Guides, only son of the late Major A. E. D. Bingham, MC (Muzzafirabad Guides) and of the late Mrs S. A. Hunter, of Singapore, and Susan, younger daughter of Lt-Colonel and Mrs John Layton, of Pankot.

1

Thus Teddie enters already marked by a fatal connexion.

Sarah Layton, subsequently describing him as a man who didn't grow on you, as one you soon got to the end of, initially gave a lone but vivid impression of vacuity, albeit cheerful vacuity. At the time, his future mother-in-law, Mildred, complained that there wasn't much to go on and although she was thinking in severely practical terms (what to tell Colonel Layton, now transferred from an

Italian to a German prison-camp, which made it seem more imperative to make an efficient and detailed report about the man his daughter Susan intended to marry), the idea of not much to go on coupled with that of his not growing on you at first led one inescapably to think of him as a person who conformed in every way with the stock idea one might have of a young man with nothing between his ears, a set of trained and drained responses and a cheerful complacency that would see to it he did nothing outstandingly silly and nothing distinguished either.

How close he came to being jolted out of complacency in the first few months of 1942 in Burma was possibly indicated by his demeanour when he turned up in Pankot a year later, on Dick Rankin's staff, 'rather disappointed' with the immediate result of his attendance at the Staff College in Quetta but 'hoping for something better' in the future. Presumably he had been rather disappointed too to discover that the Japanese had proved 'more useful in a scrap' than the British and Indian armies together and, as he trudged through the jungle back to India with the remnants of his unit (because that was the direction everyone was going in who still could) hoped for an improvement presently.

One could picture him marching out, tired, dirty and hungry, carrying more than his quota of small-arms (to relieve a couple of exhausted sepoys of their weight), keeping *on* and smiling because being personally blameless for what he supposed had to be summed up as a stunning defeat, a complete disaster, there was no call to look miserable and every reason to give an example of how to keep going, even when every limb was attached to the trunk by things that felt like loose hot rubber bands.

Between this picture of Teddie leaving Burma and the one of him arrived in Pankot a year later there is a gap, but it is one of many and it plays a perfectly proper schematic part in an account of him because to Teddie himself his whole history seems to have been a series of gaps linked by a few notable events if one is to judge by

115

the extraordinary difficulty Mildred had in getting anything out of him except a few bare and not very encouraging bits of information and a slight frown of concentration,
which could have been the effect had on him of his
realization that between them he and Mildred had a duty
to do.

'I do have an uncle,' he said; and added, 'In Shropshire
actually,' as if this made the uncle more lively and
identifiable. Teddie had lived with the uncle when sent
home from India to school, just as Sarah and Susan had
lived with their Aunt Lydia, Mildred's elder London-
based sister. Teddie's father had been in the Muzzafirabad
Guides which was why Teddie was in them now but had
broken his neck hunting when Teddie was fourteen. His
mother married again, a commercial chap called Hunter
(which was odd when you thought of the cause of the first
husband's death). They lived in Singapore until Hunter
died. 'I don't mind telling you,' Teddie told Mildred,
'people said she had a rotten time with him.' She died
suddenly in Mandalay on her way back to Muzzafirabad.
All this was before Teddie came back to India himself to
join the regiment. In due course he went to Burma, tried
but failed to find her grave and worried a bit about it until
he remembered she'd been cremated. In due course the
Japanese arrived in Burma too and presently Teddie
marched out.

And that was about it. He had red hair and sandy
eyelashes (which Clara Fosdick said she thought a sign of
untrustworthiness). He was twenty-five but had that elon-
gated bony English look of not yet having completed the
process of growing-up and filling out which meant that in a
few years he would suddenly appear middle-aged as well
as beefy because to men like this everything seemed to
happen at once round about the age of thirty; everything
except white hair which was reserved for retirement and
was equally sudden and the only sign that old age had
arrived.

School, military academy, regiment, baptism of fire,

staff-college: the next logical step was marriage so that the process could be repeated through a continuing male line. Arrived in Pankot Teddie metaphorically cleared his throat, put up his head and looked round for a girl with whom to take it. It could not be any girl. The choice had ideally to be made among girls in the range labelled Army which more or less knocked out Carol and Christine Beames whose father Colonel Beames was in the civil branch of the IMS. It knocked out several others whose fathers' regiments did not in Teddie's opinion match the standard set by his own, the Muzzys, to which none of course was superior but with which one or two might claim equality. This opinion was one Teddie's father had held and Teddie had acquired it in much the same way that he had acquired a bit of private property in the shape of an unearned income, although the capital from which the income came had been filtered to him through his mother and therefore been diminished somewhat by the commercial chap Hunter, who fortunately died of drink before his mother died of what Teddie always assumed had been shame and sorrow, otherwise he might never have seen a penny of it and have been forced either to go into some sort of business or join an inferior regiment, which would have been pretty awful he supposed. He doubted that his uncle would have 'stumped up'. He believed that his uncle hadn't liked his father. His uncle had been the elder brother.

'I suppose you'll get money from your uncle eventually,' Mildred said. She believed in coming to the point and came to it stylishly, using her languid but abrasive first-two-drinks-of-the-day voice.

'Oh, I shouldn't rely on it,' Teddie said. 'He's a bit of an old skinflint. I'm not looking beyond the six hundred a year. And my pay of course.'

'Well it will be years before Susan gets anything from us,' Mildred warned him. 'So you'll just have to buckle to and rise to dizzy heights.'

'Yes, Rather.'

'Have you a photo or a snap?'

'What of?'

'Of you. So that I can send it to John in prison-camp. I think he'll want to know what you look like, don't you?'

'I'll get one done, shall I?'

'That would help.'

'Full length or head and shoulders?'

Teddie had a practical turn of mind. It made up for his lack of imagination. He would never have thought to offer Mrs Layton his photograph but knowing that she wanted one and suddenly understanding why he saw that it was important to get it right. In uniform or mufti? Postcard size for easy handling or something larger? With or without his cap? Since he seemed to have no personal vanity the questions had to be taken seriously. He couldn't be palmed off with a casual reply such as, 'Oh anything so long as it looks like you.'

He had the kind of thick skin which managed to fall just short of suggesting insensitivity. Mildred became bored with the photograph long before the details were agreed. Teddie did not notice she was bored or that she drank too much. Perhaps he did not really notice people. There were times when he did not seem to notice himself. For instance he didn't appear to be at all put out by what another man might have thought of as the delicacy or awkwardness of his position in a household where he constantly bumped into Sarah. Before he took up with Susan he had taken up with Sarah and shown every sign of not being aware of the younger sister's existence. His attentiveness to Sarah now suggested he might at any moment explain why he'd cooled off her in spite of the fact that Sarah had not encouraged him sufficiently to make his cooling off actually require an explanation. His attentiveness would have struck an outsider who knew nothing of their history as the kind a man felt he had to show the girl whose sister he was about to marry; anything apologetic in it being an apology for taking Susan away not for giving Sarah up. Perhaps that was how he saw it too.

118

There were several explanations given in Pankot, though, of his defection, change of mind or change of heart. Had he known about one of them he might have been surprised (at last) because it is unlikely that 'fickle' was a word he would ever expect to hear used to describe him. Had he known about the other two explanations he would have agreed with the first of them, that he had finally been unable to avoid seeing how pretty Susan was and unable to resist the strong emotion with which the sight suddenly affected him. The other explanation he would probably not have understood at all and he certainly would not have cared to hear it.

Little Mrs Smalley had described Sarah Layton in terms which were sufficiently accurate for the inaccurate conclusions she then drew from them in regard to Teddie's defection to be accepted as coming close to the mark. But Teddie would have made nothing of the Smalley image of Sarah. He surely never felt that she didn't take him seriously as a person; never felt that she took none of 'it' seriously ('it' meaning India, the British role in India, the thing the British were in India to do); never felt that she laughed at 'it' and consequently at him; never felt, being a man and therefore much more serious about 'it' than a woman had to be, that Sarah was the kind of girl who although admirable in every other way lacked the attitude which men thought it important for a girl to have underneath everything else and that this explained why after a bit men felt more comfortable in the company of the younger sister. He might have agreed with Mrs Paynton when she gathered all these potentially damaging Smalley threads into a single sensible one and declared that what Sarah needed was to settle down and that she would be all right then, being fundamentally sound and a veritable rock so far as Mildred was concerned.

Getting Sarah to settle down as Mrs Bingham was exactly what Teddie had first hoped for. For him the question of her soundness never arose. Seeing her come into his office at Area Headquarters with some confidential files he had asked his friend and fellow Muzzy, Tony Bishop, Dick Rankin's ADC, who the WAC (1) corporal with the fair hair and slim figure was. The answer was tremendously satisfactory to him one assumes. Failing a Muzzy Guide girl a Pankot Rifles girl would do very well, in fact rather better because Teddie probably thought that there was something vaguely incestuous about marrying into one's own regiment. His father had done it and it really hadn't turned out at all well. If fate had at first disappointed Teddie, bringing him to a static headquarters as a mere captain when it might just as easily have sent him to an active formation perhaps as a G2, it now looked as if in bringing him to Pankot it had done so with the sole and excellent purpose of introducing him to this girl from the station's favourite regiment.

Chasing or wooing would be the wrong words to use about Teddie's activity in regard to Sarah Layton. He applied himself to her as he applied himself to any task that fell within the area of his competence. But because he was unable to think of more than one thing at a time he appeared to everybody to have mounted a frontal attack on a girl who had caught his eye and awoken feelings in him of a tender and passionate nature.

This was the light in which if he gave it any thought he must have appeared to himself and he must have given it thought, and found nothing amiss. After all chaps fell in love every day. There was nothing peculiar about it. And she was awfully nice. His father would have approved.

The most interesting gaps, perhaps, in Teddie's history are those through which one could have traced the progress or lack of it of his relationship with women. At twenty-five one assumes some heterosexual experience, but the questions – with whom? in what circumstances? are impenetrable enough to leave about him a pure aroma of cheerful male virginity tainted only by traces of something more pungent, the odour of voluntary or involuntary nocturnal emission, which does not alter his expression but does emphasize the underlying shadows of modest perplexity.

Tony Bishop had no recollection of Teddie ever having been 'mixed up' with a girl before he applied himself so wholeheartedly to the business of being mixed up with Sarah Layton. Bishop knew him before Burma and after Burma but not during Burma, so his recollections did not cover a possibly important phase of Teddie's development. He had the unit-image of him rather than a private one. The Muzzy Guides (so Bishop said, fondly mocking) was one of those regiments which not only had a rule about never mentioning women in the mess but stuck to it with such iron resolution that an outsider could have been persuaded to believe that its young subalterns not only stopped mentioning them but stopped thinking about them too until a certain age was reached and they came face to face with a situation that called for a tricky decision: whether to remain a bachelor or get married. This question was usually settled by another of the regiment's unwritten rules which was that an officer had to have a wife before he was thirty unless he wished to enjoy a reputation for unseemly frivolity.

Since Teddie was deeply attached to his regiment – it was the one thing he may be thought of as taking seriously – the regimental aura of ambiguous monasticism probably explained Teddie's own aura of either never having sown wild oats or of having sown them so far out of range of the regimental eye that they didn't count as his but as those of someone whose body he had borrowed for the purpose. Whatever the reason for this aura, it shone behind his approach to Sarah which was that of a man whose physical appetite had never bothered him before but promised to be really rather adequate, as if it knew all about itself.

What it finally came to was that Teddie was in pursuit of an idea. The idea was initially embodied in the person of Sarah Layton. After three weeks he was close enough to her to feel that all he need do next was pop the question and settle the matter. He had, one imagines, few doubts about the outcome. She had been awfully amenable and absolutely available. He hadn't kissed her yet but he had

121

held on to her hand and made other gestures claiming physical possession. They had played tennis, gone riding, swimming, dancing, to the pictures, the Chinese restaurant and Smith's Hotel for supper. He had called for her at the club, at the grace and favour bungalow and once at Rose Cottage where an elderly woman (something to do with missions) had talked rather a lot about Muzzafirabad but not about those aspects of its life which he knew. Sarah and he had walked together, shared tongas, and the front bench of a staff car when he had been able to log it out as on official duties and get rid of the driver.

The next step was therefore clear. He must arrange for them to be alone so that he could put an arm round her, kiss her and say something like You know I'm most awfully Fond of You? which sounded a bit dull but was certainly the truth and once he had said it he could logically follow it up by suggesting they might Sort of Get Engaged If She Felt Like It; which was as far as one needed to go because once one had gone that far everything else surely fell into place of its own accord.

At first (Sarah says) she thought Teddie Bingham no different from other young officers who assumed that because she was there and they were there something should be done about it. But after a while she realized he was different. He had been wound up and wouldn't stop and she wasn't sure what she could do about it except hope that he suddenly ran down or noticed Susan as so many other officers had. She did not find him unattractive but this was somehow proof of what she thought of as his negative transparent quality; he was not unamusing, not unpleasant to talk to and not uninteresting up to a point which was soon reached.

When the moment came she knew instinctively that it had and was in as great a state of uncertainty as ever about how to deal with it. He encircled her and kissed her and became rather elaborately excited. She noticed that he smelt of Pears' soap. This heightened her impression of him as being transparent because suddenly he was not, having worked himself into a lather. His excitement was a bit embarrassing because he failed utterly to move her to any kind of response and she wondered whether this was his fault or hers. She had very little fear of Teddie attempting anything more serious. Apart from his lips which were glued to hers he was not actually doing anything to any part of her with any part of him which he could not have done in a ballroom or would be ashamed of in the morning.

She thought too, that his excitement was caused less by the effect kissing her had on him than by the feeling he had of breaking out, to the degree that was allowable, from the strict confines of his normal pattern of behaviour. But a man like Teddie didn't kiss a girl as he was kissing her just for the hell of it. At any moment, she thought, he would make a declaration. She considered this imminent event as calmly as she could. She had no intention of accepting a declaration from Teddie Bingham but for an instant she understood the awful ease with which the whole business could gather momentum and overwhelm them both. If she had not been cursed with a mind that questioned everything she could at this very moment have been within an inch or two of becoming the future Mrs Bingham because she couldn't think of a single practical reason why things should not take this course, providing one discounted the question of whether they loved one another, which wasn't a question anyone seemed to take very seriously.

In any case Teddie on the face of it was doing well enough on that score for the two of them. Or had been doing well. But Sarah realized she was bored and had been bored ever since he began and suddenly she felt that he was bored too. She would have understood his becoming depressed or cross at finding his amorousness was not infectious but she had a distinct impression of his boredom. He kept the kiss going but it had taken on a remote and pointless quality, like a breath-holding contest, which it was to some extent. She had a stubborn inclination not to be the first to give in.

Just as she decided she couldn't go on he came unstuck and breathed deeply. They stared at each other in the dark of the motor-car. Surprisingly it was a serious , even tender, moment and she was afraid that in spite of everything he would make his declaration; but he didn't. For Sarah it was as if they had both drawn back in the nick of time from being involved in an association neither of them wanted but which Teddie had thought they ought to want.

Presently he resumed a proper position behind the steering-wheel, looked at his luminous watch and said, 'I say, I think we ought to be getting back.'

Two days later he turned up at the grace and favour at a time when she wasn't there but Susan was. And that was that. He was still wound up, still working. She thought he would run down and disappear like Susan's other young men whose numbers remained more or less the same while their names and faces altered. But within a month he was engaged to Susan to be married. It was this that so surprised Sarah. One day he had been just one of the crowd round her sister; the next he was the only one. Susan seemed to have put out her hand and picked out the toy she decided she liked best. Sarah had a picture of Teddie held upside down with his wheels racing and the spring whirring, his eyes closed in the ecstasy of being singled out and taken to Susan's heart forever.

But in real life Teddie was upright, on his feet, and his eyes open, alight with the pleasure if not the pain of being in love – or what passed for it in his opinion; and his opinion was the only one that could matter to him and was in this sense as good as anyone else's. Allow him that happiness, and the illusion that it sprang from Susan and not from an idea. The moment in the car with Sarah could possibly have been a turning point but the effort of making it would have been tremendous, virtually impossible. It would have involved treachery to his upbringing, a complete rearrangement of the ego, a thorough breaking-out, an entry into an unknown and rather frightening world. Besides it is better to accept the explanation that lies nearest and easiest to hand: that Sarah's lack of interest eventually got through to him as a failure of physical response, as a personal rebuff, not as a general pointer to the boring artificiality of the situation that could have prodded him alive to the fact that to date his life had been one protracted grinding experience of boredom after another because he never did anything, never would do anything, except according to the rules laid down for what a man of his class and calling should do and for how and why he should do it.

There was of course that little gap (characteristic) between getting Sarah home and turning up a couple of days later to take up with Susan. Perhaps the gap in this case represented a dark night of Teddie's soul (a whiff of that pungent odour?), a battle between a disturbing new instinct, only half felt, and an old safe and happy one which was familiar and reliable and inevitably the victor. In that case the spoils were Teddie, not Susan.

'I'd rather they waited,' Mildred told Sarah. It was apparent that she had in mind a long period; waiting until Colonel Layton was restored to them, in other words until the end of the war. But Susan would not wait. Neither would Teddie. Together they seemed to recognize a sense of urgency as if they wanted to abide by the rules while the rules were still there to abide by. The announcement of their engagement appeared on the same day as those other two announcements which advertised the fact that one of the rules had already been broken. It was the first coincidence and perhaps it was significant. This was in the second week of May. Mildred agreed to put the notice in the *Times* because Susan insisted and Mildred saw no harm in putting in what could easily be taken out by a second announcement of the cancellation she expected at any moment – for instance when Teddie produced the photograph and Susan looked at it and imagined herself left with that and nothing else after Teddie had gone back to the war as he was bound to eventually.

But the photograph turned out surprisingly well. Teddie's smile was rendered down to a quirky upward twitch of one corner of the lips which gave the lower part of his face a look of even-tempered manly resolution. The stilted professional studio lighting had for once worked on a fortuitously inspired level and produced a sort of subdued halo that was reflected again by a dreamy look in the eyes, so that his face was amazingly that of the soldier-poet, the man of action capable of making sensitive judgments. When Susan saw it she at once demanded a cabinet-size copy and had it framed for her bedside table. Towards the end of May, publicly acknowledging that there was not another thing she could do to delay matters, Mildred announced that the wedding would be shortly after Susan's twenty-first birthday, which fell in November. It was the most she could do to relate the affair to circumstances beyond her control. She wrote to her sister Fenny in Delhi who came up at once to inspect Teddie. Aunt Fenny thought him 'rather sweet'. Apart from Susan she was the first person, perhaps, to see anything below the surface.

2

Before making the necessary imaginative readjustment to see most of the rest of the short life of Edward Arthur David Bingham almost entirely from Teddie's point of view one minor and possibly irrelevant aspect of his behaviour is to be noted. His experience of combat conditions had coarsened his vocabulary.

In certain circumstances in male company he nowadays permitted himself to use words he had seldom found it necessary to use before going with the first battalion to Burma. The standard of vulgarity he reached never rose above that acceptable in an officer of his type and standing and he would never have dreamed of swearing in the mess let alone in front of women. The Muzzys had been as strict about bad language in the mess as about references to the weaker sex, if anything stricter. Damn was allowed, in fact it did not count, but bloody was frowned upon if used by anyone below senior field-rank. Teddie therefore found the conversation in the junior officers' mess at area headquarters alarmingly and disagreeably lax. He was quite shocked. Regular officers from good regiments could still be relied on to do as Teddie did – reserve bad lanugage for private or office occasions – but this mess was full of curious unmilitary fellows with emergency commissions and civilian habits. Fortunately as he thought it he seldom had to eat there. He and Tony Bishop together with an officer of the engineers and a gunner lived in a chummery a few bungalows down the road from Nicky Paynton and Clara Fosdick. In the chummery mess he maintained formality of manner and speech and once rebuked the gunner for the terms in which he expressed an opinion about the origin of the woodcock toast.

But in private, in the bedroom he shared with Tony Bishop and in the daftar, Teddie's otherwise predictable statements and responses were enlivened by certain rich images and expletives often enough for Bishop to have marked them down as something new in Teddie dating from the Burma experience, indicative of the kind of wildness even a cheerful and level-tempered fellow like Bingham would have found bubbling up in him when (as he now described it) the shit hit the fan and he had to duck.

Bishop went so far as to see two Teddie Binghams: the one who stood upright encased in the armour of the mystery of being a Muzzy Guide and the one who in moments of office crisis stepped out of the armour's support with no warning whatsoever and emphatically but unvehemently announced his opinion that the situation was balls-aching, only just short of a fuck-up, and that he had no intention of being buggered about.

The signal ordering him to a place called Mirat to take up a G3(O) appointment at the headquarters of a new Indian division had originally been sent to Muzzafirabad. The delay and confusion caused by this administrative error led to a further signal, peremptory in tone, which managed to give the impression that Teddie was to be blamed for not being where he was not and must make up for it by leaving for Mirat immediately.

This second signal which was the first Teddie knew of his default was brought round to the chummery by special messenger on an evening in the middle of July*. There was a thunderstorm in progress which lent the occasion an apt touch of flashy drama. Teddie was lowering his long ribby body into the tin tub in the ghusl-khana. It was 6.15. He had had a hard day at the office. He was due at the grace and favour at 7.30 to take Susan to the Electric Cinema and had just bitten his bearer's head off because the dhobi-wallah had failed to turn up with his second suit of khaki-drill. Allah Din had gone grumbling into the storm. Meanwhile the bhishti had heated the bathwater above the degree Teddie enjoyed, had left no tin of cold and was presently nowhere to be found.

As Teddie's buttocks made contact with the steaming water his thighs came out in goosepimples to compensate. His knees smelt of leather, which reminded him of when he was a boy having a hot bath after a game of football. He completed his submersion and breathed out slowly. He reached for the Lifebuoy soap (Pears' was for face and hands) and just then Tony Bishop walked in with the fatal signal and the messenger's pad for Teddie to sign.

Teddie had one sterling military quality. He never panicked. The word immediate had no galvanizing effect on his intellectual machinery. Immediate meant as soon as possible because nothing could be sooner than that. In the past year he had become aware that there were people in positions of authority who pretended otherwise. They put texts up on their office walls and issued directives advocating the strangest beliefs: for instance that what was difficult could be done at once whereas the impossible might take a little longer.

Teddie thought this showy and undeserving of serious consideration. He was inclined to blame the Americans, who mistook activity for efficiency, and those civilian elements in the wartime army who were naturally anxious to get it over and done with and go back into commerce where they belonged. Between them the Americans and the civilians were trying to dictate the pace of army operations and run them like a business. And they were being encouraged in this by the careerists and odd-men-out in the regular army who saw the war as an opportunity to promote themselves and their eccentric ideas.

Teddie distrusted anything to which the word flamboyant could be applied. On the other hand he admired what his Shropshire uncle called style. Not knowing quite what style was he sometimes had difficulty in distinguishing it from flamboyance and thought his uncle must have been right when he said style was on the wane and went unnoticed in an age in which vulgarity was admired more often than it was detested. Teddie took pride in having some style himself. At the moment it meant sitting on in his bath for at least five minutes after Bishop had opened and read the signal, after he had dried his hands to read it himself, sworn, signed the book and sent Bishop away.

Quite unfairly behaviour like this gave rise to an idea that Teddie was a bit slow-witted. His confidential report at Quetta, while paying tribute to his cheerfulness and capacity for work, had mentioned lack of 'verve'. The phrase had caused him no lasting pang.

Actually Teddie grasped all the implications of the posting at once. Where the slowness came in was in the method that came most naturally to him of considering them one at a time in a roughly ascending order of priority; for example: where exactly was Mirat? How long would the journey take? Should he take his own orderly with him? Did he really want to in view of the fact that the fellow couldn't organize his laundry? Who was the divisional commander? Had he heard anything at the daftar about this particular formation? Would he be able to get leave in August to join Susan and her family on the late holiday they were planning to take in Srinagar? Would he be able to get leave later in the year to come back to Pankot for the wedding? Would Susan kick up a fuss about changing the arrangements if a change was necessary? Since the posting did not bring him any promotion would it be worth while having a word with General Rankin to see if it could be cancelled? Did he want it cancelled? Was it fair to marry a girl when it looked as if he was in for another dose of active service? He had thought of that before but had she? Should he ask her whether she would like to be released from their engagement?

The prospect of her saying she would suddenly looked very likely to him because it would bring his world in ruins about his head; and there on that July evening in the tin tub Teddie – one may fancy – could not rid himself of the idea that he might be turning out to be the sort of man around whom things collapsed, not noisily but with a sort of slithering, inexorable, folding-in and -over movement. He scrubbed his back vigorously to kill this notion but stopped when he found that in getting rid of it he had got hold of another. The friction of the bristles was making him feel randy. This feeling was persistent. It continued after he had put the brush down. It had in fact been pretty persistent on and off for some time, ever since he had set his heart on getting married.

Teddie was a firm believer in cold water. He yelled for the absent bhishti. Unexpectedly the old boy staggered in with two full cans. Teddie camouflaged himself with a

130

sponge, swore at the bhishti for not having been available earlier and told him to leave the cans near the tub. Alone, Teddie stood and dowsed himself. There was no significant change. In fact the cold water had a setting-up effect. He shut his eyes and said, 'Oh, Christ,' stepped on to the duckboard and wrestled himself dry with a towel.

Susan was an absolute brick. Kissing him in front of Mildred and Sarah she had said, 'Congratulations', as if being a G3(O) in a new division was something pretty terrific. For a while he felt it was. On their way to the cinema he had an ugly but exciting thought about the journey home. He felt heroic and felt that she felt he was heroic. He didn't understand the film but became physically alert each time the girl with the enormous tits got manhandled which was every few minutes. At the end of one scene there was almost nothing left of her dress. There hadn't been much of it at the start. The other ranks down in the body of the hall whistled and stamped. The film ended with her disappointingly fully-clothed kissing the fellow with the jaw who was lying on the steps of a church riddled with bullets. For some reason it was also snowing.

In the tonga Teddie held Susan's hand – the ungloved one – and surprisingly she let him and even seemed to want it. His thoughts stopped functioning in anything like a logical order. Normally when they were alone the chaste kisses and affectionate gestures Susan allowed in public were somehow made difficult as if she disapproved of what they might lead to.

'We could have coffee at the chummery,' Teddie said.

'Aren't we going to the Chinese?'

'I mean after.'

'Oh,' Susan said. Then: 'Yes, we could.'

Like that. Teddie's neck prickled. They had never been in the chummery alone. His hand and hers were clammy. He did not dare squeeze in case it frightened her. His heart was pumping nastily. It took only two minutes to get

131

from the cinema forecourt to the restaurant. All the bazaar shops were open and brightly lit by electric bulbs or naphtha lamps. The street was full of British Other Ranks. Some were lounging against the pillars of the arcade in a slovenly manner with their hands significantly in their trouser pockets talking to Eurasian girls in white high-heeled shoes. In one shop a radio played Indian film music. The tonga stopped outside the restaurant.

Teddie got down. Susan's face was coloured faintly by the lights. She looked marvellous. But she wasn't looking happy.

'Teddie, I'm not awfully hungry.'

'Oh.'

He climbed back in. A muscle in his left cheek twitched of its own accord.

'Just coffee then?'

'Yes.'

He twisted round and spoke to the wallah. The tonga was turned in the street, causing trouble to other vehicles. The wallahs shouted at each other. For a while all the tongas were stationary. The wallahs waved their arms. Teddie felt put out because he and Susan were at the storm centre. He hated scenes but in any case this one was like having everything advertised.

He hit the wallah on the shoulder and told him to get moving.

The wallah obeyed but continued to exchange insults with each of the wallahs in the line of tongas whose free passage he had blocked. And the driver of the tonga immediately behind their own, coming in their wake, shouted insults too, presumably at their driver but in effect at them. The damned fellow was grinning too, as if he knew.

They did not hold hands. When the tonga left the lighted area they continued not holding them. There were puddles at intervals reflecting the infrequent street lamps. Between lamps the night was promisingly dark and humid. On other occasions when he had invited her to the

132

chummery she had always managed to work the conversation round to the question of who else would be there before accepting. It was becoming clearer and clearer to him that tonight she had no intention of asking and that she anticipated finding exactly what she would find: nobody. Tony Bishop was dining at Flagstaff House. Bruce Mackay, the engineer, was down in Ranpur, and Bungo Barnes, the gunner, had gone round to see the QA sister, Gentleman's Relish. He would not be back until the small hours. Teddie had seen Gentleman's Relish only once. Her other name was Thelma and he thought her extremely unattractive and alarmingly common for a girl who ranked as an officer. Since Bungo had a reputation for never wasting time on a girl who – as he put it – didn't, Teddie assumed that Gentleman's Relish did, and more often than seemed reasonable because Bungo had been out every night for two weeks and looked washed out at breakfast. Where they did it he had no idea. He disapproved of Bungo Barnes. He also envied him.

When they reached the chummery he envied Bungo more than ever because he knew that the whole thing was hopeless. Susan wasn't that kind of girl. Her trim little body was protected by some sort of absolute statement about its virginity this side of the altar. She might wish otherwise but that was how it was for her, for him. As usual lights were on in the porch, entrance-lobby and living-room. Prabhu, Bungo Barnes's equally lascivious servant, came out pander-like from the dining-room to see what was happening.

'Oh, you're duty-wallah are you, Prabhu? We'd like coffee.'

'May I change my mind and have tea?' Susan asked. She stood in front of the screened fireplace dealing with her gloves and handbag in that stunning way girls had.

'Anything you want, old thing,' Teddie said. 'Matter of fact I thought I'd have a peg. Would you prefer that?'

'No, tea is what I'd like. I've got rather a head.'

'Oh, Lord, you'd better have an aspirin.'

'No, I don't want an aspirin, Teddie. Just tea.'

'Strong or weak?'

'Just as it comes.'

'It usually comes like dishwater in this place.' He told Prabhu to bring tea but make sure that the water boiled.

'I say, do sit down or something.'

'I will in a minute.'

They stood, apart, smiling at each other. The room had always struck Teddie as a bit chintzy for an all-male establishment. He thought it awfully nice tonight because she was in it. Her dress had white and navy-blue flowers on it.

'I say is that new?'

'Yes.'

'It's awfully nice.'

He had not noticed it at the grace and favour because he'd been worried about how Susan would take the news. After that it had been dark most of the time. He reached out, stroked her shoulder. Her flesh was warm and cushiony under the thin silky material. The neck of the dress was cut square. He could just see the beginning of the division between her breasts. The skin was dotted with tiny little freckles. Her arms were freckled too. Delightfully. He slid his hand down the arm to the soft flesh on the inner side of the elbow.

He said, 'It's rotten going away, leaving you.'

'I know.'

Since he touched her shoulder she had not looked at him. Her eyelashes were wonderfully long. The tips curled up. There were a few freckles near the bridge of her nose. He felt tremendously moved and protective. Her beauty was so simple, so artless. She glowed with health. The freckles came out because she was always in the sunshine. She was made for a clean, healthy, simple and loving life. He clutched her suddenly, pressed her to him. Her hair smelt sweet. It tickled. He kissed her forehead through it. She was awfully tensed up. Her whole body seemed to be a skull. If he kissed and kissed her she would melt.

Through their clothes their bodies would flow into each other. He kissed her again and again until he had the most shamefully majestic erection. He didn't care. She was still protected by that absolute statement. The erection was a statement too and just as absolute but in a negative way.

'Su, I love you so much.' He clasped her head, kissed her closed lids. Soft, marvellous, living warmth. The melting would begin here. 'So much, honestly, honestly.'

He heard the tea-things clunking like monks' sandals and broke away, turned his back on her and the approaching Prabhu and walked, sweetly bitterly crippled, to the drinks cabinet. When he heard the tray set down he said without looking, 'Thank you, Prabhu. Just leave it, will you.' He opened a bottle of Johnnie Walker and poured a stiff measure. His eyes felt hot and hollow. His limbs were steady but felt as if they were not. He wasn't sure if there was enough blood in the soles of his feet. His knees were awkwardly placed in his legs, a shade out of true. He didn't really want soda but wasn't yet ready to face around to things so popped a bottle and poured a long one. He thought therapeutically about liquor; of what it could do to your liver. His mother's second husband, Hunter, couldn't have had any liver left.

When he came away from the cabinet Susan was sitting on one of the chintzy chairs staring at the tea-tray which Prabhu had put down on an ornate and untrustworthy mother-of-pearl encrusted table. It was maddening how easy it was to get worked up, how difficult to do anything about it if you cared about things like marriage and doing right by each other. She looked pretty pale. He hadn't yet asked her if she'd prefer to be released from their promise and come to an understanding that they weren't actually bound to each other while he was away; and now didn't dare, not because she might jump at the chance but because it would be a damned insult after the way he'd just pressed up against her. When she suddenly reached for the teapot, using both hands, the little cluster of engagement diamonds glittering balefully. The line between

135

self-sacrifice and acting like an unspeakable cad seemed perilously thin.

He sat on the sofa at the end near her chair and watched her perform her womanly little tasks. A lifetime of tea-trays stretched ahead of them. Or might. With luck. He felt a draught as of a premonition that he'd drawn a dud chit out of luck's hat and had been given Susan either briefly to make up for it or to give him a sniff of what he was going to miss. He was on the point of declaring an intention to talk to Dick Rankin in the morning about pulling strings to keep him in Pankot when to his great relief (because the intention was a callow quivering hand with a sleek shiny white feather in it) Susan said:

'Of course it was bound to happen, this proper job I mean. I hoped it wouldn't happen so soon which was silly of me, but it doesn't make any difference does it?'

'Difference?'

'Difference to us.'

'What difference could it make?'

'I thought you might think we should wait, not make definite plans. Settle for a long engagement.'

'Do you think we should?'

She glanced into the pot to check how full it was. 'No,' she said, 'if necessary I think we should speed things up.'

She raised the cup to her lips and Teddie raised his glass. They were both trembling. Teddie couldn't think why but it seemed touching and very serious. Just then they heard a car on the gravel and in a moment Tony Bishop came in looking done up. The Rankins had been entertaining visiting top brass but Tony had been able to mention Teddie's posting-order. General Rankin said Teddie's new commander was a fire-eater by all accounts, a youngish man with a reputation for unorthodoxy.

Teddie groaned. 'I suppose I'd better talk to the movement people first thing tomorrow,' he said.

'There's no need, it's all arranged. Mirat was on the blower asking where you'd got to. They said to get you down to Ranpur tomorrow and out to the airfield at Ranagunj and they'll fly you down to Mirat tomorrow night.'

'Fly? But I've never flown in my life! Supposing I'm sick?'

'I think you'll have to get used to it. Your new general's tremendously keen on his officers flying whenever they can. He's air mad.'

'What about my kit? Aren't they awfully strict about weight?'

'Pretty strict. You'd better go as light as you can and I'll send your trunk on directly you tell me to.'

'What about Allah Din?'

'Sorry, no personal servants. We'll get him back to Muzzafirabad.'

'What am I going to do without Allah Din?'

'You'll probably share an orderly. I'm afraid you're in for a rather Spartan existence.'

'It's indecent. I mean hang it all Mirat's only another military station. We might be there for months. It's not like buzzing off to the Arakan.'

He felt hollow again and indignant. The new general probably had a text on the wall saying: Do it Yesterday. This turned out not far from the case. Actually it said: Do it Now.

He took Susan home in the car which Bishop had been using to ferry the Rankin's guests and had efficiently kept waiting as soon as he saw a tonga at the chummery and guessed whose it was. Unlike the tonga-wallah, who complained at being deprived of the fare back to the grace and favour, the lance-naik driver was quite happy with the arrangement. He was obviously one of those Indians who was tireless when behind a wheel and didn't care how late he worked so long as an officer signed for the journey. Teddie and Susan sat in back-seat comfort. They held hands. Teddie had stopped feeling randy and started to feel emotional but chipper too because they were together in the same emotional situation: last night out for some time to come, last few minutes, probably, of being alone together.

'It might be fun, flying,' he said.

'Yes, it might.'

'I'll tell you what would be.'

'What?'

'Flying back, for the wedding.'

'You'll tell them directly you get there, won't you?'

Practical Susan!

'Of course. I'll speak to the Gee One first thing.'

'What will happen if the division's going away almost at once?'

'It's pretty unlikely. If we do it'll be for working-up. Anyway they'd always give an officer leave to get married. Don't worry.'

'I'll try not to.'

He cuddled her. She was still very tense. But what a girl! No scene, no shilly-shallying. Just tremendous pluck and determination. As the car turned into Rifle Range road a cold night breeze blew in through the lowered window from the open spaces of the Pankot Rifles lines. It flirted a lock of her hair against his cheek. Behind the southern ridge of the hills the sky was suddenly illuminated. Down on the plains the monsoon was loose like an electric beast.

His uncle in Shropshire always said that a thunderstorm made the milk go off in the pantry. It occurred to him that his uncle was rather a lonely sort of chap being able to notice things like that.

3

The other, empty, bed in Teddie's room had begun to make its presence felt. A plain wooden charpoy like his own, its mosquito net, folded up, was taped to the four bamboo poles tied to its legs. Three biscuit mattresses and a ticking pillow were piled at its head. Otherwise the bed was bare to the cords, awaiting an occupant.

In Mirat the rain was incessant. Violent storms were nightly visitors. They woke Teddie up. The empty bed seemed lit by St Elmo's fire; it rode the night rock-firm, half-ship, half-catafalque. In the peaceful early mornings its message was simpler but still to be reckoned with.

Ten nights after his arrival the electric beast lay quiet and he enjoyed uninterrupted sleep but woke before the orderly Hosain came in with the chota hazri. His eyes recorded the fact that the other bed was fully shrouded by its mosquito net several seconds before this struck him as new. He raised his head from the pillow and stared through the mesh of his own net. The other bed was occupied. He raised the net. How awfully odd. He thought back over his sleep and dreams but could recall nothing which the presence of the recumbent figure explained. His sleep had been wholly undisturbed. It was as if the figure had slowly materialized during the night and had now reached a stage of total conviction about itself and its surroundings. Teddie frowned. He was unused to thinking in imaginative terms. He glanced towards the window.

His own clothes were in their usual place: jacket thrown carelessly over a chair back, trousers on the seat, under-clothes on the floor. The other chair held clothes too but these were neatly arranged. Nearby stood a large leather suitcase and a bedroll which had obviously been opened to remove sheets and pyjamas then rolled up again but left unstrapped. The chap couldn't have done all that in the dark. And he must have had an orderly to help him, if not young Hosain.

Teddie reached for his slippers, automatically tapped them by the heels on the floor to dislodge any lurking scorpion gone into hiding during the night, set them side by side, swung his legs out and slipped his feet into them. The bed creaked. The other chap must have moved like a cat. Obviously a considerate sort of fellow. Teddie

139

grabbed his robe. The humidity was high. The ceiling fan was whispering round at its lowest number of revs a minute. He clicked the dial a couple of notches higher and was rewarded by a faint and regular blowing on his forehead. Leaving the switchboard and going to stand under the fan he inspected his new companion's jacket. Captain's rank. Punjab Regiment. But a green armband hung over the chair back. Intelligence. Scholarly sort of fellow probably; not a real Punjab officer at all. The uniform and the pips looked new. The luggage looked very old though. Teddie twisted his head to find a name on it. The bedroll was set in such a way that any stencilled name on the canvas cover was hidden from view. The suitcase was more revealing. But initials only. R.M. There was no tin trunk. Like himself, R.M. had travelled to Mirat light. By what method though?

The writing-table caught his eye next. Set out upon it with noticeable precision were a briefcase, a field-service cap and a leatherbound swagger cane. The cane was parallel to the base of the briefcase and the cap lay between them with its badge facing front, squared up on an invisible line parallel with the other two. The three items were placed to the left of the blotter as if marking out that side of the desk as the new arrival's, to correspond with the placing – on the left-hand side of the room facing the window – of the chair with the new occupant's clothes on it and the bed in which he was asleep. A white line drawn from the middle of the window to the opposite wall would have defined the area which seemed to have been meticulously but silently claimed in the small hours.

But on the blotter on Teddie's side of the line there was an intruder: a piece of paper tucked into one of the leather corners. Teddie recognized it as a page torn from a Field Service Notebook. In clear rather tight handwriting it read: 'I hope I didn't disturb you. The man who helped me find my quarters said our orderly is called Hosain. I should be grateful if you would ask him to wake me with tea at 0830 but not before as I did not get in until 0300

The train was badly held up. I'm told breakfast is between 0800 and 0930 but I shall skip it. I look forward to meeting you later in the day, perhaps at lunch if we are messing together. Meanwhile my thanks and my apologies for any noise last night. Ronald Merrick.'

In this note Teddie thought there was as much self-assurance as consideration. He went to the mess and on to the daftar by push-bike. At 1130 he was back in his quarters hastily packing his bedroll – Merrick was not there – and at midday was driving with the G1, Lt-Colonel Selby-Smith, to the airfield. At 1230 he was airborne in an RAF Dakota for Delhi where he would meet the divisional commander for the first time. He was away for six days. When he returned, feeling run off his feet but happy to have come daily under the general's eye as the 'young Muzzy officer who wants to get married', he found that Captain Merrick was away on a course. In the interval Teddie's tin trunk had arrived from Pankot; so had Merrick's, from somewhere else. Merrick's was just as old and battered as Teddie's. The rank of captain was freshly painted in, however, and a band of new black paint obliterated something that had been written underneath the surname.

Teddie, who never gossiped to servants only just managed to resist the temptation to ask young Hosain what Captain Merrick Sahib was like. He noticed that the boy took considerable care with the things Merrick had left behind and he resented this in an ill-defined way that made him feel generally at odds with his domestic arrangements.

He was feeling similarly at odds with his work. There was a looseness as yet about the organization of divisional headquarters which made it difficult for him to grasp what was going on. In Delhi the general had talked a lot about what he called fluidity and about the fellow Wingate who had recently been behind the enemy lines down the road in Burma with a specially trained brigade, trying to play havoc with the Japanese lines of communication and being

141

supplied by air. Teddie thought that this operation sounded like a costly and showy variation of the old cavalry role of sometimes penetrating enemy-held country, beating up their baggage trains and galloping back home: useful, an antidote to boredom, but hardly a pukka strategical operation of war. And the supply by air thing had reportedly become a fiasco once Wingate's troops were out of the jungle and into the plains and having to move so fast to escape being trapped that stuff was dropped to them long after they'd had to leave the place they'd asked for it to be dropped to them in. Which meant the Jap got it. Worst of all, Teddie thought, when the operation petered out Wingate had told his chaps to split into groups and get the hell out by any means they could. From Teddie's point of view this was like an officer abrogating his responsibility at the very moment when he was most responsible. That it had been the wisest thing to do only showed how unmilitary the whole affair was.

Even so, the casualty list had been alarming. More alarming, to Teddie, was the way his own general talked about the Wingate expedition having provided the key to the problem of defeating the Japanese. Teddie had a professional soldier's contempt for anything that came under the heading of guerrilla tactics. He did not want to swan around in the jungle with a beard and bag of rice blowing up bridges. And now he was not sure that he much wanted to play messenger-boy in a top-brass outfit like Div. HQ. He missed the comradeship of his old battalion. He missed the good feeling of knowing every sepoy's name, the name of his village, the number and ages of his children, the state of health of his wife, all the things that turned the fellow from a number or a statistic in an order of battle into a man whose personal welfare was a prime consideration.

But then Teddie thought of Susan, of the dizzy heights advocated by her mother, and accepted his present status as an essential trial and testing of his ability to rise to them. A chap, worse luck, couldn't remain a cheerful subaltern or company commander for ever.

'Delhi was pretty hectic,' he told Susan in the first of the biweekly letters which his return to Mirat enabled him to resume. 'I didn't manage to drop round to see your aunt and uncle, Major and Mrs Grace, until the last evening. I told them it's clear there isn't any hope now of my joining you all in Srinagar either in August or September. Naturally I'm disappointed but we didn't really expect it, did we, darling? As for the wedding the form here seems to be that we go ahead with the plans already made but stand ready for a rearrangement perhaps without much notice. It was nice to see your Aunt Fenny again. She got rid of the cold she caught in Pankot as soon as she got down into Delhi again. I also enjoyed meeting your uncle Arthur. He said he was glad to have the opportunity of seeing the chap he's going to give you away to. He gave me the name and address of the houseboat contractor who's fixing you all up in Kashmir so I can send a letter to await your arrival. You'll have a lovely family holiday, I wish I were coming too but I'll be too busy to mope, so don't worry. I'm enjoying Mirat and beginning to feel my feet. I still haven't met the man I'm sharing quarters with. Please thank Tony for me and tell him the trunk's arrived safely. Now I can settle in properly. The rain's been terrific here but there's a lull at the moment. If my letters become a bit irregular you'll know it's only a matter of business before pleasure.'

He had been about to write: 'You'll know it's only because we're out and about on schemes and exercises,' but even news about training was useful to spies. Teddie had been fairly security-minded ever since in Burma his battalion (he could have sworn) had been infiltrated by fifth columnists.

Through the curtain of rain the distant fort looked like a stranded battleship. The general's artillery had been pounding its walls for two hours with 5.5. In four minutes when the barrage lifted his airborne commandos would parachute in to the south to establish a perimeter, cut off the garrison's flight, block advancing enemy reinforcements and mop up pockets of local resistance. The tanks would advance from the north in the van of lorry-borne infantry. Two battalions had already moved in a wide arc to launch an attack from the left and another was holding the right flank.

The general stood, wrist cocked, eyes on watch, rain dripping from the peak of his red-banded cap. Inside the command lorry the R Toc crackled. Suddenly the general's arm dropped, he turned his face up into the rain and after a few seconds smiled beatifically. A score of officers, including Teddie astride his motor-cycle, looked up into the sky. A vicious fork of lightning ripped across it. Teddie winced, blinded by the flash and deafened by the explosive bounce of thunder. When the thunder had gone tumbling and rolling out into the deep field where old Jove had thumped it, he heard a more homely sound which the general's sharper ears had caught earlier: labouring aero engines. A lone Dakota appeared out of the monsoon clouds, roared overhead low enough for them to see the figure of a man standing in the open port; the air liaison officer presumably; and then flew back into them.

'Well, gentlemen,' the general said. 'I think we may safely assume that we've taken Mandalay. Let's go home.'

Teddie muttered, 'Good.' They had been out on the ground for two days. He looked forward to a hot bath and a man-size scotch in the mess. As Div HQ sorted itself out into its several kinds of rough-country transport Teddie kicked his machine into life and went bumping and slithering down the muddy track to make sure that the general's staff car was waiting at the crossroads. A couple of officers representing the reserve brigade were standing miserably under thin branched trees. The fort at Premanagar had vanished entirely behind the curtain of rain.

It was dark when Teddie got back. A light in the window of his room showed that the servants' quarters had been alerted and that Hosain was prepared for him. He entered

144

unbuckling his rain-sodden equipment, yelled for the boy and then, dropping his belt, holster, straps and pack on to the floor, paused – observing the signs of renewed occupation: a row of highly polished shoes, fresh underclothes and socks – not his own – already laid out on a chair for the morning, both beds with lowered nets and pairs of slippers within foot reach; and on the other officer's side of the writing-table a pile of books and pamphlets.

There was something else on the table on Teddie's side: a round chromium tray, a jug of water and a glass each with a beaded muslin cover – a tray such as could only be got from the mess bar by signing a chit and sending an orderly over with it. He heard Hosain at the back calling for the bhishti. There was a note under the tumbler. He slid it out. 'I would have waited and joined you for dinner but I have an appointment. In view of the kind of weather I hear you've had on the scheme I thought you'd need this as well as a hot bath. R.M.'

The tumbler held three fingers of whisky.

'I say,' Teddie said.

What an extraordinarily decent thing to do. He sniffed the whisky and drank some of it neat then yelled for Hosain again and sat in a wicker armchair with his damp legs stuck out. The boy came in with a newly pressed suit of KD.

'Well done, Hosain,' Teddie said. But the suit was Captain Merrick's. Teddie had to wait until it had been hand-flicked and hung in one of the almirahs before he could get Hosain to come and unlace his boots. He'd had them on for thirty-six hours. Relieved of them his feet felt alternately hot and raw, cold and raw. He smoked, drank and listened to the swoosh of water as the bhishti poured it from cans into the tin tub in the adjoining bath-house. He picked up one of Merrick's books, opened it and stared at the incomprehensible Japanese text on the right-hand page. On the left-hand page there were questions in English and, underneath, the same question in phonetics to show you how it would sound if you asked it in

145

Japanese. What is your army number? What is the name or number of your regiment? In what division is your regiment? Tell me the name of your divisional commander. What unit had the position on your unit's left flank when you were captured?

'Some hopes,' Teddie said aloud. If you ever got close enough to speak to a Japanese soldier one of you would be dead a second later. That was how poor old Havildar Shafi Mohammed had been killed, reporting a wounded Jap lying out in the open and volunteering to bring him in. The Jap had had a grenade in his tunic. He must have pulled the pin surreptitiously when he saw the Havildar get within a few paces. They both went to Kingdom Come. Merrick was wasting his time learning a bit of Japanese.

Teddie turned the page and displaced a piece of square-ruled paper which must have been marking the place Merrick had got to. In the tight neat handwriting was written: Lecture Note. 1942, approx. 10,000. Berlin, Tokyo, Singapore, July '43. Mohan Singh. Bangkok Conf.

'Sahib,' Hosain said. He motioned shyly in the direction of the bath-house. Teddie replaced the marker in the book, carried his whisky into the next room and began to shed his clothes.

He came back from the mess early. He was too tired even to write to Susan. He scribbled a note and pinned it to Merrick's mosquito net. 'Thanks for the drink. Have one on me tomorrow.' He left Merrick's bedside lamp burning, turned off his own, climbed inside his net and was asleep almost at once.

Hosain woke him at 0700. He brought only one tray of tea. Hosain indicated Merrick's huddled form, put both hands to his cheek, inclined his head, shut his eyes. Teddie scratched his head, understanding himself requested to be quiet, and went off to the wc. When he left for the mess at 0800 Merrick had still not moved.

It is possible, perhaps, for death to come slowly, even gently, civilly, as if anxious to make the whole thing as painless as possible. One thinks of death at this juncture because Merrick represented Teddie's. Coupled with the civility and consideration a certain reluctance could be detected, almost as if Merrick knew and kept giving Teddie a chance to pack his bags and go before a meeting actually took place. A final opportunity occurred that morning because Teddie saw Merrick and heard him talking for a good twenty minutes before the moment came to claim acquaintance and establish the specific relationship. But there was nothing in Merrick's appearance that caused Teddie to feel uneasy.

After his schemes the general held post-mortems behind locked doors in the Garrison Theatre. During his career Teddie had sat through countless hours of what in common with other junior officers he called prayers. He found that what distinguished the general's prayers were brevity, deadly earnestness and the presence – among the hybrid ranks of divisional, brigade, battalion and supporting arms officers – of VCOs and senior British and English-speaking Indian NCOs, who were seated not quite under the general's eye but in constant danger of attracting it.

One of Teddie's jobs, he discovered, was to make sure that the NCOs from the British battalions did not sit in stiffnecked seclusion but were properly mixed up with their Indian colleagues. According to Selby-Smith the general had a bee in his bonnet about mutual trust and also about making the ordinary soldier feel he had a 'share in the company'. Teddie thought that mutual trust was a matter of respect for each other's achievements in the field more than of sitting next to a chap you didn't know and hadn't got time to get to know, and he wasn't convinced of the value of the share in the company business when it involved the risk of an officer giving a silly answer to the general's questions and making a fool of himself in front of non-commissioned ranks.

The post-mortem began at 1100 hours. Since one brigade

headquarters was stationed twenty-five miles to the east of Mirat and another twenty miles to the north and some of their battalions farther away still, most of the officers attending had had an early start. Some of them had stayed in Mirat overnight and looked the worse for it but neatness and formality of dress were among the things to which the general seemed to attach little importance. The general himself was wearing a set of cellular cotton overalls cut to look like battledress jacket and trousers and made in the new jungle green material that was not yet on general issue. His feet and shins were encased in black dispatch rider's boots. This morning to Teddie's horror he had a Paisley patterned scarf at his neck.

He spoke from notes at a lectern on the stage. His aide and an NCO from the intelligence staff produced beautifully drawn giant-scale sketch maps which they pinned efficiently to the blackboard one after the other to illustrate the points the general was making. After a while Teddie had to admit that everything began to make sense to him. For the first time he fully understood what the scheme had been about. He was even aware that it had a kind of beauty. Formless, almost shapeless, the beauty consisted in the subtle cohesion of what seemed like disparate parts and in the extraordinary flexibility of each arrangement made to bring them together.

Suddenly withering in his mind were the stiff and predictable patterns that made traditional military affairs so easy to grasp on paper, so difficult to put into operation when the real thing was all about you. His blood stirred momentarily with a new sense of excitement in his occupation. The general, direct and thrusting, was filling Teddie's mind with poetry. Teddie sat physically composed as usual, wearing the rather blank expression of a man not naturally receptive to any idea which took time to be expounded. Had the general noticed him particularly and glanced at him every so often to judge what sort of impression he was making on the young man he might have thought he was making none and so made a note to tell the G1 to replace him with a more alert and aggressive officer, in which case he would have done Teddie an injustice because Teddie's soul, uncommitted a short while ago, had risen to its feet and was gallantly attempting to expose itself totally to the revelation.

If recognition of talent had been the same as having it Teddie might have blossomed under the general's eyes. When the general threw the meeting open to questions Teddie's soul sat down, finding itself dumb, unwilling to expose itself further, but it had planted a hopeful flag. Teddie had been won over, to what he was not sure, but the boots and the Paisley scarf were now part of the man whose man he felt he could become. You couldn't call the boots and the scarf stylish but they were not really flamboyant, Teddie decided. They were idiosyncratic marks of identification.

The post-mortem was wound up by the general with a quick but comprehensive summary of the main lessons learnt and a look into the future from which Teddie got a fleeting but satisfactory glimpse of his own as one that involved no immediate move from Mirat. The formation was still in the process of working-up exercises. These would lead to a period of intensive training for jungle warfare.

'I think you may assume,' the general ended, 'that our role will be there, to the east. Some of us are familiar with jungle conditions. My advice to you is to forget them because we knew them at a bad time. We have the wrong picture. Fortunately I don't think any of us is affected by the myth of Japanese invincibility. Man for man there's no problem. That's all I have to say this morning but I ask you now to give your attention to one of my junior officers, a man recently appointed to my Intelligence staff. If any senior officers wonder why they should stay to hear what a mere captain has to say they may restrain their natural impatience if I explain first that what he will tell you is confidential and of importance to the picture we need of the enemy we may expect to meet, and secondly that he has been in the service of the Indian government for longer than quite a number of the officers present today. He is something of a rare bird, an officer of the civil authority who has managed to persuade his department to let him into the army for the duration of the war. Captain Merrick's civilian rank was a senior and responsible one. I scarcely believe him when he tells me that there was so little going on in his district that even his superior officers agreed he might be more usefully employed. I do believe him when he tells me he first applied to join the armed forces as far back as 1939 and has continually renewed his application and I suspect it was not a case of nothing much going on but of his department deciding that if they wanted any peace they would have to let him come to the war. The kind of work he was doing meant that the most suitable branch for him to serve in was intelligence and his civilian rank would have qualified him for a more senior army rank than the one he holds. I happen to know, and I have no wish to embarrass him, in any case he is now stuck with what he's got, that he had a choice between this appointment and one elsewhere which would have given him more glamorous epaulettes. He chose the more active role and the lower rank because it was an active role he was looking for. I am glad to welcome him to this formation. I repeat that what he has to tell us is confidential. There should be no general discussion of the subject inside units and certainly not outside. Although Captain Merrick will perform the ordinary tasks of a G3 this particular subject is likely to become one of his special interests and he will continue to keep in touch with brigade and battalion intelligence staffs in regard to it and to the level at which it remains a restricted subject. Brigadier Crawford, Captain Sowton and I will not stay to listen to his address because he gave us a full and detailed account last night after dinner. Thank you gentlemen. No standing if you don't mind, it only makes for disruption. Colonel Selby-Smith, will you take over please?'

The general came down from the stage, was joined by

150

Crawford and Sowton, and left by the main aisle. From the foyer on the other side of the doors came the sound of boots stamped on the tiled floor as the men on guard duty came to attention. Selby-Smith got up and now made a gesture of invitation. On the far side of the right-hand second row of seats Teddie saw his elusive room companion rise. At first sight he looked younger than the general's reference to seniority had led Teddie to expect. Tall, fair-haired, slim and well-built, he moved with a sort of snap that Teddie would have expected in a smart cadet or a young hard-case sar'major. But once on the platform, behind the lectern, in stage-lighting, the fairness of the hair faded and the used quality of the face was revealed. He could have been any age between thirty and forty.

The hall was remarkably quiet. The general's recommendation and explanation had alerted an old instinct to dislike on sight anyone about whom there was a faint mystery, a difference, anyone who was not fully defined by rank, occupation and regiment, who appeared to have an obscure but real advantage over his fellows. Teddie was aware of this because he felt a prick of resentment himself. *I would have waited and joined you for dinner but I have an appointment.* Dinner with the general. How and when had that been arranged? The general would have got back in his staff car from Premanagar two or three hours before Teddie spluttered in on his motor-bike after playing messenger-boy over several square miles of bloody awful country and then helping off-station officers to find accommodation in Mirat for the night. The three fingers of whisky represented something ambiguous like the postcards his mother used to send from Singapore saying 'Miss you' while all the time she was having a high old time with that chap Hunter.

For the first few minutes of Merrick's address the silence persisted, but during these minutes it lost density, became riddled with receptive channels drilled one way by Merrick's strong and resonant voice and the other way by the audience's growing interest in what the voice was saying until the two sides met like tunnellers who had worked from opposite sides of a mountain and come face to face at the centre point of a clear uninterrupted passage. As if he knew that contact had been made Merrick now made a dry joke and was rewarded by more laughter than the joke deserved. Thinking about it afterwards Teddie believed that most men would have attempted a joke right at the beginning to break down the unfriendly atmosphere. Merrick must have been conscious of the critical silence that greeted his appearance on the platform. But he ignored it, simply started to speak, standing at the lectern removing his papers from his briefcase then dropping the case on a nearby chair and sorting out his notes, apparently in no hurry to look like a man giving a lecture but already giving it.

'In December 1940 an eminent member of the All India National Congress whose extremist views had become something of an embarrassment to other members of the Congress High Command, not to say an annoyance to ourselves, escaped from India, so far as we can ascertain through Afghanistan. His name was Subhas Chandra Bose. Although arrested early on in the war he had been released to his home after staging a hunger strike in captivity which the Indian government feared might lead to his death. In spite of rigorous surveillance by the police and CID of the house he now lived in he managed to get away presumably in some sort of disguise and make his way to Kabul where it seems he was in touch with the German consulate. Thereafter, quite logically, he turned up in Berlin with the declared intention of carrying on what he called India's fight for freedom from there. There are two points worth noting about this situation. The first is that a man who has such a high opinion of himself and his talents as to believe that single-handed he might achieve what the Congress as a whole has not managed to and takes the trouble to put such a great distance between himself and his jailers, is in all likelihood

152

suffering to some extent from delusions of grandeur. The second point to note is the direction of his flight and its final destination. Berlin. The two factors, the kind of man one may think Bose is and the place he went to are not incompatible as factors in our assessment of the meaning of the situation. Indeed, all this makes a perfectly sensible pattern. Hitler, Ribbentrop, Goebbels, Subhas Chandra Bose.

'At this stage of the war of course, in 1940, Mr Bose might have been excused for believing that the Germans were going to win it anyway and that his mission was a merciful step taken to minimize any suffering Indians might have undergone following a British defeat. One can quite see that the appearance of Mr Bose as Gauleiter of India could have militated against the excesses of storm-troopers in cities such as Delhi. Once again one learns the lesson that historically a man's actions – however questionable they appear at the time – can usually be satisfactorily explained away afterwards as altruistic. No doubt Mr Bose has been sacrificing himself in the interests of his country. His is an odyssey that deserves to be better known and no doubt will be because it is not over yet. Like many great adventures it has its marginally amusing elements. I am assured on the best authority that although Mr Bose stumbled most of the way through Afghanistan on foot he effected his entry into Kabul in a tonga.'

The laughter swept the hall at this point. Teddie laughed too. He was not sure he knew just who Subhas Chandra Bose was. There were so many Indians called Bose. His interest in Indian politics and politicians had always been minimal. He had a generally comic idea about them. The picture of a portly chap in dhoti, shirt and Gandhi cap bumping up and down in the back of a rickety horsedrawn two-wheeled trap on his way to meet the German consul struck him as perfectly splendid. Teddie folded his arms, always a sign of his contentment. This Merrick fellow certainly knew his stuff even though

153

his voice, confident and carrying, was – well – not quite pukka, a shade middle-class in the vowel sounds.

'Nothing I've said so far is confidential. The business of Bose's escape and activities in Berlin, although soft-pedalled by Government, is known to many people – perhaps better known to civilians than to army personnel and to Indian officers better than to British. Civilians have more time to gossip and read the minor items in the newspapers. Indian officers are probably more interested in what an Indian politician gets up to than their British colleagues are. But by and large the Bose situation is treated more as a joke than a threat. He has broadcast from Berlin and has made as little impression as the Anglo-British commentator Lord Haw-Haw. Men like Bose tend to appear to live, publicly, in isolation from what we are inclined to think of as the realities. What he actually did in Germany may therefore come as a surprise to some of you. With Hitler's permission, to assist Hitler in fighting us, he raised a unit of battalion strength from Indian prisoners-of-war who presumably volunteered for this distinction.'

The temperature in the hall seemed to drop perceptibly. For an instant the barrier between audience and speaker rose again. Teddie looked at the necks of the two Indian officers in front of him and wondered what on earth it felt like being one of them.

'This unit,' Merrick continued, 'is first reported as officially in existence in January 1942. In other words it took Mr Bose at least a year to find eight or nine hundred men to accept the bait of ostensible freedom from prison-camp and to form a group which no doubt he described as the nucleus of a great army of patriotic Indians whose quarrel was with the British and no other nation. Whether Hitler was disappointed at the feeble response or was merely amused to have his views of Mr Bose confirmed we do not know. The unit does not seem to have survived as a fighting force or even as a coherent one. It is reported scattered around Hitler's Europe, particularly in the Low Countries, doing the odd spot of beach defence, police and guard duties. But before we criticize these men, remember that as prisoners-of-war forcibly separated from their company and battalion commanders, and very far from home, they were deprived of the one thing the Indian Army has always been especially rightly proud of – the high level of trust between men and officers which is based on the real concern shown for the men's welfare by those officers, be those officers British or Indian. It is clear that Bose's failure in Germany stems from the fact that he simply couldn't find enough Indian King's commissioned officers to help him in his work of suborning cold, hungry and miserable Indian sepoys.'

There was an appreciative murmur from the front row where the most senior British officers sat.

'Bose was still in Berlin when the Japanese launched their lightning attacks in the Far East, on Pearl Harbor, Malaya and Burma. Intelligence reports reveal that he was in touch with the Japanese ambassador in Berlin and it takes little imagination to work out that one of the things he must have suggested to that gentlemen was that the Japanese should encourage the raising of similar forces from Indian prisoners-of-war to assist them in their operations in the Far Eastern theatre. But now we come across yet another gentleman with the name of Bose – '

Teddie smiled. There you were. Common as Smith.

' – Rash Behari Bose, an old Indian revolutionary living in exile in Japan. Rash Behari Bose also approached the Japanese with a scheme of this kind. He was unsuccessful in his first contact, with Field-Marshal Suguyama, who took the practical soldier's view that since India was part of the British Empire Indians could never be anything but enemy subjects. He had more success with the Japanese war ministry. Rash Behari was already head of a thing called the Indian Independence League in Japan. With the backing of the Japanese government he was now in a position to extend this as a going concern in all the invaded territories. A branch of the Indian Independence

155

League, or IIL, was set up for instance in Bangkok and it sent representatives with the Japanese forces that invaded Malaya. You see which way the wind begins to blow. Mr Rash Behari Bose probably makes great play with the fact that the IIL saved Indian lives and property during the period of hostilities. Indeed there are many instances reported of Japanese soldiers having approached Indian civilians in Malaya asking them if they followed the Mahatma and leaving them unmolested when hearing that they did.

'But the dividing line between saving innocent civilian lives from Japanese bestiality and suborning Indian troops was very thin. You could say it was non-existent. At this stage of our story there emerges I'm afraid not a cold and hungry sepoy but an officer, Captain Mohan Singh of the 1/14th Punjab Regiment. Captain Mohan Singh was captured in Northern Malaya very early in the campaign in, so the report we have states, Alor Star. The next thing we hear about him is that he is head of a small group of Indian officers working with a Japanese intelligence officer called Fujiwara. Fujiwara also had with him a representative from the IIL in Bangkok. Consequently one can trace a direct line from Rash Behari Bose through Bangkok and Fujiwara to Captain Mohan Singh. Mohan Singh proceeded to organize captured Indian soldiers into small fighting groups which accompanied Japanese forces during the rest of the Malayan and Burma campaigns.

'Here again evidence exists of lives of Indian soldiers and civilians having been saved. But to what end? The answer comes to us unequivocally in the extraordinary event which took place in Singapore in February last year on the occasion of General Percival's surrender to the Japanese commander. Contrary to normal procedure Indians – that is to say Indian officers – were separated from British officers as well as Indian troops from British. The Indian officers and troops were congregated in Farrer Park and there publicly handed over by the Japanese commander – to whom? To none other than our old friend, no longer Captain, but General Mohan Singh who thereupon addressed these troops, blamed the British for losing the battle and deserting their Indian comrades, announced that the days of British imperialism were over and that it was the duty of every patriotic Indian to form an army to help the Japanese drive them out from India for good and all.'

For the first time Merrick paused and glanced at the audience as if to judge its temper.

'Circumstances ideal for both the Boses' purpose now obtained, a potential – numbered in thousands – of well-trained and experienced Indian soldiers who only had to be persuaded to abandon their allegiance to a regime which appeared to have been utterly, perhaps one might say disgracefully defeated, and muster into a force of the kind envisaged by Rash Behari in Tokyo and Subhas Chand in Berlin, the army of new India, of free India. The Azad Hind Fauj. The Indian National Army. An army that would march alongside the Japanese not as traitors and stooges but as patriots and men of destiny. I think we should be clear about that – about the emotional feelings that lie behind an act of what in strictly legal terms must be defined as treachery. I have named Captain Mohan Singh. There were others with him whose names are also known. Perhaps it is unfair to single him out and his subsequent actions do not all contribute to the portrait of a man without a sense of honour, a man on the make. He has in fact suffered what we call vicissitudes. But history must name him as the King's commissioned officer who stood on the wrong side of the rail at Farrer Park and accepted a gift from the Japanese, the gift of command over men who were prisoners but still soldiers of the King-Emperor.

'We don't know how easy or difficult it was for Mohan Singh to come to the decision he obviously came to back in Alor Star at a time when even if a British defeat looked likely it had not yet been suffered. The timing of his transfer of allegiance and its apparent swiftness are rather damaging as I'm sure you will agree, but one must not forget the presence of that man of Rash Behari Bose's, the civilian representative of the IIL from Bangkok. Surely a persuasive fellow when talking to Indian officers taken prisoner. Possibly though, Mohan Singh had been brooding for some time on the situation he was in as an Indian who held the King's commission. He may finally have felt that incompatible with his nationalist ardour. Information come to hand shows that during his time as head of the Indian National Army he made great play with allegations that in Malaya the Indian KCO had always been treated as a second-class officer with a lower rate of pay and fewer privileges than his British comrade, that British officers arrogated superior status to themselves as members of a ruling class on whom the security of India mainly depended, that during hostilities with the Japanese and quite apart from the so-called gross incompetence of the high command, British officers panicked and thought of nothing but their own skins, in short got the hell out whenever they could and left Indian officers in the lurch by putting them in command of rearguards covering retreat.

'Since Mohan Singh's own British battalion commander is known to have been captured with him at the same time and in the same place, his views are not in this instance notably supported by the evidence. Nevertheless, I think we must say that Mohan Singh had decided to be disenchanted, to believe that the Malayan catastrophe destroyed forever the myth of the *raj's* supremacy and therefore its right to remain even a day longer in control of India's future, and furthermore to believe that it was now his duty to think only of how best to serve his country and his countrymen.

'Here in India in some Indian nationalist circles there has been as you know a curious and to most of us naïve argument that the Japanese have no quarrel with India and Indians, that it is only the British presence and the use of India as a base for armed operations that forces Tokyo to adopt a threatening attitude to the sub-continent. It was a Gandhian idea and it lay behind the serious civil disturbances of twelve months ago.

'If Mr Gandhi can believe this about the Japanese and make millions of Indian civilians believe it, Captain Mohan Singh presumably had no tremendous difficulty in making thousands of naturally apprehensive Indian prisoners-of-war believe it. Perhaps the remarkable thing is that for the many he seems to have persuaded as many – indeed many more – have remained unconvinced. I say remarkable because the consequences of resisting persuasion cannot have been, cannot be pleasant. In front of the eyes of your stubborn prisoner, officer, NCO or sepoy, things doubtless happened which made the decision to remain a prisoner and loyal to the crown a difficult one. Additionally they saw erstwhile members of the *raj*, the white sahibs, submitted to all the indignities we now know the Japanese are adept at devising. Add to the sight of these indignities the threats of hunger, thirst and physical coercion and it obviously requires a special stoutness of heart to resist the blandishments of men who yesterday were your leaders and comrades and who offer to be leaders and comrades again in an enterprise which is projected as patriotic. A prisoner is always homesick too and here is Captain Mohan Singh, supported now by many other Indian officers I'm afraid, promising to lead him home in a particularly glorious way, to a home from which the British have gone forever, to a home where the old national leaders, many of them worn and thin from prison, will greet him as a hero, as a liberator, as a true son of the India they too have fought for.'

Again Merrick paused.

'The question of what loyalty is isn't easily answered.'

The remark only deepened the silence. Merrick referred to his notes.

'The Indian National Army under Mohan Singh consisted of approximately 10,000 ex-prisoners, officers and men, but according to our information little more than

159

half of them had arms. However, if there had been arms and equipment readily available that number of 10,000 would have been considerably increased. Broadly speaking, Indian prisoners-of-war fall now into three categories – those who have so far resisted all persuasion and continue as prisoners, those who have not resisted but have indicated readiness to serve, and those who have actually been mustered in. This information is restricted. As you will appreciate when bearing in mind that figure of 10,000, and official Indian government comment and counter-propaganda, the policy is to deflect attention from this situation by minimizing its importance and ridiculing claims made by the enemy. But enemy broadcasts are regularly listened to by those civilians in this country who are rich enough to have wireless sets capable of receiving them. Foreign broadcasting is of course the one form of communication upon which Government cannot place an embargo. There have been instances of Indian families recognizing the voices of relatives who were officers in the Indian Army but who are now officers in the INA and who give stirring accounts of the great things which the INA will presently do.

'The question is, will they? I mentioned vicissitudes. Right from the beginning there appears to have been not unexpectedly an element of Japanese contempt for the Azad Hind Fauj matched by an element of Azad Hind suspicion of Japanese intentions, and some resistance to Japanese attempts to treat the INA as a mere appendage of their own imperial army. Under Mohan Singh the INA was theoretically the military arm of a civil independence movement headed by Rash Behari Bose, and after a conference in Bangkok this movement dedicated itself to take actions which would be wholly in line with the nationalist policies adopted here in India by the All India Congress.

'From February to August 1942, you'll recall, the Congress in India was demanding that the British quit India, that they should leave India, in Gandhi's memorable phrase, to God or to anarchy. What would happen if the British didn't quit was left, on paper, not very clear. But that is by the way. What did happen was clear enough.

'What I think important to bear in mind is the effect the news of Congress's demands, and of the outcome of those demands, must have had on Indian prisoners-of-war in Malaya and Burma, particularly upon those who had now committed themselves to the INA. It must have seemed to them that India was about to rise and throw the British out, that great events were afoot, that history was making their decision for them. True, their technical allegiance was to King and Country but if the mother country did not want the King and was about to get rid of him that left them with the country alone. They certainly belonged to that. It was their country after all. But apart from the matter of the British there was the matter of the Japanese. What truly were their intentions? Would they really leave India alone if the British were got rid of? INA officers have openly said to their troops that whereas the troops must be ready to fight the British – even their own old officers and comrades – they must be just as ready to fight the Japanese if the latter showed any signs of substituting the Rising Sun for the Union Jack. And there was another great INA uncertainty. Would *Congress* really approve of the Azad Hind Fauj?'

Merrick stopped to give the question time to sink in, it seemed. Perhaps that was his prime intention but suddenly he looked down at Colonel Selby-Smith and said, 'Sir, I believe the No Smoking signs are intended to apply only to the period of discussion about the scheme. I expect quite a number of people would appreciate it if you felt inclined to give permission to smoke.'

Presumably Selby-Smith nodded because Merrick glanced up and nodded to the hall, which now came stealthily alive. Teddie opened his own case in nervous gratitude. In a few seconds the hall looked like an Indian bazaar during the festival of Divali, but the business of lighting up was completed with unusual rapidity. In less than half a minute the hall was quiet again.

'This was the question. Would Congress really approve of the Azad Hind Fauj? Would they give their blessing to an operation that might lead to a bloody meeting between a rebel nationalist army and the regular Indian army? The INA assumed that upon its appearance on Indian soil the Indian army proper would disintegrate and its sepoys join hands with their rebel brothers. But even if Congress also assumed this could they accept the INA as a legal instrument of their own policy of achieving self- government?

'Quite apart from the views of the moderates and constitutionalists, the kind of Congressmen who had thought their fellow Congressman Subhas Chandra Bose an extremely dangerous man, there was the other Gandhian principle of non-violence to consider. To find out the answer to this question then, it was decided to send a group of INA officers into Burma, well-equipped with means of radio communication, to infiltrate secretly into India and contact Indian political leaders. This was done in August 1942. The enterprise was a total failure because one of the chosen officers took the first opportunity to abandon the group and to contact us and thoroughly spill the beans. The rest returned to Malaya disillusioned and the officer who reneged on them brought with him very useful documents and information. This officer is not named, but he is a bright spot on a somewhat dark horizon. It is his belief that more than a few officers and men joined the INA with the same intention as himself of either wrecking it from within or of coming back to their loyal duty directly contact was re-established with the Army to which they really belong. In other words it is suggested that they used the INA as a rather specialized means of escape from prison-camp which as we all know it is a soldier's duty to try to effect.'

An officer at the front said, 'Hear, hear.' Someone clapped. Merrick waited. He kept his eyes on the lectern and turned a page of his notes. Resuming he said:

162

'The spot on the horizon would be brighter however if all the officers in the infiltrating party had done precisely the same thing. We must have fairly deep reservations about the extent to which this joining up as a preliminary to returning to duty represents a significant factor in the constitution and motives of the INA. Nevertheless in any future confrontation with INA units and formations in the field it must obviously be borne in mind that not all INA soldiers on the other side of the wire, so to speak, are necessarily intent on attacking us. Some of them may be looking only for an opportunity to come in with their arms to turn them against the Japanese. Just how many we shall have no way of knowing until the time arises – if and when it does.

'But there will be a natural tendency among Indian sepoys and among other ranks in British battalions to resent these apparent deserters and traitors quite intensely, a tendency not to extend to them those military civilities we are required to show in the field to the fallen, the wounded and the captured.

'One of the main purposes of this talk is to establish certain facts and to provide what is hoped will be useful background knowledge so that we can avoid the worst effects both of minimization and exaggeration of the problem presented by the existence of this army. My own view is that whatever one's personal reactions, corporate judgment must certainly be suspended until all the facts are known. Meanwhile the restricted information presently given can settle quietly in our minds and may help us to exert a steadying influence on the men under our command if and when this division finds itself in action against units or formations of the INA. I will end this survey with an account of what has happened since the failure of the infiltrating party.

'There's no doubt that political events in India in August 1942, culminating in the severe riots that followed the detention of members of the Congress Party committees and subcommittees, had at least a potentially vitalizing

163

effect on recruitment of prisoners-of-war into the INA, but the INA itself seems to have suffered a fairly severe crisis of confidence, in regard to Japanese intentions and in regard to its own. The major question whether the Congress Party would approve had gone unanswered and with all Congress's influential policy-makers in jail there was now no hope of getting it answered.

'Captain Mohan Singh was naturally at the storm-centre of this crisis of confidence. Without going so far as to say that he personally agreed with the stand the Azad Hind Fauj was making he was as its head inevitably indentified with it and we may give him the benefit of the doubt here, credit him as I hinted earlier with a certain stubborn adherence to what may be called honourable principles. The main stand that seems to have been made was over areas of responsibility. What the INA was saying was that it and it alone must deal with India. Correlatively it was saying it would have nothing to do with Japanese operations elsewhere – for instance against Burmese nationalist guerrillas. To those people in the Japanese Imperial army who thought contemptuously of the INA as a mere appendage this attitude was totally unacceptable and we can assume that considerable pressure was brought to bear on Mohan Singh to conform, to put his forces at their disposal without reservations. Equal pressure was doubtless brought to bear on him by INA officers who stood by the policy of working only according to Congress principles and who saw these as integral to the principles of action and thinking in the INA. One has a picture here of the whole organization of the INA trembling on the brink of disruption.

'In December last Mohan Singh was arrested by the Japanese. The actual reasons remain to be discovered although it is believed that Rash Behari Bose was at the bottom of it. As a politician, Rash Behari presumably had a talent for bobbing like a cork on the stormiest waters, for his own position was not immediately affected. But for the first six months of this year the Azad

Hind movement and the INA had a look of being something of a broken reed. It needed a strong man to mend it, a man talented enough to satisfy both sides, the Indians and the Japanese, with his views, policies and capacity for leadership.

'Who else but Subhas Chandra Bose? But he was in Germany. *Was* in Germany. Just a few weeks ago in June this ubiquitous gentleman turned up in Tokyo. The information we have is that he came out by submarine – a typically glamorous, apparently hazardous enterprise – but, let it be marked, not one he could have embarked on without the approval, indeed the wishes, of the government in Tokyo. From Tokyo he has broadcast speeches which leave no room for doubt he is in his own eyes the man of destiny whom the Azad Hind movement and the Japanese have been waiting for. In Singapore last month he was elected President of the Indian Independence League, the other Bose – Rash Behari – having resigned to make room for him. So there we have it: Mohan Singh a prisoner, we believe in Sumatra, and Rash Behari gone into the retirement which is the reward of failure. In their place, Subhas Chandra Bose.

'He has not yet formally assumed command of the Azad Hind Fauj but that can only be a matter of time. We can indeed expect Mr Bose to claim authority over all Indian nationals in the Far East and manipulate a kind of legality for the entire proceedings by the establishment of a form of free Indian government in exile, recognized on paper anyway by the Japanese and their allies in what they call Asian co-prosperity. He is that kind of man. His qualities of leadership must not be underestimated. These were qualities that frightened several senior Congress politicians off him in the past. He was thought by them to have the makings of a dictator. One feels inclined to agree.

'This survey ends, therefore, on a note of some assurance about the continuity and enlargement of the INA as a machine of war that it would be as foolish to underestimate as it would be to allow its existence and inevitable growth to distract attention from the principal and still very dangerous and highly ambitious enemy, the Japanese. It seems to me to be very unlikely that even under Bose, who will almost certainly enjoy outwardly cordial and co-operative relations with the Japanese high command, the INA will ever slot anything but uncomfortably into the Japanese military machine and this may well contribute to its downfall. The other contributory factors to this likely downfall are of course its logistic problems and the mixed psychology and motives of its members. In terms of its capacity to equip itself either in co-operation or competition with the Japanese it must rank as a low-priority organization. In terms of its psychology and motivation it must rank as something less than an army capable of achieving a high and durable morale. How much less capable will depend on the magic of Mr Bose. But even the most skilful magician cannot sustain for long an illusion of common purpose when the purpose itself is so riddled with complexity. This will emerge as an important factor when Indian soldiers of the INA – intent on liberating India – come face to face with Indian soldiers who are under our command and are loyally determined to defend it from whomsoever dares set foot on Indian soil aiming a rifle at them.'

Merrick picked up his notes and had retrieved his briefcase before the audience quite realized he had finished. Although the applause broke out before he actually left the platform he did not remain to receive what might then have looked like a personal ovation, and was down the steps and returning to his seat when the applause was at its peak.

Selby-Smith rose and climbed on to the stage. As he stood at the lectern he clapped his hands about four times to demonstrate his own approval and to give a lead in the matter of bringing the ovation to an end. When he stopped clapping he seemed to be requesting silence and quite quickly got it.

He said, 'Although this meeting has now gone on for longer than many of you anticipated, what we have just heard so ably and interestingly presented was certainly worth staying to hear. I think there is no disagreement on that score. On your behalf I thank Captain Merrick for the trouble he has taken to present a clear picture of this rather sticky subject. In bringing the meeting to a close I would firmly reiterate that the subject of the INA is not one that the divisional commander wishes to have generally or casually discussed among you. In other words keep what you've heard this morning under your hats. Junior officers and NCOs have a particualr responsibility to be alert for gossip and rumour among the men and to report its existence without taking steps to squash it until they've had advice on the line to take. That is all, gentlemen.'

A bit stunned by what he had heard Teddie did not seize the opportunity that now presented itself to meet his room companion. He found it easier to go with the stream making for the doors than against it down to the front where Merrick stood alone doing up the straps of his briefcase. At the foyer doors which had been swung open and latched back by the guards Teddie nearly changed his mind because the idea of Merrick standing by himself made him feel he was not being as friendly as he should be, but someone spoke to him and when he next thought about Merrick he was climbing into the back of the 15 cwt Chevrolet – the last man of a party of five. The driver put up the tailboard and in a moment or two the truck was entering the queue for the exit from the forecourt.

In B mess he sat with two other officers in the anteroom and ordered beer. At five to one he saw Merrick come in. This time he wasn't alone. An Indian and an English officer accompanied him, guests from one of the brigades. Again he hesitated but just then Merrick's glance fell on him and seemed to stay. Teddie stood up and went across and offered his hand.

'I'm Teddie Bingham,' he said. 'What'll it be?'

For a second or two he had a feeling that Merrick was wondering whether he should find the name familiar. His hand came out rather tentatively as if casual physical contact with someone not intimately known was ordinarily unwelcome. The handshake failed as such. Teddie was about to explain who he was when Merrick said, 'We meet at last then.' He still had Teddie's hand and suddenly, unexpectedly, exerted grip, then quickly broke contact.

Between the man on the platform and the same man close to Teddie found a kind of discrepancy. When he thought about this afterwards he decided it was the same sort of discrepancy he'd noticed years ago in London when he was about twelve and his mother took him to a matinée and backstage afterwards to meet a man who'd played one of the character parts and still had his makeup on but spoke in an ordinary voice and seemed shy, but made up for it when they left by putting his arm round Teddie and giving him ten bob.

'Whisky or gin?' Teddie asked. 'Or are you a beer only man at tiffin?'

'It's very good of you,' Merrick began. Teddie now noticed that the blue of the fellow's eyes was made particularly vivid by the steady way he considered you with them. 'But I'm rather pressed. I'm supposed to be somewhere else at two o'clock so I'll have to go right in. Could we make it this evening?'

'Yes, of course – '

Merrick nodded. 'Good. It's time we got to know each other.' He smiled, turned, then turned back again. 'By the way. Congratulations.'

'Congratulations?'

'Hosain tells me you're getting married soon.'

'Oh. Did he? Well yes, I am. Thanks.'

He watched Merrick steering his guests to the dining-room, ushering them through the doorway with a guiding hand on each of their backs in turn. The bearer brought Teddie's beer. The man standing next to him was the adjutant of the British battalion of the brigade up near Premanagar.

'Interesting that, this morning,' the adjutant said. 'No idea anything like that going on but then I've only been in the country six months. What was he, do you know? I mean in the Indian government?'

The chap meant 'in the Civil'. Amazingly ignorant. Teddie said he had no idea which should have been good enough but apparently wasn't.

'A sort of spy do you reckon?' the adjutant asked. He had a plebeian voice and manner. He was the sort of chap one found in the bars of Tudor-style roadhouses back at home in the vicinity of Kingston-on-Thames. The fellow actually winked as such fellows did. The vulgarity of modern English life suddenly overwhelmed Teddie. It was flowing into India, blighting everything. He smiled distantly at the adjutant and murmured an apology for leaving him. He intended to swallow his beer and go into mess but, warned by a mild but sudden sensation of inner instability, put his glass down and made his way across the room to the door that led to the lavatories. Secluded there he discovered that his normally healthy and regular motions had become unpleasantly loose, untrustworthy. His forehead came out in a sweat. He felt rather unwell. The thought of food didn't much appeal. He must have picked something up.

He left by a side entrance and entered the complex of covered ways that connected B mess building to the junior officers' huts. The whole place had a temporary feeling about it. The last occupants of these particular lines had been members of the staff of a chemical and psychological warfare school. They had left a smell of gas capes and propaganda. Teddie had heard someone say that. It struck him as apt. Reaching his own room he found the door padlocked. Hosain was on mess duty. Teddie cursed his present domestic arrangements. He fumbled for his key and then paused, having noticed something extemely odd. Leant against the wall under the window there was a

169

push-bike, or rather the remains of one. For an instant he thought someone had been in the room, taken either his own or Merrick's bicycle, removed one wheel and buckled one of the mudguards for a joke. But that wouldn't account for the rust. And then, the wreck under the window was without a cross-bar: a woman's bicycle. Nevertheless he hastened to take the padlock off the door and open up.

Bicycles were kept inside rooms because of the danger of theft. Both bicycles were where they should be. He went out for another look at the useless and mysterious object and in doing so noticed something else: chalk marks on the floor-boards of the verandah, decorating the threshold. Some sort of design. The effect was cabalistic.

He sniffed the air for the lingering scent of an ill-wisher, wondering whether he would be able to isolate such a smell from all the others to which he had become used. He could not. He stepped over the chalk marks and went to the verandah rail. There wasn't a soul; just a perspective of doors like his own, each with its padlock, and beyond the hut a space and in continuing perspective another hut. Straight ahead across the bare earth compound the prison-camp style wire fence divided the lines from waste ground. Nobody could get over the wire but nobody needed to. The lines were always full of unexplained people. They came in at points where the PWD had either got fed up with erecting the fence or run out of material. It was not a security area. It might once have been some-one's intention to make it one.

He reconsidered the broken push-bike. Perhaps Hosain had found it dumped and placed it there to show that he was an honest boy. He could have got a few annas for it from the cycle-shop wallah in the cantonment bazaar. But there had to be a connexion between the bicycle and the chalk marks. The marks could have been made by Hosain. If the boy had been a Hindu Teddie would have more readily believed that this was the explanation; that the bike and the chalk marks were some odd form of puja or offering for the welfare of the rooms' occupants to ensure them a safe journey, wherever they were going, through intercession with some modern addition to the Hindu pantheon: the god of mechanical transport.

But Hosain was a Muslim. It was unlikely that either the bhishti or the sweeper took sufficient interest in any of the officers they served to make such a well-meaning gesture to one or two of them. Besides which the marks had an inauspicious feeling to them. Teddie hesitated, controlling an urge to obliterate them. His bowels began to move again. There was a griping pain in them and the sweat broke out on his forehead. He stared down at the cabalistic signs which suddenly seemed to be responsible for the disorder in his guts, for the disruption of his life which he now felt the whole morning had somehow plotted to bring about. He scuffed his rubber-soled shoes across the marks, blurring the outlines. He continued scuffing and scraping until only an ashy smear was left. He felt better.

Back in his room he found a letter from Susan on his side of the desk. He ripped it open. It was dated five days ago. 'Dear Teddie, Tomorrow we're off to Kashmir. Aunt Fenny and Uncle Arthur will meet us in Delhi and then we'll all travel together up to 'Pindi.' They would be in Srinagar by now. He stuffed the letter into his jacket pocket and went round the back to the privy. Things were no better but he had stopped sweating. He hoped he was not going to be really ill. He read Susan's letter right through. When he returned to his room he lay down on the bed hoping to catch forty winks. After ten minutes, still wide awake, he sat up and lit a cigarette and read Susan's letter again. Srinagar would be full of officers on leave. He saw the danger he was in of losing her to some fellow with more to offer, a fellow with talent and money, a fellow who had the measure of things as they were, the kind of fellow who would understand everything Merrick talked about this morning and be able to believe it without feeling that if it was true nothing was sacred any more and nobody could be relied on, that everyone was living in a bloody jungle.

Teddie got off the bed and stubbed his cigarette. He felt emotional but couldn't work out what he felt emotional about except the prospect of being jilted or of hearing that the whole of the Malayan battalion of the Muzzys which had been captured near Kuala Lumpur had gone over to that Bose character. What he did work out was that everything that was wrong for him was really the fault of that bounder Hunter who had drunk away his mother's money and then her vitality and when he was dead hounded her to her own grave. Except that there wasn't a grave. He would have felt more settled knowing there was a grave.

It was raining again when he was ready to go back lunchless to the daftar. He couldn't face putting on a sweaty cape and cycling. He stuck his cap on and pad-locked the door behind him. The ruined bike struck him as ridiculous. He walked through the covered ways until he got to the front of the mess where he was able to whistle up one of the cycle tongas whose drivers congre-gated outside the main gate.

4

During the afternoon Teddie forgot about the bicycle and the chalk marks but remembered them at six o'clock on his way back to the hut. Hosain was squatting on his hunkers outside the room, whose door was open, latched back against the outer wall leaving the mesh screen exposed. The orderly got to his feet when he saw Teddie coming up the steps. He had been sitting on the spot where the chalk mark smear was. There was no sign of the bicycle.

Teddie asked where it was. Hosain indicated the room, entered ahead and pointed at the two serviceable machines. Teddie explained about the broken bicycle.

Hosain went outside, looked and came in saying there wasn't a bicycle.

'I know,' Teddie said. 'But there was. What time did you get back from mess duty?'

Hosain said he was back at 1430 but had gone straight to his own quarters, changed and gone to the bazaar for Merrick Sahib. He came back from the bazaar at 1630 and opened the room. There hadn't been a bicycle then. If there had been a bicycle earlier someone must have taken it, probably the person who left it there in the first place. He would ask some of the other orderlies and the bhishti. But what was the good of a bicycle with only one wheel?

'Quite. That's the whole point.'

Teddie felt cross because Hosain was looking at him as if he thought Teddie was trying to cause trouble for the servants over something he had only imagined seeing. Suddenly Merrick called from the bath-house. Hosain shouted, 'Sahib!' and went with alacrity. It wasn't Merrick's fault but, no doubt about it, since his arrival Hosain had given Merrick preferential treatment. It was ridiculous having to share an orderly. Come to that it was bloody stupid having to share a room.

Teddie sat in his armchair with his legs stuck out in the shoe-removing position. Presently he heard Hosain laugh and a warm friendly sort of noise from Merrick. Less than a minute later he heard the back door being unbolted and Hosain shouting for the bhishti and then Merrick clomped in wearing unbuckled chappals and nothing else but a towel tied round his middle. He was rubbing his head with another towel.

Teddie's immediate reaction to the sight of Merrick was admiration shot darkly through with envy because Merrick had one of those bodies in which every sinew was clearly and separately defined, properly proportioned and interlocked. The fellow didn't seem to have an ounce of fat on him. You could count the pads of muscle that made up his abdominal wall.

'Ah, there you are,' Merrick said. 'I'm sorry about

lunchtime.' He stopped rubbing his head and stuck the towel round his neck. 'We seem to have been Coxing and Boxing for days one way or another. I didn't see you come into mess, by the way.'

'As a matter of fact I got rather taken short.'

'Oh. Mirat tummy?'

'Sort of. But I think it's gone off.'

'I have some stuff that will settle it if it hasn't. I expect you've been sitting under the fan or drinking too much iced beer. Take a dose anyway to be on the safe side. Hold on and I'll get it.'

Teddie felt reluctant but grateful. It was like being jawed by an older boy about looking after your health; like being taken to the San because someone had noticed you were suffering in silence. Merrick came back with a small bottle and a spoon. Hosain followed him in. 'I'll pour,' Merrick said, 'because it tends to come out in a dribble and then in a rush.' He poured a couple of drops. The drops were followed by a dollop. It was brown and looked nasty. Merrick leant forward and obediently Teddie opened his mouth. The stuff tasted like very strong cough mixture. It seemed to grip his throat all the way down.

'It cements you up,' Merrick explained. 'If you have another dose in the morning you'll be right as rain.'

'Thanks.'

Merrick made a gesture at Hosain who knelt and untied Teddie's shoes. He took the medicine bottle and spoon back to the bathroom and returned rubbing his head with the towel again.

'It must be the humidity,' Teddie said. 'Not used to it recently. I've been stationed up in the hills the past few months.'

'Well you'd notice it then. Actually the humidity's fairly low here. Ever been in Sundernagar?'

'I've never even heard of Sundernagar.'

'It's where I was before they let me into the army. Your shoes go green overnight. I had an inspector who swore he was getting webbed feet, and *he* was an Indian.'

174

'An inspector? Were you in the Indian Police then?'

'Yes. I was DSP Sundernagar. Most of it's tribal area. Pretty boring for anyone who isn't an amateur anthropologist. My predecessor was. He was desperate to get back. I was just as keen to get out.'

'Were you there long?'

'Too long.'

Teddie nodded. DPS meant superintendent, the top man in a district after the collector and the judge. He was glad Merrick wasn't ICS. The few ICS men he'd known had been remote clever fellows, too intellectual for his tastes. The police were different, easier to get on with. Some of them envied you if you were Army. Merrick was now satisfactorily placed and explained and in spite of his high police rank Teddie felt pleasantly superior to him in occupation as well as in type, background and – as was clearer the longer he listened – in class. The police weren't always quite as particular as the other services.

He forgot about the bicycle and chalk marks until he was in his bath and then he had a flash of inspiration about them. Having arrived at an explanation that connected the whole incident to Merrick rather than to himself he was reluctant to mention it but decided he ought to, for security reasons.

Returning to the room, already dried and wearing clean underclothes under his robe, he said, 'I say, Merrick – ' and then stopped, struck by a sense of having intruded upon a situation between Merrick and Hosain which he could not describe but which seemed full of potential for an intimate kind of anger or violence. Hosain was looking sullen but also tearful. He went out. Merrick, now fully dressed, appeared momentarily distracted, deprived by Teddie's entrance of the opportunity to press home some kind of point that a moment ago had been important to him to make.

Merrick said, 'I'll see you in B mess in a few minutes then. What will you drink?'

Surprised, Teddie said, 'No, it's on me – '

'Well, we'll see.'

Merrick went. Teddie looked round the room expecting to see something that explained what he found inexplicable. He shrugged, called Hosain and began to dress. When he got to the shoe putting-on stage he called Hosain again. Putting on and taking off his own shoes and boots were activities at which he drew the line if there was a man available to perform these services. He had learned to draw the line in Muzzafirabad where his first CO, Colonel Gawstone, advised him never to stoop if he could help it. The climate wasn't right for it. Mrs Gawstone had stooped to pick up a glove and keeled right over and never got up. They had buried her the next day.

'Everything comes suddenly in India, Bingham.' Teddie remembered old Hooghly Gawstone saying. 'Sunrise, night, death, burial. Nothing keeps in the heat.' And in Shropshire in sultry weather the milk went off. Extraordinary chain of thought. He had forgotten why Gawstone was called Hooghly but vaguely remembered a story involving an elephant and the floating body of a dead sadhu. Or was that another story? Even two stories?

He went to the door and looked out. Not a soul in sight. The chalky smear was indiscernible because the light was going and the glow of the lamps in the room pushed his shadow across the place where the smear was. A man appeared suddenly round the corner of the hut. It was Merrick. He came up the steps saying, 'I left something behind.'

It sounded rather feeble. Something. What? Key? Wallet? Why not say? Had he come back to find out whether Hosain was telling Teddie what the row had been about? If it had been a row. There'd been no sound of a row.

'Did you send Hosain on another errand?' Teddie asked.

'No. Isn't he here?'

'No, he bloody well isn't. He's just buggered off.'

'Anything special you want?'

176

'Only for the little blighter to put my shoes on for me.'

Teddie went back in, sat down, and began to slip his feet into the clean pair of shoes.

'Here,' Merrick said, and threw him a long tortoise-shell shoehorn. It made the job easier but Teddie was too irritable to mutter more than an almost inaudible 'Thanks'. It irritated him to have to do the job himself and irritated him to have Merrick watching him. At one point in his exertions he could have sworn the man was about to come and help him. The idea made him nervous. He fumbled with the laces. He went into the bathroom to wash his hands. When he returned to the room Merrick was standing in the open doorway as if looking for someone but presumably just waiting patiently for Teddie to finish.

'I'm ready now. Did you get what you came back for?'

'Yes, thank you.'

'We'd better lock up at the back too, I suppose. The whole thing strikes me as a bit bloody much.'

'What does?' Merrick asked Teddie when Teddie had bolted the bath-house door from inside and the door connecting bath-house to living quarters and rejoined him at the doorway on to the front verandah.

'What does what?'

'Strikes you as a bit much.'

'Having to put on your own shoes and lock up your own room. The little blighter has practically fuck-all to do. I've a good mind to boot him in the arse when I see him again, buggering off like that.'

Teddie wanted to get out of the room now into the open air and over to the mess to have a couple of burra pegs; but Merrick was standing in his way. There was an expression on his face which Teddie interpreted as disapproving. Perhaps Merrick was one of those chaps who had moral objections to strong language. Teddie wasn't very happy about it himself but there were pressures building up inside him these days which he didn't understand and using words like that helped to reduce them; or did if they weren't silently rejected, crammed back down your throat by someone like Merrick. Perhaps the fellow was religious.

Merrick said, 'I think I'm to blame for Hosain making himself scarce. I had to tick him off. It was the first time and he got quite a shock.'

'And what was the ticking off about?'

'A small enough thing.'

It may have been the way Merrick looked at him (in that manner Teddie would have called calculating had it not been for the tentative friendly smile) but now he felt exposed to the accusation he believed Merrick had intended to spare him. He said, 'Was Hosain complaining about me?'

Merrick seemed in so little hurry to reply that the answer became unnecessary. Merrick dressed it up, though. He said, 'I got the impression he found working for two officers – onerous. I wasn't conscious of anything so strong as a complaint against one of us in particular.'

'But that's what it came to.'

'Only if you assume it's more natural to raise the subject of overwork with the one officer you'd be willing to go on serving. But the natural way isn't always the one they choose, is it? He may have been making a subtle complaint about me, to my face.'

'I wouldn't call Hosain a subtle sort of chap.'

'All Indians have subtle minds if you put it like that. Often I prefer the word devious for uncultured fellows of Hosain's stamp. I'm sorry if that offends you. You regular army people are rather touchy on the subject of army personnel, aren't you? But I'm afraid my experiences as a police officer have blighted any enthusiasm I ever had for the idea that the simple fellow from the village is eager to prove his devotion to the *raj*.'

'Oh.'

There seemed to be nothing else to say. On the other hand Teddie did not feel as shocked or unhappy as he guessed he ought to be. In the back of his mind there were

178

crammed scores of case-histories which showed the relationship between white man and Indian in a holy, shining light; but none was pre-eminent, none actually came pushing through to the front to make him articulate in defence of this relationship. Merrick stood aside and Teddie hesitated, then went out on to the verandah. In any case Hosain was not a good example of the kind of man he wanted to be thinking of. He waited while Merrick closed and padlocked the door.

'That was interesting, what you were talking about this morning,' he said.

'I'm glad you thought so. One courts a certain amount of unpopularity with that kind of thing. Myth breaking's a tricky business. To make the facts at all palatable you have to leave people with the illusion that the myth is still intact or even that you've personally restored it.'

Teddie hadn't the least idea what Merrick meant. He fell into step.

'For a moment,' Merrick said, ' – towards the end – I was made to feel I had the honour of the Indian Army in my hands entirely. The relationship between a man and his subject is very close. People tend to confuse them. It was impossible to leave the facts to speak for themselves. They had to be presented in the most charitable and acceptable light. Not necessarily so that people would leave the hall thinking well of me in spite of what I'd told them but leave it thinking optimistically about the future. One has to produce a positive response not a negative one. And the facts about the INA are a negation of most of the things the army, people as a whole, have believed in as a code of *possible* conduct.'

'I can't help feeling,' Teddie began, and because he hesitated Merrick put a hand on his shoulder, to guide him. They had reached a radial intersection of the covered ways. It was quite dark now. They steered by instinct, usage and the star patterns of lit buildings. Continuing along the correct path to B mess Merrick allowed his hand to remain.

'What? What can't you help feeling?'

'Well. That ninety per cent of the chaps who've joined the INA intend to come back over at the first opportunity. As you suggested.'

A moment or two elapsed before Merrick said, 'But I suggested no such thing. You heard what you wanted to hear. You've proved the point.'

'What point?'

'That the facts aren't as important as the light they're presented in. What's chiefly interesting about all this is that a lot of those men may persuade themselves they joined the INA because they saw it as the quickest route back to base, but I doubt very much whether that's the true reason in more than a handful of cases.'

'What do you think is?'

'Herd instinct. Self-preservation. At the top among men like Bose it's a combination of herd-*leader* instinct and self-aggrandizement. Patriotism doesn't come into it. So neither does the question of loyalty. It will end up as a simple matter of two opposed views of legality, and even that's going to be settled on a purely theoretical basis.'

'How?'

'You can't hang ten thousand or more traitors.'

'You can shoot the officers.'

'Or just Bose? To encourage the others?'

'Perhaps they'll save us trouble and shoot themselves.'

'Would you?'

'Good God, yes. It would be the only way out, wouldn't it? I mean if I'd done that and got recaptured.'

'Even for a man who thinks himself a patriot?'

'You said that didn't come into it.'

'I don't think it does, but a lot of them will think they are patriots.'

'Well, I'm sorry. But there are still a few things one just doesn't do. I don't blame the other ranks so much but I find the idea of King's commissioned officers leading their men – our own men – against us utterly unspeakable.'

'Beyond the pale?'

'Yes, beyond that. Whatever it means.'

'It means outside,' Merrick said, taking him up rather too literally. 'Pale, fence, boundary. Where you draw the line between one thing and another. Between right and wrong for instance.'

'The line's already there, isn't it? We don't have to draw it.'

'There was a British officer at Farrer Park too,' Merrick said. 'He told the Indian prisoners that from now on they had to obey the Japanese as they'd obeyed the British. I don't think he meant obey in quite that sense, but it's something that may cause trouble when the legal rigmarole begins, which it will, when the war's over. Assuming we win it.'

'A British officer?'

'A senior British officer.'

'You didn't mention that this morning.'

'I thought it wiser not to.'

Teddie nodded. He felt oddly light-headed. He had a sensation of not being quite himself and at the same time of recognizing Merrick as one of the most unusual men this other self had ever met. He felt himself being drawn out, enlarged. This was dangerous because if you were enlarged there was more of you and the world was still exactly the same size. It didn't get bigger to make room for you.

The anteroom of B mess was almost empty. It was not a place in which you would ever feel at home. Its atmosphere was transitory like that of a waiting-room. Teddie was glad to have Merrick with him. He ordered scotches and sodas and thought it would be pleasant to get mildly drunk. Or even quite drunk.

'When is the wedding?' Merrick asked.

'December, or earlier.'

'Earlier, surely? We'll be gone from here in a couple of months. Once that happens you're unlikely to get an opportunity.'

'I thought sort of of leave during our jungle training period, or just after it.'

181

'I shouldn't count on it. If you've really decided to marry I'd advise going ahead as soon as possible. Here in Mirat, for instance. There's a hill station called Nanoora not far away. You could go there for the honeymoon. If you're lucky you might get a second honeymoon about Christmas or just after, but my guess is you won't.'

'You seem well-informed.'

'Well-advised. You've talked to Selby-Smith presumably?'

'Oh, yes. Well, I've raised the subject. He knows and so does the General.'

'I'd press it if I were you. Ask for a clear statement. Of the situation.'

He emphasized the last two words. They began to repeat themselves in Teddie's head. The situation. The situation. What situation? Getting married was the simplest thing in the world. All you needed was the girl, the ring, a padre and a few minutes to spare; and that was it. The catch was in getting the few minutes and in extending them to hours, days, a week or two. The situation was one of time; not having enough of it to be able to call any of it your own, expect by arrangement, by permission. Your whole life was subject to permission one way and another.

Teddie frowned, gulped his scotch and soda. Everyone's life was lived by permission. Whose? There were plenty of people around whose permission you had to seek but to give permission they had to have it themselves from somebody else. Where the hell did it all lead? Where was the highest, the final authority? One ought to know because logically it was this highest final authority that was creating the situation that made a simple thing like marrying Susan so damned difficult.

He called the bearer over again, ordered two more burra pegs, smiled aside Merrick's attempt to make the second round on him.

He said, 'I suppose one's wedding should be the most important day of one's life. To other people it's a sort of irritation, isn't it?'

The belief that he had made an unexpectedly profound statement about the comparative unimportance of the individual in the wider general scheme of things pleasantly aggravated the notion he had this evening of not being quite the man his friends would recognize. Merrick, he thought, was looking at him with the intense regard of someone more finely attuned than most to another person's potential. He felt encouraged to further profundity but found the way down to it blocked. He said, 'Are you married, Merrick?'

Merrick was drawing on a cigarette. He took his time, inhaling and exhaling. 'No. I'm not.' Each word was marked by a wreath of ejected smoke. Teddie was left with an impression of a sad history in this respect, of what they called a torch being carried. Perhaps the heat of the torch explained the cool bright blue of Merrick's eyes. Everyone had his defence. He supposed cheerfulness was his. Recently he had found the smile on his face a bit on the heavy side. Underneath it there were these pressures. Mostly sexual, he imagined. He recollected the soft flesh of Susan's inner arm, just near the elbow. He signed for the second round, raised his glass and said, 'Cheers.'

Unaccountably the second whisky went straight to his head. Denied physical intimacy with Susan who at this moment represented all women he craved the substitute; intimate accord with some man, here represented by Merrick who sat admirably composed, self-possessed, with all those hidden muscles relaxed but doubtless reassuring to him, sources of self-confidence as they were of Teddie's envy and grudging respect. It occurred to him that Merrick was – how could he put it? – a mystery that attracted him. He found himself telling Merrick about his parents, about Hunter and the abortive search for his mother's grave in Mandalay. On Merrick's clear, handsome but experienced face he saw an expression that encouraged him to feel more in control of his affairs, more intelligent about the significance of a history which it surprised him to discover he had rather a lot of. Talking to

183

Merrick made him feel that he'd almost made a contribution to the totality of the world's affairs. He believed that Merrick cottoned on to this and was assessing the contribution accurately and appreciatively. It pleased him that Merrick continued to look interested and to ask him questions because this suggested to him that Merrick didn't dismiss the contribution as negligible. With his third burra peg, which Merrick signed for, Teddie acquired a certain self-conscious tenderness towards him.

He also felt sick; rather suddenly. The medicine had cemented him up at one end perhaps but not at the other. He wondered whether the feeling would go away if he ignored it. He embarked on a description of Susan and said what a marvellous girl she was, what a lucky fellow he was. The more he thought about it (he said) the luckier it seemed to him he was. Pretty girls were usually frivolous weren't they? She was damned pretty but terrifically sensible as well as fun to be with. 'I'd like you to meet her,' he said. 'You will if we do what you suggest and get married here.' That sounded like a good idea: to show people in Mirat what a fine girl he'd got hold of. His forehead was damp.

'Are you feeling bad again?' Merrick asked him.

He said, 'It'll go off in a minute. It had better because I've decided to get pleasantly pissed tonight and that always takes me a fair time.' He signalled the bearer for two more scotches but Merrick said, 'Not for me. I'm not a great drinker. In fact there was a time when I hardly touched it. It used to amaze me how much some people could put away. It was Sundernagar that got me into a regular habit. But two in a row is still about my limit before eating.'

'My uncle actually taught me to drink.' Teddie began, remembering himself at seventeen and the evening session in Shropshire with the decanter and his uncle's dedicated but critical eye; but then stopped short of explaining why: that his uncle said that a good head for good liquor was one of the few things that still distinguished a gentleman from others. But Merrick appeared to cotton on to that too. He said, 'Mine was the kind of family that never kept drink in the house except at Christmas and then it was port.'

'My uncle's a port man,' Teddie said, intending to encourage. 'He's always talking about putting some down for me, but I'll be surprised if he does.'

Merrick smiled. 'This was the sort that doesn't get put down. Australian port *type*. When I was a boy I thought all wine was port and that all port came from Australia. It's the sort of thing that makes life difficult for clever children from humble families. One suffers disproportionately. The young are extremely unkind to each other and their elders aren't always free from prejudice. I doubt there's a more unattractive sight than that of a schoolmaster currying class favour by making fun of the boy in his form whose background is different from the others. It's the kind of situation in which it's as well to be tough as well as clever. Fortunately I was both.'

'What school was this?'

'A grammar school. But my natural element would have been the local county. I got into this other place on a scholarship and my people were very proud of that. They weren't exactly poor but they were poverty-stricken in comparison with other parents. And lower-middle-class. By those standards. I took up boxing and found my own level.'

'Do you still box?'

It was the only thing Teddie could think of to say.

'No. But it was my athletic skill as much as my academic achievement that got me into the Indian Police. Those and the interest taken in me by the assistant headmaster. He taught history which happened to be one of my best subjects. I owed him a lot. We kept up a correspondence after I came out, right up until the time he died.'

'I was an awful duffer at school,' Teddie confessed. Like his confidential report from Staff College, recollection of his scholastic stupidity and only average capacity at games caused him no regret: certainly no shame. School, after all, was only part of the adult arrangement to keep children out of the way while they were growing up. He supposed it was different for people like Merrick's parents, but he imagined there was a similarity somewhere. In any case here they were, the two of them, arrived on the same sofa in the same place with the same rank and the same privileges, sharing the same room and the same servant who, as it happened, preferred Merrick who hadn't been born in a world where servants figured and port got put down.

At once he remembered the bicycle and the chalk marks and the idea he had had that these were a message to Merrick, a warning to Merrick by an INA sympathizer who had found out that Merrick was taking a detailed interest in the subject and perhaps that he was lecturing on it that morning. But just what a bicycle and cabalistic signs had to do with either the subject or Merrick's involvement was a mystery.

He said, 'Does a bicycle have any special significance for you, old man?'

He had never seen such a change in a fellow. At least, he couldn't remember seeing one. It was brief but – there was no other word for it – electrifying. The tingling sensation communicated itself to Teddie. For a moment Merrick looked as if he had been made by a machine and was waiting for someone to come and disconnect him so that he could collapse back into his component parts because there was no possibility of his being galvanized by the vital fundamental spark. Subsequently what puzzled Teddie was that he should have thought about the change in Merrick in such terms. He wondered whether he was becoming over-sensitive, whether he had picked up something that had attacked his nervous system, speeded up his reactions and sent his imagination out of control. Something odd had been happening to him ever since he arrived in Mirat. There was that peculiar fancy he had had about the spare bed as a burning ship or catafalque. Perhaps he had been affected by the aeroplanes. The height had hurt his ears and after each flight it had been a day or two before his hearing was really clear again. That sort of thing could upset your physical balance so there was no reason why it shouldn't upset your mental balance too.

'A bicycle?' Merrick asked. 'What do you mean, special significance?'

'Well I don't know. Is it a sort of symbol of the INA?'

'Not that I'm aware of. Why?'

Teddie told him.

'Just that?' Merrick said, when he had explained. 'A broken bicycle?'

'Well there were these chalk marks. I'm afraid I scuffed them out.'

Presently Merrick said, 'What a pity.' He sipped some of the scotch remaining in his glass. 'Do you remember the marks in any detail?'

'I'm afraid not. I say, do you think I was right?'

'About what?'

'The INA.'

Merrick did not reply for a while. He was inspecting the palm of his left hand. He said, 'Possibly. Have you told anyone else?'

'I asked Hosain. He didn't know what I was talking about. I expect the beggar thought I was accusing him of something.'

'I see. Well that explains that. He did say or at least imply you'd questioned his honesty. But I never listen to complaints from servants about other officers. That's why I was ticking him off. Have you mentioned the bicycle and marks to anyone else?'

'No.'

Teddie, sensing a secret, felt privileged.

'Then I shouldn't.' He looked at Teddie's glass. 'Let me get you another of those before we eat. To kill the bugs.' He called the bearer over. Ten minutes later when they got up to go into the mess Teddie felt euphoric. At dinner

187

he drank beer. Afterwards he drank several brandies and Merrick drank one. Without Merrick to guide him he might have lost his way in the maze of covered walks. By the time they got back to their room Teddie was satisfactorily several over the eight but still on his feet. He protested when Merrick helped him take off his shoes. He did not remember getting into bed.

He woke with a thick head when Hosain roused them at half-past seven with morning tea, and recalled a dream that had been so vivid it couldn't have happened that he woke in the middle of the night and saw an Indian – a Pathan in a long robe – standing in the middle of the room.

When he pressed the subject of his marriage, as Merrick had recommended, he was unable to ignore a moment longer its grand irrelevance to the position in which he and every other officer at divisional headquarters were placed. He found himself having to treat it with the same sympathy and impatience that Colonel Selby-Smith showed (wrinkling his face and temporarily detaching his mind from the main stream of his multiple concerns) so that it was not until Teddie was alone in his room that he fully appreciated the fact that he was none the wiser but somehow committed to panic-action. He had no idea how to conduct his affairs on such a basis, nor how to break it to Susan and her mother. He wished he had left the subject unpressed but at the same time realized that to have done so might have been disastrous. His feelings towards Merrick were now ambivalent. He was grateful to him for the advice but couldn't help identifying him with the unsatisfactory result of taking it.

Between mid-October and Christmas, Selby-Smith had said, there was now no likelihood of getting away because the serious business of working up would be done during those few weeks, probably in one of the stickier areas of Bengal. After Christmas, leave was anyone's guess. Selby-Smith's own was that there wouldn't be any. The battalion and brigade leave rosters were at the tail-end stage. With the exception of Teddie every officer at divisional headquarters had had leave before joining. The general had been very keen to establish what he called a pattern of full working continuity once the division was formed. He would be adamant about not granting leave to any officer unless the circumstances were exceptional. Selby-Smith promised to have a word with him at lunch because Teddie's circumstances were, if not exceptional, at least different. In the afternoon Teddie received the general's ruling. He could either postpone his wedding until after Christmas and risk not having it at all or he could get married in Mirat at any time he wished between now and the third week in October and have seventy-two hours' leave to enjoy the consequences.

At first he felt bucked. Cycling home from the daftar he saw Mirat through the honeyed eyes of an ardent young husband, but suddenly its strangeness imposed itself on him and he could not picture her there. All kinds of practical details about the wedding presented themselves for consideration and for once he found it impossible to deal with them one at a time. He arrived at his quarters incapable of coherent thought and wondered how best to get hold of Tony Bishop whose job it should be, as best man, to do his thinking for him. Hosain brought tea and he began a letter: Darling Susan –

The blank paper only emphasized the immense distance she was from him and it was a distance he did not feel he could cover. He abandoned the letter in favour of a List which began after an entry or two to look suspiciously like a staff officer's note to the Q side. He had just written the word accommodation which was all right as an idea – in fact as such essential – but the ramifications of the word now began to be exposed; the names and faces of people requiring accommodation sprang up argumentatively claiming attention, comfort, indeed some reasonable degree of luxury. The bride; the bridesmaid (Sarah); the bride's mother; the matron of honour, Mrs Grace (Aunt

Fenny); the chap to give the bride away, Major Grace (Uncle Arthur); the best man. It would be simpler for him to go to Pankot. But that would take forty-eight of the miserable grudging allowance of seventy-two. There would hardly be a night he could call his and Susan's own.

He yelled for Hosain, told him to tell the bhishti to get a move on with the bath water. A thunderstorm broke. For fifteen minutes the electricity was off. He fanned himself with the writing-pad. The solution came to him dressed in its own perfect grey and respectful logic. There would be no wedding until after bloody Christmas and bloody Bengal. There would probably be no bloody wedding. He went out to the closet and sat miserably hunched, resting his forehead on both fists.

As a boy in his first year of English exile, in the house of his Shropshire uncle, he had often retreated to the unfriendly privacy of the cold English lavatory to consider the extraordinary miseries of life. His eyes blurred in sympathetic remembrance. It was several seconds before he realized that the most shameful thing was happening. He was blubbing.

Darling Susan, he began again a few days later when this unusual and useful man Merrick had solved the problem for him. And broke the news to her. With enthusiasm. 'As for arrangements here,' he continued, 'they're simple enough. Rather exciting in fact. Can't remember whether I mentioned that Mirat is a princely Indian state' (he hadn't; the fact had escaped his notice; Merrick had told him). 'The palace and all that sort of thing are on the other side of the lake' (he'd hardly noticed the lake either), 'but it seems the old Nawab has a guest house there that he's made available to the station for special visitors who can't get decent accommodation. I've had a word with the SSO and the guest house is available for the October dates I suggest. I've booked it anyway because I can always alter it if you can't manage it. There's tons of room for all of you, apparently, including Aunt Fenny and

190

Uncle Arthur. The SSO says it's very comfortable, even luxurious. And apart from the commissariat which one arranges oneself it's all free as air. It seems the old Nawab likes having English people there. It's in the grounds of the palace but quite separate and of course guarded, so don't worry. It should be fun. There's a nice old church in the cantonment, which is where it'll be, and afterwards we can shoot up to the Nanoora Hills in just a few hours . . .'

He stopped, gazed at the rain outside, living the eternity after the word hours, or trying to. Not having been to Nanoora he found it difficult to conjure a background to Susan's hair which he could see and smell. The background to her hair kept coming out as Pankot. Nanoora might well do so too, in fact. One place looked much like another once you were used to it. He bent over the desk again and wrote: 'I'll drop a line to Tony Bishop but perhaps you or your mother would too. I'm sure General Rankin will give him long enough leave to accompany you all down, even if you come a week before the wedding. I can get him a room at the club. So don't worry on that score. Darling Susan. Enjoy Srinagar. How I wish we could have been there together. But it was not to be.'

One other thing was not to be either. Five weeks later, a week before the wedding party was due in Mirat, Susan rang from area headquarters in Pankot to divisional headquarters in Mirat, got put on to Teddie personally and told him that Tony Bishop was in hospital with jaundice and had to be written off as best man. Teddie felt disturbed, less by the news and the problem it presented than by the business-like and utterly unromantic tone of Susan's voice which he had not heard for a long time and which quite clearly commanded him to take firm steps to ensure that there was no other hitch.

Teddie's desk was endways on to a window that looked out on to the main verandah of the Ops block. Susan was saying, 'So Teddie, you'll have to detail someone at your end to hold your hand in Tony's place,' and just then Ronald Merrick walked past.

191

Teddie smiled. 'Don't worry, old thing. Easy as wink. I'll probably get the fellow I share quarters with. He's a helpful and willing sort of chap.'

Coda

I've got a terrific favour to ask old man he had said but really it had been the other way round the favour being done to Merrick who as a boy could not have dreamed ever of supporting an officer of the Muzzafirabad Guides as best man at a wedding: a dignity not to be taken on lightly and certainly not to be repaid like this with a cut cheek and a piece of sticking plaster, an impediment to the tender conviviality of skins.

Shaving, the sensation of having been taken advantage of, of having had a casual friendship presumed upon, settled like a claw between his shoulder blades (which were otherwise unscarred, unmarked by the talons of physical desire. Her fingers had conveyed a reluctance which he supposed was a degree better than distaste). Teddie dabbed his cheeks and chin with a towel, cut a fresh piece of sticking plaster and applied it to the wound.

Merrick's wound. Teddie had borne it with an equanimity that disguised incredulity. This morning however the face in the mirror was that of an acquaintance well enough known, taken enough interest in, to make an explanation of what had happened at the wedding obligatory and, in advance of getting it, unconvincing, in fact unbelievable, part of an especially sly confidence trick. The face in the mirror was that of a man Teddie felt he couldn't trust. The eyes were too narrow, shifty under sandy lashes. The cheeks were drawn, as by some vice lately attempted and come to nothing. The bones shadowed them with a mixture of shame and unaltered intention.

Yesterday they had arrived in Nanoora. Tomorrow they must return. Their one complete and uninterruptible day had begun. The hours were almost too many for him to hold because the whole weight of them seemed to be on his back. It was as if he had invented the day for his own convenience. He went back into the bedroom where Susan lay, crumpled, asleep or wishing she were. He couldn't be sure. She appeared discarded, not by other people but by herself. The curtains were still drawn across the too large window which was bordered by breaking and entering bands of vagrant sunshine. The room was otherwise still part of the private revelations of his wedding night and would be until the bearer brought morning tea and pulled the curtains back: an event that was not due for another forty minutes.

Showered and shaved he was conscious of thirst and hunger. But there was this other more insistent appetite; so intense it seemed that it would never be satisfied. He could never get enough. The mere sight of her sharpened and hardened him. His genitals ached but were totally in command again, engorged. His mind was frozen. He stripped and clambered in, without making a sound; it felt to him nevertheless as though he had whimpered. His arms trembled, anticipating exertions. She was night-scented, a warm aromatic combination of breasts and thighs and rucked transparent nightgown which gave his spoiler's hands no rest but racked them with endless exhausting domineering tensions.

She cried out softly, apparently rudely awoken. With an abrupt gasping acquiescence she opened her legs but not her eyes; offered what assistance she could think of; but the duality of their enterprise did not connect them. Only his flesh did that and there was an improvement in her in that direction, the only one that mattered for the moment, having been earned, worked for with a kind of tight-lipped patience. The contest over, detumescent, he lay licking her wounds with kisses.

Later he drew her bathwater, poured in generous handfuls of sweet, silly pink salts. For half-an-hour he sat by the bedroom window, considering the unknown prospect of Nanoora which was surprised in its own daylight.

He drank tea and listened to the irregular but confirming sounds of the sponge dipped and squeezed. He tried to believe that the bathroom was not her refuge but a place of preparation for the business of giving and sharing and taking up her part of the day which somehow had to carry a whole future in its mouth – like a mother-beast with her cubs, to a place of safety.

What had he done? Hurt her physically? Shocked her with his carnal approach? Had he been while exercising consideration and patience inconsiderate in showing vigour, making no attempt to hide this extreme of happiness? His own shock had been the shock of joy that was legitimate, endorsed, blessed, with nothing murky or restricting perched on its shoulder. He had discovered a private area of freedom inside the stockade. She had not entered it with him. He must be at fault. He had failed to arouse her. He had a miserable impression that she did not like him. His body ached for her affection.

PART THREE

The Silver in the Mess

1

Barbie had never known the wilder secrets of life nor held the key to its deepest sensual pleasures. The mystical element in a wedding was therefore real to her. She observed with pleasure the grace and stillness which became Susan's chief attribute the moment her engagement was announced. The girl was different. Her realization of her love had driven everything else from her mind and left her body in repose. Where once she had worked so hard at being the centre of attraction she was now, as of right, at a centre and stood there smiling out at the world; even that part of it which Barbie inhabited.

Barbie watched Sarah closely and was satisfied that there was no broken heart. She had not believed Teddie and Sarah well suited in the few short weeks they were going everywhere together. She thought of these girls as her own girls, born of her womb, dramatically separated from her but now living near her in ignorance of her maternal claims. It was a harmless act of self-deception and hurt nobody, except perhaps herself.

It was a great disappointment to her when the Laytons returned early from the family holiday in Kashmir and announced that the wedding was not to be in Pankot in December but as soon as it could be fixed, in Mirat where Teddie had been posted. She had intended to be at the church even if Mildred had not found it in her heart to invite her to the reception. She had persuaded herself that she would in fact receive an invitation and had ordered through Gulab Singh's a set of twelve Apostle teaspoons for the wedding gift. She planned to have a new costume made in some festive colour. She inspected bolts of cloth at the durzi's. A heliotrope caught her eye. She believed in planning early but said nothing to anyone. Her fear was that in spite of the instructions she had given him the durzi would turn up at Rose Cottage and scatter all these colourful materials on the verandah and so give away her hopes and expectations.

Which is what he did, on the evening of the day the Laytons got back from Kashmir and, uninvited, assembled at Rose Cottage with Clara Fosdick and Nicky Paynton to discuss the problems of the sudden change of plan; so that at first it appeared to them all that the durzi had heard the news and was prompt off the mark, anticipating an urgent order for a trousseau as yet only half-heartedly bespoken.

'Full marks for information and method,' Mildred told him. 'Show us what you've got.'

He set the white-sheeted bundle down, but at Barbie's feet, and opened it, perplexed by so large and interested an audience, and revealed bolts of woollen cloth in colours and patterns that would have killed every woman there except one: who stood exposed. The durzi twitched the heliotrope material between thumb and finger and said, 'Pure.' He said it to Barbie.

'It's a material I've been looking at,' she told them. But the truth was all too clear. She never wore 'colours'. The material was for a special winter occasion. 'I can't make up my mind and he's trying to do it for me, the wretch. What do you think?' She took refuge in the dog. 'Panther now. What do *you* think?' She got a desultory wag. In this climate pets faded even quicker than women.

'The question is, could I carry it? That's what my mother used to say to her clientele. I doubt you can carry it, or, It wouldn't do for everyone but you could carry it. I always imagined a difficult material as an immense *load*.'

Which it was. She would have liked to lighten the load and at the same time obliterate the embarrassing scene; and saw how this might be done – by swooping on the bolts of cloth and throwing them like huge unwieldy paperchains until the verandah was heaped in heliotrope, electric blue, bilious emerald and garish pink. She grinned in frustrated exultation.

'I suppose it *is* somewhat festive. Christmas Day perhaps or would that be carrying it too far?' She laughed at her unintentional pun, turned, looked down at the durzi. 'No, take it all away. Some other time perhaps but this is not the place.'

'Aziz,' Mildred said, 'tell him to call at the grace and favour tomorrow at eleven.'

Aziz did so. Satisfied, the durzi did up his bundle, salaamed and was away; an old bent man ever ready to exercise his skill at both sides of his trade – selling and stitching. His cloth was better and cheaper than the stuff at Jalal-ud-din's. At night in his open-fronted shop he sat cross-legged on his platform under a naphtha lamp and an oleograph depicting the Lord Krishna fluting maidens by moonlight. He wore half-spectacles on his nose and looked up at you from above them and smiled, pressing his palms together, as if in a predominantly Muslim bazaar it required alertness and good manners as well as predestination to be Hindu. Barbie pictured him spreadeagled under the bundle, strangled on the way home by *thugs* as a sacrifice to the Goddess Kali; his bloated tongue the colour of the rejected cloth, and listened in now to Mildred talking to Clara Fosdick and Nicky Paynton.

It seemed that in Kashmir, at Mildred's insistence, the houseboat had been moved from its original site – a noisy berth between two others that were rented by American officers who played portable gramophones until the early hours and had Eurasian girls draped on the sundecks under awnings. They had tried to involve Sarah and Susan in these late-night parties.

Mildred ordered the boat taken to the remote spot where she and John Layton had spent part of their honeymoon, and moored it one hundred yards from someone who had got there sooner but whose boat seemed quiet, hardly to exist in fact; muted to the point of creating its own illusion of itself as though at any moment it might break up into component parts of air and light and water.

Or so Barbie conjured it, absorbing all the separate pieces of information from Mildred's account and re-assembling them. To begin with she had never been to Kashmir and had to imagine this entirely for herself, helped out by recollections of pictures in books and on postcards. She thought of Kashmir as snow and apples at the same season and a deep lake into which the snow melted and the apples fell. In Spring there were sheep from which the fine wool shawls came; and then in Autumn the smell of carpentry. The water was always placid but grey and misty. At night there were stars and heaven looked very far away, far behind the stars, as it did in places where there were mountains. For the first time, listening to the story, she admitted the actual quality of colour and sunshine so that the water now looked green as well as deep, shaded by willows whose fronds brushed the ornate fretted wood of houseboat roofs.

And in this long warm sleeping afternoon a cry came, across the one hundred yards of water, the cry of a child, which seemed odd. Only an elderly woman, apart from servants, had been noted. To this woman, after discussion, cards had been sent and the cry of the child at first sounded like the ambiguous answer and continued to do so until the arrival of the tiny reciprocal rectangles of pasteboard with that name in copperplate, engraved.

Lady Manners.

The lake was still placid; no ripple. Distantly the mountains still erected sharp outlines. Shade remained dark like indigo velvet. Butterflies hemstitched this tangible material, and Barbie – living it – watched them and heard the cry repeated, felt the fascination of the situation before she understood the predicament created by the proximity, the awful nearness to the untouchable condition that attached to that name, Manners, which was the name of the woman and, with her inexplicable permission, of the child whose father was any one of six disgusting hooligans. There she was, the old woman, once distinguished, once elegantly in occupation of Government House in Ranpur and the now virtually disused Summer Residence in Pankot, at ease upon the sundeck of a houseboat; isolated from the world her niece and now she had scandalized.

The girl, the Manners girl (poor running panting Daphne) had paid the price of her folly by dying, bearing the tiny monster of the Bibighar that should have been destroyed in the womb and, it was once suggested, thrust down the throats of the culprits or their bloody priests. Miss Manners had not had, surely, religious scruples about abortion? More likely a conviction that she knew the father. The implications of this conviction were almost too astonishing to imagine, as were the old woman's motives in announcing the death, the birth, to a world that thought it better to forget.

Of course, Mildred said, it wasn't possible to follow up the ritual begun in ignorance with the exchange of cards. She let her slightly hooded eyes stray explanatorily towards the garden where the girls innocently played with Panther in that permitted zone originally marked out by Barbie. But, she added, there had been odd moments of hiatus: shikaras setting out from both houseboats at the same minute, or unable to avoid what only a few yards of water stopped from being an actual confrontation, but close enough to demand an inclination of heads, since the occupants of each had met by pasteboard and they could not accept the burden of uncivilized pretence that this had not occurred, could not assume that they were total strangers, even if it were tacitly agreed there should be no development of an acquaintance from which neither side could benefit, and from which one side (that of the girls, playing there with the ball and the dog, those appendages of unsullied English life) could only incur positive harm.

199

'What did she look like?' Nicky Paynton wanted to know.

'One couldn't see. We were never, thank God, *that* close, and even under the shikara awning she wore an old topee and a veil.'

Teddie's letter about the new arrangements for the wedding had been almost a relief, giving as it did a conscientious reason for ordering the boat away (even if it looked like embarrassed retreat) back to its original mooring to be closer at hand for unexpectedly early last-minute shopping and the making of arrangements for an early return to 'Pindi by cars, to Delhi by train (where Aunt Fenny and Uncle Arthur became detached), and on to Ranpur, back to Pankot, and the excitement as well as the slight hysteria of bringing the wedding forward and somehow transferring it to Mirat: a place of palaces, mosques and minarets.

Guests of the Nawab! Barbie's visions were now coming to her through the fretted stone screens that embellished so much Moghul architecture. Through these she peeped at lawns and lakes and fountains and saw Susan, standing in her new-found stillness, in bridal white, her veil lifting in rose-scented breezes that had blown across deserts.

Quite quickly she detected a mystery about the book but put it down to the curious evasiveness Sarah had brought back from Kashmir with her, like something caught and not yet shaken off.

The book was an elegant affair of dark red leather, gold tooling and paper in which you could see flecks of the wood from whose pulp the paper had been made. The text was printed in the Arabic script which Barbie, fluent in spoken Urdu, had never learned to decipher. But she could see it was poetry.

The book was to be the Laytons' thank-you present to the Nawab of Mirat in whose palace guest house they were to stay. Mildred mentioned the book and now Sarah had brought it up to show to Mabel. She unwrapped it and offered it as if it were a gift she had received not one the family were to give.

'It was a bit of luck really,' she said.

'Why luck?' Mabel asked, hearing.

'Luck to discover the connexion.'

'Connexion? Who are the poems by?'

'Gaffur.'

'Oh!' Barbie interrupted. 'Gaffur. He's a classic Urdu poet. I used to know several quotations. What connexion do you mean?'

'He was court poet to a Nawab of Mirat in the eighteenth century. A relation. The same family as the present Nawab. A Kasim.'

'"It is not for you to say, Gaffur,"' Barbie suddenly recalled, '"that the rose is God's creation. Howsobeit its scent is heavenly." Oh, how does it go on?'

'Yes,' Sarah said. 'How?'

Her face was very pale. This was unusual.

'I don't know. But I do know that in each poem they address themselves by name, just once, I think. Not their real names. Their pen-names. I didn't know Gaffur was a Kasim.'

She hesitated, held up one finger. 'It is not for you to say, Gaffur, that the rose is God's creation. Howsobeit its scent is heavenly. Something something something. It's quite useless. I've lost it. Is there a connexion between the Nawab and Mr Mohammed Ali Kasim the politician?'

'Yes,' Sarah said. 'The Nawab and he are kinsmen as well, but fairly distantly.'

'How extraordinary, and well – fraught. I mean, is that the word?'

'What are you saying, Barbie?' Mabel asked. Barbie answered from her abdomen, a schoolroom trick that did not strain the throat. Her whole body acted as a sounding board.

She said, 'The Nawab of Mirat is related to Mohammed Ali Kasim who is presently in gaol.'

'Oh,' Mabel said. 'Is he?' So that it was not clear which

201

he she meant or which condition – the relationship or the incarceration.

'The Congress ex-chief minister in Ranpur,' Barbie emphasized.

'I know,' Mabel said. 'My second husband was once a colleague of *his* father.' She turned to Sarah. 'Who thought of the book?'*

'Someone we met in Srinagar.'

'What was their name?'

A pause.

'The idea just emerged in conversation. We met so many people,' Sarah eventually said.

As Sarah took the book back into her hands Barbie remembered the old parlour game in Camberwell. I open the book. I look at the book. I close the book. And I pass the book along. The catch had been to cross your legs as you passed the book to the next player otherwise you were out. It was a game which like others of its kind scared her until she was old enough to think it silly, and even then the icy little hand would touch her low down on the back of her neck, the hand of the invisible guest, the demon-spirit of the party who knew the answers to all the conundrums and puzzles and who presided over the gathering with a thrilling kind of malice, totting up the scores and marking down for ridicule, if not worse, special victims: the foolish

---

* It is not for you to say, Gaffur,
    That the rose is one of God's creations,
    Although its scent is doubtless that of heaven.
    In time rose and poet will both die.
        Who then shall come to this decision?
        (Trans. Edwin Tippitt (Major. I A. Retd))

You oughtn't to say, Gaffur,
    That God created roses,
No matter how heavenly they smell.
      You have to think of the time when you're both
        dead and smell nasty
And people are only interested in your successors.
        (Trans. Dmitri Bronowsky)

aunt, the sickly cousin who cried when Barbie's father did his grotesque babes-in-the-wood act, sitting in a tub, under the table, with only his bare knees showing, and on each knee a grinning face sketched with burnt cork, the eyes closed.

Sarah, having taken the book, looked at it herself. Her grace was a different kind from Susan's. If grace was the right word then Susan had the look of imminent entrance to it, Sarah the look of being born there, of merely having to wait for it visibly to form itself around her, when she and it would exist in a state of mutual recognition. It had not happened yet, but something had happened, in Kashmir, which had heightened the other look she had always had of taking very little on trust, of preferring to work things out for herself; heightened the look and presumably her realization that it was far from easy. It then occurred to Barbie that Sarah could have seen the child, talked to Lady Manners, taken one of those opportunities when characteristically alone to pay the visit her family steered clear of.

Barbie pictured it: this young girl and the old woman, and the child somewhere in the vicinity. I came, the girl was saying, because I couldn't go without saying hello. So said hello and talked and later was shown the child. One of God's creatures. Although, as Gaffur for some reason would have it, that was not for one to say. The idea of the book could have come out of this visit because the conversation could have turned upon the imminent journey to Mirat, and the reason for the journey. It was the kind of thing the old woman would know: the connexion between a poet and a prince and an imprisoned politician.

Convinced that she had hit upon the solution to the mystery of the book Barbie gazed at Sarah with awe and curiosity; fear for her toughness and temerity. Sarah had her father's dignity but it was committed in a different cause, or seemed to be; committed to discovering where she would feel it earned, where her duty was. On the score of duty her father obviously had no questions. His dignity was therefore unqualified. It was this difference in dignity that people saw and in Sarah misinterpreted; people like the Smalley woman who saw the difference as something perilously close to 'unsoundness' – a condition which led to an inability to retain the affection of suitable and dignified young officers. Barbie thought: More fools they, Sarah's worth ten of most of them; lucky the man who gets her but he will have to be pretty special. She looks at my old fond and foolish face and sees through it, I think, sees below the ruination, hears behind the senseless ceaseless chatter, sees right down to the despair but also beyond to the terrific thing there really is in me, the joy I would find in God and which she would find in life, which come to much the same thing. But if she's not careful she'll find herself not living, just helping others to. Perhaps that's all I've ever done. If so it isn't much, it isn't enough I don't suppose. Especially if I ask myself: How many of those children did I ever truly bring to Jesus?

Sarah glanced at her.

'What did you mean, Barbie, fraught?'

'I suppose I meant odd, difficult, to be the guest of a man whose kinsman we've put in clink, but India is full of oddities like that isn't it and perhaps the Nawab disapproves of his politician kinsman. Or if he doesn't he obviously doesn't disapprove of us. But then the princes like us better than the rest of them do, don't they? We've bolstered them up and some of them one gathers hardly deserve it. One of my friends belonged to what's called a zenana mission and she once spent a year in a palace of a tiny state in Rajputana. Actually I forget but I think it was Rajputana. Her job was to try to give the rudiments of a modern education to the ruler's wives and daughters who were all in purdah or going to be in purdah. She adored the children but said there were times when she actually went in fear of her life, not that it was ever threatened but she heard such terrible things, quite barbaric. But I'm sure Mirat's not like that.'

'No, I'm sure it isn't,' Sarah said. 'I must go.'

She got up, leant and kissed Mabel who thanked her for bringing the book of poems. Barbie went with her to the front where the tonga was waiting.

'She did appreciate it. She would have liked to be at the wedding, but Mirat's so far. Too far. It was awfully nice of you to come up specially to show the book. Shall you invite the Nawab to the wedding?'

'I expect so, Barbie. You would have liked to come too wouldn't you?'

'Oh yes. But I couldn't leave Mabel. Has Captain Bishop been given permission to accompany you?'

Now seated in the back of the tonga Sarah looked down at Barbie. 'Well he was, but he's just been taken to hospital. We believe it's jaundice. Mother's gone to see him this afternoon to find out.'

'But whatever will you do?'

'If it's jaundice Susan's going to ring Teddie and tell him to find another best man quickly.'

'But what about the journey?'

'We'll be all right. We're meeting Aunt Fenny in Ranpur and all going on together.'

'And your Uncle Arthur, Major Grace?'

'He can't get away from Delhi until the Thursday before the wedding.'

'All that way, with no man to look after you?'

Sarah smiled. 'I'm sure there'll be lots of officers on the train. We shall be quite safe. Don't worry.'

There are these spoons, Barbie wanted to say. The twelve Apostles. They came today. My gift to Susan and Teddie. Twelve witnesses to love of the sublimest kind. But having got them she was at a loss how and when to offer them. She watched the tonga turn and waved to Sarah's retreating figure. Sarah sat holding on to the struts of the hood with one hand and on to the book on her lap with the other.

It is not for you to say Gaffur that the rose is God's creation, even if, though, its scent, its scent is of Heaven, heavenly. 'My memory,' she said aloud, turning back in, 'Is not What it Was.'

She wondered what happened to all the thoughts which once having had you stored up, and especially what became of those that seemed to be lost which you couldn't put your hand on. She stood in the middle of the room, one repository inside another, and was filled with a tiny horror: the idea of someone coming to claim back even one item of what was contained in either. The idea was horrifying because if you allowed the possibility of one claim then you had to allow the likelihood of several and then many of them, and finally of thousands; so that the logical end to the idea was total evacuation of room, body and soul, and of oneself dead but erect, like a monument marking some kind of historical occasion.

2

The disappointment people had felt at missing an event that would have added some necessary glitter to life was lifted a bit when the Laytons got back from Mirat and it became known that the wedding had been dogged by a series of minor misfortunes.

Mildred's initial attempts to dismiss these as being of no importance only succeeded in making the misfortunes seem major and presently the word disaster entered people's heads and was actually used on several occasions.

If Susan herself had looked downcast the idea of disaster would have gained currency; but, as if making up for what Pankot had missed, she glittered for it, trailing the absent ceremony and reception behind her like a diaphanous shadow that sparkled in the pure late October light, a shadow which was a degree or two darker than was really fair but causing her no trouble, a fact that attracted the kind of new regard to which she was entitled: a girl who had left Pankot pale and beautiful and come back flushed, happy, quite her old self, but with this extra dimension of having entered the honourable company of grass widows, with the bloom of the orange blossom still on her cheeks and her husband already gone on the first leg of the journey back to the front to fight for the preservation of the sterner world she now inhabited.

And when the misfortunes had been pieced together in some sort of chronological order, when they were looked at calmly, then even the stone that had broken the glass that cut Teddie Bingham's cheek on the way to the church could be seen as an acceptable symbol of the attacks to which people who merely tried to get on with the job in hand were only too well accustomed.

The stone, it seemed, had not been meant for Teddie but for his companion, the last-minute substitute for Tony Bishop, an extremely interesting man whatever way you looked at it, a man who had apparently incurred such intense dislike among Indians of a certain kind that they persecuted him, kept track of him wherever he went and then chose a moment to embarrass or harass him. On the day of the wedding it had been two moments: on the way to the church and on the platform of Mirat station just as Susan and Teddie were about to wave good-bye from the window of their honeymoon compartment.

Between these two moments there had been another for which Captain Merrick was hardly responsible unless you expected a best man to think of everything in addition to the groom's state of nerves; but from the point of view of the wedding this middle incident had been the worst, or very nearly. In a way nothing could be worse for the bride than to be told within a minute or two of leaving for the ceremony that there had been a hitch which meant a half-hour delay, and then, on coming up the aisle at last, see her groom standing at the head of it, pale, smiling lopsidedly, with a large piece of gauze padding stuck to one cheek with sticking plaster.

'You have to admit,' Lucy Smalley said, 'that it has its comic side,' but no one else was prepared to admit that it

207

did when a Layton girl and a Muzzy Guides officer were the central characters in the affair.

It was the involvement of a Layton girl and a Muzzy officer that weighed most heavily against the substitute best man, an otherwise virtuous target for despicable attack. He ought to have made it clear to Teddie who he really was.

Mildred said that after the wedding was over he had admitted persecution of one kind and another ever since leaving Mayapore for a dreary backwater called Sundernagar, where he had continued in his police rank as District Superintendent until making his escape into the army for the duration. It would, she supposed, have been rather difficult for him to anticipate a demonstration against him on the day of the wedding, but if he had made it clear, if he had said to Teddie right at the beginning, Look, I'm the policeman who was made to seem to have put up a black in that ghastly Manners case, the fellow who actually arrested those blighters, then even if he hadn't added, And I'm still being tracked down and messed about by Indians who think I arrested the wrong men and treated them in some sinister sort of way; even if he hadn't added *that* useful bit of information, then when the stone came sailing through the window of the car taking Teddie and him to the church, he would have been able to say, That was meant for me, and explained why then or later. And boring as it would have been, a perfect bloody nuisance, everyone would have known what was up and Teddie wouldn't have been able to say he'd never been warned that his best man was someone who'd been unpleasantly in the limelight. Teddie had always had a horror of being mixed up in vulgar scenes, apparently. He thought at first that the stone was meant for him because he was a British officer or that it had been chucked by someone demonstrating against the Nawab because all the cars used at the wedding were lent by the palace and had crests on the doors. And in either case, of course, it made him feel perfectly miserable. Not to mention his poor cut cheek.

And there, in regard to the stone, Mildred left it with a

sound of shattering glass and an impression of Teddie making just a little bit of a fuss, and of Mr Merrick having failed by a perceptible margin to act quite like an officer and a gentleman; an impression which she hardened by reporting him by no stretch of the imagination out of the top drawer, so that it had seemed almost a special kindness to have chosen him for best man, an unconscious repayment to him for the poor way the authorities had treated him in the Manners affair, after all he had done to try to solve and settle it.

After the stone there had been the incident at the club, and it was reasonable to suppose (Mildred suggested) that if there had not been the incident of the stone nothing dire would have happened at the club.

The Nawab and his party had been refused entrance to the reception by the British military police who were stationed at the front. The MPs were a last-minute precaution, only there in case there were further untoward or unexplained incidents. Assuming that no Indian was persona grata at the Mirat Gymkhana, they stopped the Nawab, his chief minister and his social secretary from crossing the threshold, which could have caused troublesome diplomatic repercussions if the club secretary hadn't got wind of it and personally rescued them, personally conducted them into the reception. It was the wedding group's first meeting with the Nawab and his chief minister, Count Bronowsky, émigré white Russian who now looked like one of those dessicated Muslims of the Jinnah stamp. The two had been away on a visit to a neighbouring state. The social secretary was a different kettle of fish, perhaps a tricky one. He was Ahmed Kasim, the younger son of the ex-chief Congress minister in Ranpur, M. A. Kasim. Heaven knew what he thought of everything. If he thought badly he'd disguised it well. He'd made himself very useful during the week – you couldn't say charming, he'd been too formal and correct for that. He accompanied Sarah riding one morning and she had no complaint about his behaviour, which Aunt Fenny had been worried about. He never mentioned his father or the fact that he was in prison. He had not struck one as in the least politically minded which may have been why his father had packed him off to work in a princely state as a hopeless reactionary case. When it came to M. A. Kasim's sons, the old Congressman had probably had to swallow political pride and disappointment, because the elder was a King's commissioned officer currently a prisoner-of-war in Malaya and here was the younger working for an Indian prince and looking after the comfort of visiting members of the *raj*.

'It was Susan,' Mildred said, 'who really saved the day. When the old Nawab finally arrived on the lawn, still bristling from the insult, she went forward and dropped him a curtsy, which wasn't protocol but made all the difference.'

Glances went admiringly to where Susan stood, or sat, wherever she was on the two or three occasions Mildred recreated this picture of her, on a lawn, in sunshine, in her wedding veil and dress, holding together a situation that had threatened to fall apart. Admirable girl. The Nawab must have been immensely flattered.

It was the third incident that most concerned and puzzled Barbie because it seemed to her from what she could understand of it that it was of a different order, one that reached outside the wedding and cast innumerable patches of light and shade. The patches of light revealed nothing because the light did not fall on anything, rather it pulsed on and off so that the patches were like mysterious glowing areas attempting to burn their way out of an imprisoning mass of darkness. They did not move; and, coming on, they had gone out before you could fix their positions or even their relationship to each other.

'What was it,' she asked Sarah, 'that actually happened at the station?'

They were walking in the garden of Rose Cottage; or rather Sarah had been walking and Barbie had come down

210

to her. It appeared that they were together but Barbie did not feel that this was the case. She was wary of the girl. She had an idea that it might be unwise to touch her. The Nawab had been pleased with the volume of Gaffur's poems, Mildred said. Sarah had not mentioned them again. She had not mentioned Mirat, or going riding with the Kasim boy, Ahmed; an excursion which Barbie would have liked to hear about. It was as though she had never been to the wedding or had been and not come back but sent only her reflexion home. She looked at Barbie now from that sort of distance.

'At the station? No more than you've already heard.'

'But I heard it without understanding it.'

'I think that's how we all saw it at the time. Without understanding it. But it was very simple really. Just an elderly Indian woman pushing through us and kneeling at his feet.'

'Captain Merrick's feet?'

'Yes.'

'Beseeching him?'

Sarah paused with her hands behind her back, looking down at her own feet as though she could see the woman there.

'Beseeching him,' she agreed. 'Yes, that's a good word.'

'But who was the woman?'

'The aunt of the Indian boy Miss Manners is supposed to have been infatuated with. The boy who was the chief suspect. He's still in prison.'

'Poor woman. What was she like?'

'Grey-haired. Dressed in a white saree like a widow.'

'In a white saree?'

'Yes.'

'And that was all that happened?' Barbie asked after a while.

'That was all. She pushed through the crowd and fell at Mr Merrick's feet and had to be taken away. Then the train was going and we were waving good-bye to Susan and Teddie.'

'It couldn't have made much sense.'

'It didn't, at least not then.'

'When, then? When did it make sense? When you knew who Mr Merrick was?'

'Oh, we knew that by then. It came out during the reception. He was embarrassed because it made it look as if he'd tried to hide it but according to him he was just trying to forget it. I suppose he wasn't really lying when people asked him what he'd been in the police and he said DSP in Sundernagar.'

'No, that's true. How did it come out?'

'Count Bronowsky remembered his name.'

'Who is Count Bronowsky?'

'The old Russian the Nawab has as his chief minister. He was talking to Aunt Fenny. He said how well the best man had dealt with the stone-throwing incident, making sure they knew at the palace that the reception would be delayed. When Aunt Fenny told him Mr Merrick had been in the police and was used to dealing with a crisis he identified him at once as the DSP in Mayapore. I gather the case had interested him or perhaps he just had an exceptionally good memory. He went to find Mr Merrick and they had a long talk on the terrace but Aunt Fenny had the news well broadcast by the time they came back in. Teddie was awfully cool with him which was a bit unfair, but I think someone had already suggested that if Mr Merrick was the DSP in Mayapore at the time of the Manners case then the stone had probably been thrown at him and not at the Nawab's car. And the thing that happened on the station capped it. But still without making much sense. I didn't really get the hang of it until that evening when Mr Merrick came over to the guest house to apologize to Mother.'

Barbie thought: Mildred never mentioned an apology.

'But I was the only one up,' Sarah went on. 'All the others were still resting. I was waiting for the dark and for the fireflies to come out. So Mr Merrick and I sat and waited for them together. He was going that evening,

212

leaving Mirat for the new training area in Bengal. He told me quite a lot of things. He seemed to want to talk about it now that it had all come out. He explained who the woman in the white saree was. He said he was sorry for her because she was what he called an ordinary decent person who had done everything for her nephew, the one who's in prison. He'd not seen her since he was in Mayapore but he'd always known he was kept track of by the kind of people who tried to make out he'd arrested the wrong men and ill-treated them, the people responsible for what happened to spoil the wedding. He said they were exploiting the woman, using her as part of a scheme to make him feel like a marked man. It all seemed a bit farfetched to me, but I expect it's the only explanation.'

'Did he remember my friend, Edwina Crane?'

'I'm sorry. I never thought to ask.'

'Well, I don't suppose he did. Although as DSP in Mayapore he'd have known all about her being attacked. But I expect one of his juniors dealt with that. He had his hands full with that other awful business, didn't he? Does he still feel he was right, or does he think he might have made a mistake after all, arresting those boys? Miss Manners seemed so positive they weren't the ones, if we're to believe all we heard.'

They had reached the shade of a pine tree that stood near the very end of the garden. From here there was the view to the farther hills and the mountains. In a week or two the snow-capped peaks would be obscured by cloud as often as not. Sarah sat down. Barbie followed suit.

'He feels he was right,' Sarah said. 'He sounded very sure. Very sure indeed. But the more he talked about it the more I felt he'd got it all wrong. And that would be terrible, wouldn't it? If he had got it wrong but is always going to believe he didn't. Do you see what I mean? I know it's terrible in other ways, for the boys who have gone to prison and for – well – but she's dead, and that's another question, another sort of terrible. But to have got something wrong, and never see it, never believe it . . .'

213

Sarah dug her hand into a cushion of pine needles, sifting them, considering them. Suddenly she went on: 'He said that he was once attracted to her himself, in love with her perhaps. He made it sound like a confession, like a determination to be honest about every possible aspect but all the time I felt it wasn't. I don't know why I felt that. But everything he said sounded rehearsed. And while he was saying it you felt him watching for the effect, even knowing what it was going to be.'

'You didn't like him.'

After a while Sarah shook her head.

'No. I don't think I liked him at all.'

Perhaps, Barbie thought, because you had seen the child and talked to the old woman, and had seen the other woman, the woman in the white saree, and felt the presence of the unknown Indian. And wonder how in all this complexity guilt can lie alongside innocence and whether it might not have been in Mr Merrick's power to separate them.

She continued to sit in spite of getting cramp because Sarah did not move and she did not want to leave her alone.

'What did you say?' Sarah asked, coming back into herself after what seemed a long time.

'I wasn't talking.'

Sarah stared at her for a moment or two and said, 'I'm sorry, I thought you were,' and then Barbie wondered whether she had been.

For years she had had real and imaginary conversations with people, with herself, with God, with anyone who was there to listen or not listen. But an imaginary silence was something new. If you didn't know you were talking then you didn't know what you were saying. She tried to remember exactly what she had been thinking in case she had spoken some of her thoughts aloud, but her mind appeared to have been blank after the image of Sarah sitting with the old woman and the child, pondering the question of guilt and innocence and the part Mr Merrick had played or not played in attempting to establish them.

'You seem to be haunted by it,' she said, 'I mean by that awful business. First in Kashmir, being so close to the houseboat, and now in Mirat, with Captain Merrick.'

'Someone should be haunted by it,' Sarah said.

And then Barbie was sure she was right: Sarah had visited the woman and seen the child. She had a concern to hold the child, to take it to St John's and see it baptized.

'Yes,' Barbie said. 'Perhaps we should.' She got up. 'Stay here. I've got something for you to take to Susan.'

She went into the house, returned with the box of Apostle spoons and the note she had written. She knelt again and offered them.

'They're a combined wedding and twenty-first birthday present. Nothing very much. A set of teaspoons. I'd be grateful if you'd take them to her.'

'Thank you, Barbie. That's very kind.'

Sarah put the box on the cushion of needles and looked at the envelope on which Barbie had written, 'Mrs Edward Bingham.'

'I may be leaving Pankot,' Sarah said.

'Oh, Sarah, why? Where?'

'Just to do something more useful. Nursing perhaps or what I'm doing now only in a place where the war's a bit closer. Do you think that's selfish?'

'Why selfish?'

'Because of leaving Mother and Susan. With Daddy a prisoner it's always seemed to be my job to help look after things.'

'Susan's a married woman now.'

'Yes. That's why I thought I could go.'

'I should miss you dreadfully, well we all should, but it would be wrong to hold you back. *That* would be selfishness.'

Sarah glanced up. For a while they looked at each other gravely. 'I wish I could see things clearly enough to be positive like that,' Sarah said. 'But I never can. I must go – '

Abruptly she rose.

'Thank you for Susan's present. Please don't bother to see me off.'

She was gone before Barbie could get to her feet. She watched her until she was out of sight and then followed slowly.

Mabel was not working in the back or on the verandah which must mean she was either at the front or gone for one of her increasingly rare but still solitary walks.

I must explore, Barbie thought; and then spoke aloud: 'I must explore this mystery of the imaginary silence,' and as her voice continued she found that she could detach herself from its sound so that it seemed to go drifting away, or she to go drifting away from it, until she was left in a state of immobility or suspended animation, surrounded by what she could only describe as a vivid sense of herself as new and unused, with neither debit nor credit to her account, no longer in arrears with any kind of payment because the account had not been opened yet.

This was very clear to her but she guessed it wouldn't be when the immobility was cancelled. She thought: Emerson was wrong, we're not explained by our history at all, in fact it's our history that gets in the way of a lucid explanation of us.

She began to enjoy the sensation of her history and other people's history blowing away like dead leaves; but then it occurred to her that among the leaves were her religious principles and beliefs, and – observing the solemn evergreen stillness of the wood-capped hills – felt reassured and wisely reinstructed.

An imaginary silence should not be used to destroy contact but to create it. She went round to the front to find Mabel but the garden was empty. Mabel's stick was on the front verandah so she was not out walking. She went inside, knocked on Mabel's door and opened it.

Mabel was sitting on the edge of her bed watching Aziz removing the contents of an old press and placing them carefully on a blanket spread on the floor.

'Hello, Barbie,' Mabel said, looking up. 'We're sorting out some winter things.'

Barbie had never watched this ritual at Rose Cottage but she knew that it took place. She came further into the room, fascinated as she had been since childhood by the prospect of viewing someone else's possessions; for these had a magic quality of touch-me-not that belonged in fairy tales and in such tales dispensation was possible but not inevitable and every invitation to come nearer was a sugared gift.

'Oh, no. Aziz,' Mabel said, as he opened layers of tissue to show the coat of a grey costume.

'*Hān*,' he insisted. 'Bond is-street.'

Mabel smiled. 'I bought it in London the last summer I was there,' she explained to Barbie, 'the summer John's grandfather died. Susan was only ten or eleven then so you can tell how out of date it is. But every winter Aziz tries to make me bring it out, because of the tag.'

'Bond is-street,' Aziz repeated. '*Pukka*.'

The whole costume was spread out now. It had the simple elegance of all expensive clothes.

'You could shorten the skirt,' Barbie suggested. 'It wouldn't spoil the line.'

'Wouldn't it?'

Encouraged by Barbie's interest Aziz said, '*Hān*. Shorten is-skirt.'

'Perhaps. If I can still get into it.'

Mabel reached down and pulled the costume towards her, twitched at it, and Barbie wondered how easy or difficult it would be to make her take an interest again in things outside Rose Cottage: in clothes, in visits, sprees. The two of them could have a holiday, a short one, not far away. They could go down to Ranpur to do some Christmas shopping. She would take Mabel round the Bishop Bernard and introduce her to Helen Jolley. For such a holiday she would have the heliotrope.

'Very well, Aziz,' Mabel said. 'Put it on the pile.'

Aziz nodded. He rearranged the costume, folded it with

217

reverence, replaced the dried sprigs of lavender whose scent mingled with that of sandalwood and mothballs. The tissue-wrapped costume was put on the smaller of the two piles. Suddenly he reached into the chest and said to Barbie, 'Memsahib!'

'No, no,' Mabel said. She made a gesture as if to stop him but it was ignored. He was intent on revealing a treasure. He lifted a package out and removed the top layer of tissue with a flourish.

'Sarah *bachcha,*' he said. Barbie went closer. A wedding veil? No, a complete garment. She could see the neckline and tiny sleeves folded across its front. Sarah Bachcha. Sarah as a baby. She got down on her knees. 'Oh, it's a christening gown. Was it Sarah's?'

'*Hān.* Sarah Mem.'

Aziz linked thumbs and flapped his splayed fingers. 'Batta fye,' he said, and laughed at Barbie's puzzled expression. He put his hand in under the creamy lace from which the gown was made. As he did so Barbie exclaimed. The hem of the fine lawn undergarment was edged with a band of seed pearls. But there was more enchantment to come. 'Look,' he said, and fluttered his hand. The lace came alive. Butterflies palpated his pink brown palm. Three of them. Five. Seven. A dozen. More than that. The whole gown was made of lace butterflies.

'Oh, but it's beautiful,' Barbie said. 'Did Susan wear it too?'

Mabel answered. 'No. Susan had something new.'

Now that the lace was exposed Mabel seemed willing to acknowledge it. But putting out her hand to touch it Barbie felt that she was encroaching upon one of the many parts of Mabel's hidden history. She drew her hand back.

'No, do take it out,' Mabel protested. 'It's beautiful lace. My first husband's mother gave it to me for when we had children, but we never did. There's a full length of it still unmade up. Enough for a shawl. Aziz, show Barbie Mem the piece.'

Aziz reached into the press and lifted out another

tissue-wrapped package. He opened it and unravelled the lace as the durzi unravelled bolts of cloth. The lace cascaded across his and Barbie's knees. The butterflies hovered, settled, rose, settled again. Some of their wings were folded, others only partly folded. Some displayed the full spread.

'It's exquisite,' Barbie said. She hardly dared touch it. 'So delicate and alive.'

'It's rather remarkable when you realize that the old woman who made it was blind.'

'Blind!'

'Not from birth. But for many years. She sat in a room in the top of a tower of an old French château that belonged to my mother-in-law's family. She called the butterflies her prisoners.'

Barbie put both hands under the lace and raised them. The butterflies quivered as in a taut web. They were part of the web.

'Yes,' she said. 'They are caught, aren't they? How carefully you've looked after it.'

'Aziz sees to that. Would you like that piece?'

Barbie let the lace free. 'It's very kind of you,' she said, 'but it's much too beautiful. I wouldn't know what to use it for. And besides it's precious and it's family.' She thought of the wedding and its possible consequences. 'And now it may come in.'

'What?'

'If Susan and Teddie have children.'

'There's Sarah's dress already made up and there if wanted. Are you sure?'

'Quite sure. But thank you very much for the offer.'

Mrs John Layton, the card began, Miss Sarah Layton and Mrs Edward Bingham, request the pleasure of your company at the Officers' Mess, The Pankot Rifles. The date was for two weeks ahead, the time midday. On the bottom right-hand side it said Buffet Luncheon and on the left RSVP. Two cards were delivered to Rose Cottage.

In the envelope containing Barbie's there was a note from Susan. 'Dear Barbie,' she had written, 'thank you so much for the beautiful set of Apostle teaspoons. I'm writing to Teddie who I know would wish me to say thank you on his behalf as well. I heard from him a few days ago and he says he is very fit but of course working very hard. Mummy and I have decided that she should give a little party here to make up for having to have the wedding in Mirat and that it would be a good idea to have it on my twenty-first. A lot of our wedding presents were to cover both occasions. I do hope that you and Aunty Mabel will both be able to come. Mummy says it's years since Aunty Mabel visited the Mess and a lot of the young officers who have heard of her but never met her are dying to because really she is quite famous, not just because of Daddy but because of all the silver her first husband presented and which is used on special occasions. We shall have the wedding presents displayed, by the way, and your spoons will look awfully nice in their blue-lined box. With Love, Susan.'

'I expect you'd like to go, Barbie,' Mabel said.

'Only if you do.'

'Well I shall have to but I'd want to come away before they start eating. I can't bear eating standing up or eating in crowds. But Mildred knows that. She won't mind. If I put in an appearance that's all anybody will want, but you stay on and have a good tuck in.'

'Eating in crowds gives me indigestion too. We'll go and come back together. We'll arrange to slip away.'

I shall have the heliotrope, she decided. When I look in the mirror and see my grey hair I know I can carry the heliotrope.

She went down to the bazaar towards evening which was the time she liked best, especially in November when it was quite cold and there were braziers and early lanterns and the smell of charcoal and incense. She stood at the entrance to the durzi's shop. A chokra beckoned her in, dusted a chair and invited her to sit and then went through the curtain which presently parted again to admit the old man and the chokra who was carrying the bolt of purple cloth.

'Ah, so you know what I've come for,' she said. He unravelled three or four yards and held it up. She gazed at it, testing for the edge of an old uncertainty and found it gone. 'The name heliotrope,' she said, 'comes from the Greek words helios, meaning sun, and trepo meaning turn. Heliotropion. A plant that turns its flowers to the sun.'

'Memsahib has decided?'

'Yes. And you have my measurements. The usual style, the skirt straight, box pleat at the back, the coat with pockets on my hips, deep enough and roomy enough for me to stick my hands in. As in the last suit, the grey one. I leave the choice of lining to you, it is always perfectly matched. When shall I come for the fitting?'

The fitting was a formality. Year by year his scissors and needle were wielded with precision, year by year she gained, lost, nothing in weight nor changed shape in any way. He had only to refer to his figures that were filed away either in a drawer or in his mind under the name Bachlev, Baba; the holy woman from the missions. The fitting was arranged for one week from that evening and the finished garment promised for delivery the morning of the day before the party. He gave her a snipping of the cloth. She put it in her handbag. It would be useful if she wanted to match up shoes, gloves and handbag, or to consider the tones of the blouse to go with it or of one of her sprays of velvet flowers for the lapel.

'How nice you look, Barbie,' Mabel had said. 'What a happy colour,' and had seemed almost eager to be off; but halfway down Club road she had suddenly turned as if she had changed her mind and would tell the tonga-wallah to take them back. In the lapel of the Bond Street costume a small diamond brooch glittered, a miniature of the Pankot Rifles badge. She wore no other jewellery. The brooch had been a gift from her first husband, who died on the Khyber. Her face was shaded by a grey felt hat with a wide brim. In place of a ribbon a fawn chiffon scarf was tied round the base of the crown. The free ends hung behind to shade her neck. Her legs, too often hidden by shabby gardening trousers, were still slim and well-shaped. Seated, the shortened skirt revealed them to the knee; to just below it when she stood. Fawn gloves covered the work-roughened hands.

We could go to Ranpur, Barbie had said the night before. To do some Christmas shopping. 'Oh, I shall never go to Ranpur again,' Mabel replied, 'at least not until I'm buried,' which had seemed to Barbie an odd sort of thing to say until she remembered that her friend's second husband was buried there, in the churchyard of St Luke's; and the way she now twisted round as if to tell the tonga-wallah to go back seemed like a momentary confusion, as if what was uppermost in her mind was the idea of going to Ranpur for that macabre purpose and the understanding that the time hadn't yet come and that the journey downhill must be cancelled, or anyway postponed. And then her eye had been reattracted by Barbie's heliotrope costume and the real object of the journey had again become clear. So that she resumed her position and watched the road unravel beneath her feet, and said nothing, but listened, or did not listen, while Barbie talked –

– or talked and was silent. God, she felt, had waited a long time for her to see that she could ignore the burden of her words which mounted one upon the other until they toppled, only to be set up again, and again, weighting her shoulders; a long time for her consciously to enter the private realm of inner silence and begin to learn how to inhabit it even while her body went its customary bustling way and her tongue clacked endlessly on: as at present, keeping time with the clack of the horse's hooves as the equipage, avoiding the bazaar, dropped down through Cantonment Approach road, making for the military lines.

'We're late,' she heard herself exclaim. In the world where she talked, where everybody talked, time was of peculiar importance. In Rifle Range road there were no other vehicles. They passed the end of grace and favour lane and in a moment or two turned left into Mess road. The geometrically laid out huts showed black against the green and the green itself was sparse, trodden. Distantly, in groups, sepoys drilled. A board painted in Pankot Rifles colours and with a huge gilt and coloured replica of the badge marked their destination. They turned at right-angles, crossing a culvert into a compound, approached the long square-pillared portico, and drove into it. When the tonga stopped Barbie could hear the uneven drone of voices inside. Servants stood at the entrance, dressed in white tunics and floppy white trousers. The ribbons in their pugrees, and their broad cummerbunds, were woven in horizontal stripes of the regimental colours. One of the servants, tall and thickly built, elderly, moved forward and saluted and stood offering his arm to Mabel.

'Memsahib!' he said.

Mabel had automatically put her hand on his wrist but the note of urgency in his voice arrested her. Her body seemed to stiffen with uncertainty or alarm. The servant spoke again and Barbie listened carefully so that she could tell Mabel louder and in English what he was saying.

'He says he wonders if you remember him now that he's old and has a beard.'

'What?'

Barbie repeated it but was not sure Mabel understood. She was looking down at the man, her hand still gripping his wrist.

'Is it Ghulam?' she asked at last. 'Ghulam Mohammed?'

The old man nodded and for a while they stared at each other. Then he turned his wrist over so that his palm touched hers.

'You are well, Ghulam Mohammed?' she asked in Urdu.

'I am well. Is it so with you?'

'It is so.'

'God is good.'

'Praise God. Ghulam, this is my friend, Miss Batchelor.'

'Memsahib.'

'Now we must go in,' Mabel said in English. He made his arm into a crook and helped them down, and then up a shallow flight of steps into the dark interior.

'Thank you,' Mabel said, and added – as if to impress the name on a memory she could not trust – 'Ghulam Mohammed.'

The hall was pillared. The voices came from a room on the left whose double doors were open. Barbie could see Mildred in a flowery hat, Colonel and Mrs Trehearne, and Susan looking younger than twenty-one talking to Kevin Coley, the depot adjutant who had lost his wife in the Quetta earthquake, was now the oldest captain in the regiment and said to be content to remain so. Barbie always thought he had a face like a medieval martyr; one of the unimportant ones who went to the stake in job lots.

And then, as they approached the doors, there was a change of rhythm in the voices, a slowing down, and a quietening; what Barbie recalled ever afterwards as a hush which spread back through the room and brought people's heads round to watch Mabel's arrival, her return after a long inexplicable absence to the place she had first entered longer ago than anyone else present, which meant that her presence now had a mystical significance. In her there surely reposed the original spirit of the hard condition, the spirit that belonged to the days of certainty, self-assurance, total conviction?

With several paces yet to go Mabel hesitated as if she would draw back and suddenly Barbie wished that they both could. But – 'It is very crowded,' Mabel said and then moved forward indomitably as Mildred came out to receive her. The brims of their hats forced distance on their embrace, but Mildred looked genuinely pleased and even grateful to Barbie whose trembling hand was taken in a gesture that implied there was greater affection than the social circumstances allowed Mildred to show. 'You both made it,' she said. 'How nice. Mabel, there are some young boys who are dying to meet you but scared stiff so go easy on them for God's sake. There's one called Dicky Beauvais whose uncle was a subaltern under Bob Buckland. I know he's particularly hoping for a word.'

'Hello, Aunty,' Susan said. 'It's so nice of you to come and thank you for the marvellous present.' She kissed her aunt and then surprisingly kissed Barbie too and said, 'What a nice colour,' and led them into the still hushed assembly where the distance between Barbie and Mabel began subtly to lengthen because the Trehearnes interposed themselves and guided Mabel gradually towards the Rankins while the Peplows claimed Barbie as their own. Mabel looked over her shoulder and Barbie felt herself forced away from the centre to the periphery. I never understood, Mrs Stewart was saying, your sudden interest in Emerson. I do not wish to talk about Emerson or indeed about anything, Barbie said, but only from inside that area of privacy and silence. Her voice was saying something quite different. Is Sarah here? she was asking Clarissa. She wasn't at the door unless I missed her, how awful if I did. No I have not met Mrs Jason, how do you do?

There were glimpses to be had of the felt hat and the chiffon scarf. They formed a point of reference. Her eye continually sought it. The room, dark-panelled and Persian carpeted, was uncomfortably warm and close. Half-lowered tattis on the porticoed verandah kept out the glare. A bearer offered a tray and she took a glass of sherry to occupy her hands. She had not reckoned with this separation and it occurred to her that it had been engineered, arranged beforehand by Mildred with the innocent connivance of Clarissa Peplow who seemed to have assumed the duty of making sure that Barbie was kept entertained, refreshed, introduced and out of certain people's way. She began to be afraid that when the time came for her to help Mabel slip away she would be unable to find her, which was ridiculous since there was only this one room in use and the verandah on the other side of the long buffet table, where the windows were open, letting in some fresh air. She looked for but could not see the display of wedding presents. Neither, now, could she see the hat with the chiffon scarf. The room frightened her.

'What a nice suit, Barbie.'

It was Sarah. Barbie clasped her hand. 'Is she all right do you think, in this crowd? I feel I ought to be with her but there are so many claims on her attention.'

'They've got her a chair,' Sarah said. 'Over in the corner there. You can't see her from here but she's all right.'

'We're slipping away, you know, before the buffet.'

'Yes, I know. Barbie, you know Tony Bishop, don't you. He's been posted to Bombay. Isn't he lucky'

'We met once at Rose Cottage but you may not remember me from among all those young people.' She offered her hand to the ill-looking man who had been Teddie Bingham's friend. 'Are you quite recovered from the jaundice?'

'Thank you, yes.'

'It is so debilitating, well so I gather, never having had

it, only heard. I've always enjoyed excessive good health which I suppose is rather indecent, a sign of diminished sensibility perhaps, a certain coarseness of constitution no doubt inherited from my father whose life was terminated by the wheels of a hansom cab or bus on the Embankment I forget which in fact I was never quite sure but everyone expected him to go from cirrhosis of the liver which given the same intake any ordinary man would have contracted. Did you change your mind, Sarah, I mean about the presents? Susan told me they'd be on display but perhaps it proved too difficult, I mean they'd need guarding wouldn't they?'

But the presents were on display on the verandah, guarded by a naik and two sepoys who stood stiffly in the at ease position not catching the eye of any guest because it was not the guests of whom they had to entertain suspicion but intruders or contractor's servants coming too near the sparkling array of cutlery, glass, tea and coffee sets, trays, table-lamps, vases and carved boxes. A kind of queue had formed, as for the rite of passing by a bier Barbie thought when fifteen minutes later she accompanied the Peplows and Mrs Stewart to inspect the remains of the wedding. The verandah was crowded too.

Trees partially screened the view across to the grace and favour bungalow which Barbie had never been inside because she had always declined Sarah's invitation to go in when – as they sometimes did – they shared a tonga from the bazaar and Barbie went out of her way to bring Sarah home. She thought she could hear Panther barking. There were cries from the parade ground. But the verandah of the mess seemed to lack conditions in which an echo could exist. Voices, sounds, had a brazen hollow quality. 'Wavell's the first Viceroy we've had who knows anything about the country and then of course he's a soldier,' someone told her but when she glanced round the speaker's face was not turned to her but to another man and she

227

did not know either of them. When they reached the loaded table she could not see the spoons.

'Absolutely splendid, I agree,' she said, taking Clarissa up, 'A splendid display.'

After a while she abandoned her feverish attempts to find the spoons and carefully, slowly, quartered the table from edge to edge and from front to back. She longed but did not dare to ask Clarissa, 'Do you see my little Apostle spoons anywhere?' She wondered if she had a wrong impression of what they looked like in their box and looked twice at pastry forks and for any box whose lid was not open; stooped to see whether they were placed where the eye could not fall on them easily from a standing position. 'Excuse me,' someone said, and straightening quickly to let a woman pass behind her had to steady herself with a hand placed too quickly and heavily on the table so that for an instant she feared being the cause of a shameful and unforgivable incident. 'Oh, Barbie, be careful,' Clarissa said. 'I think we'd better stand back.' 'It wasn't my fault,' she said and then came away to be out of danger and free of the risk of other people's anger.

It was humiliating to think it might be realized what she had been looking for. But the spoons were not displayed and that was humiliation enough and one from which she could not retreat. The line of escape from the toppling towers of her words was blocked. 'There's such a crush,' she said, 'and I've forgotten how to cope with crowds. Also I can't hear myself think, not that I suppose you imagine I ever can.' She grinned at Clarissa who was looking worried. With such a look Clarissa would observe the good Samaritan at his work.

'Do you know,' Barbie went on, 'I have never been in a Mess before. I mean Mess with a capital M. Isn't that odd, or don't you think so? I suppose the room in there is the anteroom, is that the correct nomenclature? Where the officers forgather before going in to dine and toast the King-Emperor and throw their glasses into the hearth, or does that only happen in kinematograph pictures?'

Oh, and I could throw my glass into a hearth, she said (but saying something else to Clarissa and so finding her way back into that blessed privacy where words actually spoken didn't matter) – dash it into a thousand sharp fragments, so that the sound would attract attention and He would say, What troubles you? What is your name? When did we last talk? Because it is to be talked to that I want above anything. I want to create around myself a condition of silence so that it may be broken, but not by me. But I am surrounded by a condition of Babel. To this, all my life, I have contributed enough for a dozen people. And He stops His ears and leaves us to get on with it.

She moved, prompted by Clarissa's charitable hand and Christian heart to re-enter the maelstrom and was granted a curious vision, fortuitous and short-lived. By chance, and people's movements, a clear channel was opened and she saw at the end of it the felt hat and the chiffon scarf and Mabel seated on the leather armchair, enthroned thus, and young men arrested in postures of deference and inquiry, one – an Indian – leaning forward while Mabel's hand was raised to her deaf ear and then folded again with the other on her quiet lap, and young men's smiles which were not as fully understanding as hers but ready to acclaim some imminent discovery; of what, only they could tell. Barbie could no longer see them because the vision was shut off again by barriers of fleshy faces, arms, bosoms, chins and epaulettes; the bark and chirrup of the human voice manufacturing the words which created the illusion of intelligent existence.

Behind this mass of people Mabel also presumably continued to exist but she would have liked proof of it and contemplated forcing a passage, gathering her friend in possessive and protective arms.

'Are you all right?' Sarah asked, reappearing. 'Can we get you another drink? Have you met Captain Beauvais? Dicky, this is Miss Batchelor, Aunty Mabel's companion.'

'I suppose companion is the right word. How do you do? I see you're Pankot Rifles too.' Captain Beauvais

229

looked very young to be a captain. He had a shiny pink skin and a little fair moustache and the enthusiastic expression of mediocrity which Barbie had learned to recognize from years of looking in a mirror. 'Have you met Mabel yet? You *are* the one Mildred mentioned who hoped to speak to her because of someone called Bob Buckland?'

'Yes, that's right, and I have,' Captain Beauvais said. 'Was it sherry?' He detained the bare-foot bearer. 'His feet,' Barbie said, 'in this crush!' And received a fresh glass which she sipped from immediately. 'Do you know Muzzafirabad?' she asked. 'I was there centuries ago but of course there's no reason why you should because you're not a Muzzy.'

'Well actually I do. Are you connected?'

'Not with the Muzzys. I was Mission not Army. Are you on Dick Rankin's staff or with the regiment?'

'I was with the regiment but Area collared me to take Teddie Bingham's place.'

'But you know Muzzafirabad. I expect it's changed. Teddie knew it but we seemed to be talking about two different places. I was Bishop Barnard, but only the infant school. A mere shack. Well, very small. The children came mainly for the chappattis. There was so much hunger. And disease of course, the two go hand in hand. And still do. One is appalled, appalled and thinks – well, can nothing ever be done, is it truly a hopeless task? The love of God can't fill an empty belly and when it's full one seldom thinks to thank Him.'

'We accept some pretty skinny fellows nowadays, but they soon fill out.' His eyes snatched at avenues of escape. 'Talking about food, I think there's some beginning to come in. May I get you something?'

'That's very kind but we're slipping away before the buffet.'

She retreated, backing away from Captain Beauvais, slightly spilling her sherry. She begged someone's pardon, put the sherry down and turned, found the crowd moving

230

inexorably forward, pressing her back towards the table on to which salvers and tureens were being placed by the contractor's scruffy servants who were coming in from the verandah in what looked like dozens. Excuse me, she said, but I must get to Mrs Layton senior. Excuse me. I do so beg your pardon. Retreating from the crowd, from the cold consommé, the pâté, the chicken and turkey and ham, the salmon mayonnaise and Beauvais's skinny recruits with the army beef already thickening their stick-thin arms and legs, and from the nameless little girl; the unknown Indian. To find Mabel. Who had retreated from all these things long ago as if she knew the whole affair was doomed and hopeless.

The channel was open and she broke through into it and saw the chair, empty, abandoned. She looked round but there was no sign of the felt hat with the chiffon scarf flowing from it. Nearby on a leather sofa two young Indian women sat in their best sarees smiling into the middle-distance, waiting for their husbands to resume responsibility.

'Have you seen Mrs Layton, Mrs Layton senior?' she asked one of them.

'Oh, no.'

'The lady in the grey hat and scarf who was sitting in the chair.'

'Oh, no. She went I think.'

She cannot have gone, Barbie said, unless she was never here and it is all a dream; and pressed into the crowd again trying to make her way back to the place she had been standing in before in case Mabel had noted it and gone there to find her and tell her it was time. Perhaps she had made for the verandah to find her and see the presents. She would not have left by herself.

She was not on the verandah.

Having walked its length Barbie re-entered the anteroom through the open door used by the contractor's servants. From here she had a clear view of the still empty chair.

She moved through the narrow passage between the straight line of the wall and the uneven line of backs and elbows. The noise was deafening. She looked for a familiar face but on this side of the room there seemed to be none familiar enough. The mouths in the faces had forks going into them. She marvelled that there should be such a volume of conversation. She became hungry both for food and chat and mercy and felt faint and then a bit sick, put her hand out to steady herself and saw that her hand rested on a door. At waist level there was a brass knob that looked gaunt. She grasped it, turned and thrust. The door was very heavy. Passing through the opening she pushed it to behind her and was surprised to find it lighter in the closing than the opening. It banged.

The sound echoed down the long corridor in which she now stood. When it died away there was a profound silence. The noise of the party was miraculously shut out. A door at the other end seemed a great distance away, as far, as unattainable as the landing at the top of the frightening stairs in the gloomy little house in Camberwell. She considered the grace which levitation would bestow but setting out on her journey in search of Mabel found herself denied it, as earthbound as ever. The corridor was filled with aqueous light from the murky fanlight windows whose long cords were looped on their hooks with military precision, their free ends hanging at what looked like equal measured lengths. Between the cords were mounted trophies. Ranged along the opposite wall stood heavy marble busts, rock-firm on stout tapering plinths. Through these she must walk the gauntlet, dare the waxen and sightless faces of Mabel's forbears, the tusks and glaring eyes of their guardian beasts: the hunters and the hunted, now voiceless and immobile but met in a permanent conjoint task of terrorism of strangers and intruders.

The floor was tiled in lozenges of black and white but down its centre lay a Persian runner which smothered the sound of footsteps. She paused in the centre of one of the blue and crimson medallion designs. A few paces ahead, on her left, there was a wide arched recess with a pair of mahogany doors set in it. One of them was half open. She was still some distance from the closed door at the end of the corridor. The closed door had a look of Mabel not being in the room it led into. The half open door on the other hand suggested her recent passage through it. She strode the last few paces, pushed the door further open and entered.

Immense. Shadowed. A long room, the length of the corridor but higher. The main windows were shuttered. Again light entered only through the fanlight windows. In the centre of the room a vast mahogany table reflected two great epergnes that floated on the dark unrippled surface like silver boats on a glassy midnight lake. On opposite banks chairs, awaiting occupants, were placed arm to arm in close formation. The walls were panelled in dark-stained wood to the height of the tall shuttered french doors. Above this level they were whitewashed. Fixed to them as thickly as butterflies to a naturalist's display board were flags, some worn as thin as mummys' rags; standards and heraldically disposed weapons of war: swords, sabres, lances, muskets. Between the window were sideboards and dumbwaiters heavy with plate. At both ends of the room were monumental fireplaces and above them gilt-framed battle landscapes. Against the wall on the corridor side of the room there were three glass-fronted display cabinets. The light slanting down through the fanlights was reflected back by the silver contained in them. In front of the furthest cabinet stood Mabel.

Barbie opened her mouth to speak but did not. Mabel stood in front of the cabinet like someone in the presence of a reliquary. She had become untouchable, unapproachable, protected by the intense and chilling dignity of the room in which (Barbie felt) some kind of absolute certainty had been reached long ago and was now enshrined so perfectly and implacably that it demanded nothing that

233

was not a whole and unquestioning acceptance of the truth on which it was based.

Still unaware of Barbie's presence Mabel turned and went to the nearer fireplace, stood and gazed up at the dark picture in which Barbie could make out a white horse with a dim uniformed figure declamatorily astride against a backdrop of clouds and cannon puffs. Like the representation of the crucifixion above an altar the picture held the room in silent celebration of the mystery of its governing genius.

I have lost her, Barbie thought. Mabel had not wanted to come but having done so she had been unable to resist the impulse to enter the inner sanctuary of the world from which she had cut herself off and, having entered, the associations had proved too powerful. Yes, I have lost her, Barbie repeated, but come to that I have never really found her.

Mabel turned round and Barbie wondered if she had spoken her thoughts aloud. Nervously she touched her cheek with her gloved hand. For a moment neither of them said anything but faced each other across the length of the inhospitable table until Barbie had the distressing impression that Mabel's first words would be accusing and dismissive.

'Is it time for us to go, Barbie?'

She nodded. If she spoke she guessed she would not be able to stop and it seemed imperative for their future that she should hold her tongue in this place.

'I'm sorry if I've worried you, wondering where I'd got to,' Mabel said. For a few seconds more she surveyed the table, the walls, the cabinets of silver, then she walked towards Barbie and when she reached her grasped her wrist as she had grasped the bearded old servant's.

'We can go out the back way through the cloakroom at the end of the corridor. If you're ready.'

'Oh, yes,' Barbie said. 'I'm quite ready.' She turned her hand round so that her palm was pressed encouragingly in her friend's. But Mabel stood immovable. Suddenly she said:

'I thought there might be some changes, but there aren't. It's all exactly as it was when I first saw it more than forty years ago. I can't even be angry. But someone ought to be.'

Barbie unhooked the dangerous spectacles and placed them near the table-lamp. She settled the pillows, adjusted the tops of the sheet and blankets so that her friend's hands were covered. And then sat for the customary ten minutes before turning the light off. In the morning at breakfast Mabel would not say : It's very strange, I went to sleep over my book but woke in the morning without book or spectacles, is it Aziz or you who tucks me up? Barbie knew she would say nothing because she had said nothing on all the previous occasions.

Tonight there was no muttering, not even a movement of lips. Barbie stood up, switched off the light and waited until she was sure that Mabel still slept. Back in her own room she approached the penitential area of the rush mat but found herself reluctant to attempt communication through that medium. I shall have an imaginary silence, she said; and sat at the writing-table, opened Emerson – her own copy, bought to replace the borrowed one – and proceeded to read aloud to the class from his essay on self-reliance.

'Society is a wave. The wave moves onward, but the water of which it is composed does not. The same particle does not rise from the valley to the ridge. Its unity is only phenomenal. The persons who make up a nation today, next year die, and their experience with them.'

And some are buried here (she thought, as her voice droned on through the essay and then off into inaudibility as her imaginary silence took hold) – some are buried here in the churchyard of St John's and some in the churchyard of St Luke's in Ranpur, as Mabel's second husband was, the one who was not a soldier and died of disease not wounds. By his side it is her eventual wish to rest because she says I shall never go to Ranpur again until I'm buried.

But who were Bob Buckland, Ghulam Mohammed and Gillian Waller?

A voice replied: Does it matter?

She clutched her throat in alarm. The voice had spoken so clearly. It was not her own voice. Her own voice was still droning on through the words of Emerson. Scared, she tuned back into it. 'In the will work and acquire, and thou hast chained the wheel of Chance, and shall always drag her after thee. A political victory, a rise of rents, the recovering of your sick, or the return of your absent friend, or some other quite external event, raises your spirits, and you think good days are preparing for you. Do not believe it. It can never be so. Nothing can bring you peace but yourself. Nothing can bring you peace but the triumph of principles.'

She cried out involuntarily, stood up, pushing back the chair. She went towards the mat and then began to tremble because she could not quite reach it and in any case her knees would not bend. She seemed fixed in this proud and arrogant position. Her jaws were locked too, her mouth still open as if to allow the cry to come back in. She could not remember what her principles were.

A few weeks later Mildred announced that Susan was going to have a baby and that Sarah, who had put in an application for posting to a forward area, had dutifully withdrawn it.

4

Romeo, if dead, should be cut up into little stars to make the heavens fine.

(Emerson's essay on Love)

Nowadays she communicated with the world outside Rose Cottage by writing letters to Helen Jolley. She had never known Miss Jolley intimately. There was the right amount of uncluttered distance between them. Miss Jolley had sent only one reply and Barbie did not expect to hear from her again so had ceased to post her own letters or write them on notepaper. She wrote them in old exercise books taken from the trunk of missionary relics. Many of these were only partly filled and had a useful number of blank pages in them. There was a considerable saving in the cost of stamps and stationery; and an ease of reference back.

24 December 1943

My Dear Miss Jolley,

On this special night you would do well to pause in your administration of the Bishop Barnard and ask yourself as I do what gifts our mission had brought to the children of India, and if – among them – has ever been the gift of love. I do not mean pity, I do not mean compassion, I do not mean instruction nor do I mean devotion to the interests either of the child or the institution. Love is what I mean. Without that gift I doubt that any can be, could have been, brought to Jesus. After many years of believing I knew what love is I now suspect I do not which means I do not know and have never known what God is either. Do you? Do not be deceived by my self-assured expression. Reject the evidence of my confident stride. Shut your ears to my chatter. They are all illusory. I question my existence, my right to it. This is not I trust despair. While you are about it by the way (prayer I mean, if indeed you submit to that discipline busy as you are with so many other things) you might pray for the soul of Edwina Crane. My own prayers are not guaranteed reception. Her need though is greater at the moment than mine or yours. On this night, especially. Most sincerely, BB.

8 March 1944

Dear Helen,

It is all right. About Edwina. Let me describe it to you while the detail is fresh in my mind. Ever since the news of

237

the enemy's invasion of Indian soil we have been alert. This morning when I rose I knew that something of vital importance to our safety had happened. I called Aziz but got no answer. I knocked at Mabel's door and went in expecting to find her still in bed because it was early. Her bed had been slept in but was empty. I searched. She was nowhere to be found. She and Aziz had gone. The servants' quarters were abandoned. It didn't take me long to work it out that everyone was making for the railway station and that a place would have been reserved for me on the train alongside Mabel. In fact I remembered that this had been carefully planned beforehand in the event of Pankot falling in danger of enemy attack.

I packed a few things, closed and bolted all the doors, windows and shutters, and let myself out. Imagine my relief when I saw a tonga waiting. The wallah flourished his whip and warned me to step on it. I thought, 'I may step on it but can the horse?' It looked more like an ass than a horse but I thought it would embarrass the driver to have this pointed out. 'You'd better jump in,' he said, 'because they're coming and everyone's gone ahead to catch the last train out.'

I stopped trusting him. He observed my hesitation and in a different tone of voice said, 'What are you waiting for, Barbie? You'd better buck up.' It was Mr Maybrick in disguise. He had piles of his organ music tied up in untidy bundles in the back. I scrambled in, made room for myself. Off we started. The horse wasn't lame as I'd feared. We made excellent progress. I felt elated, as in those days when my father took me on a spree and I had to hold my hat on. (It had a wide brim with artificial flowers Mother made out of coloured scraps of velvet.) As we bowled down the hill past the golf-course I thought there were people there all wearing hats like this but then realized they were holding up umbrellas, coloured ones, made of paper. Mr Maybrick told me they were fifth columnists and that the golf-course was the rendezvous. We were in danger of being cut off and there was no time to catch the train. We would have to seek refuge in St John's Church.

It was at this stage that everything became weird. You say I dreamt. But what is a dream? Everything 'happens' in the mind whatever the source of the event. Now four-in-hand, first Mr Maybrick and then I whipped the horses down Club Road making for the haven of the church. My short grey hair flew black and long and I was filled with joyful longings and expectations. I was not myself.

I felt capable of dealing with every eventuality, calm in anticipation of the Lord's help. We arrived at the site of St John's but a change had come about. It was not the churchyard which I and Mr Maybrick (now back in his ordinary clothes but with a dogcollar like Mr Cleghorn) were standing in but the compound of the mission school in Muzzafirabad. My servant Francis was calling the children to school by tolling the bell. He tolled it eleven times. We had a view across the golf-course. The number of paper umbrellas had increased and the fifth columnists had now been joined by the Japanese. We could see their yellow faces and the guns they carried in place of golf-bags. Mr Maybrick also had a gun. He looked at me and said, We must save a last bullet each. I did not believe such a terrible step would be necessary. When I looked again I did not see the enemy but troops of children marching to their lessons. I called out, wishing to hurry but not to frighten them. Francis whispered to me that the danger had not passed. I was afraid his expression would show how desperate he felt so I smiled and said to each group of children as they passed through the school doorway, 'It's quite safe now.'

At last all the children were inside. Mr Maybrick and I went to join them. And then I was Edwina no more but myself and the schoolroom was the church after all and I was alone. Mr Maybrick was at the organ playing. The church was otherwise empty, still, safe, happy. I knelt in a pew to give thanks for our deliverance and as I did so the most benign thought entered my mind. A voice said to me: I'm all right now. I knew it was Edwina. She wanted me to know that God had forgiven her that mortal sin and received her into His everlasting peace and mercy.

This was a form of communication, wasn't it? From Him, about Edwina. Which means I am not abandoned, although I think that now Edwina has gone from me in this life forever I am not unlonely. But this is a loneliness I can support.

28 April 1944

Dear Helen,

Do as I have done. Go to the window when it is dark and look at the night sky and ask yourself this question: Are the heavens finer than they were?

Teddie Bingham is dead, killed in action. The house still rings with Susan's single cry of anguish and on the edge of my bed remains the imprint of her body where she sat afterwards in stony silence, cut off from all human correspondence. My poor Susan. Heavy with child. Weighed down by her loss. Scarcely more than a child herself. In front of the other women here I couldn't restrain my tears.

I shed tears at my father's death. I felt he had died through some fault of mine. I was so plain and gawky and not clever in the ways a little girl is meant to be. Over the seams I sewed, for instance, my mother pursed her lips, and blacking his boots I fumbled so badly his socks became smeared and he said, Heavens, child! but the Heavens were not open to receive me and shield me from his forgiveness. His funeral as is the custom among the London poor was more splendid than his life. So many flowers! A crowded church. Men I had never seen in the house, stiff in black and with the formality of respect for a life gayer than it should have been but now gone and leaving wisps of secret masculine camaraderie behind it that had no business either in our family or the house of God. And there was one young woman, in passing whom

240

on our way out my Mother sparked with ebony lights and an electric stiffness in that corset which made her waist a tower of strength but not particularly of affection.

At home in the midst of ham and stout she placed her hand warningly under her heart and thus announced the approaching years of her martyrdom and her patient claim on my body, soul and memories, and I was aware of the peculiar poetry and diversity of life and its intricate loyalties which left me bereft and determined to arrive at a source, as it were at a conclusion, which the mirror announced in advance of the event. God, anyway, would have me; therefore I yearned for Him. But was it He who answered?

I look at the night sky where Teddie is scattered and am awestruck at this kind of immensity. Unthinkable distances. Surely no prayer can cross them. I am humble in the face of such sublime power. But in the next instant I try to imagine what existed before it was created. I try to imagine no universe. Nothing, nothing. Try to imagine that. In all that terrifying blackness try to imagine no blackness, nothing, not even vacuum, but nothing. Nothing even as a thought. Space deprived of space in which to exist. Draw in the billions of light years of space and stars and darkness, compress and compress until all existence, all space, all void is the size of a speck of dust.

And then blow it out.

The mind cannot conceive of this situation. The mind demands that there be something and therefore something before something. Is the Universe an unprincipled design? Does God weep somewhere beyond it crying to its prisoners to free themselves and come to Him? If it is all explained by chemistry, that chemistry is majestic. It can only lead to the most magnificent explosion, to which God will harken while we burn and disintegrate and scatter into pieces.

I am worried about Mabel. She talked once not about God but about the gods as though some kind of committee were sitting, one before which she had become weary of giving evidence. At night she falls asleep over her book with her spectacles on her nose at a dangerous angle. I have nightmares in which I see her turn into the pillow, crushing and splintering the lenses, cutting herself, bleeding slowly from closed eyelids so that she appears to be crying blood. She waits with Spartan fortitude for her life to run its course. Her days are spent in celebration of the natural cycle of seed, growth, flower, decay, seed.

One day she said to me, 'No flower is quite like another of the same species. On a single bush one is constantly surprised by the remarkable character shown by each individual rose. But from the house all one sees is a garden, which is all there is to it anyway in the long run.'

Perhaps that is how she sees the world. She puts her hand on my arm and I am imprisoned by her capacity to survive. A sentence of life, suffered with patience and forbearance and with small pleasures taken by the minute, not the hour. Is that tranquillity? She is not so tranquil in sleep. Bygone things press on her then.

The fighting in Manipur has been very fierce but it looks as if we shall drive them back, doesn't it? There will be no paper umbrellas on the Pankot golf-course. As Mabel said, everything will be just as it always was.

5 June 1944

My Dear Miss Jolley,

Shortly after the Memorial service that was held here for Captain Bingham a mysterious event took place. A name appeared in the visitors' book which is kept at the gate of Flagstaff House. The person signing gave no indication of her whereabouts in Pankot, contenting herself with the word Rawalpindi after her signature, as if to leave no room for doubt while withholding opportunity for contact. It was as though she wished to say: I am here in your midst, think about it.

But no stranger has appeared. No one has seen her or seen anyone who might be her. Yesterday evening I raised the question discreetly with Sarah, suggesting to her that

242

since they were so close to her in Kashmir they would recognize her; but Sarah said they would not. I did not think it a good idea to press her, to face her directly with the question whether in Srinagar she had visited the woman, spoken to her, seen the child.

Is the child here too? Unbaptized? You will know to whom I refer, whose signature it is that has appeared in the book. You will not know, none of us does, why she is in Pankot or where she is staying. Unless the signature was a practical joke, as has been suggested, she must be hidden away in the area of West Hill where there are summer residences that belong to rich Indians from Ranpur, an area which people from East Hill never visit. Her arrival and simultaneous disappearance serve to emphasize the stark division there is between our India and theirs. She has made herself one of them. The division is one of which I am ashamed. I have done nothing, nothing, to remove it, ever. My poor Edwina sat huddled by the roadside in the rain, holding that dead man's hand. That, I continually see, was significant. For me that image is like an old picture of the kind that were popular in the last century, which told stories and pointed moral lessons. I see the caption, 'Too Late.'

Sarah came to the cottage yesterday evening to say goodbye. She went to Ranpur today to catch tonight's Calcutta mail. Only for a short visit, but for a special reason, and for Susan's sake, to see and talk to Captain Merrick who is in hospital there, having been wounded – Susan believes badly – in the same action in which poor Teddie was killed. It seems in fact that he was with him on that occasion at the height of the fighting on the Imphal plain and performed some sort of heroic act whose object, although it failed, was to save Teddie. An officer from Teddie's division wrote to Susan and told her of Captain Merrick's bravery, since when she had had a letter from Captain Merrick himself, in hospital, but not in his handwriting. This weighs on Susan's mind. If ever she blamed him for the disturbing events that spoiled her wedding day she is determined to forgive and forget and in any case, as a soldier's daughter, sees it as her duty to extend the hand of gratitude to her dead husband's comrade. She has asked Sarah to ask him if he would stand as godfather to the child, when it is born.

For this I am thankful. In the past few weeks she has been, many of us feel, dangerously withdrawn, lying here on the verandah at the cottage day after day, as she used to before Teddie's death when her pregnancy curtailed her activities, but without that look of living inwardly. I heard a woman here, Lucy Smalley, say that poor Susan reminded her of the daughter of a woman called Poppy Browning, but she shut up when she saw I was in earshot; and tonight I asked Sarah who Poppy Browning was. She did not know. Nor does she know who Gillian Waller was, or is, for I was silly enough to ask that too and then had to explain, to expose myself as a stupid old woman who tucks another old woman up, one who mutters in her sleep.

A little while ago I mentioned to Susan the existence of the lace and when Sarah and I had done talking tonight she went in to Mabel and received that exquisite christening gown to take to her sister. The child is due next month. In Calcutta, Sarah is to stay with her Aunt Fenny and Uncle Arthur. They have moved from Delhi. He is now a Lieutenant-Colonel. I longed to go with her, to have a chance to see our old headquarters again and to see the wounded man, who perhaps knew Edwina. Will Sarah remember to ask him this time?

Yours,
Barbara Batchelor.

She scrawled the signature, closed the exercise book that had belonged to a little girl called Swaroop. She undressed, put on her gown and opened her door to listen and judge the state of affairs. It was past midnight. She crossed to Mabel's door, opened it silently and stood arrested. Mabel, propped against her pillows, must have watched the door opening.

'Can't you sleep either?' she said; and Barbie recalled the day nearly five years before when she had gone out to the verandah and found Mabel working there, the day she had expected to be told she must go when her holiday was over. Can't you sleep either? Mabel had said. I don't blame you. It's such a lovely day.

Mabel had already put her book aside and replaced her spectacles in their case, and Barbie felt pleased with her as she would have been pleased to find that a pupil had learned a difficult lesson well.

'Oh, I haven't tried yet,' she said. 'I've been writing letters, catching up, and time just slipped by. Can I get you anything?'

'No, thank you, Barbie. There's nothing I want. I'm not sleepy though. It's rather close, isn't it?'

'Just a bit.'

Mabel nodded, apparently glad to have her impression confirmed.

'It won't be long before the rains get here,' Mabel said. She glanced at the curtained windows as if through these an approaching rain might be discerned. 'Did I tell you it was raining the first time I came to India? I remember being very disappointed. I'd expected brilliant sunshine and it seemed such a long way to come just to get wet and see grey sky. But then I'd not experienced the heat. So I didn't appreciate the contrast.'

'It's not so marked up here.'

Barbie went further into the room and then to the bedside, checked the muslin-covered water jug even though she could see that the tumbler hadn't been used.

'Stay and talk to me,' Mabel said. The request was so unexpected that for a moment Barbie wondered whether Mabel was making fun of her. But her friend's face betrayed no irony.

'Talk? What about?'

'Anything. About when you were young. I always enjoy that.'

'Do you? Do you?'

She sat on the edge of the bed. She could not remember, now, ever being young. And then did. 'I was always a bit afraid of going upstairs to bed. So I hummed a song which I fear Mother disapproved. That is to say the first line of it. I don't mean she disapproved only of the first line and of course I don't mean hummed because you can't hum words, but I sang it under my breath over and over. And in the end I couldn't ever remember the rest of it and never have. Isn't that strange? I've seen a deal of gaiety throughout my noisy life.'

'Throughout what?'

'Throughout my noisy life.'

'Oh.' Mabel smiled. 'One of your father's comic songs.'

'He was passionately fond of the music hall. And often promised to take me but of course never did, he was afraid of what my mother would say if she found out and anyway he was always short of what he called the ready. There was the Christmas when he lost the presents for my stocking on the journey home. As white as a sheet when he came in at the door and very very late, but not drunk, that's what Mother said years later when she told me, when he was dead and she had forgiven him, and told me there wasn't any Father Christmas anyway. I never knew I once nearly didn't get a stocking. I don't remember a Christmas when there wasn't something in it. Mother said that when he came home and said: I've lost the stocking things, poor Barbie's stocking things: they set to and turned out drawers and cupboards looking for odds and ends for hours so as not to disappoint me and that I said it was the nicest stocking ever. But perhaps that's only how she remembered it. But it showed they loved me. I adored Christmas mornings. I always woke while it was still dark and worked my toes up and down to feel the stocking's weight and listen to the rustle and crackle. And then I'd sit up and sniff very cautiously to smell the magic, I mean of someone having been there who drove across frosty rooftops and had so many chimneys to attend to but never forgot mine.'

246

'Yes,' Mabel said. 'I remember that – the idea of a strange scene in the room, but I don't think I put the idea into words.'

'I don't suppose I did either. It's how I describe it now. As children we accept magic as a normal part of life. Everything seems rooted in it, everything conspires in magic terms.' She laughed. 'Even the quarrels in our house had the darkness of magic in them, they were strange and incomprehensible and threatening as magic often is. I expected to find toads hopping on the staircase and misshapen things falling out of cupboards.'

'Poor Barbie.'

'No! My life was never dull '

'Is it very dull now?'

'Now least of all.'

She had a sudden strong desire to lower herself gently and be taken into the older woman's arms and to lie there in peace and amity until they both fell asleep. She would be content then not to wake but to dream forever, enfolded, safe from harm; and for an instant it seemed to her that if she sought harbour in this way it would not be closed to her; that Mabel would accept her and go with her happily into this oblivion of cessation and fulfilment.

But Mabel slowly closed her eyes as if shutting that avenue of escape and said very quietly, 'I can sleep now thank you, Barbie,' and Barbie got up, smoothed the top of the sheet and was careful to make no disturbing contact with her friend's hands. She whispered, 'I'll deal with the light,' and when Mabel nodded reached for the ebony switch and turned it. She felt her way in the dark back into the hall and her own familiar room and circumstances.

A meditation. St John's Church. 4.30 P.M. 7 June 1944

i

You said: Stay and talk to me because I can't sleep. So I stayed and talked. I told you about the stairs and a

247

Christmas stocking and after a very short while you said: I can sleep now.

The next time I saw you was in the morning. You were on the verandah drinking a cup of tea and you apologized for having had breakfast without me. I never thought to ask Aziz what you had eaten. Perhaps he would not have told me because you'd already instructed him not to in case I said: That's no sort of breakfast. And began to fuss and bother. As it was I sat down and drank tea too and said nothing because I had noticed nothing.

This was yesterday. I must search for clues to moments when you may have been on the point of making an appeal like that of the night before. Stay. Talk to me. Those few moments on the verandah drinking tea were not one of them. When Aziz called me to breakfast you said nothing. You resumed reading a seed catalogue. But you were still there when I came back. I thought that you were absorbed, planning next year's garden.

I said: I'll do the accounts this morning. If you do the cheques after lunch I'll take them down to the bazaar and settle them on my way to Mr Maybrick's

I had to repeat it. But that wasn't unusual. In case you had forgotten I reminded you that I'd promised Mr Maybrick three days before to go to his bungalow for tea and mend his volume of Bach. You said: Oh I thought that was tomorrow. So I said: No, it was fixed for today, the sixth of June.

Is that the date? you said. And looked towards this year's garden.

I went inside and sat at your bureau and began the accounts for May. After a while I heard you stirring and saw you through the window putting on your straw hat and going out into the sunshine with the pannier. At eleven Mildred came with Susan and shortly afterwards Mrs Fosdick and Mrs Paynton arrived. Aziz was worried. He said to me: Memsahib said nothing about lunch for so many. I assured him that only Susan was staying for lunch, that presently Mildred and the others would go down to

248

the club and be there all day playing bridge, and that Mildred would return at about six o'clock to take Susan home.

He said: Memsahib, when will *you* be back?

I thought of the volume of Bach and of the difficulty I always had persuading Mr Maybrick to let me get on. Perhaps seven o'clock, I said. Or seven-thirty. But certainly by eight, in time for dinner.

When the others had gone I went out to where Susan lay. Her smock was taut over her swollen stomach. I said: Did you like the christening gown? She said: yes, it was beautiful. So I told her the story of the blind woman who made the lace, of how she called the butterflies her prisoners. After a while Susan said: I like things that have stories to them, somehow it makes them seem more real: and then closed her eyes to show that she wanted me to go away. I returned to the bureau and finished the accounts. I made out the cheques so that all you had to do was sign them. We had another visitor then, Captain Beauvais, who brought Susan a book. Aziz gave him a drink and Susan and he talked in a low voices. He had gone before you came in from the garden at lunchtime.

At lunch you said: When will Sarah be back? And Susan laughed and said: Oh, Aunty, she's only just gone, she was only due to reach Calcutta this morning.

You said: So she'll be gone for a few more days.

After lunch I helped Susan to settle on the verandah again. I tried to get her to walk for a bit in the shady part of the garden but she said she was tired. I found you at the bureau signing the last cheque. You said as you always did: Thank you for coping with all this. I took the cheques and the bills and went to my room. I lay down for a bit. At three o'clock I asked Aziz to send the mali's boy for a tonga. Then I tidied myself for Mr Maybrick and looked for you to tell you I was off. You were in the garden, but not in the shade. I said: Aren't you awfully hot? You said: No, I like the sunshine. And then: Will you be long? I said: I should be back soon after seven. This seemed to puzzle you. You'd forgotten again about Mr Maybrick. I had to remind you. You said: Oh yes, so you are. Have a nice time.

When I looked back you were watching me. And lifted your hand. Which wasn't usual. But pleased me. I waved back. I went round the side of the house so that I wouldn't disturb Susan.

Isn't it very close? Stay. Talk to me. Is that the date? When will Sarah be back? Will you be long?

These were your appeals. Which I did not hear. I did not hear Aziz's appeal either. When will *you* be back? He saw the sunlight and the shadow and in his heart interpreted them correctly. But followed your mood and example. When I left in the tonga he made Susan some tea. No one knows what he did after that. The kitchen was neat and tidy. He always kept it so.

ii

Mr Maybrick waves his arms in the air. Pages of Bach fly from his hands, swirl, swoop, drift, fall. His face is contorted by the anguish of a man who requires order but cannot keep it. We stand erect in this tempest of paper music. Then I turn, pretending to go; having only just arrived. He waits until I am at the door and cries: Come back! I am no longer even a little afraid of Mr Maybrick but I obey because it pleases him to act the martinet. I can see him terrorizing coolies who grin when his back is turned because he never harms them. I can see him ordering his wife about, before she began to ail, and see her, one hand shading not just her eyes from the light but her smile with which she commences to perform what he demands but in her own way and to her own satisfaction, which she knows will be to his as well.

What a pickle you are in, I tell him, and sit on the one chair that is not cluttered with things that have no business on chairs. We are ankle deep in Bach. The situation looks hopeless, more hopeless to him than to me because the pages are numbered and it only requires patience and application – qualities he does not normally possess – to restore them to their proper order. The problem will be the rebinding. He complains about the quality of the gum I used last time, about the quality of the original binding, about the climate that makes things fall apart anyway, about the decline in standards of workmanship, about the fact that, as he says, nobody gives a damn any more; and finally – the rub, because it explains why he has scattered the pages in a childish rage – about a double sheet that is missing.

Have you looked in the organ loft? I ask. He declares that the missing sheet cannot possibly be in the organ loft. He says: It's no good sitting staring at it, what are you waiting for?

I tell him: Tea. I tell him I require a cup of tea first and that after that I will walk down to the church and look in the organ loft while he makes a start clearing up the mess he has made.

On my way to St John's I see suddenly what a vast improvement my time in Pankot has wrought in my character. Application I had, and patience, but of a questionable kind. Confronted in the old days with the ruins of the Bach I would have fallen avidly upon the scattered pages and somehow contrived to make greater confusion than before. And I would not have dared insist on Tea.

I see that I have acquired qualities of leadership and command. For a moment my pride in this achievement is disproportionate to its degree. I feel a deep glow of satisfaction. I lengthen my stride. Although it is a very hot day I have on the heliotrope. The sun is lowering towards West Hill. I turn my face to it. I am happy. I have, I feel, always done my utmost and now enjoy my reward on this earth whose beauty is serene towards evening.

As I turn into the churchyard the clock strikes the half-hour after five. I enter and go straight to the organ loft. The light is not good. I crouch down, searching, convinced I shall find the missing sheet. And I find it in a corner. It bears the dusty imprint of Mr Maybrick's shoe. I smile. And then I hear a sound, the sound of the latch lifted on the little side door through which I too have just entered, the slight squeak of the hinges, the sound of the door closing. Mr Maybrick has followed me.

I stand up and cry: Eureka! and look down to where he should be. But there is no one. The church is empty. I call again, less boldly. No answer. I have the missing sheet in one hand. With my other I seek my neck, automatically, and then the chain, the pendant cross.

I leave, unhurriedly. I tell myself my entrance must have disturbed someone at private devotions, someone whom I did not see when I came in and who has taken the opportunity of my climb to the organ loft to leave unnoticed. Slowly I follow this solitary worshipper out and down the path past the gravestones, but he – or she – is still invisible. I walk back to Mr Maybrick's.

I find him sitting on the floor, the scattered pages all around him untouched. He is listening to the news on the wireless and shushes me when I begin to protest at his idleness. Resigned, I throw things from the chair which has now become cluttered. He shushes me again. I subside. For a while I do not listen to the news but then do so and become aware that it is important. I cannot pick up the thread, though. It ends. But the announcer repeats the opening and this is followed by martial music.

It seems that British and Allied forces have invaded Normandy. They have opened the second front. Mr Maybrick shouts for his bearer and then heaves me out of the chair and does a little jig. His enthusiasm is infectious. Poor Bach is in danger of being trampled underfoot. Mr Maybrick tells his boy to bring sherry. He says that when the Germans are defeated the whole weight of the Allied armies will be thrown against the Japanese and then we can all live civilized lives again.

And all the prisoners in Germany will be freed! I cry: I must phone the cottage – I go into the hall, pick up the receiver and wait impatiently for the operator to answer. I am anxious for Susan to know, because of her father. I ask for the number and continue to wait. The operator tells me the number is engaged. Crestfallen I go back to the living-room. I work it out that Mildred has heard at the club and is already on the phone to Susan. We drink sherry. Ten minutes later I telephone again but the operator says there is still someone speaking. Mildred is probably back at the cottage and ringing all her friends. I resign my role as the bearer of good tidings. Come, I say to Mr Maybrick, let us begin on poor Bach.

iii

'Perseverance,' Barbie said, 'which was incidentally one of my father's favourite words if not one of his virtues, unless you count perseverance with the bottle and the cards, perseverance – Mr Maybrick – wins the day.'

She slapped the last page of Bach, straightened her bent back and cried out partly from the pain of easing the ache and partly from astonishment at Mr Maybrick's firmly planted kiss. Only on the forehead. Nevertheless. She felt her face and neck grow hot.

'Angelic Barbie,' he said. 'Ham-fisted with glue but angelic. What would you say to mutton curry and rice?'

'I should say no.'

'Is that all?'

'Had you been more complimentary about the glue I should have added thank you. You may help me up.'

'I will if you say yes. It was planned. Mutton curry and rice. For two.'

'Planned by whom?'

'By me.'

'Mr Maybrick, you have been overdoing the sherry. At your age it is ill-advised.'

'You've not done so badly yourself. You can knock it back.'

'Two glasses are all I've had.'

'Refilled occasionally without your noticing, between fugues.'

'I see you are determined to be difficult.' She got up unassisted. Her joints were very stiff. She looked at her watch. It was seven-fifteen. She had been crawling across the floor and kneeling sorting pages for over an hour. Mr Maybrick had been more of a hindrance than a help.

He said, 'If you stay to supper you could start the binding afterwards.'

'If I stayed to supper I should do no such thing. The binding will have to wait. Meanwhile I should be obliged if you'd send Kaisa Ram for a tonga. I'm going to tidy myself and when I come back I'll expect to hear that a tonga is on its way.'

'You've become a hard woman, Barbie. I'd set my heart on it.'

'Then you should have said so three days ago and not left it to chance and your powers of persuasion. And if I said yes you know very well you'd have to dash into the kitchen and tell Kaisa Ram to throw some more meat into the pot, and that he'd complain, that you'd shout at him and that you'd have a burnt supper, bad temper for the rest of the evening and indigestion all night.'

She turned to the door that led through the single bedroom to the bathroom.

'It'll take fifteen minutes for Kaisa Ram to get a tonga,' he said, 'but only five to cut off another chop.'

'And an hour for it to cook properly. So please send him down to the stand. When I come back I'll have another sherry. I don't believe a word of your story of surreptitious refills.'

She left him but caught the flicker of the smile he was doing his best to disguise. The bedroom, crammed with

254

the monumental furniture of his spacious tea-planting days, was even more untidy than the living-room and overpowered by the majestic bed that filled the central space. As always, this bed was shrouded by the regal canopy of a faded white mosquito net. In Pankot there was no need of one and if there had been Mr Maybrick's would have been inadequate because it was full of holes and rents which Kaisa Ram neglected to mend. But Mr Maybrick said he couldn't sleep in a bed that had no net. She sympathized with this peculiarity, remembering that whenever she had moved from a mosquito-ridden area to a cool and airy one she had always found the absence of a net initially alarming, a source of apprehension, of fears of falling out at least, at worst of attack by night-intruders.

The bathroom was cheerless. A single unshaded bulb illuminated its dingy whitewashed walls and concrete floor. In one corner there was a cubicle and in this an ornate commode of which Mr Maybrick was very proud. The commode, fortunately, was always spotless but the bathroom itself was grimy. There tended to be cock-roaches.

Normally, when visiting Mr Maybrick, she hurried through the business of tidying herself. But tonight she found herself slowed down, struck by the significance of her surroundings, the reality of this ordinariness, this shabbiness, this evidence of detritus behind the screens of imperial power and magnificence. The feeling she had was not of glory departing or departed but of its original and continuing irrelevance to the business of being in India, which was her and Mr Maybrick's business just as much as it was the business of the members of the mess in whose inner sanctum she had stood last year, intimidated by the ghostly occupants of those serried ranks of chairs.

She paused between soaping and rinsing her hands, riveted by an image of the captains and the kings queuing to wash their own hands in Mr Maybrick's bowl after relieving themselves in Mr Maybrick's mahogany com-mode with its rose-patterned porcelain receptacle, and finding no fault, nothing unusual, feeling no hurt to their dignity; and going back through the unholy clutter of Mr Maybrick's bedroom without a glance at the half-opened drawers festooned with socks and vests and shirts that wanted mending, because the one thing to which the human spirit could always accommodate itself was chaos and misfortune. Everything more orderly or favoured was a bonus and needed living up to.

She closed her eyes and was back in the Camberwell scullery and then in the dark hallway, taking the first rise of the stairs, with all the captains and kings behind her waiting to do the same. Why, she said, the mystery at the top of the stairs is where we're all headed, willy-nilly, which is what my father but not my mother understood. She opened her eyes. The lather had begun to encrust her hands with a creamy rime. She rinsed and dried them on the week-old roller towel. She dabbed her wrists with cologne from her handbag phial and resprinkled the fine lawn handkerchief. Chaos, misfortune. Punctuated by harmless escapes into personal vanities. She clicked her handbag shut. The click was as satisfactory as a decision.

'Mr Maybrick!' She called, re-entering the living-room.

He came in from the hall.

He said, 'Oh, there you are, Barbie. Arthur Peplow is here. He has something to tell you.'

iv

'I said, I will take heed to my ways: that I offend not in my tongue. I will keep my mouth as it were with a bridle; while the ungodly is in my sight. I held my tongue, and spake nothing, I kept silence, yea, even from good words; but it was pain and grief to me. My heart was hot within me, and while I was thus musing the fire kindled and at the last I spake with my tongue; Lord, let me know mine end, and the number of my days: that I may be certified how long I have to live.'

V

Where the rime had been was Arthur Peplow's hand. In the pause between the word 'stroke' and the words 'it was very sudden', she heard down the road the chime of the half-hour after seven.

Mr Peplow said, 'I think we must believe that she felt no pain, but went very peacefully. Susan was tremendously brave. The poor girl was quite alone. When she realized what had happened she rang Colonel Beames at once, and then her mother. She couldn't find Aziz anywhere. Have you any idea where he could have gone?'

'Aziz?'

'Never mind. In a moment or two Clarissa and I want you to come down to the rectory. Captain Coley's going to spend the night at Rose Cottage to look after things there for Mildred. Clarissa's having a bed made up for you.'

'I have a bed,' she said. And removed her hand from Arthur Peplow's to take the glass of sherry from Mr Maybrick's hand which was shaking. She held it, but did not know how to deal with it. Some of the deep brown liquid spilt on to the heliotrope skirt. 'I don't want it,' she said. 'After all.' Arthur took the glass. There was nowhere for him to put it down.

'The thing is,' he said, 'we all think it best if you stay the night with us. You can come straight away. If you don't mind borrowing some things Clarissa can lend you what you need. Beames or Travers will look in later with something to help you sleep. I asked Beames myself, I thought it would be wise. You'll need a good night's rest.'

'It's very kind of you, Arthur. But I must go home at once. If someone will fetch a tonga.'

She watched Arthur Peplow get up. Some of the books

257

and magazines which he had pushed aside to make room on the sofa for the two of them slid back into place. She observed the glance he exchanged with Mr Maybrick before parking the glass of sherry on top of the grand piano. Glad of the momentary relief such a prosaic detail provided in the mountingly oppressive nightmare, she recalled that the piano was badly out of tune because it had not been played since Clarice Maybrick's fingers were last upon its yellowed, mottled, keys. Another thing she remembered Mr Maybrick telling her was how Clarice always took her rings off before playing and placed them on the ebony ledge at the bass end of the key-board.

Arthur Peplow went out into the hall. She heard the ping that accompanied the lifting of the receiver. You could not get a tonga by ringing the exchange. Suddenly the door between hall and living-room closed, which meant that Arthur didn't want her to hear what he was saying or know to whom he was saying it. She stayed where she was, readopting an old habit of mind; that of believing in the good sense and good will of established authority; although the waves of rebellion had already risen and were – she guessed – only temporarily subdued. Mr Maybrick came to the sofa and sat beside her, pushing the books and magazines to give himself room. He sat with his elbows on his knees and his hands clasped in the space between and looked down at the worn bit of carpet.

'When I left this afternoon,' Barbie said, watching the door that led to the hall where Arthur's voice had begun to drone, to vibrate, to punctuate longer periods of silence, 'she watched me and waited for me to look round, and then lifted her hand to wave.'

Mr Maybrick nodded but said nothing.

'You do understand, Mr Maybrick that I can't possibly sleep at Arthur's and Clarissa's or anywhere but at the cottage. There will be no need for Captain Coley to be there. In fact I find the idea quite unacceptable. Aziz and I will manage everything. I quite see that Mildred can't stay. She'll have to take poor Susan home and look after

258

her. But Captain Coley's presence is not necessary. I am prepared to wait here for a bit but eventually, no – quite soon, I must go back.'

'I'll come with you if you like.'

'Thank you. That would be kind. So long as it's understood that I stay there.'

She grew rigid with impatience. There was much to be done. And quickly. In India these things were always done quickly. They had to be. And the problems of making special arrangements were likely to be many. She herself must be prepared for the journey to Ranpur. Packing was something that would occupy her.

'And I must pack,' she said. 'I must be ready to leave tomorrow. The man at St Luke's in Ranpur used to be the Reverend Ian Wright and still may be. Arthur will know.'

Again Mr Maybrick nodded. She did not know whether he was listening but his mute agreement was encouraging. The door opened and Arthur came back in smoothing his head with one hand. He asked Mr Maybrick whether Kaisa Ram could produce some tea or coffee. Mr Maybrick got up and went out saying he would see. Directly they were alone Arthur said, 'That was Kevin Coley at the other end. I told him you want to go up to the cottage and he's had a word with Mildred. She's still there with Susan and I think she'd be grateful if you'd let her get Susan away first, because the girl's in pretty much of a state. In fact she's suffering badly from reaction. Colonel Beames left about an hour ago and Susan was fairly all right then but he said he'd have a word with Travers because it's Travers who's been attending to her during her pregnancy. Well, they've been waiting for Travers to turn up and Coley's trying to get him on the phone now. Mrs Fosdick and Mrs Paynton are there helping Mildred cope. There's nothing you can actually do, Barbie, and frankly I think the best thing is for you to wait here a while and then if you feel you must just go up and collect some things for the night. I'll take you.'

'Mr Maybrick has promised to do that.'

'Well, that's fine. Coley said he'd ring me as soon as Mildred's got Susan away. Please don't misunderstand. Mildred knows how upset you must be and that you can only be more upset the moment you set foot in Rose Cottage. Just now she has her work cut out keeping poor Susan on an even keel. The danger is premature labour brought on by shock. And you *do* appreciate how much of a shock it was, don't you?'

'Yes, Arthur.'

'Coley says Aziz is still missing. It's very odd. When I mentioned it before I don't think you took it in. But he's not been seen since he brought Susan out her tray of tea. She had a cup and then noticed it wasn't yet four o'clock so she dozed off again and was only half awake when Mabel came and sat down and seemed to nod off.'

'What time was that, Arthur?'

'About five. Beames got there at five-thirty.'

'More than two hours ago. I don't understand. I don't understand why I wasn't called at once.'

'No one knew where you were.'

'Aziz knew.'

'But Barbie.'

'I'm sorry. I keep forgetting. But Susan knew.'

'She said she only knew she'd seen you making out cheques and imagined you'd gone down to the bazaar to pay them.'

'Yes, I see.'

'Clarissa was out when Mildred rang and asked me to go up. Otherwise we might have traced you sooner. She rang me at the cottage when she got home at seven and found my message. She said she thought you might be here with Edgar. So I came straightaway.'

That was very kind of you, Barbie intended to say; but she could not because it was being borne in on her that Arthur Peplow was deeply implicated – even if he didn't realize it – in a plot to keep her out of the way, to stop her from going to Rose Cottage. She could not judge whether punishment or kindness was intended. If punishment,

260

then Mildred was probably at the bottom of it. If kindness, then Mabel's death could not have been the quiet and peaceful passing Arthur had described.

She saw her friend with blackened face, protuberant tongue, and limbs stiffened in the final gesture of total and absolute terror; and Susan backing away, clutching her swollen belly, shrieking for Aziz, getting no answer qnd then – with space achieved between her own body and the horror – scrabbling at the telephone and shouting incoherently for help, making for the door, running down the gravel drive to the rockery-bordered exit to Club Road, clasping the pillar of the open gateway and screaming until the whole of Pankot echoed and trembled.

But this was not the way it had been, nor the way it ever could have been. The convolutions of the petals of this rose are dissimilar to the convolutions of this, Mabel must have said; and, leaning towards it, to examine more closely the miracle of its individuality, become aware of a corresponding shadow leaning over her, so that she straightened carefully to absorb the shock and leave the rose to its freedom and perfection; and turned, holding the basket, walked cautiously towards the short flight of wooden steps to the verandah. Here there was a promise, briefly kept, of continuation. A figure sleeping. Within it another; patiently achieving its human shape. Briefly too, a green leaf, one of many sprouting from stems in pots on the balustrade, adumbrated the shape and texture of its successors to fingers still occupied by love and custom.

But again the shadow leans and the hand that touches the leaves is arrested by another which is more grandly and fearfully informed. And a voice – the same that said: Does it matter? – says, That's all, that's all.

She sits. The favour granted to someone like her. A rock. The seas pound. One wave scarcely distinguishable from any of the others puts out the faltering spark. But in that place there is no visible difference between sleep and death. She had nodded off. And out. The dear indomitable body remains. Marking the place.

I have a concern, Barbie thought, to see if the eyes are open. She felt that they should be but didn't know why except that in Mabel's case this would somehow be seemly.

'Barbie,' Arthur said, taking her hand to his cold but well-intentioned comfort. 'Don't try so hard not to cry. You loved her and cared for her. You did it well.'

'But not today. She wanted me to be there. But of course she would never have dreamed of asking. If she could have made it back to her room she would have, for Susan's sake.'

'There, there. That's better.'

'Forgive me.'

But before she could disgrace herself she became free of the encumbrance of Arthur Peplow's sympathy. She got up, grabbed her handbag and went into Mr Maybrick's bedroom and shut the door. The physical exertion closed the gate on useless grief. From what appeared to be a considerable distance away she saw Mabel waiting. She achieved levitation and floated without trouble through the apex of the regal canopy of the mosquito net and left the room filled with the dark bat-wing flapping of the ghosts of her sorrow. She longed now only to escape and destroy the distance between the terrible little bungalow and Rose Cottage.

She switched on the light in the bathroom and closed the door, crossed, reached up and unbolted the side door. Warm night air stroked her cheeks. She stumbled, surprised by an unfamiliar dimension – a high step – and saved herself from falling. She pressed on through an opening in what appeared to be a trellis. There was a sickly odour of sweet jasmine in the night and charcoal fumes from the outhouse where Kaisa Ram was cooking mutton curry. At the front of the bungalow she moved cautiously but, gaining the road, planted her feet firmly.

She hastened past the rectory bungalow, squat behind its partial screen of trees, showing but one lighted room, and walked down the hill, past St John's. Where Church

Road joined Club Road she would with luck find an empty tonga making its way back from club to bazaar, but reaching there she found the road deserted and, having no time to waste, set off on the uphill climb. Presently two tongas went past, both laden; and then she had to stand still and hide her eyes from twin glares that loomed and roared and went past leaving dust and petrol fumes and echoes of singing male voices. At the milestone she paused to rest. She heard the clock of St John's strike eight in another world. She got up and plodded on.

Captain Coley was in the front porch, waiting, which meant that Arthur and Mr Maybrick had discovered her escape and telephoned a warning.

'We're waiting for Travers,' he said. 'It's Susan. We think she's started.'

'Then she should be got to hospital.' She glanced into the lighted hall. Already the place had the look of not belonging to anyone. 'They should have taken her home long before this,' she said. 'Colonel Beames should have insisted. Where is she?'

'With Mildred in the spare bedroom.'

She went into the hall. Just then Susan cried out. At the same instant from some quality of sound and echo Barbie realized that the thing she had come to look at wasn't in the house. She turned, intending to raise the question of where Mabel's body had been taken but was forestalled by Mildred calling Captain Coley's name and then appearing in the living-room doorway.

Barbie noticed that Mildred's hair was still immaculately set. She would have expected something of the last few hours to have left a mark of itself in the form of disarrangement however slight. She noticed the hair because its groomed perfection set the tone of Mildred's whole appearance. She searched for signs of wildness in Mildred's face and in doing so realized that for a perceptible count, even if only in fractions of seconds, she and Mildred were staring at each other like old enemies who knew that the truce by whose terms they had both faithfully abided was now officially over.

'I'm sorry to have arrived before you've got Susan home,' Barbie said. 'But I won't get in anyone's way, unless of course there's something I can do.'

'Thank you,' Mildred replied. 'But I think we can cope. Providing Travers gets here pretty soon. What's the form, Kevin?'

'The form is he should be here any minute now. Probably with an ambulance.'

Mildred nodded, made to go back in but paused. She looked at Barbie. She said, 'Have you any idea where that bloody man can have got to?'

'Which man, Mildred?'

'Aziz,' she said; and repeated it. This time the sibilants struck like snakes. 'Aziz.'

'I think, yes, I'm sure it was for today, he had permission to visit a relative in one of the villages.' The cautious lie came pat. But Mildred wasn't fooled.

'A sick relative, I suppose. No. I don't think so. The other servants know nothing about it. Well, if and when he ever shows his face again, Kevin here's promised personally to boot him in the rear.'

'I don't think you understand, Mildred. I don't think you understand at all. About Indians like Aziz.'

'I understand only too well. My God, I understand! He knew what I presume none of us knew. That she was ill. And bloody well funked it. Let's see how far he gets. I've asked Beames to have a word with the police.'

'The police! Whatever are you saying?'

' – not that there appears to be anything noticeably missing. But there hasn't been time for a proper check.'

Another cry from Susan cut her off. For an instant her eyes closed and one hand gripped the jamb of the doorway. A voice which Barbie recognized as Clara Fosdick's called Mildred's name. Mildred went back towards the little spare.

Behind Barbie Coley said, 'Terribly upset. Don't take

police business too seriously. No one really suspects the old chap of pinching anything but it's a necessary precaution, at least until Beames is satisfied about the cause of death.'

She faced round to Coley upon whose martyr's face there already seemed to be the reflection of flickering flames.

'What do you mean?'

He looked pained by so direct a question.

'Only a formality. Feels he should have a pathologist's report to confirm his opinion that it was a stroke.'

The sound of an engine revving, of a driver changing into a low gear to negotiate the entrance to the drive, rescued him from further explanation. He went quickly out to the porch. Barbie hesitated, then approached Mabel's bedroom. She grasped the handle of the door and had confirmation that it was locked. In the dining-room she repeated the process. The door between Mabel's bedroom and the dining-room was locked too.

And there was something new and peculiar about the dining-room itself. It took Barbie a few moments to pin it down. The few pieces of silver normally kept on the sideboard were no longer there. Aziz, Aziz, she cried out silently; but almost immediately knew that Aziz had had nothing to do with it. She tried the cupboard doors in the sideboard. These were locked too. Doubtless the silver was inside.

She heard Travers's voice, and Coley's, and stood erect and still while the voices moved from hall to living-room and to the spare bedroom. Then she opened the french window on to the verandah which was illuminated by the light cast from dining-room and living-room and little spare. Susan's lounging chair was there, with its cushions. The book brought by Captain Beauvais lay unopened on the floor together with another book and a copy of the current issue of the *Onlooker*. A tray of tea on a low stool was on the other side of the place where Susan had lain dozing, and several paces beyond on the other side of the french window into the living-room, but near the balustrade, another chair: upright and empty, with the pannier-basket beside it.

She moved closer to it and then stooped and picked up the basket. It contained secateurs, dead rose-heads, a hand fork to whose tines particles of earth clung. She touched all these things, assuring herself of their existence; consequently of her own.

Then she saw lying on the floor where she supposed Beames had let it drop after removing it the old frayed-brim straw hat. She stooped and picked this up too.

'But it can't have!' Susan cried out. Barbie heard her clearly, 'It can't have started. The baby isn't *finished* yet.'

Barbie moved into the shadow but saw through the uncurtained open window of the little spare. They had Susan on her feet. Travers held one arm and Mildred the other. Clara Fosdick had her own and Susan's handbags. Nicky Paynton held open the door into the living-room. The girl seemed to be a dead weight. Travers said, 'Come along, Su, you don't need the stretcher. Just keep on your feet. We'll have you right as rain, you'll see.'

Her resistance went. Meekly but cautiously as if every step she made was an opportunity for the baby to make a dangerous bid for its freedom she let Travers and her mother lead her out.

When they had gone Barbie waited, giving them time to get out to the ambulance. Then she moved into the area of light and went back to Mabel's chair, still holding the basket and the straw hat.

She sat down.

But there was no way in.

Presently she was aware of a shadow fallen across her feet and she felt the little shock-waves of someone's fear or agitation. She glanced up. It was Kevin Coley. He thought he had seen a ghost.

He said, 'Mr Maybrick's here to take you down to the Peplows for the night.'

266

'Very well, Captain Coley. Thank you. I'll pack a few things.'

In the living-room she realized what she carried that was not hers and what was missing that belonged to her. 'I think I left my handbag on the sideboard in the dining-room. Would you look? There are some things in it which I ought to hand over.'

He came back with the handbag held high, as men held such things. She put the pannier and straw hat down, took the bag, got out the receipts and crossed to the bureau. The lid was locked and the key missing. She stood until the flush of humiliation had come and gone and then turned and offered the receipts to Coley saying, 'Will you see that Mildred gets these?' Coley took them. Leaving hat and pannier behind she went into the hall where Mr Maybrick was waiting.

'Barbie – ' he began.

'No recriminations,' she said. 'I'm going to pack an overnight bag. I take it you have transport of some kind outside.'

'Only a tonga.'

'That will suffice. Do one thing for me first. Find out from Captain Coley where they have taken Mabel.'

In her bedroom she collected nightgown; slippers, dressing-gown, a change of underwear and toilet articles. She crammed these into an old fibre suitcase whose handle was mended with string. Back in the hall ten minutes later she found Mr Maybrick and Captain Coley standing several feet apart and not talking.

'If Aziz should come back, Captain Coley, you will tell him where I am, won't you? And you will treat him with the same courtesy he and Mabel always showed one another, I trust.'

Coley looked hunted. And then she realized that he was a coward, and always had been, in spite of that uniform, that precious insignia. She turned the screw.

'Well? I have your word? The word of a British officer to an Englishwoman?'

Coley flushed, aware of her mockery, and – with his fingers tainted by keys and valuables – of its justification; that she mocked him not only for himself but for the whole condition. She did not care. The charade was finished. Mabel had guessed the word years ago but had refrained from speaking it. The word was 'dead'. Dead. Dead. It didn't matter now who said it; the edifice had crumbled and the façade fooled nobody. One could only pray for a wind to blow it all away or for an earthquake such as Captain Coley's wife had died in. Barbie saw how perhaps with one finger she might topple him, because there was nothing to keep him standing except his own inertia.

But she had other things to do. She decided not to wait for his reply; and in any case the silence that followed her demand revealed how little she would be able to count on any promise that he gave. She marched out to the tonga with the fibre suitcase.

'What was the answer?' she asked when Mr Maybrick joined her.

'We should go to the general hospital and inquire there.'

'Then please tell the wallah.'

'I'm bound to say Coley didn't think there would be much point.'

'Naturally. Captain Coley sees little point in anything. He should have died in the rubble of Quetta. In most ways he did. The Lord alone knows for what purpose the remains are preserved.'

She waited in the reception hall of the general hospital seated on an uncomfortable highly polished bench, watching. Mr Maybrick making things difficult for one of the girls at the inquiry desk, a fair-skinned Eurasian who kept on lifting the receiver of her telephone, presumably trying yet another extension at Mr Maybrick's insistence. After ten minutes something definite seemed to be decided and the girl suddenly looked impressed and helpful. Mr Maybrick came over to the bench. He sat down.

'Beames is over at the nursing home annexe. If we go

268

across now he'll have a word with you. The nursing home is where Susan's been taken, and Mildred will be there too.'

'My business is only with Colonel Beames. I'm sorry you're being put to so much trouble, Mr Maybrick. If you want to go home to your supper I can manage on my own.'

He stood up, grabbed the suitcase and said, 'Come on, we can walk it, it's not far.'

They came out and followed directional signs along the asphalt path. They both knew the nursing home well. They had visited Clarissa there the year she was ill with pleurisy.

The reception hall was less forbidding than the one at the main hospital. There were rugs and bowls of flowers. The woman behind the desk was a VAD. Her grey hair was blue-rinsed.

'Miss Batchelor?' she asked, ignoring Mr Maybrick. 'Colonel Beames is engaged but won't keep you long.'

Barbie and Mr Maybrick sat together on a leather sofa. The blue-haired woman made notes on a file of papers with a very sharp looking pencil. Whenever she answered the telephone she said, 'Pankot Nursing Home, can I help you?' She had a miniature switchboard on the desk with red and green switches on it which she manipulated with dexterity and self-assurance. Once she banged a bell and was answered by an Indian porter to whom she gave a folded note and a brisk instruction. Ten minutes later another VAD came through the hushed swing doors.

'Miss Batchelor?'

Barbie stood up. She followed the woman through into a polished corridor and round a corner into another where they stopped at a white painted door marked Private. The woman knocked, opened and stood aside after announcing Barbie's name. The room was carpeted. The civil surgeon got up from behind a large desk and crossed the carpet silently. In the few years they had passingly known each other they had exchanged not many more words. He was a tall man with a nose and eyebrows and jaws that looked as if they had champed bones.

'I'm sorry to have had to keep you waiting,' he said. He pulled a leather chair close to another, waited for her to sit and then sat himself. He subjected her to a kind of remote scrutiny. His was a face that accepted nothing and gave nothing. 'It will perhaps have been an even greater shock for you than for any of us. I am so sorry. But I do now have my pathologist's report which confirms my assumption of cerebral haemorrhage. I suppose one must be thankful that it wasn't the kind of stroke that would have left her paralysed but alive. Had she complained of feeling unwell lately?'

Barbie shook her head.

'Well if she felt out of sorts I don't suppose she'd have said so or called any of us in. She was very much a law unto herself wasn't she? I'm sorry that there had to be this very slight delay in giving the certificate but in the circumstances I really had no alternative. I've told Mildred – Mrs Layton junior – the result of course. She's here with young Susan, as I expect you know. You're staying the night with the Peplows?'

Barbie nodded.

'Mrs Layton has phoned Arthur Peplow and given him the all clear to go forward with the arrangements. It's unfortunate Sarah's in Calcutta. Mrs Layton is going to telephone her sister but even if Sarah starts back first thing in the morning she won't be here until the day after tomorrow. I'm afraid Susan's in for rather an arduous time from what Travers says, so her mother won't be able to see to the other business personally. Fortunately Arthur Peplow and Captain Coley have undertaken to deal with it.' He brought a small envelope out of his pocket. 'I want you to take the two tablets in this packet with some warm milk when you go to bed tonight. To give you a proper night's rest.'

She accepted the envelope. She said, 'Thank you, Colonel Beames.' She would not take the tablets. 'That is very kind of you, and very practical. There is a great deal to do and one must be on one's feet to do it.'

'Well, yes, but it's all being done. Don't worry. Sleep is the best thing for you.'

'Can you tell me anything about the arrangements, for instance about the arrangements for transportation?'

'Transportation?'

'To Ranpur. I imagine there will be a service here at St John's, especially as Mildred won't be able to leave Pankot while Susan is having her baby. And perhaps some kind of brief ceremony the next day at St Luke's. But I'm concerned about the transport. You see, I should wish to accompany.'

'Did you say St Luke's?'

'Yes. St Luke's in Ranpur. That's where the actual burial is to be. At St Luke's in Ranpur. She wished to be with her late husband, Mr James Layton. Hasn't Mildred mentioned that to you?'

'No.'

She waited for him to say more. But his face had gone out entirely. The heavy jaws were clamped shut.

'Then I had better see her and remind her,' Barbie said.

'Are you sure those were the elder Mrs Layton's wishes?'

'Quite sure.'

'I see.' Beames paused. 'Then I'll mention it to Mrs Layton junior. Interment in Ranpur is not among the impressions I have about the arrangements but possibly I haven't a complete picture. I do know that a service at St John's late tomorrow afternoon has been talked of.' He looked at his watch. 'I have to leave now for Flagstaff House but I shall be coming back later to see Mrs Layton. I'll mention it to her then.' He stood up. 'We've given her the room next to Susan's and she's resting on my orders. She's had a very trying time which would explain why she might overlook a point such as the one you've raised – if she has overlooked it. I'm sure that she'd know about it if it is an established wish or a definite instruction. You may depend on my letting her know what you've told me.'

She got up. She had no intention of depending upon

Colonel Beames: but that, she thought, need not concern him. She allowed him to lead her to the door.

'Are you accompanied?' he asked.

'Mr Maybrick is with me.'

'Good. And have you transport?'

'We have a tonga.'

'It's curious about the servant, isn't it? But I know a similar case. I suppose it's a kind of sixth sense coupled with this odd fatalism some of these old fellows develop. But it's not proof of unfeeling.'

'The opposite,' she said. 'Quite the opposite.'

They stood at the open door now.

'I wish to see her, of course,' Barbie said. 'Can I do that now?'

He observed her without reacting visibly to what he saw. She felt the same expression moulded upon her own face.

'I'm afraid not. But if you ring the general hospital in the morning and ask to speak to Doctor Iyenagar or to his assistant I'm sure it could be arranged, should you really wish it.'

'Doctor Iyenagar?'

'Or his assistant. Extension 22.'

'Thank you, Colonel Beames.'

He made as if to accompany her but she assured him she could find her way. She walked back along the corridors to the waiting-room. Mr Maybrick stood up. She went to speak to the blue-haired woman at the desk.

She said, 'Colonel Beames tells me that Mrs John Layton is staying the night. I may want to telephone her in the morning. Is that fairly easy?'

'Yes, there's a telephone in every room.'

'What extension should I ask for?'

The vicious-looking pencil ran delicately down the list.

'Extension eight. Mrs John Layton.'

'Is that also her room number?'

'That is correct. Her daughter Mrs Bingham is in number seven.'

272

'Thank you so much. Goodnight.'

'We should have left the case in the tonga,' she said as they walked back along the asphalt path.

'And let the fellow run off with it,' Mr Maybrick replied. As if it contained things of value. 'He's probably gone away. It's not like the old days. They'd wait all night to get paid what they were owed. What did Beames say?'

'It was a stroke. So nothing need be delayed. They can go ahead with the arrangements.'

'That's a blessing.'

'What *are* the arrangements, Mr Maybrick? Did Arthur tell you?'

'He was hoping everything could be ready for a service at five o'clock.'

'And then?'

'Then? The interment.'

'In St John's churchyard?'

'Yes. He was relieved Mildred didn't insist on cremation. So many people do nowadays and he doesn't hold with it. But she asked him to go ahead and select a site himself.'

'Are you absolutely sure?'

'Oh, yes. He was quite relieved. He hasn't had a burial there for some while.'

They came to the end of the path. 'I'm afraid it will have to be stopped, Mr Maybrick.' She halted and held his arm. They now stood on the broad asphalt area in front of the main entrance to the general hospital. The tonga-wallah called to them and then the tonga emerged from the dense shadow of a clump of trees whose branches overhung the drive.

'What do you mean stopped? Aren't you satisfied with Beames's opinion?'

'It isn't that.'

'What then?'

'The burial has to be at St Luke's in Ranpur. I told him so but I'm afraid that might not be enough. I must see

273

Mildred. I think I must see her tonight. Either she's forgotten or Mabel never told her. She couldn't deliberately disregard a wish like that, could she?'

'What wish? Whose wish?'

'Mabel's. She wished to be buried next to her late husband James Layton, at St Luke's in Ranpur.'

'And you said so to Beames?'

'Yes.'

'What did *he* say?'

'He said he'd mention it to Mildred tonight when he gets back from Flagstaff House.'

'Then he will. If it's all that important you can tell Arthur when we get back and one of you can ring Mildred in the morning to check whether Beames kept his word. Come on. You need some food and something warm to drink and to get to bed and try to sleep.'

He swung the case up beside the tonga-wallah.

'I'm sorry to be a stubborn nuisance to you, Mr Maybrick, but – '

'For God's sake!' he said. 'Call me Edgar, can't you, after all these years?'

'Yes, all right.' She nodded her head. 'Edgar. Edgar.' She began to laugh and covered her face. She could not stop. She laughed for sorrow and for his name because it didn't suit him and presently she was laughing for Mabel because the alternative to laughter was shriek after shriek of wild and lonely despair because Mabel had gone and she had lost her occupation and she saw how it was and would always be for everyone.

'Barbie!' Mr Maybrick (Edgar) was saying; he had her by the shoulders but she could not allow herself to be enfolded, admonished or cherished. She forced her body away and began walking towards the steps that led to the glass door through which shone the lights in the main entrance hall of the hospital. She scrabbled in her handbag and found her cologne-scented handkerchief and dried her cheeks and eyes.

'Now where are you going?' he called.

'It's all right. You go back home.'

He caught up with her as she placed her foot on the first step. 'Barbie, what are you doing?'

'I have to see a Doctor Iyenagar.'

'A doctor what?'

They were at the door now, each pushing one immaculate sheet of framed glass, so that the arrival had all the force of an important emergency. The Eurasian girl glanced up, startled. Barbie went to the desk without hesitating. The spirit of the hard condition had entered: an inspired visitation.

'Colonel Beames will have rung,' she announced in a penetrating voice. 'Please tell Doctor Iyenagar I am here.'

'Oh, but Doctor Iyenagar has left.'

'Then his assistant, Doctor whatever his name is. Extension 22.'

The girl swung round in her swivel chair, fumbled with plugs, She said, 'It's Miss Batchelor, isn't it?'

'Yes. I am to see Doctor Iyenagar or his assistant in connexion with the death this afternoon of Mrs Mabel Layton. Colonel Beames should have rung before he left for Flagstaff House.'

'Yes, I see. I don't remember – ' She responded to a voice in her ear. 'Get Doctor Lal, please.' She looked up at Barbie. 'Doctor Lal will come. Please sit down.'

'Is he on the other end now?'

'Not yet. I will tell him.'

'There's no need for him to come. Just tell him I'm here as arranged by Colonel Beames and then be good enough to have someone show me to his office.' She turned to Mr Maybrick. 'Edgar, why don't you go back to the rectory bungalow and tell Clarissa I'll be there in half-an-hour. You could send the tonga back for me. It oughtn't to take me half-an-hour but if there's any snarl up here I'll have to get on to Isobel Rankin and ask her to get Beames to sort it out from that end.'

'I'll wait,' Mr Maybrick said, then added, 'You may need me if you have to deal with people called Iyenagar or

275

Lal or whatever it is.' He glanced at the Eurasian girl who looked at him as if she agreed. He looked back at Barbie. His face was redder than usual, but grave. He understood.

'Doctor Lal?' the girl said. 'I'm sending Miss Batchelor to your office in connexion with the late Mrs Mabel Layton. It is arranged by the civil surgeon. Please see her urgently. Thank you.' She removed the plug and banged a bell. A chaprassi came. She gave him an order.

'Doctor Lal will be waiting, Miss Batchelor,' she said.

'Thank you.'

She followed the chaprassi through into a corridor and found that Mr Maybrick was accompanying her.

'Barbie, what are you doing, for heaven's sake?'

'Something I have to,' she said. The chaprassi indicated a flight of steps leading to basement level. On the half-landing there was a directional sign. It said: Mortuary.

Mr Maybrick grabbed her shoulder. 'Barbie, you can't!' But she shook him off. The basement corridor was low-ceilinged and very hot. She glanced back up the stairs and saw Mr Maybrick leaning against the wall holding his elbows. He shook his head. His mouth moved. She did not think badly of him. Because of Clarice. Who had ailed in Assam. And died slowly. And been unrecognizable. According to Clarissa. Who knew.

The chaprassi opened the door. A thin young Indian in a white coat got up from a stool at a bench littered with white enamel trays and large glass jars. The walls were of whitewashed brick. In one corner a fan whined on a chromium stand. There was a smell of formalin.

'Doctor Lal?'

'Yes, I am Doctor Lal.'

'I was expecting to see Doctor Iyenagar but I'm told he's left.'

'Oh, yes. Half-an-hour since.'

'Then you are in charge.'

'Yes. You come from Colonel Beames, isn't it?'

'Yes. I do. Obviously Doctor Iyenagar told you to expect me. Upstairs I was afraid there'd been a tiresome lack of liaison. May we please proceed without further delay, Doctor Lal? I should have been at Flagstaff House ten minutes ago.'

The young man looked tubercular. His eyes were enormous. He had studied too hard. He had not eaten enough. He had his qualification. Which should have opened a world to him. But the way into that world was blocked by Beames and his fear of Beames upon whose good opinion his career depended. Contrasting his delicate night-animal's features with Beames's bone-fed face she felt instinctively that he had no sanguine expectations of that opinion.

'Oh, yes,' he said. Did his lower lip tremble? Necessity made him frank. 'Proceed with what? I am sorry, but Doctor Iyenagar – '

'What about Doctor Iyenagar? Are you saying you've no instruction in this matter? If so we'll waste no more time. Ask the switchboard for Flagstaff House. I'll speak to Colonel Beames and ask him to repeat to you what he's already said to Doctor Iyenagar.'

For a moment she feared that a habit of acting upon the last order given would send him to the telephone. But almost at once he said, 'It should not be necessary if you tell me what is the problem.'

'It's not a problem. Or at least it wasn't. It's a question of identification.'

'Identification? Of what, please?'

'Doctor Lal, you're making this extremely painful and tedious. The business is bad enough without prolonging it. I have to see and identify the body of the late Mrs Layton.'

He looked relieved. And then puzzled. He said, 'Oh, yes. But no one mentioned to me this necessity. Are you a relative?'

'Yes.'

'One moment.'

He went towards a door, then came back, moved a chair a few inches from the wall. 'Please sit.' She did so.

He opened the door and went through. She closed her eyes to pray for grace, for the continued suspension of Doctor Lal's disbelief. And abruptly opened them, warned by the blankness behind her eyelids. She got up, opened the door he had gone through. The corridor on the other side of it was narrower and lower than any she had been in this evening. But chill. At its end there were closed double doors flanked by fire extinguishers. In each door there was a circular window.

The corridor floor was covered with tiles of some kind of rubber-like composition. She walked silently to the doors and opened them upon an enclosed winter that hummed faintly on a high note so that she seemed to be both deafened and desensitized, projected into a season of frost, a landscape and a time unknown to her. Entering it she became inhuman, like Doctor Lal, like the two white rubber-clothed figures who seemed to be chafing the naked body in a farcical attempt to bring it back to life. The body was on its side with its right arm raised, held by brown hands. There was a yellow pigment in the arm and in the shoulders. It ended just above the pendulous white breasts but spread upwards across the face which was framed by tousled grey hair. The eyes were open and looking directly at the doorway. The mouth was open too and from it a wail of pain and terror was emitting.

'You should not have gone in!' Doctor Lal shrieked. 'It is most irregular. Please go back and wait.' He stood guarding the doors through which he had just pushed her with feverish hands, back into the corridor. 'Nothing is ready yet. Doctor Iyenagar is saying nothing to me about identification. I am telling the men. But suddenly you come in without permission upsetting everything. It is not allowed. And now you are in a state. Please, please you must sit somewhere and wait to be patient. Why should I be blamed for this?'

The wall supported her. She felt its hardness against

the back of her head. She closed her eyes and breathed in deeply through her mouth.

'No one is blaming you, Doctor Lal. No one will blame you. I shall say nothing. You would be wise to say nothing too. I've seen all I need. Just forget I was ever here.'

She went up the corridor and through the still open door into the laboratory. When she got out into the main corridor she saw Mr Maybrick sitting on the bottom step of the flight that led up to the ground floor. Their glances met. She felt that they were people who had known each other a long time ago, too long ago for either of them to presume upon an old acquaintance by speaking first. They ascended silently: he from his reminder and she from her first authentic vision of what hell was like.

The blue-haired woman was still on duty. Barbie approached her alone. Outside, in the tonga whose driver had been persuaded to come by the narrow asphalt path prohibited to vehicles, Mr Maybrick sat, still speechless from the shock of that word: Mortuary.

'I'm afraid an emergency has arisen that makes it imperative for me to see Mrs John Layton at once. It's in connexion with the death this afternoon of Mrs Mabel Layton.'

'Oh, yes. Well, now.' She glanced at her watch. 'Mrs Layton isn't a patient so I expect it can be arranged. I'll have a word with Sister Page.'

'You'd better tell her I've come on behalf of Captain Coley and the Reverend Arthur Peplow. It's really extremely urgent. It affects the funeral arrangements and of course Mrs Layton has to be informed at the earliest possible moment.'

The blue-haired woman nodded. She had already lifted the phone, pressed one of the red switches and turned a little handle. She asked to speak to Sister Page. It seemed that Sister Page was with a patient. The blue-haired woman gave a careful message, repeated everything that Barbie had told her but had to say names twice. She

279

waited. While she did so the box buzzed. She manipulated switches and said, 'Pankot Nursing Home, can I help you?' And then, 'Just a moment.' She pressed more switches, turned the handle, listened and then presumably switched herself off from the conversation and back to Sister Page's extension.

'Hello?' she said. She listened. 'Well, will you do that? Meanwhile I'll have the visitor brought up.' She replaced the receiver, banged a bell and said, 'Sister Page is with Mrs Bingham but Mrs Layton hasn't gone to bed yet. A porter will take you to the second floor. If you wait at Sister's desk in the lobby, Sister Page or Sister Matthews will meet you there and then take you to Mrs Layton's room.'

She told the porter who had come in answer to the bell to accompany Memsahib to Wellesley. Barbie said, 'Thank you,' and followed the man. They went up by lift.

Sister Page's desk was unoccupied. It was surrounded by vases and baskets of flowers taken from the rooms for the night. A clock on the wall behind the desk showed ten minutes to ten. To the right, painted in black, was the legend: Rooms 20-39; with an arrow. To the left a similar legend pointed the way to Rooms 1-l9. Barbie turned left along the broad corridor. As she turned a corner into a narrower one a nurse came out of a room half way down it and walked towards her. She had wide hips and thick legs.

'Sister Page?' Barbie asked.

'No, I'm Sister Matthews. Are you lost?'

'I don't think so. I'm here to see Mrs John Layton. They told me downstairs to come up.'

'Oh.' The girl looked put out. But then smiled. 'I understood it was a Captain Coley with a message from a Mr Peplow.'

'Then they've got it slightly muddled. It *is* a message, and a very urgent one, which concerns Mrs Layton, Mr Peplow and Captain Coley.'

'Yes, I see. And there I've just told Mrs Layton it's Captain Coley. Well never mind.'

'How is her daughter, Susan?'

'Mrs Bingham's just as well as can be expected.'

'It isn't a false alarm?'

'No. But the pains have settled down a bit. I'm afraid it's not going to be an easy delivery, she's so tense. But who can blame her? We've been trying to get her mother to take something to get a good night because Captain Travers says it won't be until morning at the earliest from the look of things. But Mrs Layton's awfully anxious to get on the phone to her sister and other daughter in Calcutta. We've been through once but a dense sort of servant answered, so we're trying again at eleven tonight. I expect they're all out celebrating the second front, which is what I should be doing if we weren't so short-staffed. I'll take you to Mrs Layton.'

'Don't trouble. I know the room number.'

'No trouble.' She turned to lead the way but as she did so a door opened and another nursing officer, coming out, said, 'Oh, Thelma, thank God, come and – ' and broke off, seeing Barbie. 'Be with you,' Sister Matthews said and then knocked at room number eight, thrust the door open, glanced round and called loudly, 'Your visitor, Mrs Layton.' and stood aside for Barbie to go in.

The room was filled with a cheerless festive odour. From what was obviously a bathroom Mildred called, 'Come in, Kevin. There's a fresh glass on the dressing-table. Pour yourself one and freshen mine, will you? I'll be with you in a minute.' A tap was turned on for a few seconds. 'What's happened?' Mildred asked. 'I warn you I can't stand much more today. Bring mine in, will you? There's an angel. I'm going barmy in this bloody place. I've been phoning Calcutta like mad but there's nobody at Fenny's except some half-witted Bengali bearer. Since you're here you might have a go and see if you can get any sense out of him.' A pause. 'Kevin?'

Another pause. The bathroom door swung wide open. As she caught sight of Barbie Mildred seized the edges of her open dressing-gown and quickly covered her nearly naked body.

For a moment she stood quite still.

Then she said, 'You bloody bitch.'

'Mildred, no. Please don't. Don't talk to me like that. We mustn't let any unfriendliness come between us and what we have to do. It's much too important. I'm sorry if there's been some kind of confusion. But it's not my fault. I had to mention Arthur's and Captain Coley's names because it *does* concern them and I knew you'd never see me just on my own. But you must realize it's not my fault if the message was wrong by the time it reached you. Do I look like someone called Captain Coley? It's pure nonsense, and very wrong of you. But I don't care. You can call me anything you like afterwards, punish me in any way you like for anything you've ever thought I've done to you or done you out of. But you must listen to what I have to say and you must do it, you must. Otherwise she'll never rest. Never. Never. I've seen her, so I know. She'll haunt me, she'll haunt you, all of us. She's in that terrible place and in anguish because she knows you've forgotten your promise or aren't going to abide by it.'

Mildred had gone to the dressing-table, and refilled her glass. Now she said, 'I've no idea what you mean. What promise and to whom?'

'The promise to Mabel to bury her at St Luke's in Ranpur.'

'What on earth are you talking about?'

'It's what she wished. She told me. She must have told you.'

'At St Luke's? in Ranpur? I know absolutely nothing about it and it's quite out of the question. If you don't want the humiliation of being asked to leave by a member of the staff you'd better go now.'

'Why is it out of the question? There's a telephone on that table. All you have to do is ring Arthur and tell him to get on to Mr Wright in Ranpur, tell him this simple thing, that it was her wish to be buried next to her second

282

husband, your own father-in-law, at St Luke's in Ranpur. Arthur and I will do everything else that's necessary. But the instruction to cancel the arrangements for St John's must come from you.'

'What you will do is leave this hospital at once and stop interfering in matters that aren't your business. I find your suggestion utterly obscene. It is June. Perhaps you've noticed it's warm even in Pankot. Quite apart from the question of the cost of the ice, I have no intention of having my husband's stepmother transported like a piece of refrigerated meat to be buried after several days' delay in a churchyard that so far as I recall hasn't been used for burials since the nineteen-twenties. And especially I have no intention of doing so at the whim of a half-witted old woman. Even if there were an indication of such a wish in my stepmother-in-law's Will, or a subsequent written instruction, I should have to override it.'

'I know nothing about a Will, I only know – '

'But I do know about the Will. I've had a copy of it ever since my husband went abroad and copies of subsequent codicils. She had a horror of people having to grub through papers. In fact she was most meticulous and thoughtful about sparing her family unnecessary bother and anxiety. The gruesome little convoy you seem to think she wanted us to become involved in is quite out of character. After five years of living on what one presumes were fairly intimate terms with her I'm surprised you didn't know her better. On the other hand – '

Mildred sipped her gin, put the glass down. And smiled.

' – I'm not surprised. You were born with the soul of a parlour-maid and a parlour-maid is what you've remained. India has been very bad for you and Rose Cottage has been a disaster. I imagine you're paid up either to the end of the month or the end of the quarter. This month it comes to the same thing. I'd be glad if you'd be out before then. As quickly as possible in fact. I'd see that you got a pro-rata refund.'

'Mildred – '

'How dare you call me Mildred! To you I'm Mrs Layton.'

'No, that is ridiculous. That's just spiteful. Mildred is your given name, your Christian name, given when you were baptized. I *shall* not call you anything else. Not in His hearing – '

'Oh, God,' Mildred said. She covered one ear and bent her body as if to ward off a blow or to ride with the flow of a physical pain. The movement brought her in direct visual contact with the table and the telephone. She moved forward and reached for it. Barbie lunged; grabbed her wrist and found herself off-balance, forced heavily and painfully to her knees. But she grabbed Mildred's other wrist and hung on, imprisoned by her own violence in this penitential position. She shut her eyes so that the surge of her strength would not be interrupted. It flowed through her arms and into Mildred and they were united in a field of force, in area of infinite possibility for free and exquisite communication.

Tears of wonder, of love and hope and intolerable desire flowed from beneath Barbie's parchment-coloured lids. For a moment she could not get feeling into her lips. They would not come together to help her form the beginning of the required first word of supplication. She had to dispense with it and begin with a confession.

'I am sorry,' she said, 'sorry, sorry. I am what you say but I loved her so much and it seemed she was my chance, my gift from God to serve Him through her when everything else had been no good hadn't come to anything and just now she was trying to say help me help me. Please, Mildred. She asked for so little but she did ask for this. Why should I ask for it? Why should I make up a story? I'll do anything everything you say but please please don't bury her in the wrong grave. Not that, not that.'

She felt Mildred's wrists force themselves free and knew the answer. She opened her eyes but could not make anything out clearly. The shock of an impact stunned her. For an instant she thought that Mildred had hit her face with her open hand. But then she felt the coldness of water soaking into her blouse and as her eyes cleared she saw the empty carafe which Mildred held.

Without water there was no ice, no frosty particle, no storm of hail. The devotional machine had come to life in the shape of Mildred and a handy jug. The bathos of this situation shocked Barbie into a perilous composure. She felt capable of killing in cold blood, of burying Mildred alive along with Kevin Coley, a pile of empty gin bottles, some silver from the mess, and one of the mummy-rag-thin flags on top to mark the place.

She held an edge of the table, getting purchase to rise which she did without dignity but perhaps honourably. Who could say? She did not know. Dignity and honour were not inseparable. At times, and this was one of them, they seemed far distant for both of them.

Without another word she retrieved her handbag from the floor where it had fallen and left the room. She closed the door gently. In the corridor she realized that limp strands of hair clung to her forehead. The front of the heliotrope jacket was blackened by water. Her chest was icy cold. She put her head up and strode past Sister Matthews and another nursing officer, said good night to their open-mouthed faces and clumped down the stone stairs that entwined the lift shaft. On the ground floor the blue-haired woman was busy on the telephone and smiled absently when Barbie called good night. She was spared the shame of a direct encounter.

Mr Maybrick was asleep. He had reclaimed the fibre suitcase from the driver's seat and sat nursing it, with his head on one side. She climbed in gently and spoke in undertones to the tonga-wallah. When the vehicle jerked forward Mr Maybrick woke, alarmed. She clutched one edge of the suitcase and he another to save it from disaster. And like this they swayed and bucked through the benevolent night guarding her possessions.

Four young officers of the Pankot Rifles took the weight
of the coffin on their shoulders. A scratch lot they could
have been better matched in height, but the angle of their
burden was maintained step by faltering step at a degree
several notches above a level that would have led to a
bizarre accident. She recognized the pink face of Captain
Beauvais, pinker from the exertion of this funeral regimental duty, and wondered whether on his way out he felt
the additional weight of a recollection of Bob Buckland,
whoever Bob Buckland had been or was. The shortest of
the four, he had the right front station and so the coffin
had an inclination downwards and moved upon a line that
drove logically into the ground beyond the open door to
the hastily dug hole for which the woman immediately
behind the cortège was responsible.

Beside Mildred walked Kevin Coley; behind these two
Isobel Rankin and Maisie Trehearne, and then Clara
Fosdick and Nicky Paynton and Clarissa. A thin scatter-
ing.

For some time after the coffin had been borne out and
the last mourner had followed it through the open door
Barbie remained seated in the shadow of a pillar far back
in the church, and in the denser shadow of her own bitter
and terrible conclusions.

There (she thought) went the *raj*, supported by the
unassailable criteria of necessity, devoutness, even of
self-sacrifice because Mildred had snatched half-an-hour
from her vigil to see the coffin into the hole she had
ordered dug. Presently she would return to the hospital
where Susan was still in labour. But what was being
perpetrated was an act of callousness: the sin of collec-
tively not caring a damn about a desire or an expectation
or a fulfilment of a promise so long as personal dignity was

preserved and at a cost that could be borne without too great an effort.

And so it will be (Barbie thought) so it will be in regard to our experience here. And when we are gone let them colour the sky how they will. We shall not care. It has never truly been our desire or intention to colour it permanently but only to make it as cloudless for ourselves as we can. So that my life here has indeed been wasted because I have lived it as a transferred appendage, as a parlour-maid, the first in line for morning prayers while the mistress of the house hastily covers herself with her wrap and kneels like myself in piety for a purpose. But we have no purpose that God would recognize as such, dress it up as we may by hastily closing our wrap to hide our nakedness and convey a dignity and a distinction as Mildred did and still attempts. She has a kind of nobility. It does not seem to me to matter very much whether she appears half-dressed in front of Kevin Coley. But I think it matters to God and to the world that she rode with him into the valley and offered matriarchal wisdom to women older and as wise or wiser than she. For that was an arrogance, the kind which Mabel always set her face against, because Mabel knew she brought no consolation even to a rose let alone to a life. She brought none to me in the final count, but what distinguished her was her pre-knowledge that this was anyway impossible. So she probably forgives me about the grave and closes her eyes. It was not everyone who saw that they were open.

'Those are for her, aren't they?'

It was Edgar Maybrick's voice. He gathered the bunch of flowers from where it lay on the pew at her side.

'They've all gone now,' he said. 'Is that your case?'

'Yes,' she said, and rose, letting him reach down and pick the suitcase up as well. He led her out. When they reached the place – a blur of fresh-piled flowers – she took the bunch from him and standing well away from the shape of the dark hole that should never have been dug cast it in.

She returned to Rose Cottage alone. As the tonga pulled

up at the porch she saw the figure of an old man come from the side of the house and stand waiting. She got out and paid the fare. The front door was open, as were the windows of her room. She and the old man watched each other for a while and then she called to him, 'Will you come and help me, Aziz? I'm very tired and should like a cup of tea.' She went up the steps and entered the hall. Behind her she heard the clunk of his sandals as he cast them off on the verandah before following her in.

PART FOUR

The Honour of the Regiment

1

Susan was delivered of a healthy male child, that looked
absurdly like poor Teddie, at five o'clock in the morning
of June the eighth, three hours before Sarah, hurriedly
summoned home from Calcutta, arrived in Pankot on the
night train from Ranpur and thirty-three hours after Susan
had cried out 'But it can't be! The baby isn't finished yet.'

For a while Susan did not look at the child. She averted
her head no matter what her mother said or Travers said
and the nursing staff said. It began to look like a classic
case of rejection. It was not until Sarah took the child in
her arms and impressed on Susan that there was nothing
wrong with it, that it was as lively as you liked, in fact
pretty obstreperous and not in the least pleased by
anything or anyone it had seen so far, that Susan turned
her head and looked at Sarah and then at the child and
said nothing but let Sarah put the screaming bundle where
she could get a view of its purple face and groping
miniature hands.

Accepting the child in her own arms her reluctance to
examine it closely was obvious. She said, 'Is it whole? Is
it?' and took some time to comprehend the evidence,
revealed detail by detail by Sister Page, that there was no
doubt of this. The effort exhausted her and she cried a bit
but smiled and touched the baby's cheek; and slept and
woke; and when the moment came applied herself to the
primitive task of giving suck with a frown of spartan
concentration which gradually eased and left upon her
brow a radiance that was too old, too heavy for her face.
But no one noticed that.

Presently her milk failed which Mildred said was just as
well because one ought not to become so physically

involved. It was bad for the child and the mother, unhygienic and potentially a bloody nuisance for everyone concerned. She had advised against it and had been surprised by Susan's insistence that at least she should try. Well, not surprised. The poor girl had done her damnedest to do everything right. She'd been a brick.

'After all,' Mildred said, 'one can't imagine more trying circumstances.' She gave up the room next door to the one auspiciously numbered seven, took herself back to the grace and favour but still spent most of the day with Susan. Isobel Rankin saw to it that a telegram was sent to Colonel Layton through the Red Cross. Letters were written. The slight unease felt about the welfare of prisoners-of-war in Germany now that Europe had been invaded was not openly admitted; instead it was suggested to Susan that her father might be home for Christmas.

'How lovely if he were,' Susan said. 'For us anyway. But it seems a bit unfair, doesn't it? All he'll want is peace and quiet and looking after and what he'll get is a screaming baby that gets all the attention.' She smiled and added, 'But I don't suppose he'll mind because it's a grandson,' and then closed her eyes so that the visitors lowered their voices for a while and thought of the need there would presently be for Susan seriously to consider getting married again to give the boy a father; preferably to Dicky Beauvais who was attentive and in every known respect an excellent choice.

Like other young men in the past Captain Beauvais had originally seemed interested in Sarah; but in his case it would have been impossible to show interest in Susan because when he arrived in Pankot she was a married woman and then a pregnant married woman. He had assumed a brotherly role and it was only since the news of Teddie Bingham's death that the brotherliness had begun to wear thin which it did in a way that suggested to some people that it had never been more than a disguise for the warmer feelings he had always had but tried to reserve and express for Sarah only.

Again it had become necessary to subject Sarah to

scrutiny. There seemed to be something wrong with the girl, something complex which was not going to be put right by a simple antidote like the safe return of her father or getting her married off to the right sort of officer, or allowing her to abandon her family responsibilities in Pankot to do a more exciting or exacting job of soldiering closer to those areas where the shooting was. Neither did that hint of little Mrs Smalley's at the time when Teddie Bingham transferred his affections to young Susan – that Sarah was perhaps just a little unsound in her views – really seem justified. All that could be said was that her behaviour was a degree less than admirable because it lacked either enthusiasm or spontaneity.

'She thinks too much,' Nicky Paynton said, 'And say what you will men don't like it when it shows. She should learn to hide the fact which shouldn't be too difficult because she already knows how to keep her thoughts to herself.'

But that was before the crisis brought on by Mabel's death and Susan's premature labour, both of which events Sarah missed by going to Calcutta. The journey back to Pankot must have been tense and exhausting. She had been fond of her aunt and tireless in her efforts to jolly Susan along after the blow of Teddie's death. Fate had deprived her of the opportunity to help at a time when her help was most needed, but she was at Susan's bedside within an hour of reaching home on the night train from Ranpur. Both her sister and her mother were asleep but she stayed in Susan's room and nodded off in a chair beside the bed, with one hand on the counterpane where Susan could reach it when she woke.

Travers, who found the sisters like this, was touched, and related how the relief that Sarah must have felt at finding her sister well and the baby safely born, had caused her to smile as she slept. The same look of happiness was on her face on the occasion she held the baby and persuaded Susan to accept it, and it occurred to Nicky Paynton who was present that at last something like an enthusiasm could have entered Sarah's life, even if it were second-hand: an enthusiasm for her sister's child. The important thing, Mrs Paynton thought, was that the soil should be tilled. Sarah, she thought, had spent long enough unconsciously making up to her father for not being a boy. At that moment the situation became clear to Mrs Paynton and so did the future which ceased to be worrying. The solution to Sarah was simple after all. What had been repressed was nothing other than a highly developed maternal instinct.

'Sarah, did you manage to see Captain Merrick?' she asked – remembering on the way out of Susan's room what Sarah had gone to Calcutta to do.

'Yes, I saw him the afternoon of the day I arrived.'

'How was he?'

'Waiting for an operation.'

'Anything very serious?'

'I suppose in medical or surgical terms it was quite straightforward. They were going to cut off his left arm above the elbow. Excuse me a second.'

Sarah went to Sister Page's desk and spoke to the girl who was sitting there. Clara Fosdick and Nicky Paynton waited near the liftgate and looked at one another. When Sarah rejoined them Mrs Paynton said, 'How very upsetting.'

'What?'

'About Captain Merrick. Does Susan know?'

'Yes, Captain Travers thought it better to say straight out because she had an idea he might have no arms at all. The letter he wrote us from hospital in Comilla was dictated.'

The lift came. Inside, the cramped conditions discouraged conversation but enabled Nicky Paynton and Clara Fosdick to study Sarah's face and agree later when they were alone that there was an uncharacteristic hardness and decisiveness in its expression, a look of impatience which made the tenderness shown for her sister and her sister's child more noticeable.

Coming out of the lift into the reception foyer Mrs Fosdick added, 'Did he agree to be godfather?'

'No. He was grateful for the suggestion but didn't think he'd make a good one.'

'Because of his arm?'

'I expect that came into it.'

'What happened to him? Did he say?'

'He pulled Teddie and a driver out of a burning jeep and got them under cover. He got bullet wounds and third degree burns. He saved the driver but was too late for Teddie. He'll be getting a medal.'

'I should think so too.'

'The police's loss was obviously the army's gain,' Nicky Paynton said. 'But I'm sorry Captain Merrick's said no. He'd have been a godfather for any boy to be proud of.'

'Later on, perhaps,' Sarah said. 'When the boy was old enough not to be frightened. His face was burnt too.'

'Oh, dear. Badly?'

'I couldn't tell. There wasn't much you could see through the bandages except his eyes and mouth. But Sister Prior said his hair would grow again and he might even look human.'

'What an extraordinary thing to say.'

'She said it to relieve her feelings. She didn't care for my Lady Bountiful act. She's the sort of nursing sister we describe as a bit off, the sort who wouldn't be an officer at home but is because she joined the QAs and came out here. I think she blames people like us for the fact that there's a war on at all. She thought it was scandalous giving badly wounded men medals. She though money would be more to the point. But she's on the wrong track there with Ronald Merrick. He's not interested in that kind of payment or in the kind of people who'd suggest it.'

'I should think not.'

'He says he blames himself for Teddie being killed. Dicky Beauvais promised to be back with the staff car. Can we give you a lift? I'm going to the daftar so it's on the way.'

'That would be nice,' Nicky Paynton said.

'I'll see if he's here.'

Sarah went into the forecourt and presently returned

and reported the car coming up the drive. While Captain Beauvais took a rupee from Mrs Fosdick to pay off their waiting tonga-wallah the three women got into the back of the car.

'Why does Captain Merrick blame himself?' Mrs Paynton asked when they were settled.

'I don't think he does really. It's his way of putting things. He'd gone forward to collect a special prisoner and Teddie went with him, although there was no need. I think Teddie was interfering, I mean not trusting Ronald Merrick to deal with a situation in the way he thought it should be handled. After they'd talked to the prisoner Teddie took the jeep when he shouldn't have and went further forward still, and took the prisoner with him because the man said he had two friends in the jungle who wanted to give themselves up too. Ronald didn't know he'd gone and when he found out he had to go after him.'

'That's okay,' Dicky Beauvais said, getting in the front. He signalled the driver to start and sat with his arm over the back of the front bench to take part more comfortably in whatever conversation was in progress.

'Sarah's telling us about Captain Merrick and poor Teddie.'

'Oh, yes,'

'But isn't it very unusual,' Mrs Paynton said, 'for Japanese soldiers to give themselves up?'

'Oh, they weren't Japanese.'

'What then?'

'Indian soldiers from Teddie's old regiment.'

The car slowed at the end of the drive and then moved smoothly and comfortably, well sprung and upholstered, out on to the road that led to area headquarters.

'Muzzys,' Sarah went on. 'Not Teddie's lot. From the other battalion that was captured in Malaya. Now fighting with the Japanese against us. They belonged to the INA we hear about but aren't supposed to take seriously. Captain Merrick says there are far more of them than is allowed to be supposed but that they're badly led and armed and half-starved because the Japanese don't think much of them, especially not of their officers. Anyway he followed Teddie in another jeep and then they found themselves being mortared and shot at by the Japs *and* the INA. The man driving the jeep Ronald was in turned it round to get back where he belonged, so Ronald jumped out and went the rest of the way on foot. When he got to Teddie's jeep it was burning and the prisoner had gone, so he pulled Teddie and the driver out and dragged them under cover, which is when he got shot up himself as well as burned. I haven't told Susan all this because although Ronald Merrick didn't actually say so I think everyone felt Teddie had been wrong and silly. I don't suppose he could bear the thought of leaving two old Muzzy Guides hiding in the jungle, waiting to be recaptured. I gather the divisional commander was rather brassed off, losing two staff-officers and a jeep as a result. But of course the *regiment* would be pleased by what Teddie tried to do, wouldn't it? Don't you think so, Dicky?'

Dicky nodded, but glanced at the driver and then warningly at Sarah.

'After all,' Sarah said, apparently not noticing, 'he was doing it *for* the regiment. Ronald says that when they were talking to the prisoner and the prisoner realized Teddie was a Muzzy officer the poor man broke down and knelt and touched Teddie's feet. So it makes you wonder how many of the men have joined the INA without knowing what they were doing. It's different in the case of the officers. Ronald said Teddie thought INA officers completely beyond the pale. I gather the same thing nearly happened in Germany, but on a much smaller scale. Isn't that so, Dicky?'

Dicky said nothing.

Again Sarah seemed not to notice his reluctance to discuss the subject in front of a lance-naik driver, but her next comment might have been taken as an oblique criticism of this attitude. She said, 'I can't think why there's so much secrecy about it. It makes it look as if we're afraid of it spreading, but Ronald Merrick said it was difficult in Imphal to stop our own sepoys shooting

INA men on sight even if they were trying to give themselves up.'

'The best thing for them,' Nicky Paynton said. 'It'll save rope later.'

'Did you hear the news on the wireless this morning?' Sarah asked, as if changing the subject.

'You mean what Dickie Mountbatten says about carrying on operations through the monsoon? I thoroughly agree. Bunny said ages ago that downing tools directly the monsoon set in was military suicide if you were fighting the Japanese, but perhaps now that Mountbatten's said it we can press on and push the little horrors right back across the Chindwin and not sit on our bottoms for three months waiting for the rains to let up.'

'I didn't mean that. I meant the news about ex-chief minister Mohammed Ali Kasim being released from jail and taken to Mirat.'

'Oh, that,' Clara Fosdick said. 'Well the poor old man's ill and there never seemed much point in locking *him* up. My brother-in-law Billy Spendlove always had a high regard for him. In fact he expected him to tell the Congress to take a running jump when there was all that nonsense about ministers having to resign in 'thirty-nine. Billy said that in 'forty-two the Governor gave Mr Kasim an opportunity to disown Congress policies because he knew he'd disagreed with practically everything Congress did from 'thirty-nine onwards but the old boy refused and said he preferred to go to jail. And it's not a pukka release, is it? He's obviously got to stay in Mirat in the Nawab's custody. At least until he gets better. It's so embarrassing when they start getting ill because the people automatically think a political prisoner's ill-health is due to bad treatment.'

'But,' Sarah said, 'someone said at the daftar this morning it's mostly eyewash about him being ill. The real reason is because the elder son who was an officer in the Army and was a prisoner in Malaya has just been captured in Imphal, fighting with the INA. The government thinks Mr Kasim's the kind of man who won't try to make excuses for his son turning coat, and that by being nice to him now he'll be very helpful to us after the war if other Indian politicians start calling INA men heroes and patriots. Which they're bound to.'

'Why bound to?'

'Because of there being so many. If there were only a few isolated cases of Indian officers and other ranks going over to the Japanese then they wouldn't be worth bothering about and we could courtmartial them without anybody either noticing or caring.'

Nicky Paynton cut in. 'It seems to me that what's good for one is good for as many as there are.'

'But that's looking at the thing from the point of view of the principle that's involved. We shan't really be able to afford to do that.'

'We should damn' well try.'

'Then we'd make fools of ourselves, wouldn't we, Dicky?'

Dicky smiled bleakly. He gave the driver instructions to turn in at the next compound.

After the staff car had left Mrs Paynton and Mrs Fosdick at their bungalow, Nicky said, 'Do you know, Clara, Sarah hasn't once said anything to me about her Aunt Mabel's death, has she to you?'

'She said thank you when I told her how upset we all were.'

'That's all she said to me, too. I thought she was probably too cut up to say anything else but now I'm not sure. I think Mildred's going to have trouble with that girl. Perhaps Lucy Smalley was right. She seemed to want to provoke Dicky Beauvais just now.'

'How, provoke?'

'Well, Clara, let's face it. Dicky's an awfully nice chap but he's not particularly intelligent is he? I got the impression she was trying to provoke him to come out with the kind of remark she could have a private little laugh at. In fact she was provoking us too. It makes one wonder – '

'Wonder what?'

'Well, put it this way. She's always had guts. Suddenly she has nerve. It makes one wonder what happened to her in Calcutta.'

'Perhaps it's just the wrong time of the month.'

'No. You can usually tell when she's having one of her bad periods because she goes quieter than ever. She wasn't quiet this morning. In fact Dicky Beauvais was dying to tell her to shut up because the driver was listening. That's why I took the line I did, about shooting them now saving rope later. But I expect she's right. If we ever do win this bloody war we might hang Bose and one or two of the bigwigs but the rest will just have to be cashiered or dismissed with ignominy. Only by then we'll probably be on our way out in any case and the bloody Indians will have to deal with them in their own bloody way, and they'll probably bloody well make heroes out of them.'

'Nicky!'

'Well, it's true.'

'But there can't be all that many.'

'Can't there? There can be and are. We all know it. But we try to pretend it's not so. But it is so. The bloody rot's set in. When I think of Bunny sweating away in the bloody jungle – '

She went to her room to calm herself and wrote a letter to her husband who had got a brigade at last. 'Darling Bunny, Hope you're in good form,' she began and looked at the latest snap of the two boys in Wiltshire, grinning into the sun with the innocence of youth. 'Mildred's younger daughter, Su, has just had a baby boy.'

2

When Mildred pronounced Susan 'a brick' Travers concurred. Seeing Susan come through, as he put it, he said this showed how wrong people had been who had thought her dangerously withdrawn like that poor girl of Poppy Browning's; and was then taken aback by the hardening of Mildred's jaw, her snapped demand and explicit rebuke, 'Who said that?' and thought it better not to mention it had been Sarah who, in case it was something he should bear in mind when treating her sister, told him what the missionary had said.

'I think it was Miss Batchelor.'

'That woman!' Mildred exclaimed. 'What can she know about Poppy Browning or her daughter?'

Poppy had been Ranpur Regiment, with a daughter married into the cavalry, a young girl six months pregnant when her dashing husband was killed in Quetta by a roofbeam collapsing on his back and on both arms of the Indian girl under him whose open mouth was choked with plaster and who was also dead, suffocated by lover and rubble, when rescuers arrived and disentangled them from the ruins of the bungalow and each other's bodies: a situation which Poppy Browning's daughter had celebrated by smothering her baby two days after it was born. The affair had been hushed up, which was one of the reasons why the daughter was now never mentioned by name but referred to as Poppy Browning's daughter, and a clean clear image preserved of Poppy herself, whose life and record and those of her husband had been unblemished. The sad scandal that brought their Indian career to a premature and obscure conclusion, no longer being spoken of directly, had elevated them to a special place in the minds of people who recognized the value of selfless service, hard work and cheerful dispositions. Poppy and her husband had been mixed doubles champions three years running, back in the 'twenties when they were in their prime and their daughter still at school in England.

Ever since the Quetta tragedy the name Poppy had blown gently, frail but hardy like the flower, brave among the stubble of the reaped field of human experience. But this section of the field was private. The name Poppy Browning was scarcely known among the younger generation and it was certainly not one to be bandied about by a retired missionary, an interfering woman whose tiresomeness had reached its apogee and was no longer to be borne. So Mildred implied. But her habit of leaving her disapproval to speak for itself, of making exclamatory denunciations rather than explanatory criticisms, as if these were sufficiently informative, left the actual details of Barbie's bad behaviour unclearly set out in the minds of people who felt their sympathies were due to Mildred and indeed assumed by her to be offered; anything else being unthinkable if the appearance of the order of things were to be preserved.

'Some wild idea,' Mildred said, 'that Mabel wished to be buried in Ranpur. Can you imagine anything more grotesque?' Imagine, no. But imagining the grotesque was not necessary when it got about that there had been a macabre and unauthorized visit to the mortuary, a visit which had involved a Eurasian receptionist and a Doctor Lal in serious trouble.

Daily, Miss Batchelor was seen aboard a tonga, clutching a bunch of roses, on her way to the churchyard, a visit prolonged beyond the time it took her to place the flowers on the grave by (it was said) a lengthy vigil in the church itself. Presently in addition to the roses she was observed to clutch a suitcase, the one in which bit by bit she was transferring her belongings from the cottage to the tiny room in the rectory bungalow where Arthur and Clarissa Peplow had offered her temporary refuge.

Neither Arthur nor Clarissa was to be drawn out on the subject of the grotesque idea Miss Batchelor had apparently had about her dead friend's wishes and on the whole people refrained from asking them because merely to do so raised the question whether Mr Peplow had buried Mabel Layton in the wrong place. Neither were many questions asked on the subject of the offer of temporary refuge which Clarissa described as the most practical way out of an unhappy situation and a Christian duty but not to be thought of by anyone as a preliminary to a permanent arrangement being come to. The room was too small.

'I am already worried,' Clarissa said, 'about the amount of stuff with which Barbara seems to be encumbered. If there is much more she will have to speak at Jalal-ud-din's about temporary storage.'

Alive, old Mabel Layton had been precariously contained; but her gift for stillness, the sense that flowed from her of old and irreversible connexions, had made the task of containing her less difficult than her detachment implied it could have been. She should no longer have been a problem but a once slightly disruptive pattern that now dissolved and faded into the fabric. But, dead, she emerged as a monument which, falling suddenly, had caused a tremor which continued to reverberate, echo, in the wake of Miss Batchelor who, bowling down Club Road in the back of a tonga, now guarded the fibre suitcase as if it were crammed with numbered pieces of the fallen tower that had been her friend, and as if it were her intention to re-erect it in the garden of the rectory bungalow or even in a more public position, in the churchyard perhaps or at the intersection of Church and Club Roads where – imperfectly reassembled – it might lean a little and dominate the whole area with a peculiar and critical intensity, make it impossible to go past the spot without having one's confidence further inpaired and one's doubts increased by this post-mortem reversal of roles. For whereas one had been in the habit of looking in on the eccentric elder Mrs Layton to satisfy oneself that the purpose and condition of exile were still understood (however idiosyncratically by her), furthered and supported, now she would look down from an eminence upon the purpose, upon the condition, accusingly, still silent; but silent like someone who knew that events could speak for themselves and would do so.

On cue, the clouds of the southwest monsoon, thinned by the overland journey across the parched, open-mouthed plain, appeared in the Pankot sky and spilt what moisture they had left, establishing the wet-season pattern of sudden short showers, of morning mist which could be dispersed by the sunshine or give way to a light persistent drizzle. When the sun came out there was a strange mountain chill that did not make itself felt upon the flesh but in the nostrils, mingling there with the pervading scents of hot mud and aromatic gum. But this year these familiar manifestations of a Pankot summer contained an element, difficult to analyse, but unmistakably felt, of something that acted as an irritant.

As if aware of a special necessity, Mildred Layton now took a day off, put on jodhpurs, and accompanied by Captain Coley set out on horseback on a day's trek to the nearest villages to thank women who had sent little presents and messages of goodwill to Colonel Sahib's younger daughter and baby; to discuss with them the now excellent prospects of the early return of the long-absent warriors from across the black water. It became known, through Coley, that Mildred had gallantly drunk cup after cup of syrupy tea, eaten piping hot chappattis, a bowl of vegetable curry, been soaked in a sudden shower between villages, held squealing black babies, patted the shoulder of an ill-favoured looking woman who was weeping because since her husband went away she had grown old and fat; discussed the crops with village elders, more intimate problems with the wives and mothers, the hopes of recruitment with shy striplings pushed forward by their old male relatives to salaam Colonel Memsahib, and returned exhausted but upright through one of the wet season's spectacular sunsets which turned her white shirt flamingo pink and the shadows of the horses brown.

There was a glow, but it was external to the affair; a bit too theatrical to penetrate to the mind where it was needed. It gave the performance qualities of self-consciousness which made it look as if Mildred's main achievement had been to draw attention to an undertaking whose only claim was a nostalgic one upon the fund of recollected duties and obligations which time and circumstances were rendering obsolete; as obsolete as Teddie's gesture, of which the division had taken a view of a kind it would not, in better days, have taken, but with which one somehow could not argue – considering the cost of a jeep

302

and the shortage of equipment, not to mention the escaped prisoner, the burnt sepoy-driver and Captain Merrick's lost left arm. The price of regimental loyalty and pride seemed uncomfortably high.

The circumstances surrounding the death of Teddie Bingham were better not discussed but it was circumstances such as these which were speaking, louder than words, sustaining the illusion of Mabel Layton grimly looking down from the eminence whose site was shifted according to the whim of Miss Batchelor, who sometimes seemed uncertain what to do with the contents of the suitcase and was seen once to get as far as Church Road and then order the tonga back up the hill to the cottage, which she had now received official notice to quit by the end of the month.

Perhaps at the height of this piecemeal removal from cottage to rectory Clarissa had put her foot down. 'She'd better not,' Nicky Paynton said, 'otherwise where will the poor old thing go?'

A comic but horrifying thought took hold: of old Miss Batchelor, homeless, seated on a trunk in the middle of the bazaar, surrounded by her detritus, unpacking and rebuilding the monument there, to the amusement of Hindu and Muslim shopkeepers who would interpret such a sight as proof that the entire *raj* would presently and similarly be on its uppers.

'She's writing to the mission,' Clarissa said, 'or so she assures me. One hopes but has doubts that they'll soon find something for her, either in the way of voluntary work or permanent accommodation. But everything points to the advisability of her leaving the station. In view of everything that's happened she could never be happy here again.'

It would have been different if over the last five years Miss Batchelor had entered more into the spirit of things; for example, Clarissa hinted, she could have done more for the church in Pankot. But shortsightedly she had subordinated all her private interests to those of the elder Mrs Layton, had become over-wrapped up in that peculiar woman's solitary affairs, 'against, I often felt,' Clarissa said, 'her true instincts which were to say the least of it for having as many fingers in the pie as possible if I'm any judge. But I'm afraid it's too late for her to revert to type. Which is a pity because Barbara was born to serve. And then there is this attitude of hers to that old man which isn't going to help her patch things up with Mildred. I mean the man Aziz. She says only she and Mabel would really understand his behaviour which is as may be, but Mildred says that if it hadn't actually happened Mabel would have invented it, if necessary beyond the grave.'

Aziz's extraordinary perhaps sinister disappearance had gone counter, utterly, to the case law, the accumulated evidence that justified a deep and affectionate belief in the dependability of old and faithful servants. In the welter of conflicting and often unsatisfactory responses of Easterner to Westerner, one simple rule had stubbornly persisted, the rule of loyalty to the man or woman whose salt had been eaten. It was an ancient law but it had lived on and been honoured countless times. Men had died for it, not only in their youth on the battlefield fighting the sahibs' wars but in their age and infirmity on the steps of verandahs in defence of their masters' women and children. Women had died for it too, ayahs for their infant charges, maids for their mistresses. The rule, uncodified, was written in the heart and in old men like Aziz could normally be assumed to have passed across the line of law and custom into the realm of personal devotion.

Well, so one might have thought; so it had seemed, as it would seem for Mildred and John Layton with their Mahmoud, Nicky Paynton with her old Fariqua Khan who wrote monthly progress reports to Brigadier Paynton; countless others, in Pankot, in Ranpur, the length and breadth of India, wherever master, mistress and servant had grown used to and fond of one another, had jointly experienced good times, bad times. A sahib's, a memsahib's death left such old bearers inconsolable and the death of a Fariqua or a Mahmoud could bring tears to eyes accustomed to the discipline of staying dry in public.

304

But Aziz had not conformed, he had not been inconsolable. He had not wept, he had not got in people's way while doing his touching best to shoulder his share of sad and necessary duties. He had not shouldered them. His desertion – no matter what the civil surgeon said about having known of a similar case – smacked of unfeelingness. His return and refusal to explain himself was like a declaration of an absolute right to answer to no one for his actions, to opt out, if he wanted to, from any situation in which there were established and desirable lines of conduct for him to follow.

So that queer thing Mildred said about Mabel inventing Aziz's disappearance if it had been necessary to do so was clear. Mildred saw Aziz's brief defection as a gesture made as much by Mabel as by him and which summed up, reflected, Mabel's long-sustained and critical detachment from the life and spirit of things. Mildred – whom it used to seem that Mabel didn't trust – had obviously never trusted Mabel, and for better reasons. While the old woman was alive Mildred had held her own criticisms in check, for John's sake, the regiment's sake, the station's sake, and even now could not descend to anything so crude as a direct attack.

Instead there had been a faint shrug of the shoulders when Kevin Coley reported Aziz unassailable, protected by Miss Batchelor's assertion that he had returned to serve *her*, that she would require, indeed insisted on, these services for the few days remaining to her at Rose Cottage, would herself pay his wages from June the first until the day of her departure for the rectory and his for his village and retirement. Mildred shrugged her shoulders too when people questioned Aziz's right to receive the small pension Mabel had made provision for in the Will.

'One must respect a Will,' she said. The impression she gave was of blaming Mabel, not Aziz, and of declining to take any tiresome action that would draw attention to the fact that one was living through a period in which general moral collapse seemed imminent, a collapse for which Mabel was as much to blame as anyone.

It was remembered how on the day of the wedding party the old woman had sat, deafer than ever, making things difficult for young officers who were anxious to pay their respects, notably difficult for young Beauvais whose uncle had been a subaltern under Bob Buckland, who, in turn, had been a fellow-subaltern of Mabel's first husband and whom she had known, been fond of and consoled by between her husband's death and her marriage to James Layton.

It was remembered too how she had left the party without a word, and apparently by a door at the back of the mess, 'feeling unwell and not wanting to be a skeleton at the feast,' according to Mildred's later explanation of an absence which, without causing any special concern at the time, had certainly made itself felt through the empty chair, like a criticism too subtle to be interpreted easily or accurately.

The truth could no longer be avoided. It had been a criticism of the foundations of the edifice, of the sense of duty which kept alive the senses of pride and loyalty and honour. It drew attention to a situation it was painful to acknowledge: that the god had left the temple, no one knew when, or how, or why. What one was left with were the rites which had once propitiated, once been obligatory, but were now meaningless because the god was no longer there to receive them. Poor Teddie! His was an end of an expository kind, like a last sacrificial attempt to recall godly favour. If there were still a glow to be had it would have spread from there, but it did not. Nor did it spread from the action of the man Merrick as once it would have done because nothing could obliterate the image of Merrick as an earlier victim of changed circumstances, of the general loss of confidence, the grave shifting of the ground beneath one's feet as the layers of authoritarian support above one's head thinned and those of hostile spirits thickened.

Somewhere along the line doubt had entered. Even on a sunny day it lay upon the valley, an invisible mist, a barrier to the clearer echoes of the conscience. A rifle shot would no longer whip through the air, slap hard against a hillside and bounce, leaving a penetrating and convincing smell of cordite, sharpening senses and stiffening the blood. It would go muffled, troubled, and its message would be garbled; and the eye would not dart alerted, Khyber-trained, to the hillsides for the tell-tale flick of a mischievous robe, but shift uncomfortably, to observe the condition of the lines, for signs of mutinous movements on the parade grounds where the Pankot Rifles went through the motions of training another generation of candidates for the rolls, acolytes for the temple.

And presently – not suddenly but with an increasing persistence – Mildred's personality began to stand out, a reminder to people of what life had meant, been like; so that an interesting counter-image to the one of Mabel began to emerge – an image of Mildred, also made of stone, splendidly upright, and revealing her true distinction through her refusal to compromise either her upbringing or her position by allowing what was irresistible to move her or what was expedient to take precedence over what in her judgment was right.

And so after all a glow came, even if it did not spread. The glow was Mildred. The famous expression shone. It could not infect but it could remind. And when she said, 'What Teddie tried to do was worth the whole bloody war put together,' it was realized that with her unerring instinct she had gone straight to the heart of the matter, cutting through such irrelevancies as divisional annoyance, the cost of a jeep, the loss of a prisoner and Merrick's arm, leaving one with Teddie's blameless death, his praiseworthy sacrifice for a principle the world no longer had time or inclination to uphold.

From the rear of the compound of the grace and favour bungalow smoke rose, between showers, as Mahmoud directed the burning of the stuff Mildred was beginning to throw out, the unwanted accumulation of the years of pigging in which were now over; over too late, of course. Rose Cottage would certainly be more comfortable, more convenient for most things, but the station had been deprived for ever of any significance that might have attached to her presence there. Now she seemed to wish it to be recognized that she was merely claiming what had become her husband's property; not, as once could have been the case, acquiring an appropriate and proper setting for her virtue. She would live there and hold it in trust for him.

'Susan has decided to give the baby all Teddie's Christian names,' she said. 'So there'll be another Edward Arthur David Bingham. On the whole I approve.'

It was the continuity, logical and unsentimental, to which she responded, the idea that in this matter of the name Teddie would endure long after the acrid smell of the lost jeep had died away and the bloody accountant-general had finished reckoning out the amount in rupees. Dick and Isobel Rankin had agreed to be godparents. Sarah would be the younger godmother and Dicky Beauvais the second godfather. The child would be well endowed. Mahmoud's widowed niece, called Minnie because her real name was unpronounceable, had gladly accepted the duties of ayah. The christening would take place at St John's, a week after the day fixed for Susan to leave the auspiciously numbered room in the nursing home.

'We shall have the christening party here,' Mildred said, meaning the grace and favour. 'I want to get it over before we move up to the Cottage, and get Su used to the idea of having the baby at home. The last time she was up at the place wasn't the happiest occasion.' At the cottage, she said, she herself would have Mabel's room, the little spare would be an excellent nursery. Susan and Sarah would share the other room, the one Miss Batchelor was in the process of vacating. Even sharing, they would have more space each than they had in the tiny bedrooms of the grace and favour.

'I should have liked to do some redecoration, but I think that will have to wait,' Mildred said. 'I'll have to keep the mali on but I've told Mahmoud to keep an eagle eye on him. It's time the mali earned his keep. You can't say that with Mabel he was exactly overworked, can you?'

She glanced down at her half-empty glass. For a while after Teddie's death, the drinking habit had been less frequently indulged, but then resumed as if she had decided that giving anything up was a sign of weakness. Now that she could afford it, with the whole of Mabel's money coming into Colonel Layton's possession, there was no reason left for anyone to question the habit at all. For a hard-drinking woman who had recently had a great deal to cope with she was comparatively abstemious. And remembering the time when it seemed as if she drank for the station's sake as much as for her own, people felt there were many good reasons, few of them identifiable, why she should actually drink more than she did. It was as if, anticipating more reasons to come, she deliberately held back, in order to be in good form for the occasion.

3

Her flesh had hardened. It had the toughness of metallic substance. When she walked she sensed her body's displacement of the air. Between herself and Aziz there was a magnetic field of force. They spoke seldom. It was not necessary. In their brief exchanges there was an undertone of parable.

'There's very little more,' she told Clarissa after several visits to the rectory bungalow; and edged out of the narrow space between the bed and the wall, catching the nailed feet of an imitation ivory crucifix with her sleeve, so that the Lord was tilted sideways as He would be if the cross weren't planted firmly enough or were lowered into the wrong hole, one too wide for it.

She straightened the sacrificial figure and turned to face Clarissa's forgiveness which was conveyed through a swift averting of the eyes as if from the sight of a near accident of an ominous, sacrilegious kind.

From the rectory she went to St John's, visited the grave and then sat down in the shadow of the pillar, in the same pew as on the day of the funeral, so that Mabel might find her without difficulty. This was a vigil she kept every day between four and five, bringing roses cut from the bushes with Aziz's help. It interested her to discover how much he seemed to have learned about the way to cut blooms without weakening the bush or spoiling its shape. She did not understand the principle but guessed there was one and allowed him to guide her by silent indication or a sudden gesture of restraint.

Returning home she faced daily the mounting evidence of what seemed like improvidence. Could one single woman have acquired so much, have needed so much? The drawers in the Rose Cottage chests were deep. Sometimes she thought of them as comically bottomless, yielding up one item more for each item removed and crammed into a suitcase.

And shoes. In serried ranks. On tip-toe along parallel brass rods at the base of the almirah, each pair polished and cared for by Aziz and the mali's boy.

'I am fond of my shoes,' she said, newly discovering this attachment. She took the favourite pairs to the rectory but found the base of the almirah an unwilling repository. There were no brass rods and in any case the skirts of her suits and dresses hung too low, right down to the bottom of the cupboard. In one angle of the wall there was a curtained recess. She placed the shoes on the floor but the curtain did not conceal them. The shoes looked like the feet of old people eavesdropping. Nowadays tears came unexpectedly. 'Crying in a happy home,' Clarissa had warned her, 'is like untidiness in a neat one, and is a worry to God.' Barbie dried her eyes and looked round belligerently.

The room was dark as well as small. She peered through the single window, craning round the side of the miniature dressing-table to see what was to be seen. The view, on to the side of the bungalow, was blocked by creeper. She pushed the window open to let in some air. There were bars on the inside, a protection against thieves. The creeper sighed and shook. Tendrils of it, in possession of the sill, groped stealthily forward, probing for a grip on the interior. She hit and pushed them away, closed the window, found one tendril trapped inside and growing. She nipped it off. It was tough-skinned like herself. Its sap was odorous. Two kinds of death she had always feared: by drowning and by suffocation. She would need to be wary of the creeper. It was an understanding enemy.

Returning along the gloomy but sanctified passage to the hall she looked for Clarissa to say good-bye until tomorrow. Clarissa was no longer speaking on the telephone as she had been when Barbie arrived and sought and received nodded permission to take the suitcase through to the place of temporary refuge.

She said, 'Clarissa?' and, leaving the suitcase on the floor, parted the old-fashioned bead curtain that hung in the archway between hall and living-room. The living-room was crowded with leather chairs and wicker-work. There were exhausted indoor ferns in brass pots which filled the air with a green spiritual miasma. An oval mahogany table covered by a bobble-fringed bottle-green cloth stood roughly in the centre of the room. By this table Clarissa was waiting, with her hands laced in the long string of sandalwood beads she wore in the afternoon but for some reason never before lunch and never at dinner.

'Clarissa, I am just going to the grave and then home. I brought a few pairs of shoes.' She clutched a bunch of roses, yellow ones whose strong sweet scent Mabel had loved best of all. Clarissa did not reply, except by nodding.

'Is something wrong, Clarissa?'

Slowly Clarissa flushed.

'Yes. At least. I have something I find it painful to say. But must say. I hope there has never been anything except total frankness in our relationship. I mean other things as well, a mutual respect and recognition of common Christian intention, but always frankness. You will have to forgive me, Barbie, but it would be totally – a totally false *position* for me if we went ahead with our arrangements without my saying what I have to.'

'What is it Clarissa? Is it the amount of luggage? It *is* a little more than I thought.'

'It is not the amount of luggage although speaking of that I am afraid you've already brought more than I can adequately provide room for and still leave the servants space to keep order. I don't wish to be unthoughtful or unimaginative but if there is anything more to come than a caseful the day after tomorrow – providing we reach that stage – I think you'll have to speak at Jalal-ud-din's about storage. They do offer some facilities.'

'That won't be necessary, Clarissa. I should not want my stuff mouldering in a native storehouse.'

'Let me say no more about luggage. Personally I always try to keep in mind the fact that we bring nothing into this world and can certainly take nothing out. Ever since childhood I have firmly rejected the tyranny of possessions, thanks to a proper unbringing in this regard. And Heaven knows that those of us who serve in India soon learn how transient our experience of home and hearth is, don't we? I doubt that we shall remove from this station before Arthur's retirement, but there is very little in this room that has been with us in other places or would go with us to our next. One is sure of but one thing, the strength and love of God.'

The scent of the roses became overpowering. Barbie supported herself with one hand on the bottle-green cloth. Its texture was harsh and scratchy. Like a hair-shirt. The flush had left Clarissa's face and neck. She was now pale as from a sense of eternity and the will to earn her place there.

'I have strayed from the point,' she said. 'The painful point.'

Barbie moistened her dry teeth with the tip of her tongue. The sandalwood beads began to clack through Clarissa's suddenly animated fingers.

'I was at the club this forenoon,' Clarissa began, still in the pedantic way she had of speaking when delivering herself of an oration or an opinion previously formed and rehearsed. 'Not alone, but with others, people whom I respect and whose good opinion I value, people whom you know but whom I shall not name. It happened, it so happened, that the question of your temporary refuge here arose, and it was said by one, it was said, well, what a pity it was that after all these years some way could not have been found of allowing you to remain at Rose Cottage to help Mildred, if only for a while, with the enormous burden she will bear at least for a time, with Susan and the baby to look after. What a pity, and how useful, what a help you might have been since you know so well the details of the running of that house.'

The beads ceased clacking for a moment, having been gripped by Clarissa's plump white fingers, in one of which the gold wedding band was countersunk. But then the fingers fluttered again and the clacking resumed.

'It was of course an impractical suggestion but well-meant. But then it was said that quite apart from it being impractical it would be most, most, unsuitable. Unsuitable especially, it was said, with two pretty young girls in the house. And I could not, no I simply couldn't believe my ears, so much not believe that the moment, the opportunity, to challenge it, to discredit it, had gone before I fully understood exactly what had been implied. But having understood what was said, what was implied, in the hearing of several, I must convey it to you otherwise my position would be intolerable both in private and in public. For should I ever hear this thing repeated I must challenge it. I do not propose, Barbara, to refer to it again of my own accord, inside or outside this house, but I require, for my own peace of mind, under this roof, I require – from you – some word – '

Barbie was confused. She could not take in a clear notion of the matter, which seemed to be a special failure since obviously it excited Clarissa considerably, 'If I knew what word, Clarissa,' she said.

'A word,' Clarissa repeated, jiggling the beads in agitation, 'a word of refutation, of assurance, assurance that there are no grounds, no grounds, for such a wicked implication.'

Clarissa had flushed again with the effort of her demand, her appeal, whatever it was. Suddenly she let go of the beads and placed one hand under her heart, so that thinking she was unwell, perhaps overcome by the humidity that often accompanied the onset of the rains, Barbie took a step towards her, but stopped, because Clarissa had taken a simultaneous and involuntary step back. And, alerted by this evidence of apparent physical revulsion, Barbie began to grasp what had been said and a flush of anger began to darken her yellowed cheeks and old throat, spreading in unison with the electric surge of intelligence that awakened a desolate withered capacity for needing affection in return for giving it.

'Yes, I see,' she said. She thought for several moments before continuing. 'You naturally wish to be reassured. But what can I say? If it were true I should probably deny it because at the moment I've nowhere to go and if this is going to be said about me I should find it difficult to go anywhere in Pankot. It's a difficult thing for an elderly spinster to refute. But for what it's worth, Clarissa, so far as I know my affection for Sarah and Susan is not of an unnatural kind, unless it is unnatural to feel maternally to them, to take pleasure in their company and care what happens to them.'

'Thank you,' Clarissa said. And then, exhaling, clapped her hands to her cheeks and sat down on a bandy-legged stool.

'Is that all, Clarissa?'

Clarissa's mouth was still open. The tips of each of her little fingers held it in that exclamatory shape. Her eyes were closed.

'Oh!' she whispered. 'It was wicked. It was wicked.'

'Am I expected, Clarissa? As arranged? The day after tomorrow?'

Clarissa opened her eyes but did not look at her. Presently she nodded her head and Barbie turned and left the room, leaving her friend to recover the sense of deep Christian repose to which she was accustomed.

* * *

314

Without touching the other withered wreaths and faded cards she tidied up the green tin vases that held her own offerings, removed prickly stems from which the last petals had fallen and placed the yellow roses in a vase of their own. The hump of clay would never settle. When she had finished she noticed it was raining. She went inside the church and sat by the pillar; and as usual prayed that there would be no letter for her from the mission in answer to her hasty request, or that if there were it would be couched in negative or unoptimistic terms. But half way through the prayer she retracted it and, remaining on her knees, opened her eyes. She thought: I do not see how I can stay, I do not see how I can face it.

And not seeing how, she understood the depth of need and desire to stay which had been forming in her mind and heart ever since the day that Mabel was buried in the wrong grave; to stay for as long as it took to right the wrong that had been done, even if that meant waiting for the return of Colonel Layton who might be moved to listen to the truth. It was Colonel Layton's father by whose side Mabel had wished to rest.

She had begun to regret the letter to the mission, her offer of voluntary services in any capacity however menial in return for a roof. She had begun to feel that bit by bit she and Clarissa could become used to and of use to one another. She had even begun to imagine the possibility of patching things up with Mildred. All for Mabel's sake. All to achieve for Mabel's soul the repose that depended on the proper repose of Mabel's body. She had believed that she should not leave Pankot while there was hope. She had felt no horror at the idea of opening the grave and taking the remains to Ranpur. The idea had filled her with a sense of the quietude that would follow.

But she felt horror now; the horror of her own shame. In front of her hovered the pale shape of Clarissa's face with hands pressed against the cheeks. She wanted to put immense distance between herself and her life. How can I face it? she repeated. How can I walk about in the bazaar or sit here on a Sunday in the middle of the congregation, knowing what has been said, what has been hinted? The shape of Clarissa's face changed into that of Mildred's and the hands were not at the cheeks but droop-wristed below the chin, holding a glass, the downward-curving lips quirked at the corners in a dismissive smile.

'How can I face it?' she asked aloud. And the face became that of yet another, chin in hand, regarding her with that compassion and patience, that exquisite desire. She trembled and leaned for support against the pillar, hiding in its shadow. She longed to be transported back to Rose Cottage. Outside the cottage she had become utterly vulnerable. When she left the cottage forever she would enter an arena of defeat from which she could see no exit. There was beauty in the quiet formality with which the trap had been set. Already she felt the onset of the last, the grand despair, the one that was awaited. Mabel, she whispered. Mabel. Mabel.

Abruptly she was cold because she had heard the sound of the latch, as on the day of Mabel's death. Far down the church the little side door had been opened and closed. The sound echoed faintly. She clung to the pillar, listening to the light-falling footsteps coming up the aisle to the back of the church. They were a woman's. Her skin prickled but her eyes suddenly brimmed, in gratitude, and awe, and loving terror. She remained kneeling, pressed against the pillar and dared not look up. Her nostrils quivered, fearfully alert for the sweet odour of the ghost, the compound of flowers and formaldehyde that must attach to the newly dead. I am here, she muttered, here, here. Bound to this pillar, to this life.

She covered her face. The stone of the pillar chilled the bare knuckles of her right hand. The footsteps had ceased, having come close. There was a faint creak, and then silence. She did not have the courage to move. But presently, astonishingly, she became peaceful, comforted. She thought, 'I can face anything if I try.' She withdrew from the shadow of the pillar. The air was cool on her overheated forehead. She glanced along the pew but could see nothing. She inclined her body backwards, bringing into her range of vision the pews in front, and caught her breath, shocked by the visible presence of the seated figure. Involuntarily her hand covered her mouth.

It was not Mabel. It was not any woman she knew. The head was covered by an old-fashioned solar topee with a veil swathed round the brim. After a while the woman became restless as if she had become aware of being watched. Upright in the pew, staring at the stained-glass window above the altar, the woman touched her throat and turned slightly, looking to left and right. Reassured, she resumed her still and silent vigil, and stayed thus until there was one of those mysterious adjustments, a small shift of the empty building's centre of gravity, as of a momentary easing of its tensions and stresses which created an illusion of echo without traceable source, so that to Barbie it seemed that the church's guardian angel had half-opened and then closed one of his gigantic wings.

The unknown visitor rose, stepped into the aisle and walked down it towards the altar. She was elderly and moved with the care of a person conscious of a duty to carry her years with dignity. Before turning towards the side door she placed a hand for support on a pew and with lowered head bent one knee. Going out, she opened and closed the door gently. A little later Barbie caught the sound of a motor-car, starting up, not on the Church Road but on the West Hill Road side.

As the sound faded, as the car took the woman away in that revealing direction, she realized who it was who had sat a few feet in front of her, but she was slow to respond. What might have been curiosity or superstitous fear of such close proximity was muted by the stronger current of an emotion which warmed her body and kept her kneeling, one hand on the pillar and the other still upon her mouth.

Within that little complex of events, the expectation of the ghost, the shock of seeing the woman, the echo from an unknown source high in the roof (above all, within that) she wondered if there had been one other thing, no more than a faint disturbance, a rearrangement of the

317

sources from which she received impressions. Fleetingly, it seemed to her, her presence had been noted by God. She stayed very still. The impression was not enlarged, confirmed in any way, but it was not destroyed.

Well, I am going now, she told Mabel. She waited. There was no answer. Carrying the empty fibre suitcase in which she had transported shoes, she left the church. Outside she put her head up and went in search of a tonga.

When she got back to Rose Cottage she filled her largest suitcase with things taken at random from the stuff remaining in her room, left space in it for her nightwear and toilet things and then emptied the drawers on to a sheet spread on the floor. Without looking at what she must leave behind she knotted the sheet, making a bundle, and called Aziz, asked him to have it removed because she wanted none of the contents and did not wish to see the bundle again. He returned with the mali's boy and the sweeper girl who between them dragged the bundle out on to the verandah and out of sight.

Directly it had gone she felt reduced, already cut off from the source of energy and power residing in the bungalow. She glanced at what remained: the suitcase, the writing-table and the metal trunk of missionary relics which this morning Aziz had helped her pull away from the wall between dressing-table and almirah into the centre of the room. She knelt on the rush mat in front of it, as at an altar, as at her life. The once-black paint was scored and scratched with the scars of travel and rough handling; and the name, painted in white roman capitals – Barbara Batchelor – had faded into grey anonymity of a kind from which a good report might be educed by some-one who did not know her; a chance discoverer in a later age.

'Poor trunk,' she said. She touched the metal. It was warm like an animal, one that relied on her, dispas-sionately but assuming certain things about their relation-ship. 'There is no room,' she said, 'no room at Clarissa's.'

She considered alternatives. One was to ask Mr Maybrick to give it temporary shelter. But it would not survive, neglected amidst all that chaos. Nor would it survive in the alien Muslim shadows of Jalal-ud-din's. She caressed the lid. Beneath it lay the proofs of her failures and successes, evidence of endeavour. Gazing down at the name it seemed to her that the trunk was all that God need ever notice or take into account; that she herself had become unreal and unimportant.

An idea began to exert itself, persuasively; to flow up from the trunk through her arm like a current: an idea that the trunk should be left at Rose Cottage where she had been happy. But where? Where Mabel could see it, or sense it, or even touch it, groping blindly for a familiar or friendly object to give her troubled spirit momentary relief in its wanderings between the cottage and the alien grave?

The brass padlock with its key was in the lower ring of the main hasp. She had but to lever up the two side hasps to raise the lid; but the prospect of looking through the contents dismayed her. She unlocked the padlock and transferred it to the securing ring, clicked it shut and used the key to lock the two smaller clasps. She put the key aside to place it in her handbag, but continued kneeling.

From behind her Aziz spoke. 'Memsahib. Sarah Mem.'

She looked round as startled by the interruption as she would have been if caught in an act of private devotion. In the open doorway she saw the two faces, Aziz's and Sarah's. The colour came into her own. She got unsteadily to her feet as Aziz stood aside for Sarah to enter. Since the evening of the day Sarah got back from Calcutta, the day after the funeral, she had not visited the cottage, and that single visit had been brief, cut short by their nearness to Mabel's death, their reluctance to talk about it and inability to find other subjects of conversation. The girl had rung subsequently to ask if Barbie was all right, opening the way for an invitation. She had now come of her own accord as if there were matters that could no longer be laid aside, but Barbie was afraid of being alone with the girl because of what had been said.

'I must look a sight,' she said, pushing back a stray lock of her short-cropped hair. 'I've been clearing up, trying to get some sort of order into things, some sort of sense. It's quite a task.'

'I'm sorry,' Sarah said. She did not say what about. 'Is there anything I can help with?'

Barbie shook her head. Sarah was in uniform. She had probably come straight from the daftar. She looked soldierly. But womanly. Perhaps Mildred genuinely suspected something 'wrong' with the girl, and 'wrong' with Barbie. There had been a book once, of arcane reputation, which she had never read; but she remembered the title. Well, Barbie cried in herself, to herself, to the quiet room, the ancient walls; *I* am lonely. Lonely. But God help me my loneliness is open to inspection. It's here in this place beneath my breast. Between Sarah and myself, between myself and any woman, there is nothing that there should not be. I have been slandered. Spitefully. As punishment. For my presumption.

She went into the bathroom, washed the grime from her hands and splashed her face, to cool her skin and the anger that hardened it and made it smooth. She chafed her wrists with cologne, combed her grey hair and called to Aziz.

'Tea! Tea outside, or – ' returning to her bedroom, 'sherry?' And stopped. The decanters were locked in the sideboard and Kevin Coley still had the keys. Sarah, arms folded, turned from contemplation of the view from the front window.

'I should love some tea, Barbie.'

'Aziz has probably anticipated. Have you not? Aziz? Aziz!' In the hall her voice rang beating against the gongs of brass trays on the panelled walls, rebounding from the implacable wood of the locked door of Mabel's bedroom. From the region of the kitchen he shouted back in simple confirmation of his presence. She led the way through the sitting-room, unbolted the french window and went out on to the verandah. The sky was clear again but the areas of sunlight were evening-narrow, the shadows long. The

320

garden scent was heady, heightened by the dampness in the air. The chair in which Mabel had sat down to die had not been moved. Fallen rose petals lay ungathered on the lawn.

'One full day more,' Barbie said, standing by the balustrade. 'Early mornings and from tea until dusk – those were always my favourite times.'

She heard the creak of a chair as Sarah sat and presently the click of a lighter. She waited for the aroma of cigarette smoke to reach her and then turned round.

'I shall be out of here after breakfast the day after tomorrow,' she said. 'Aziz will be ready to go too. I don't know what his travelling arrangements are. He and I will say good-bye here but if he's required to do so he'll wait until someone arrives to take over his storeroom keys. Mahmoud or Captain Coley. Otherwise he'll lock up and leave the keys with the mali.'

'Yes, I see. I'll tell Mother.'

Aziz brought tea out. When he had gone Barbie said, 'Will you pour?' Then she sat down and took her cup. She asked how Susan was. Susan was well, Sarah said. They were taking her back to the grace and favour. The day after tomorrow. Minnie, Mahmoud's widowed niece, who had never had children of her own and was scarcely more than a child herself, was excited but also fearful of her new responsibility. For a while Sarah would have to help her.

If there was a feeling of constraint between them, Barbie thought, the fault was her own. The girl's manner was if anything less indrawn than it had been in the past, and beneath the pallor, the marks of strain, there was a faint flush, a look of contentment in the flesh of the face as if she had reached a firm decision about the situation she was in.

'Clarissa told me your news about poor Captain Merrick,' Barbie said.

'Yes, I didn't mention him last time I was here. I meant to tell you that he talked a bit about Miss Crane. He didn't know her very well, I'm afraid.'

'I imagined their paths were unlikely to have crossed.'

'He knew her by sight of course, and visited her in hospital after she was attacked. They weren't able to talk much because she was so ill, and afterwards one of his assistants dealt with it. By then he was involved in the other business of Miss Manners.'

'And later still? When Edwina took her life?'

'Yes, he dealt with that. He was at her bungalow. That's what he remembers. He talked quite a lot about an old picture he found there. From the way he described it I think it must have been the one you had a copy of and showed to people.'

'It would have been that one, I expect. I still have the copy in my trunk.' Barbie thought back to that day on the verandah nearly two years ago. 'I don't remember your being with us when I showed it.'

'I heard about it.'

Barbie nodded. She had made an exhibition of herself over the picture. She said, 'Why did Captain Merrick talk about the picture?'

'He seemed to see a connexion between the picture and Teddie. Has Clarissa Peplow told you how Teddie was killed?'

'She said he was trying to bring in some Indian soldiers who'd deserted. I'm afraid I didn't listen very hard.'

'Man-bap,' Sarah said, after a pause, but abruptly.

'What?'

'Man-bap.'

Man-bap. She had not heard that expression for a long time. It meant Mother-Father, the relationship of the *raj* to India, of a man like Colonel Layton to the men in his regiment, of a district officer to the people of his district, of Barbie herself to the children she had taught. Man-bap. I am your father and your mother. Yes, the picture had been an illustration of this aspect of the imperial attachment; the combination of hardness and sentimentality from which Mabel had turned her face. If Teddie had died in an attempt to gather strayed sheep into a fold she saw why Captain Merrick might remember the picture. But Sarah's reasons for referring to it were otherwise obscure to her. And she did not wish to probe. She did not want to talk about Edwina, or about Teddie and the ex-police officer who had lost an arm and whom Sarah had never liked.

But – 'It's interesting about Ronald Merrick,' Sarah began. 'He'd like to be able to sneer at man-bap but he can't quite manage it because actually he'd prefer to believe in it, like Teddie did. If he did. Do you think he did, Barbie?'

'I don't know.'

'Did Miss Crane?'

'Why do you ask that?'

'Because Ronald Merrick thought so. He talked about her sitting at the roadside holding the dead Indian's hand. He thought that was man-bap. Was it?'

'No.'

'What was it?'

'Despair.'

For a moment Sarah looked stricken by the bleak word as if it was the last one she had expected; but then she smiled briefly in recognition.

'Yes,' she said. 'That makes sense.'

Again they became silent but it was the silence of matched temperaments.

'What happened between you and Mother, Barbie?'

'If you don't know I expect it means she'd prefer that you shouldn't.'

'She said you had an idea that Aunt Mabel wanted to be buried in Ranpur.'

'Then you know all there is to know.'

'That's all it was about?'

'That's all.'

'What about Aziz?'

'That wasn't a bone of contention. Although your mother can't have liked my saying she didn't understand.'

'No, she wouldn't like that.'

'I didn't really understand myself, in the sense of being able to explain it. But I didn't feel the need and your mother did. That was the difference. I'm sorry for any annoyance I caused her. She had a great deal to attend to. I had only this – one thing.'

Sarah nodded. She put out her cigarette. Barbie thought she would get up, make an excuse to be off home; but she settled back in the wicker chair.

'How were your aunt and uncle?' Barbie asked her.

'Very well, thank you.'

'You can't have seen much of Calcutta.'

'No, not much. A bit. I was taken dancing at the Grand, and then to a place where they had Indian musicians.'

'By Aunt Fenny and Uncle Arthur?'

Sarah smiled. 'No, by one of the officers who attended the course Uncle Arthur's running. He and Aunt Fenny live a much gayer life than they used to in Delhi. They have one of these large air-conditioned flats and it's usually full of young people, mostly these young men who do the course.'

'What kind of course?'

'About how India is run in peace-time. It's supposed to attract recruits for the civil service and the police among men who've liked India enough to want to stay on after the war.'

Barbie tried to consider this. But she was giving Sarah incomplete attention. The image of the trunk was super-imposing itself on the image of the verandah, the tea-table, and Sarah on the other side of it smiling as if waiting for her to smile back.

'Is the course a success?' she asked.

'I suppose one or two of them might be tempted. Having them back to the flat is part of the attracting process. You know. The ease and comfort of lots of servants but in modern surroundings, the kind they have to admit are pretty decent. But I should think they're more likely to try for one of the business firms where the future's more secure and they can get transferred home to the London office when it begins to pall or if they want to get married and have a proper family life. Otherwise I get the impression they think the course is rather quaint.' Sarah paused. 'They were the kind of young men I was just beginning to get to know before Su and I came back out in 'thirty-nine. My sort of people. The sort of people we really are. There's such a tremendous gulf, I mean now. More so from their point of view than from ours.'

'Well,' Barbie began, intending to say something about Sarah's sort of people, her own sort of people, but she could not apply herself to the subject. She said, 'I'm glad you had a bit of fun.' She recalled Sister Matthews's explanation of the solitary presence of a Bengali bearer in the Calcutta flat on the night Mildred had tried to ring her sister from the nursing home: that everyone must have been out celebrating the second front. She wondered at what hour the news of Mabel's death and Susan's premature labour had reached Sarah; and pitied the girl, imagining her returning to her aunt's place, flushed with the excitement of a night in the city in the company of those young men, men of her own kind, men whom she understood or had once understood and now envied because they were part of 'home', and her aunt saying: Sarah, your mother rang, it's bad news I'm afraid. Had the girl's thoughts immediately turned to her father, far away in prison-camp?

Had the Layton girls missed a 'proper family life'? What did that mean, anyway? Was it important to have one, significant if one missed it? As in other Anglo-Indian families the discipline of separation of children from parents had presumably marked Sarah's childhood. With such a separation Barbie had never had to contend. The separation she had suffered had been permanent and presumably more tolerable as a consequence since there was no arguing with death: her father's and then her mother's. But she was full grown when she came out and she came out as a treader of new ground, not old, and in her own behalf and, so she had thought, in God's, and had never married, never had children.

Knowing Sarah and Susan was the closest she had ever been to knowing what it felt like to have daughters. If they had been her own children, could she have borne the separation? Would Susan eventually have to bear it, or would the whole condition of life in India for English people have changed by the time the child had reached the age of seven or eight, which brought the first, the childhood, phase of Anglo-Indian life to a conclusion? It was not many years ahead. But the condition could well have changed by then. The child might be lucky.

But not its parents. Not Susan. Nor Sarah. Nor young Dicky Beauvais whom Clarissa Peplow hoped Susan would marry. Looking at Sarah Barbie felt she understood a little of the sense the girl might have of having no clearly defined world to inhabit, but one poised between the old for which she had been prepared, but which seemed to be dying, and the new for which she had not been prepared at all. Young, fresh and intelligent, all the patterns to which she had been trained to conform were fading, and she was already conscious just from chance or casual encounter of the gulf between herself and the person she would have been if she had never come back to India: the kind of person she 'really was'.

Reaching towards the table to replace her cup Barbie hesitated, completed the movement with conscious effort, to keep her hand steady, and then leant back in her chair. There had been a disturbance, another quick displacement of air, but this time a faint whiff of the malign breath, of the emanation. Alert, she watched the verandah and then the garden which was in sharp focus but seemed far away, hallucinatory, dependent on the human imagination rather than on nature for its existence, wide open to the destructive as well as creative energy of mind and will.

She heard herself say to Sarah, 'I have what I think nowadays you call a problem in logistics,' and then stopped, hearing as well a gentle exhalation which presently she decided must have been her own sigh of relief, of renewed patient anticipation.

'My little room,' she said, 'I mean of course my little room at Clarissa's. It has its limitations. Quite serious ones. And Clarissa has said there cannot be, apart from myself, more than another suitcase. Which leaves two

326

items. Important to me but not to anyone else. To begin with there is the writing-table.'

She looked at Sarah who looked back at her without the concern and commitment suitable to the occasion. But then Sarah was still very young. She would not have learned as yet to understand the grave impediment to free movement which luggage represented in one's affairs.

'Well my writing-table,' she went on, 'in a way, yes, that can be managed because it folds. Like a wing. It is portable. It can stand against a wall, go under a bed. I think I can get my writing-table past Clarissa. And quite apart from a silly affection I have for it I also have use. I expect I shall conduct quite a heavy correspondence. And I can unfold it, sit on the bed and write without worrying whether Clarissa's room is put out of shape, because its shape can be quickly restored, but the trunk – '

She paused, collected her ideas.

'The trunk is a very different kettle of fish. Unlike a writing-table, unlike one's clothes, one's *shoes*, it is of no use. But it *is* my history. And according to Emerson without it, without *that*, I'm simply not explained. I am a mere body, sitting here. Without it, according to Emerson, *none* of us is explained because if it is my history then it is yours too and was Mabel's. But there is no room for my trunk at Clarissa's, no room for my explanation.' She grinned. Sarah's brow had become creased. Barbie could not blame the girl for being puzzled. The situation was very complicated and she was not sure she understood it herself.

'I had thought,' she continued, 'of asking permission to leave my trunk in care of the mali, until I can send for it. It could be put in the shed in the servants' quarters where the gardening implements are kept. But – '

'But what?'

'But if I asked permission of the person fully qualified to give it – asked permission of your mother – it would certainly be refused. Would honour be satisfied if I were to ask it of you?'

'I should think so.'

'If I asked should I obtain?'

'I'll look after your trunk, Barbie. It can stay in the room. Susan and I are going to share it but it can stay in my half.'

'That is kind. Very kind. But if you are to share the room with Susan you can't also share it with the trunk. Let the mali have it. Let him keep it in the shed. Then there should be the minimum of fuss for all of us. The alternative is Jalal-ud-din's. Clarissa has already mentioned it. But I should not be happy to think of my trunk in a heathen storeroom. The trunk is packed with relics of my work in the mission. It is my life in India. My shadow as you might say.'

Sarah nodded, readjusted the hold she had of her own arms, then said, 'You'll let me visit you at Clarissa's, won't you, Barbie?'

For several seconds Barbie did not reply. Then, 'It might be better if you didn't,' she said. 'At least not for a while. Not until I've found my feet. The room is too small to be a suitable place in which to receive guests and I am myself merely a guest, albeit a paying one. You may of course always visit Clarissa and anticipate seeing me as well but I do not want, as the saying is, to push my luck. I do not want to incur Clarissa's wrath by filling her house with wild and extravagant parties. I shall have to learn, have to learn, yes, to be as quiet as a mouse. Which won't be easy. Clarissa does not hold the key to imaginary silences. Shall you tell Aziz about the trunk now, Sarah? So that he can tell the mali? And it will be official?'

Sarah nodded and Barbie called the old man. When he came Sarah spoke to him. Presently he went away and returned with the mali and Sarah spoke to the mali too. When they had gone and Barbie had thanked her Sarah got up to go. The light was fading quickly.

'There is one thing else,' Barbie said. 'Mabel once told me that she had made provision for Aziz in his old age.'

'Yes, she did.'

'And it will be – respected?'

'Yes, Barbie.'

'Forgive me for mentioning it. I feared perhaps she may have meant to make provision, meant to remember him, but failed to put it into words.'

'No, she remembered Aziz. She remembered you too, Barbie.'

'What?'

'Only in a little way. A small annuity. To help out with the pension. You should hear from the Bank in Ranpur soon. Although of course they always seem to take ages.'

'Yes, I see. She should not have.'

'Why not?'

'She should not have. It's taking it away from the rest of you. And I didn't expect anything. But it was very kind. Very kind.'

'Oh, Barbie, don't.'

'Kind,' Barbie repeated. 'So kind.'

She felt in her jacket pocket for the cologne-scented handkerchief. She blew her nose.

'My mother,' she said – laughing – 'was always terribly impressed by the word annuity. She thought it a mark of true gentility. It's odd how these things come back to one. She would have been very proud. My daughter, she would have said, need never concern herself about money because she has her annuity.'

That evening before supper she sat on her bed and watched Aziz and the mali measure the trunk for its shroud of stitched gunny-sacking, which the mali said his wife would cut and help him to sew round it. Later, holding a lantern, she followed the *cortège* round to the mali's shed and saw the covered object stowed in one cleared corner. As she left, holding the lantern high, she heard the clink of the spades and forks as the mali carefully replaced them.

On the morning of the day she left Rose Cottage she woke early, before Aziz brought the pot of tea, the banana, the thin slice of bread and butter which usually made up her chota hazri. The previous night she had drawn back the curtains in order to be able to distinguish between a clear morning and a grey one. It was scarcely light but she could hear the whisper of fine steady rain. She rose and walked bare-foot to confirm it and saw the hunched blanketed figure of the chaukidar who at night guarded Rose Cottage and the next bungalow down the road, patrolling between the two but usually to be found asleep on their own front verandah. The rain was dripping from the verandah roof but there was a lightness in the shadows of the garden that indicated a clear, perhaps sunny, morning later.

She turned back into the room, gazed at the rush mat and then impulsively knelt to say a morning prayer. The prayer turned out to be as full of information as requests. Thank You for Your many blessings and for the years of Rose Cottage. Please guard this room where my two girls are to sleep and admit to Your kingdom the troubled soul of my friend Mabel Layton. I have left my trunk in the shed. I am going to Clarissa's. It is not far.

Rising she inspected the roses gathered yesterday. She had meant to cut many more but a further and final visit from Sarah had interrupted her, put her off her stroke. Seeing the girl crossing the lawn in the late afternoon she feared she had come to cancel the arrangement about the trunk. But she had not.

Barbie had kept the roses in her bedroom all night; young buds, because she had wanted them to begin to unfold and absorb the substance of her dreams and waking meditations, so that they could express upon the grave a special love and particular gratitude. Leaning close to them now it seemed to her that they had absorbed little, perhaps nothing; that each bud was merely a convoluted statement about itself and about the austerity of the vegetable kingdom which was content with the rhythm of the seasons and did not aspire beyond the natural flow of its sap and the firm grip of its root. The bushes from which these roses came had been of English stock but they had travelled well and accepted what was offered. They had not wished to adapt the soil or put a veil across the heat of the sun or spread the rainfall more evenly throughout the year. They had flourished.

'You are now native roses,' she said to them. 'Of the country. The garden is a native garden. We are only visitors. That has been our mistake. That is why God has not followed us here.'

Like a departing guest she opened the drawers in dressing-table and chest just enough to show that they had been dealt with and were empty. For a similar reason she opened the almirah, took out her travelling costume and left the door ajar. After she had bathed she found the chota hazri tray on the bedside table. She sat in her underwear and dressing-gown and sipped and munched, kept glancing at her watch, already alert for the sound of the taxi which Mr Maybrick had guaranteed to send up not later than eight o'clock. She had told Aziz that she would not wait to eat a proper breakfast.

At a quarter to the hour she began her final preparations. At five to she called Aziz. Between them they upended the writing-table which she had locked the night before and folded the legs in. He carried it into the hall and came back for the suitcase. He brought newspaper in which to wrap the roses; and then gave her a key.

'What is this, Aziz?'

He told her he had found it on the floor, that it must be the key to her trunk. She recognized it now. She put it in her handbag and then sat alone until she heard the car arrive.

The rain had stopped. Outside, below the verandah, the other servants stood. She had tipped them all the night before for the last time. Now she shook hands with the mali and his wife, ruffled the boy's hair, smiled at the sweeper girl who kept in the background. Last in the line was Aziz. He had on his fur cap and carried a shawl over one shoulder, ready for his own journey.

'Good-bye, Aziz.'

'Good-bye, Barbie Mem.'

'Have you far to go?'

He indicated a direction, his arm straight and stiff, the

hand open, pointing vaguely towards a mountainous distance. A day's journey. Two days'. More than that? She did not know. The name of his village and district written for her in uneven block capitals on a scrap of paper had meant nothing to her. One day she would borrow a large-scale map of the area and search for the name among the contours that showed the greatest heights.

'God be with you,' she said.

'And with you,' he answered. Briefly their hands met and clasped; and then she entered the taxi whose door was held open by the mali's boy.

4

On the first Sunday after Barbie's arrival at the rectory bungalow Arthur Peplow conducted the morning service as one of thanksgiving for the defeat of the Japanese attempt to invade India at Imphal, for the news that the last Japanese soldier had been driven from Indian soil, and for the continuing good reports from France of the allied offensive against the Germans. Having announced that this should be their theme in all their hymns and prayers he said that they would begin with a rather more intimate kind of thanksgiving. He moved towards the front pew where Susan sat with her sister and mother.

'Forasmuch as it hath pleased Almighty God of His goodness to give safe deliverance to this our sister, and hath preserved her in the great danger of childbirth, We shall give hearty thanks unto God and say: Except the Lord build the house: their labour is but lost that build it. Except the Lord keep the city: the watchman waketh but in vain.'

As if blissfully unaware that several members of the congregation (the Smalleys for instance) raised their eyebrows at his inclusion of the form for the churching of women in a service attended by Other Ranks and young and impressionable officers, he announced hymn number 358; and it may have been that towards the back of the church where a group of young British soldiers on church parade got noisily to their feet, one of them glanced at the elderly woman next to him, on the other side of a pillar that rose between pews, alerted by a strangled sound such as might be caused by a sudden constriction of the throat. If so he must then have been reassured. No incident was reported. And the service got off to a rousing start with Bishop Heber's missionary hymn: From Greenland's icy mountains: which everyone knew and could sing happily without bothering much about the words.

The hymn chosen to close the service was Onward, Christian Soldiers. People felt that Arthur Peplow had done the station proud.

Outside, shading her eyes from a splendid burst of Sunday sunshine, Nicky Paynton said that there was nothing so cheerful as a good rollicking morning at church. It set you up for the day. Ahead lay an equally cheerful session in the club bar and a luncheon there of Madras curry guaranteed to bring cleansing tears to the eyes and an overall feeling of well-being. In the evening Clara and Nicky were dining with the Trehearnes. They asked if they could stop in on the way and see the baby. Mildred assented. Kevin and Dicky were dining at the grace and favour. They could all have a drink together before Clara and Nicky went on to Maisie's.

'The baby will be asleep,' Susan warned them. 'I shouldn't want him woken. He falls asleep as soon as he's had his six o'clock bottle. It's his best time.' She plucked at her mother's sleeve. 'We ought to be getting back. Has Mahmoud brought the flowers?'

'I'll check,' Dicky Beauvais said and walked off briskly down the path through the lingering groups of worshippers.

'We sent Mahmoud up to the cottage,' Mildred explained, 'to get some roses for Susan.'

'For Aunty Mabel's grave,' Susan said. 'Because I missed the funeral.'

Dicky was coming back, self-conscious with a large bunch of roses. Presumably Mahmoud had been waiting outside the churchyard gate. Susan went to meet him. She looked slim and pretty and very young. Dicky took her round the side of the church to place her offering on the grave Arthur Peplow had chosen for Mabel's resting place: a secluded spot. It was plucky of Susan to come to church so soon after her return from the nursing home, Clara Fosdick said; and thoughtful of her to arrange for the flowers.

'But she's anxious to get home now,' Mildred said. 'Minnie's not been in sole charge before. But it seemed wise to start as one means to go on. Minnie's quite capable of making sure the brat comes to no damage even if she's hamfisted with the paraphernalia. And Panther's taken a shine to him. He growls if old Mahmoud goes near. He knows the ghastly thing belongs to Su. He doesn't mind Dicky taking a peep because Dicky brought them home. But he took an unpleasant interest in poor Kevin's ankles last night, didn't he Kevin?'

'One can protect ankles. Throat's what you have to watch out for.'

Susan and Dicky came back but were detained within earshot by Lucy and Tusker Smalley.

'Lots of congratulations, Susan,' Lucy said. Tusker added, 'Rather.'

'Thank you. And thank you for the lovely flowers you sent. I'm afraid I haven't yet written to everybody.'

Lucy said, 'I hear you're calling the baby Teddie.'

'No, not Teddie. Edward. It's very important to get it right. I've got not to care for nicknames and diminutives for men.'

She glanced at Lucy's husband. 'Why do they call you Tusker, Major Smalley?'

Smalley indicated his regimental insignia, the Mahwars: a bull-elephant from whose back, howdah-like, sprang a tuft of toddy-palm.

'Mahwars. Tuskers, regimental nickname.'

'Yes, I know that. But why do they call *you* Tusker?'

'Bit of a long story.' Tusker looked modest but pleased.

' – after all,' Susan continued as if he had not said anything, 'we never called my husband Muzzy Bingham. Nor daddy old Pankot Layton.'

There was a pause. A breeze riffled the skirts of the women's dresses.

'Which regiment will you want little Edward to belong to?' Lucy Smalley asked. 'That will be quite a decision, won't it? Between the Pankots and the Muzzys. You'd have to be making it now if you could put a boy down for a regiment like you have to for a school.'

Mrs Smalley's voice drifted away, caught by the tail of the breeze and chased by the stronger following gust that whipped through the churchyard and prompted Susan into action. She appeared almost to be spun round by it, so that no one could have said that she turned her back on the Smalleys nor that she pushed through the group headed by her mother, but there was what amounted to a convulsive movement, a rearrangement of positions, a making way for her which was ended abruptly by her touching her sister's elbow as if finding base and going off then slightly ahead of her, down the path at a pace quick enough for Dicky to have to start off rather fast and lengthen his stride to catch up with them.

'The children are having tiffin at home,' Mildred said, 'and they have their own tongas.'

'Is Susan all right?' Nicky Paynton asked.

'Susan is fine.'

She anchored the group round her by not budging until the Smalleys approached. And then, turning her back, snubbed them as if so far as she was concerned Susan had been perfectly behaved until they managed to upset her; Lucy by mentioning Teddie's name and Tusker by saying the word regiment which was the very thing Teddie had died for; and then slowly led the way down the path between the ancient gravestones: a woman making a point, one that was less well defined than it was felt – the point, perhaps, that if Susan's behaviour could be seen as a further demonstration of how time was running out for people like Mildred then anything like a scramble was vulgar, too tiresome to consider let alone join.

The next time Mildred walked along that path would be for the christening, the admission as a lively member of holy church of little Edward Arthur David; and that would bring to a formal close a difficult phase of the responsibility she had shouldered during her husband's absence. From things she said it was gathered that there could be no question of Susan marrying Dicky Beauvais or anyone until John Layton came home. The implication was that the same must apply to Sarah. One dead and never-seen son-in-law, one live grandson, and two still healthy daughters were sufficient evidence of life having gone on for Colonel Layton to come back to and not feel that things had fallen apart for want of a firm hand. Now Mildred was digging her heels in. She would not be rushed again. She had been rushed once and the result had been pretty disastrous or nearly so. Real disaster had been averted by Susan not letting the baby die on her or herself die on the baby.

According to Nicky Paynton, Mildred's off-hand manner towards the child, her use of a word like brat, did not disguise the fact that she was bucked at the prospect of having a grandson to hand over to Colonel Layton when he resumed his position as head of the family. The boy was half a Layton. John must have often regretted having no son of his own to bear his name, though he had been proud and fond of both his daughters. And he had been pleased about the marriage, quite taken, so Mildred said, by Teddie's photograph. How stoically he received news of Teddie's death wasn't known. His letters took a long time to reach Pankot and there was proof of letters going astray in both directions. It was possible that he would get news of the child's birth and not know that his son-in-law was dead. It was possible that he was ignorant of both events. They had heard nothing for some time and with the opening of the second front they perhaps had to be prepared for a period of silence and uncertainty.

But they were inured to both and Mildred without dropping her characteristic guard infected her friends with a spirit of optimism. The christening party to be held at the grace and favour after a quiet family ceremony at St John's promised to be a jolly affair, rather like a picnic amid (Mildred warned) the packing crates that were already being filled as the process of separating Layton private possessions from stuff belonging to the army and public works department got under way.

When it was all over there would be little left to delay the move up to Rose Cottage. The christening party had its valedictory aspect. In spite of all its drawbacks the grace and favour bungalow had served its turn and deserved a good send-off. The accommodations officer was already nagging for possession so that he could turn the bungalow into a chummery for officers of the new emergency intake and relieve pressure elsewhere. From being full of women it would become (Mildred said) 'full of chaps' and presumably they wouldn't object so much to being woken at the crack of dawn by bugles opposite or, if they did, would have less cause.

And (at the club during midweek) Mildred smiled, directed the bearer's attention to her glass and said, 'Although I'm afraid Edward's going to be even more effective than a bugle. He seems to have an instinct for getting everybody on parade at six A.M. prompt. Doesn't he, Su?'

'Most children wake at six,' Susan said. 'I used to wake at six at Aunt Lydia's in Bayswater and at great-grandpa's in Surrey. They never had bugles.'

'But then you're Army,' Nicky Paynton said.

'Yes,' Susan said. She sat very upright on a club chair watching the clock and everybody who came in and went out. She had not been inside the club for months, not since she had begun, as she put it, to 'show' and took to smocks. This morning her mother had persuaded her to put in an appearance, to take up the reins of a proper routine.

'Relax, darling,' Mildred said. 'You simply must learn

337

to trust Minnie. And you ought to change your mind and have a drink, even if it's only a nimbo.'

'All right.'

The bearer brought her a nimbopani. She sat holding the tumbler in both hands and used both hands to raise it to her lips. 'Are you cold?' her mother asked. It had been raining hard all morning and the temperature had dropped. No, Susan said, she wasn't cold.

'I thought you shivered,' Mildred went on. 'I hope you're not sickening for something.' No, Susan said again. She was quite all right, she wasn't sickening for anything. She put the glass on the table and made an effort to take part in the conversation by giving her attention to the person speaking; but after a while her glance strayed to the clock again and to the people coming in and going out and back to the clock and then to her wristwatch. She reached for the glass one-handed, lifted it and then lost her grip.

The glass fell, wetting her skirt and legs with the nimbo, and broke into sharp fragments on the floor at her feet. She stayed seated. There was a hush in the room, then talk was resumed. A sweeper was sent for. Clara Fosdick examined her stockings and pronounced them unladdered and only a bit damp. On the other hand Susan, she said, was soaked.

'Well,' Mildred said, 'that *was* clumsy of you, wasn't it? You'll have to change when you get home. Are you madly uncomfortable?'

'No, Mother.'

'Perhaps you'd better go to the cloakroom and mop up with a towel. Then come back and have another nimbo. There's loads of time.'

'I shan't want another nimbo.'

'Well go and dry off.'

'I'm more comfortable sitting still.'

The sweeper came with brush and pan. Mrs Fosdick, without getting up, shifted her chair and gave him room to get at all the splinters but Susan did not. She watched him sweeping gingerly round her feet. After he had gone

Mildred ordered another drink but the conversation lagged and Susan had not looked up again. Irritably Mildred said:

'Darling, what on earth's the matter with you?'

'Nothing's the matter. I'm relaxing.'

She smiled and suddenly leant back with her arms folded. She asked Nicky Paynton whether she had heard recently from the two boys in Wiltshire. Nicky said she had. The elder was looking forward to being eighteen, finishing with school and joining the RAF of all things. 'But I expect we can talk him out of that,' she added, 'unless he's really set on it as an alternative career to the army and it's not just the temporary glamour of the boys in blue at home that's attracting him.'

'And what about the other?'

'Oh, it's the Ranpurs for him. But then he's still at the stage of thinking his father's the cat's whiskers.'

Susan had not stopped smiling but the others were aware of the avoidable subject having once more cropped up and conjured Teddie's shade. Again their conversation lagged and presently Mildred looked out of the window, finished her drink and said, 'It's stopped. We'd better get you home and out of that damp frock.'

'Yes, I should like to go home now, if you don't mind.'

But she waited until the others had got to their feet before rising herself. She walked, arms still folded, behind her mother and her mother's friends, past the pillars and the potted palms –

– and into her inner life, her melancholia; an inexplicable business, worse than that of Poppy Browning's daughter because that girl had had a certain justification for what she did: an unfaithful husband dead in the arms of his Indian mistress. But Susan's husband had died gallantly and tragic as the circumstances were then and later in the matter of the premature birth she was surrounded by love and devotion and the child was surely a lively reminder to her of this fact and of the duty she had to cherish him, show him at least as much affection as she herself had been shown.

And she had done so. Therefore the incident that

occurred at the grace and favour bungalow on the afternoon of the day before the christening ceremony was even further beyond anyone's ability to understand than it would have been had she continued to show signs of rejecting the child. But the rejection had been of a brief duration. Her subsequent concern for the child's welfare was both charming and touching; a bit exaggerated but no more so than the other traits and characteristics that went to make up the bright little personality in whom there had always seemed to reside a spirit of particular determination to do the right thing, but with style and youthful freshness; no doubt drawing attention to herself in the process but also to the purpose and condition of a life based upon a few simple but exacting ideas.

Now through a single action she shattered her own image as a child might destroy its own carefully constructed edifice of bricks. Indeed there was in her behaviour a disagreeable element of play, of wilful destruction of a likeness of the adult world she inhabited. At first her action was said to be one that had endangered the child's life but once the facts were known the idea of tragedy narrowly averted was replaced by a suspicion that if mockery had not been intended it had been accomplished; and this suspicion proved as strong as the pity felt for a girl in the grip of such a deep post-natal depression that there was little to distinguish it from madness.

But the word madness did not help. If she had gone off her head presumably she had done so because she found everything about her life unendurable. Meaningless. It did not help either to remember that she had not only fitted in but had been seen to fit in. She had tried. Trying should not have been necessary. Apparently it had been, for her; and suddenly she had stopped; not only stopped but symbolically wiped out all the years of effort by her extraordinary gesture.

On the afternoon of the day before the christening when her mother was at Rose Cottage supervising the measurement of new curtains, and Sarah had gone back to the daftar and so left Susan in sole command, she sent

340

Mahmoud to the bazaar to buy some blue ribbon for the christening gown – Sarah's old gown which Mabel had kept in a trunk for years and only handed over a day or two before her death. She made Mahmoud take Panther whom she complained was getting fat and lazy through lack of exercise. Ten minutes after he had gone, dragging the reluctant dog, she called Minnie from her task of sorting sheets and pillow-cases for the dhobi and told her to run after him and tell him she wanted white ribbon, not blue.

So Minnie set off, but turned back. Questioned about that later she said that in spite of all the little offerings she had made since the little Memsahib became a widow, the bad spirits had not been appeased, they had not gone elsewhere, they still infested the bungalow and the compound, and this particular day – the day before the alien rite of christening – was especially inauspicious. And from certain things the little Memsahib had done – taking out the christening gown, smoothing it, holding it, talking to it; looking at the baby but not touching him as if afraid to – she believed the little Memsahib was also aware of the bad spirits. She had turned back at the gate partly because she was afraid of what might happen if she deserted her post and partly out of curiosity. She thought little Memsahib intended to make a special Christian puja of her own.

Although, like her uncle, Minnie professed the Muslim faith, the rigours of that austere religion lay lightly on the people of the Pankot hills. Wayside shrines to the old tribal gods were still decorated with offerings of flowers and here and there in places believed to be inhabited by bhuts and demons – a tree, a crossroads – there might sometimes be found dishes of milk or clarified butter. For some time now in secret places of the grace and favour compound Minnie had prepared and kept replenished such tokens of appeasement. It would interest her to see how little Memsahib might go about a similar enterprise.

She returned to the bungalow but stayed hidden and was rewarded by the sight of Susan, seated now on the verandah, dressing the child in the lace gown, talking to it to reassure it and then – the dressing completed – continuing for a while without speaking and looking not at the child but straight ahead, so that Minnie assumed she was engaged in some kind of silent incantation.

And then quite abruptly Susan had risen and carried the child down the verandah steps and across the grass towards the bare brick wall that divided the garden from the servants' quarters. Minnie thought that perhaps there were a number of magic paces which mother and child had to take together and automatically she began to count. The alarm she might have felt when Susan suddenly stopped and placed the child on its back on the damp grass was momentarily stilled by the fascination exerted by the whole strange process, for there could be no doubt now that she was the spectator of a ritual which no other Indian had ever witnessed, otherwise she would have heard tales about it. When Susan walked away from the child, along the wall, towards the place where the wall ended, again Minnie counted the paces taken, and when she bent down, picked up a can and walked back, it was the whole action that exercised Minnie's imagination and not just the can, the reason for the can, which she recognized as one full of kerosene Mahmoud found handy for lighting his bonfires of accumulated rubbish. Kerosene was oil. Was it holy oil to people like little Memsahib?

Susan's next action was the most fascinating of all. She walked round the child in a wide circle tipping the can as she went on sprinkling the oil. Then she put the can down near the wall, approached the circle again and knelt. With the can there must have been matches because she had a box in her hand and was striking one and throwing it on to the kerosene. Flame leapt and arced in two directions, tracing the circumference until the two fiery arms met at the other side, enclosing the sacrifice.

Minnie did not understand but she had stopped trying to work it out because she understood the one important thing. She understood fire. Crying out, she snatched a sheet from the dhobi's bundle and ran. The grass inside the circle was too wet for the flames to catch hold and spread towards the middle where the child gazed at the sky and worked its legs and arms. But Minnie did not understand that either. She acted instinctively, flung the sheet over the flames which were already turning blue and yellow, dying; and used the sheet as a path to reach the child. Picking it up she backed away calling out all the time to little Memsahib who continued kneeling and gazing at the centre of the ring of fire where the child had been. She seemed not to notice that the child was no longer there and that Minnie was crying out to her.

She was still there when Mahmoud got back from the bazaar and found Minnie on the verandah hugging the now crying child, not daring either to approach her mistress or let her out of her sight. She was still there when, summoned by Mahmoud, Mildred returned. She ignored all her mother's orders and entreaties to get up. When Travers arrived she ignored him too. She stayed where she was until Sarah, driven home by Dicky Beauvais, went out and talked to her. She let Sarah take her indoors and presently into the ambulance that Travers had called to take her back to the nursing home. In all this time she had looked at no one, spoken to no one, but smiled as if happy for the first time in her life.

In the servants' quarters up and down the station the tale spread quickly. It reached the bazaar and the nearer villages that same night before the last fire had been damped down and the last light extinguished. The little Memsahib was touched by the special holiness of madness and her melancholy cries could be heard in the hills, scarcely distinguishable from the howling of the jackal packs that disturbed the dogs and set them barking. The sound could be heard all night but faded out as morning came leaving a profound, an ominous, silence and stillness that seemed to divide the races, brown-skinned from pale-skinned, and to mark every movement of the latter with a furtiveness of which they themselves were aware if their aloof preoccupied expressions were any guide.

Certainly an air of furtiveness hung over the ceremony

343

of christening which Arthur Peplow at Mildred's insistence conducted as arranged at eleven o'clock in the forenoon, ushering the participants in and speaking to them in a whisper as though the ritual were forbidden and every one of them a potential martyr, fearful of God but also of discovery. The child's feeble cries were a constant threat as were the nervous coughs, the scraped feet, Arthur's mumbling, their muttered responses.

There was no party afterwards. Mildred had cancelled it. How she managed to attend the ceremony was considered a marvel. Outside the church the Rankins, having done their duty as godparents, thoughtfully went back to Flagstaff House leaving Mildred to be taken home by Sarah and Dicky. To the innermost circle gathered for lunch, Isobel reported Mildred composed but uncommunicative except in one matter. 'What was that bloody woman doing in church?' she had asked, meaning the Batchelor woman who had been observed by all of them seated as far away from the font as it was possible to get, in the very front pew where she had never been seen to sit before; and on her knees praying as if her presence were going to make all the difference between a christening that 'took' and one that didn't.

'But I'm really not sure,' Isobel said, 'that Mildred hasn't become over-obsessed by Miss Batchelor.' Asked by Nicky Paynton just what she meant she showed some reluctance to answer. Things were bad enough, she said, bad for the station, without their being aggravated by criticism and gossip. But in the end she revealed that Clarissa Peplow who like Isobel herself had called at the grace and favour the previous night to see if there were anything to do to help had been forced by Mildred to take a box of teaspoons which the old missionary had given to Susan as a wedding present. Clarissa had tried to get out of it but Mildred became 'extremely agitated'. She swore that nothing had gone right since Susan received them and said she didn't want them in the house a moment longer. Clarissa could throw them away if she couldn't face giving them back but she must take them with her. All of which,

Isobel said, suggested that Mildred had got it into her head that Miss Batchelor was a bad influence and to blame for everything.

In fact (Isobel went on to say) Mildred had come as near as dammit to accusing Barbara Batchelor of deliberately turning Mabel against her family. She said that if Mabel hadn't been cosseted and flattered by Miss Batchelor right from the start she would have got rid of the damned woman and moved into the spare and let Mildred and the girls take over the rest of the house and that if that had happened Susan would probably never have married Teddie Bingham who had been a decent enough chap but not the husband Susan deserved. He would probably never have risen above junior field rank. Pigging in at the grace and favour had distorted the girl's outlook, it had got on her nerves, completely unsettled her, until suddenly she had seen marriage as a way out, chosen Teddie without thinking properly and married him only to find herself back where she started, a grass-widow, then a widow, and then a mother with a fatherless child. And now God knew what was to happen to her.

'According to Travers, Susan hasn't spoken a word to anyone but just sits in the room they've given her staring out of the window and *smiling*,' Isobel ended.

It was this that seemed so appalling: to have done what she had done and yet to smile. But what had she done? The more one thought about it the more incomprehensible it became. Even the mechanics of the act – let alone the motive – were meaningless until one of the men, Dick Rankin himself, said it reminded him of the kind of thing kids did to scorpions to watch them sting themselves to death rather than be burnt alive. 'It's not true, though,' Rankin pointed out, 'if you pop a scorpion into the middle of a ring of fire it arches its tail and looks as if it's stinging itself to death but it's only a reflex defensive action. The blighters scorch to death because in spite of what they look like they've got very tender skins which is why they mostly come out in the wet weather. In the hot dry weather they hide under stones.'

But God knew why the girl should use the child as a kid might a scorpion. She must be completely off her rocker. Perhaps in her deranged state she had been trying to re-enact the circumstances of Teddie's death, which had been by fire. But why the carefully described circle? When you looked at it logically the child had never been in danger except of catching a chill which the little ayah had taken the first opportunity to ensure he didn't, by bathing and wrapping him up warmly.

'Well,' Rankin summed up. 'I suppose the psychiatrists will make something of it. You can't apply ordinary logic in a case like this. But it's damned embarrassing for the station.'

And back you came to the smile and through the smile to the uncomfortable feeling that Susan had made a statement about her life that somehow managed to be a statement about your own: a statement which reduced you – now that Dick Rankin had had his say – to the size of an insect; an insect entirely surrounded by the destructive element, so that twist, turn, attack, or defend yourself as you might you were doomed; not by the forces ranged against you but by the terrible inadequacy of your own armour. And if for armour you read conduct, ideas, principles, the code by which you lived, then the sense to be read into Susan's otherwise meaningless little charade was to say the least of it thought-provoking.

5

'I am sorry, Barbara,' Clarissa said, having given her the spoons. 'I know it was wrong of her. They were not her spoons to return. But I had no choice and have none now. Dearly as I should have liked to refuse, I felt I could not. Dearly as I should like to hide them and forget them, I cannot. I hope you will take the exceptional circumstances into consideration and forgive her.'

'Blessed are the insulted and the shat upon,' Barbie

said. 'For they shall inherit the kingdom of Heaven, which is currently under offer with vacant possession.'

'What did you say?'

Barbie did not repeat it. She said, 'Forgive me, The circumstances are indeed exceptional. I am not myself. Mildred is not herself. Thou art not changed and God is not mocked.'

Clarissa's mouth hung open. She clutched the rosary of the afternoon sandalwood beads. Barbie put the box of spoons by her side on the bed. With Clarissa in the room there was scarcely sufficient space for the two of them to stand. From the bed she could see the old people concealed behind the curtain in the angle of the wall.

'I had a letter from the bank in Ranpur this morning, Clarissa. The annuity Mabel has left me will amount to one hundred and fifty pounds a year. It will take some time for the first quarterly payment to reach me because it all has to be done in London. But it is considerable additional security. It means I can afford to pay you more for my board and lodgings.'

'For a temporary arrangement I am adequately repaid,' Clarissa said. 'Your suggestion is generous but I cannot accept it.'

'I had another letter too, Clarissa.' She opened her handbag, got out the letter and gave it to Clarissa to read: 'Dear Miss Batchelor, Mr Studhome in Calcutta passed your letter to me because he himself had no suggestion to make in regard to employment in the mission on a voluntary basis. But he asks me to tell you to write to him again if the matter of accommodation remains unsettled at the end of the year. He says that he has no immediate solution to offer because during the past five years there have naturally been other retirements and the continuing difficulty of arranging passages home has led to more demand for places in Darjeeling and Naini Tal than there is a supply. However the main reason for his passing your letter to me was the possibility he thought there might be of our having a suggestion to make at this end both about accommodation and employment. Unfortunately we have none. I hope that you will soon find somewhere suitable to live. It is very kind of Mr and Mrs Peplow to take you in meanwhile. I trust you are well. Yours sincerely, Helen Jolley.'

Clarissa gave her the letter back, said nothing and began clacking her beads.

'I called at Smith's Hotel after the christening this morning,' Barbie continued. 'Because the annuity means I might have afforded their price for a while. But they have no vacancies and the accommodations officer has what the manager calls a lien on any room that falls vacant.'

Clarissa released the beads and turned to go.

'What news is there of Susan?' Barbie asked, not wanting her to.

'There is no news. She looks out of a window and smiles.'

'Smiles?'

'Smiles.'

'Why then she is happy.'

'Happy? How can she be happy when she is out of her mind?'

'Perhaps she has entered it,' Barbie said and then raised her voice because Clarissa had gone. 'Perhaps that's why she's happy and why she smiles.'

She lifted the lid of the box and stared at the twelve rigid identical apostles. One of them, Thomas, was said to have reached India and to have preached near Madras at San Thome which was named after him. Which spoon was Thomas? She wondered what she would make of them and they of her if they were suddenly made manifest and stood before her, laughing and lusty; simple hard-working men, good with nets and boats, swarthy-skinned, smelling of sweat, of fish, of the timber-yard; men who worked with their hands, most of them. 'You'd get short shrift in Pankot,' she said. 'I wouldn't give tuppence for your chances, least of all if you tried to get into that place where the silver is and asked permission to sit at that table and break your bread and drink your wine.'

She began to shut the lid but stopped, held by the picture she had just conjured of the apostles in the mess and by the fact that the spoons were silver, solid silver. They had cost, in her terms, a lot of money and had been given with pride as well as love. She realized that Susan had probably looked at them once, written her thank-you letter and forgotten them, making it easy for Mildred to ensure that they were left out of the display of presents. She did not blame Susan but she could never offer them to her again, she would never be able to say to the girl, Your mother sent these back, don't you want them? It would be for Mildred to tell her should she think of asking where they were. It would be for Mildred to tell her the truth or to lie.

She did not want to keep them herself but they were too good to throw away. She could hardly offer them to Clarissa. The home they must find should at least be appropriate and she believed she had hit upon the most appropriate of all.

She shut the box, dragged the writing-table from its place against the wall, unfolded the legs and set it up by the bedside. Having unlocked the drawer she took out some crisp blue writing paper and matching envelopes which were lined with sky-blue tissue.

Dear Colonel Trehearne,
I am sending today *via* the adjutant a small gift of silver teaspoons which I should like to present to the Regiment for use in the Officer's Mess, in memory of the late Mrs Mabel Layton. I hope that this small gift will be acceptable to the Regiment.
Yours Sincerely,
Barbara Batchelor.

Dear Captain Coley,
I have written today to Colonel Trehearne to say that I am delivering to you this box of silver spoons which I am presenting in memory of the late Mrs Mabel Layton for use in the officers' Mess.
Yours Sincerely,
Barbara Batchelor.

Before sealing the letters she considered carefully whether she should bother with Coley. She could deliver the spoons direct to Commandant's House without involving him; but she wanted to involve him because she wanted Mildred to know where the spoons were going before they actually got there and she was sure that Coley would tell her and that if he did she would try to make him send them back. And this he would be unable to do if he knew about the separate official letter already on its way to Colonel Trehearne. He would have no alternative but to pass the spoons on. She believed that even Mildred would be afraid to arrange for them to be lost in transit and would shy away from asking Trehearne to be so ungallant as to decline them.

In the hall she checked the address of Commandant's House in Clarissa's directory. She looked for Coley's too but could not find it. There was a telephone number with the words 'Adjs Office' written in beside it. She would have to go to the Pankot lines and inquire. Back in her room she sealed the letters and addressed Trehearne's and at half-past two set out stoutly shod, macintosh over her shoulder, stick in one hand, the box of spoons and the two letters in the other.

In the bazaar which she could reach within ten minutes of leaving the rectory bungalow she bought stamps and posted the letter to Colonel Trehearne. As the letter disappeared into the box she thought: No going back now! Nothing for it now! March! To the barricades! She strode facing the oncoming traffic which seemed uncommonly heavy but with next to nothing going in her direction so that she began to feel like someone moving against the flow of columns of refugees. The shouting tonga-wallahs, the bobbing head-load carriers, the gliding cyclists and the lurching soldiers in the open backs of uncovered trucks and lorries might have been calling: Wrong way! Wrong way! The notion exhilarated her. For the first time since leaving Rose Cottage she felt strong and free because the intense vulgarity of Mildred's gesture in returning the spoons had released in her a vulgarity just as intense but of greater splendour. I, Barbara Batchelor, she declaimed, daughter of Leonard and Lucy Batchelor, late of Lucknow Road, Camberwell, am about to present silver to the officers of the Pankot Rifles. And as my father used to say, storming out into the night or into the morning, bugger the lot of you.

Half way down Cantonment Approach Road she transferred the remaining letter and the box of spoons to her macintosh pocket because her palms were sweating in the humid afternoon. The cloud level was low. There was no rain as yet but the light was strange: bright under a dark sky and then dark under a bright one as if there were a single band of luminosity which bounced, throbbing, between earth and heaven. She did not mind if it rained. She had her sou'-wester in the other pocket of her mac. The umbrella, her mother used to say, take the umbrella. Horrid umbrella. Black cotton cave. Dead Bat. God is weeping for the sins of the world, her mother said. Laughing, you mean, her father replied, laughing fit to bust. But rain was only rain: sea sucked up and sprayed on the parched land by the giant elephant, the elephant god.

She paused opposite the main entrance to the grounds of the general hospital. The nursing-home wing was hidden from view by trees and the lie of the land, She walked on attended by a faceless wraith whose Susan-pale arms opened the way for her, parting misty curtains, one after the other, as if insisting on a directiom, an ultimate objective, a sublime revelation at the end of a tricky and obscure path.

The light became apocalyptic. Puddles in the road shone white reflecting a purity whose source was not visible. The landscape was now bleak, the ground on either side of the road waste: areas of wind-shorn turf broken by rifts and channels. The last refugee had gone by and she was alone, resolute in an alien territory, entering Rifle Range Road that ran straight full-tilt across the valley towards the hills. Suddenly, as if they had cracked under their own weight, there came a report then another, as many as a dozen. The air shifted under the duress of a wind of panic from the hills and the first drops of rain began to fall. The panic did not touch her but the rain would. She put on her macintosh and sou'-wester, patted the pocket where the box of spoons nestled, and strode on past the entrance to grace and favour lane with scarcely more than a glance in the direction of the bungalow to make sure it was still there. Presently she turned into Mess Road. It was the day of the wedding party. We could go to Ranpur, Barbie had said, to do some Christmas shopping. Oh, I shall never go to Ranpur again, Mabel had answered, at least not until I'm buried. But on that day it was sunny. Coming from the shade of the portico into the glare the white of the servants' uniforms dazzled the eye and the emerald leaves of glistening plants in terracotta pots shone like scimitars and cast razor sharp indigo blue shadows. Is it you, is it you, Ghulam Mohammed? Mabel said. And Barbie knew for whom she might ask. She walked into the mess compound. The pebbles in the path gleamed in the rain. Ahead, level with the entrance, there was a parked military truck and as she gained the shelter of the long portico a group of young officers came out laughing and began to climb up over the tailboard while one stood smoking and calling to the absent driver.

Turning, he saw her, and two of the three now settling in the back of the truck and slapping wood and metal with boisterous good-natured impatience saw her too. She filled her old schoolmarm's lungs, grated her Memsahib's voice into gear, and called: 'Good afternoon. Can one of you help me?'

Close to them she noticed that their faces were tight and youthful. Their single subaltern's pips looked painfully new. None of them could have been at the party eight months before. She guessed the thought stiffening their necks and minds: Careful – You never know who she is.

'Do know if Captain Coley is in the mess?'

'Coley? The adjutant? No, I don't think he is.'

The officer who had been shouting for the driver

glanced at the three in the truck who shook their heads. One of them said, 'He wasn't in the daftar this morning.'

'Oh, dear. How dreadfully inconvenient.' She smiled, mimicking the bright brassy manner of women like Nicky Paynton and Isobel Rankin which she noted tended to make the men put themselves out and do things without actually being ordered to.

'I'll ask,' the young officer said and began to go inside but remembered his manners in time and invited her to precede him into the building. Inside, his newness and uncertainty were even more apparent. There was no one about and he seemed unsure of what to do next. Barbie said, 'It's my own fault. I ought to have rung. But I was coming this way and thought I'd kill two birds with one stone. The trouble is I've never visited him in his quarters and have no idea where he hides out. Have you?'

'No, I'm afraid I haven't.'

She got it then: the unmistakable London accent. It came out in the word afraid. It warmed her heart. So did the rather over-greased black hair, the stubby plebeian but not unhandsome features beneath it. As a soldier he must be confident and efficient otherwise the regiment would not have accepted him even at this stage of the war when regiments were taking the best they could get, which she had heard was very good, but having to close their eyes to social shortcomings. As a gentleman he obviously fell short of the Pankots' traditional requirements, and knew it, was far from happy in this silent mausoleum.

'The fact is we only got here from OTS last week,' he said. A bearer crossed the hall, carrying a tray. The subaltern stopped him and asked in inaccurate Urdu whether Captain Coley was in the mess. He didn't understand the bearer's reply but Barbie did. Captain Coley would not be in the mess until after the week-end. She asked the servant if he knew where Captain Coley lived because she wished to see him quite urgently. He gave her directions but they were very muddled and she did not understand the references. She said, 'Is Ghulam Mohammed here?'

The bearer said he did not know Ghulam Mohammed.

There was no Ghulam Mohammed. There was no Ghulam Mohammed in the mess.

She asked him how long he had worked in the mess, and the answer was disturbing. Since last November.

'Ghulam Mohammed was here then,' she insisted.

No, he had never worked with a Ghulam Mohammed. If Memsahib wished he would ask the head steward.

'It doesn't matter,' She turned to go. The officer followed her. He probably hadn't understood a word. She was glad. Her hold on things had begun to be undermined.

All the same he grasped the situation. 'No luck?'

'No, none. But I'll be able to find it.'

'The driver will know, won't he?'

'Oh, I'd forgotten the driver. How clever of you. The driver's bound to know.'

When they got outside, the driver had turned up and was waiting by the cab door. Asked if he knew where the adjutant sahib lived he said nothing but inclined his head to one side and kept on doing so in answer to every one of her questions.

'He knows?'

'He knows.'

'Can we take you?'

'How kind. But shan't I be making you late for a parade.

'It's only the munshi.' He led the way round to the passenger seat, warned her about the height of the step.

'Adjutant Sahib bungalow,' he told the driver after he had slammed the door shut for her. A few seconds later he knocked on the back of the cabin and shouted, 'OK.' As the truck engine started she thought she heard men's laughter. She smiled. The cabin smelt of petrol and other peculiar metallic odours. The truck, one of the snub-nosed variety, gave her the feeling of riding in a tank. It bucked and growled. The windscreen wipers swung like metronomes but squeaked on the glass. She expected it was against the rules for a civilian to ride in it. She wished she had insisted on getting into the back. She would have liked to gossip to the young officers and to have found out

354

where they all came from and what they thought of India. Were they the kind of young men Sarah had met at her aunt's and uncle's in Calcutta? If you're ever stationed in Cal, she might say, watch out for a man called Colonel Grace, he'll be after you to sign on for *ever*.

She glanced at the driver. Thin cheeks. Hawk's nose. And a skin so sunburnt that the usual Pankot copper-colour was, in this light, blue sheened. There were minute red veins in the whites of his eyes. She was startled by the clarity of her vision. He smelt powerfully of garlic. His khaki was immaculately starched and pressed. His marbled brown legs were covered by fine dark hairs above and below the knee, between the tops of the socks and the hem of the knife-edged shorts. Tucked above the windscreen was a faded postcard, a photograph of a chubby wide-eyed smiling beauty with a caste-mark between her thick eyebrows; an Indian film star, she supposed. She imagined a smell of jasmine, a thin nasal voice. How remote his life from her own, But he could have come from the same village as Aziz, or Ghulam Mohammed.

She had never asked Mabel who Ghulam Mohammed was. Now he had gone, like Poppy Browning's daughter, like Gillian Waller, with Mabel to the grave, the one that should not have been dug: crying out soundlessly like the unknown Indian on the road from Dibrapur and the girl in white whom she imagined running in the dark from a martyrdom, or from something unimaginable, which might even have been love. She thought: Perhaps I should have given the spoons to the old woman in the veiled topee, have waited in St John's for her to arrive, and kneel or sit staring at the altar unconsciously sharing my vigil, and called to her softly: These are for the child. And given her the twelve little apostles. But perhaps she isn't in Pankot any longer. Perhaps she was never here. In any case it's too late. I'm presenting the spoons to the mess.

She clapped her hand against her pocket. Yes, the box was still there. She gazed out of the streaming windows. The speed of the truck made the rain seem heavier. All this area of Pankot was new and strange to her. It looked unwelcoming. Rows of huts, squat and dark, parade grounds, basket-ball pitches. Distantly, clutches of figures silhouetted against the white light running for cover. It was very hot in the cabin. The window in the door on her side was misting up.

At a crossroads marked by military signposts the driver turned left. This road after a while became tree-lined. They were going past bungalows up a slight incline and then down into a dip at the bottom of which the driver stopped. There was no bungalow visible, only a dirt track leading off to the left through a kind of copse.

'Adjutant Sahib,' the driver said and pointed at the track. She noticed a square white board on a short post aslant in the hedge, but could not read it. The young officer appeared and opened the door. 'Is it far up the track, do you think?' he asked. 'The truck could get up there. It's muddy to walk.'

'Oh I don't mind. Not in the least. I'm dressed for it.'

'What about when you leave? I've not been this end before. Do you know where you are?'

She asked the driver how far she would have to walk to get a tonga. He indicated ahead and said half-a-mile. She thanked him and got out. She put her sou'-wester back on but did not bother to tie the strings under her chin.

'It's been very good of you. I hope I haven't made you late for the munshi.' She offered her hand. Before shaking it he took off his cap She could hear the others talking. 'My name's Barbara Batchelor, incidentally. At present I'm staying with the Peplows, that's at the rectory bungalow next to St John's church. Arthur Peplow's always glad to see new faces. People sometimes look in for a beer after Sunday morning service, before going up to the club. So don't forget. And good luck to you all, if I don't see you again. Don't get wet. I'm all right. Well protected.'

She went and stood at the end of the dirt track. The door slammed. She waved, watched the truck turn in the road and waved to the men in the back when a full view of them was presented by the truck's manoeuvres. When it had gone out of sight she turned and studied the board.

A foot square, two feet off the ground, it had been painted white some time ago. The paint was peeled, the black letters had faded and the first letter had come off with its background. The notice read: apt K. Coley. Under the name an arrow pointed up the track or would have done so had the board been straight. Its tilt directed the arrow downward into the mixture of gravel, pebbles, earth and mud and tyre-marks which made up the track's surface.

From the path there was nothing to be seen of the bungalow where Coley lived. It was an appropriate setting for a man whose military ambitions were said to have been smothered ten years before in the tumbled bricks and masonry of Quetta. One could imagine him choosing it for its isolation, its proximity to the lines and to the office he was content to occupy for the rest of his working life. He stirred himself, Barbie had heard, only when threatened by promotion and posting to another station. There was nothing he did not know about the running of the regimental depot. Successive commandants had connived at his schemes to stay put.

At the entrance to his hidden retreat Barbie felt a pang of remorse. She could never like Coley but the air of melancholy emanating from the faded tilted board and from the whole area persuaded her to make allowances, to forgive him for behaviour that perhaps had not been natural but forced on him by Mildred. Perhaps he had been afraid to resist her, fearing the power she potentially wielded. Mildred's husband – if he survived prison-camp – was Trehearne's likely successor as depot commandant. Or so Coley might anticipate. And presumably he had only a slender stock of pride. Most of it would have gone with his ambition. If acting the part of the dog at Mildred's heels secured his future, he would play it.

The track curved and came to an abrupt end: a corrugated iron shed, a garage. To the right a gateway without a gate opened on to the steps of rough-hewn stone that led up into the copse.

She climbed the stone steps. What she entered was a

compound planted with hedges, shrubs and bushes that had grown wild among the trees. She identified rhododendron among other more exotic leaves and could see that the path had originally been laid out with an eye to withholding for as long as possible a view of the bungalow that lay at its end; so that the revelation of what was ordinary and ugly stunned her for an instant into acceptance of it as rare and beautiful. Walls, windows, roof, verandah – entirely commonplace, mean even – moved her with the austere poetry of their function. Here a man sheltered from and diminished the horror and vulgarity of the world by the simplicity of his arrangements for living in it.

The path had brought her within a few feet of the front verandah steps. The verandah was narrow. From where she stood she could see the padlock on the hasp of the closed doors. Eden was unoccupied. But perhaps round the back she would find a servant capable of being roused from mid-afternoon torpor. As she moved a gust of wind blew leaves upward. At the back of the bungalow she found a small grassed compound, a servant's hut, also closed and padlocked, and an open-sided byre in which a tethered goat was munching vegetable stalks.

The rain was still not heavy. She hesitated before climbing the steps to gain the temporary shelter of the back verandah, then went up stealthily, conscious of trespass during the occupier's and the servant's absence. This verandah was deeper than the one at the front and was furnished in the familiar way with wicker chairs and table. The windows were shuttered. There were no french windows; only plain narrow doors, also closed.

She prepared to wait for the rain to reach its peak and die out or settle into a persistent Pankot drizzle through which she could walk in search of a tonga without getting too wet. The darkness of the sky suggested a heavy·fall. Already the air seemed thick with mutterings of storm and the distant warning murmur of tempestuous forces gathering in the hills to strike through the valley.

But after that single gust of wind no other came and the

rain continued to fall modestly. Nothing in nature confirmed as real the restlessness in the surrounding air. She clenched her fist and put it against her chest; her heart was not pounding, but there was a pressure round about her, a pulsing. She turned and stared at the shuttered windows and then at the narrow doors which when not closed would be hooked back to the outside walls. The hooks hung loose. But the hasps were not in position. The doors were not locked. Cautiously she tried the handle on one of them. It opened without a sound and the screen of wire mesh yielded to a touch.

'Captain Coley?' she said, and cleared her throat, meaning to call again, more loudly, but the interior was dark and so hot it seemed to suck the breath out of her lungs and at the same time to whimper with relief like a creature deprived of liberty who sensed release. 'Captain Coley?' she repeated. The words came out unsteadily and made no impression on the creature's distant incoherent supplications, its scarcely audible gasps and cries. The mesh screen swung back; she was not aware of pushing it. 'Captain Coley?' she said again and something folded her in its sticky arms and drew her into the interior; not the creature but its keeper. It held her for a moment and then was not there and the illusion of hot darkness was splintered. Her flesh tightened, attacked by frosty particles of fear, the shuttered bungalow was filled with subterranean light and at its centre the creature was imprisoned in a room divided from the one she stood in by swing ornamental shutters that filled no more than the central space of the open doorway. It was like being back again in that chill corridor approaching other doors that gave a view through oval windows. She was drawn to them by the creature's moans and cries until she stood in a place where over the top of the shutters she saw in the gloom the creature herself, naked, contorted, entwined with another, gaunt and male silently active in a human parody of divine creation.

It was not the stark revelation of the flesh that caused Barbie to gasp and cover her mouth for in her own body she guessed the casual ugliness that might attach to a surrender to sensuality. What filled her with horror was the instantaneous impression of the absence of love and tenderness: the emotional inertia and mechanical pumping of the man, the cries coming from the woman who seemed driven by despair rather than by longing, or even lust. It was as though the world outside the subterranean room was dying or extinct and the joyless coupling was a bitter hopeless expression of the will of the woman for the species to survive.

Turning, groping, Barbie regained the verandah, closed the door and leaned on it, head back, mouth open like a swimmer breaking surface; and then fearing she must have been heard made for the steps, stumbled in going down them and blundered round the side of the bungalow, terrified of discovery, of turning and seeing Mildred and Kevin Coley bearing down on her, naked, raw-eyed, determined on her destruction as the sole witness of their act of adultery.

She ran down the path and – misjudging the twists – was whipped by twigs and obstructed by branches. Going down the rough-hewn steps she misjudged again and wrenched her ankle, falling. Scrambling up she ran down the track. It seemed endless. When eventually she came out on to the lane she turned left into the unknown.

The ankle did not begin to hurt until, after walking for fifteen minutes without coming upon a landmark or a wider road that might lead her back to familiar surroundings, she stopped, knowing that something was wrong. She felt in her pocket – but the spoons and the letter were still there. The wrongness was in the other pocket. There was no sou'-wester but it wasn't on her head either. Her hair was sopping wet. She turned, intending to go back and look for it but at that moment became aware both of the pain in her ankle and of the futility of such a search. The sou'-wester must have been torn off her head by the overhanging branches in the garden. She could not remember that happening. But then she could not remember either whether she had taken the hat off on the verandah and left it on the table. Her name was written in indelible pencil on the white lining of the headband.

Limping, punishing the stick, she struck out again through what had become a downpour, not daring to stop and shelter in case her ankle seized up and she found herself unable to move, marooned in this inhospitable region.

PART FIVE

The Tennis Court

1

Miss Batchelor was taken to the civil wing of the general hospital on the day Nicky Paynton heard that her husband had been killed in the Arakan.

For three days Clarissa had sent meals into Barbie's room, spoken to her from the doorway but otherwise kept clear in order not to be infected by the awful cold the old missionary had caught as a result of walking about in the rain, without a hat, getting lost, returning home like a drowned rat and then refusing all advice and offers of hot balsam.

But on the fourth morning, alarmed first by the sight of Barbie's flushed face and the fact that she opened her eyes but seemed unable to speak or rouse herself, and then by the feeling of hot dry skin under her own cool hand, Clarissa rang Doctor Travers who, after a brief examination, sent for an ambulance.

'How long has she been like this?' he asked while they waited. Clarissa confessed that she hadn't actually seen her since before lunch on the previous day when she thought she looked better but not as well as she insisted. 'I made her promise not to get up and she said she wouldn't. After that I was busy all day but the boy said she ate all her meals, except her supper. She was asleep when he took it in. She hasn't touched her night drink either.'

Travers said, 'I wish I'd known sooner. Actually it's risky moving her but I don't think we could save her here. I ought to warn you it's ten to one against her making it. She's got broncho-pneumonia and the heart's pretty weak. What on earth's the poor old thing been doing?'

Clarissa said she didn't know but described the state Barbie was in when she came back into the house on the afternoon of the day of the christening. They went back to the room and for a moment Clarissa thought Barbie had gone in the few minutes she and Doctor Travers had been talking in the hall.

He sat on the bed holding Barbie's wrist and then listening to her chest again through his stethoscope. 'I suppose she's quite alone in the world?' he asked presently.

'Until she came to Pankot she lived only for the Mission,' Clarissa said. 'She talks about getting back into harness but of course she's past it. I think it was the letter she had from them saying they wouldn't have her back that did it.'

Travers looked round, surprised because Clarissa Peplow's voice sounded very unsteady. He had always assumed her to be emotionally dehydrated.

'Will *you* have her back, Mrs Peplow? That is, if the question happens to arise?'

Clarissa nodded.

'I ask because it could be important. I mean if we get her over the pneumonia. People don't die only because of diseases, you know.'

At that moment the telephone rang and thinking it might be the hospital warning him of a delay Travers got Clarissa's permission to answer it. It wasn't the hospital but Clara Fosdick, asking for Clarissa. She said she was glad to be speaking to him, however, because Nicky Paynton had had this telegram about poor Bunny being killed in action and Clara had already thought of ringing Colonel Beames to suggest that he should look in. Clara said she thought Nicky was taking it too well and being over-conscientious about not breaking down in front of people. Nicky and Bunny had absolutely adored each other and it was awful, Clara said, to see Nicky going about the house as if nothing had happened and even trying to get ready to go to the club to play bridge in order not to let Isobel and Maisie down, because with Mildred temporarily dropped out it was difficult to make up a four at short notice if, as she had last night, Isobel indicated that she had a free afternoon and wished to play.

'I'm not sure whether I should cancel it or not,' Clara

said. 'I mean I know I should. In fact must. But she seems set on keeping her promise. She says Bunny would have understood.'

There was of course no bridge. But neither did Nicky Paynton ever break down in front of anyone. She adopted a manner that made her in the eyes of her friends curiously immune from their sympathy although not from their admiration. After sending a telegram to her friend Dora Lowndes in Wiltshire (who was married to the boys' housemaster and looked after them during the holidays) and then following the telegram up with a letter to the boys themselves, she continued her daily routine, not as though nothing had happened but as though it had and was over and wasn't to be mentioned because it concerned no one except herself and her sons.

Bunny's death, she implied, was entirely her private affair. Even from the start, although still referring to him and saying his name, she used the past tense, which made people feel he had been dead for years and that her widowhood had been the determining factor in her personality for a long time – the one everybody had missed noticing before and had to get used to quickly if they were to stand a chance of remaining on friendly terms with her.

Everybody agreed that it was an astonishing performance; the best ever put up in a society that prided itself on being able to do exactly what Nicky Paynton was doing if the need arose. That it was also a farewell performance was understood. It could only be a matter of time before Nicky announced that she was packing up and going home by the quickest means available, to be with her sons. No one else had any claim on her. With one stroke India was finished for her and although she would probably assure her friends that she'd be back, this was one of those crystal clear cases of a woman leaving and knowing that her chances of seeing India again were slim enough to be non-existent. She would never be able to afford the fare. If either boy eventually came out she might be tempted to scrape together enough to come and visit him and renew old acquaintanceships, but she would be foolish to do so. It would be unbearable.

Already you could see her looking at things as if trying to fix them sharply enough in her memory to carry away indelible impressions of them; and then beginning not to look at all because she was only making things worse for herself, knowing she was looking for the last time.

Nicky had had the worst kind of luck. If the children had been grown up or if there had been no children the decision to go home could have been postponed at least until the end of the war, even indefinitely. Perhaps – as in the case of her friend Clara Fosdick – the question would never have arisen. All her closest friends were in India. They would have rallied round as Clara's friends – Nicky and Bunny in particular – rallied round when Freddie Fosdick died of cancer in his own hospital back in '36, leaving no children but a wife rather younger than himself; although not young enough to have further expectations, even if she had had the inclination to marry again, which she had not. As it was between Nicky and Bunny so it had been between Clara and Freddie.

Clara knew that Nicky's loss affected her as much as anyone because the moment Nicky packed and went she herself would be homeless. The bungalow they shared was occupied officially by Nicky as the wife of Colonel Paynton of the Ranpurs. Clara was merely a paying-guest. The obvious solution would be for her to go to live in Ranpur with her sister and brother-in-law, Mr Justice Spendlove, but she didn't care much for Billy Spendlove and her sister knew it and stuck up for him whenever she thought he was being criticized, They usually managed to quarrel during Clara's short visits.

And so, stoically but without being able to disguise her inner preoccupations, Clara waited for Nicky to make the inevitable announcement.

She made it at what was from Clara's point of view an unsuitable moment; at Rose Cottage and to the company assembled there as in the old days on a sunny Saturday morning.

Mildred's sister Fenny had come up from Calcutta to be at Mildred's side during Susan's illness and to help with the move to Rose Cottage; a move finally achieved a few days after Nicky received the telegram – if anything so piecemeal, so incomplete, could be reckoned an achievement. It was piecemeal because spread over several days and incomplete because Susan's things were in Miss Batchelor's old room along with Sarah's, and Susan's baby and the ayah were in the little spare; but there was no Susan. And Panther had escaped twice from Mahmoud's custody and twice been found outside Susan's old room at the temporarily empty grace and favour bungalow, his head resting on one of his two outstretched forepaws, too far gone in his animal misery to keep up the whining and whimpering which in the first few days of Susan's absence had made Mildred lose her temper and say that the wretched creature would have to be put down.

After the second escape during which he seemed to have torn his hindquarters on what the vet thought was barbed wire Mildred ordered the dog to be tethered in the servants' quarters of Rose Cottage. He turned vicious. None of the servants dared approach. It was Sarah who risked being bitten, trying to calm and feed him and bathe his wound. She left water and a meaty bone within his reach. He did not touch them. It looked as though he intended to starve himself to death to prove his loyalty to Susan. His deterioration was frighteningly rapid. The tether became pointless. He hadn't the energy to stand. No longer capable of snapping and snarling he trembled when Sarah stroked his head. She fed him warm milk and brandy through a pipette given to her by the veterinary officer from the old Remount Depot, Lieutenant Firozeh Khan. Lt Khan said that the kindest thing would be to have the dog destroyed. It hadn't acted like this when Susan was away having the baby. It was possible that the dog thought Susan had been taken away and the baby left in her place as a substitute. It might be dangerous to have it around.

'No,' Sarah said. 'That's pure imagination. Panther's got to be saved. Captain Samuels says Panther may be important to my sister when she's a bit better.'

Samuels was an RAMC psychiatrist attached to the military wing of the hospital. He hadn't been in India long and was used to dealing with men, chiefly British other ranks. Mildred had already said she didn't see what good he could do since most of his work was confined to treating slackers who thought they had nervous break-downs because they were deprived of fish and chips. Her friends agreed that perhaps there was something disagree-able about Susan being talked to, questioned, by a man; particularly by a man like Samuels who might be consi-dered clever at home where psychoanalysis was fashion-able, but who was after all a Jew. But the alternative was the Hospital of the Samaritan Mission of the Sisters of Our Lady of Mercy in Ranpur, a mental home staffed by Catholics; Eurasians and Indians mostly; the same ghastly kind of place with a small wing for Europeans such as poor Poppy Browning's daughter had ended her days in, screaming obscenities at her mother who used to go home from her weekly visits and wash in Lysol because they'd given up bathing the girl forcibly, except once a month, and Poppy used to touch and hold her close in an attempt to show her she was still loved.

Susan, thank God, was reported quite the opposite; clean, well-behaved, silent. She had said a few words to her mother and to Sarah and presumably more than a few to Captain Samuels who told Mildred her daughter was 'beginning to adjust' whatever that meant. Adjust to what? Mildred had apparently not bothered to ask. She distrusted the whole psychiatric process and had no time at all for the jargon. She said Travers had acted precipi-tately, sending Susan back to the nursing home. There was nothing wrong with the girl that a good rest, a change of air and the company of young people wouldn't put right. She wasn't getting any kind of rest at the nursing home with Captain Samuels visiting her sometimes twice or even three times a day. Mildred managed to make these professional visits sound as though something un-wholesome was going on.

'I'm sure Millie is right,' her sister Fenny said on this particular Saturday morning when Mildred had gone indoors in answer to Mahmoud's announcement that Captain Coley Sahib was on the telephone. 'I think it would be a good idea for her to come and stay with me in Calcutta and bring both girls and ayah and the baby. There wouldn't be room in the flat but Colonel Johnson and his wife who are friends of ours have a simply huge old eighteenth century John Company house and would gladly put them up. Or we could spend October in Darjeeling with old Dogra friends of Arthur's and come back down to Cal in November when the weather's really nice. Sarah would benefit as much as anyone. In fact I've suggested she and I could go down to Calcutta together quite soon. She's been up two nights with that dog as well as making sure ayah looks after little Edward properly and she visits Susan at least once a day, *and* still reports to the daftar whenever she can in spite of Dick Rankin telling her she can have extended station leave for as long as she wants. She's gone there this morning.'

'How *is* the dog?' Maisie Trehearne asked.

'Sarah says it's on the mend. She's got it in the mali's shed. I haven't looked myself. I can't bear the sight of sick animals but then I'm no good in a sick-room of any kind which is why I never visited Sarah's friend Captain Merrick, although the hospital's practically visible from the flat. But I did ring before I came up to Pankot and they said he was fine and quite cheerful considering he's lost his left arm.'

Fenny stopped and conscientiously avoided looking at Nicky Paynton, presumably in the belief that the subject of wounded officers was to be avoided. Fenny had become stouter since her last visit to Pankot at the time of Susan's engagement, when she pronounced Teddie Bingham 'rather sweet'. She filled the chair she was sitting in, which happened to be the one Mabel died in. The others wondered whether she knew but supposed she didn't in view of her confessed inability even to visit someone who was ill.

And she was smarter than they remembered. Arthur Grace's belated elevation to a Lieutenant-colonelcy and appointment in Calcutta seemed to have given her a sort of cosmopolitan gloss. She belonged, as though in default of having arrived sooner at a desirable peak, to a new order of Indian authority and had apparently, as a result, absorbed and smothered a multitude of sins. For Rose Cottage she was slightly over-dressed. Of the three women sitting with her, Maisie, Nicky and Clara, only Maisie remembered her as the youngest and prettiest of the three daughters of General Muir who had lived in Flagstaff House in the years immediately following the end of the 1914–18 war. Lydia, the eldest, had been cold and rather snooty, very intelligent and not at all ena-moured of Anglo-Indian life. Her fiancé had been drowned in the Atlantic by German submarine action, a loss that had brightened the northern, arctic, gleam in her critical eye. She had gone home, got married and settled in Bayswater. Fenny in those days had a reputation for charming silliness, Maisie recalled, and in spite of being chased by scores of personable and promising fellows had married a man who turned out something of a failure. But all three knew well enough the Fenny to whom in middle-age an air of portly dowdiness had attached; a dowdiness she had combated by being vigor-ous in her opinions. Which had been comfortingly con-servative. The vigour remained but now suited her. Fenny was particularly welcome just now. She radiated self-assurance.

'I'm so glad to have got Millie out of that poky little bungalow,' she said, making a sign to Mahmoud to replenish glasses. Mildred was still on the telephone indoors. 'I don't mind telling you I had to prod her a bit. At the last moment she said she didn't want to come. But she didn't want to stay in the grace and favour either and anyway she no longer had a choice. She said that if it wasn't for the girls she'd ask Dick Rankin to pull strings

369

and get the airforce to fly her home to wait for John there.'

She looked over her shoulder to be sure Mildred was still indoors. Then lowering her voice slightly she said:

'She's awfully against that missionary woman, isn't she? She told me she's been going through Mabel's papers because the money looks like being less than she expected. I thought she meant Miss Batchelor had been cooking the books and feathering her nest but she said there wasn't any sign of that, only what she calls influence.'

'What sort of influence?' Clara Fosdick wanted to know.

'Payments to charities. *Indian* charities. Orphanages, famine relief funds, child-widows, that sort of thing, and always *anonymously*. There are all these letters from the bank in Ranpur, dating back *years*, acknowledging her instructions to make anonymous donations to this and that – hundreds of rupees at a time, and advice notes about transfers of sterling from London which means she was selling securities at home as well as having the interest sent out.'

Maisie said, 'I don't see where the influence comes in if it's been going on for years. Unless you mean only five. Miss Batchelor came here at the end of nineteen thirty-nine.'

'I know. But according to Mildred although Mabel had been giving money to Indian charities for ages, long before Miss Batchelor came to live with her, it almost doubled afterwards, especially in the last couple of years. And there was one donation to the Bishop Barnard Mission which isn't an Indian charity but does help to educate them. Not that I'm against it, any of it, but Mildred says the Bishop Barnard was the mission Miss Batchelor worked for, which proves it – '

'Proves what?'

'According to Mildred, that Mabel was influenced to dish out all this dough *by* Miss Batchelor. On top of which the estate has to fork out to buy an annuity for the woman and if she dies soon after it's bought it's hundreds or thousands of rupees wasted.'

'Perhaps she won't live long enough for it to be bought at

all,' Nicky said. 'Clarissa Peplow told me Captain Travers doesn't expect her to pull through.'

'But she's been in hospital well over a week, nearly two, and she hasn't popped off yet. Don't tell Mildred, for Pete's sake, but Sarah's been over to the civil wing once or twice to see her when she goes to talk to Susan. Sarah says she only seems semi-conscious but reckons she's a tough old bird and will get over it.' But whether she does or doesn't Mildred says the idea of an annuity could only have come from *her* because it's a typical lower-middle-class idea of upper-class security and respectability.'

'Isobel Rankin says Mildred is over-obsessed by the idea of Miss Batchelor as an eminence-grise,' Maisie Trehearne said. 'I don't know whether that's true or not but if it is we oughtn't to encourage her. The whole situation is becoming very – unhappy.'

Particularly in regard to spoons; about which Maisie's husband had received what he called a charming and touching letter from the old missionary, but not, as yet, the spoons themselves, which had puzzled him until he heard she had gone into hospital. It still puzzled him a bit. Maisie did not know what to tell him. For some years he had lived in an old-fashioned chivalrous world of his own. If it hadn't been for the war he would have retired in 1942. Sometimes, she thought, he acted as though he *had* retired. He had become fond and foolish and sometimes querulous. He couldn't understand why Coley insisted he'd received no spoons but only a sou'-wester, and he inquired every day after Miss Batchelor's health. The position was not an easy one for her to support. He lived for the regiment. Silver for the mess was as much an obsession with Mildred Layton. When it came to choosing between Mildred's and her husband's obsession there was no question which side she would support. He wanted the spoons. She hoped no one would tell him the spoons were originally Susan's and that Mildred had returned them in a fit of the extraordinary pique that generally possessed her nowadays. Another puzzling feature was that Mildred had said nothing about the spoons. Presumably Kevin Coley hadn't mentioned Miss Batchelor's intention to present them. But Maisie thought this strange too because Kevin and Mildred were so thick. Perhaps he was telling her now, on the telephone.

'Of course,' Fenny went on. 'I've told Millie there's absolutely no proof and certainly no reason why Mabel shouldn't have forked out all that money without prompting. Millie seems to have forgotten, but I don't suppose you have, Maisie, I mean about Mabel's attitude to Jallianwallah.'

'Attitude to whom?'

'Jallianwallah. The General Dyer business in Amritsar in 1919.'

'Well I have forgotten. What was her attitude?'

'Don't you remember how we all collected money for Dyer when Government should have stood by him but didn't and issued that report that he'd exceeded his duty, firing on the unarmed mob in the Jallianwallah Bagh, and the poor old boy was disgraced and retired on half-pay?'

'Well of course I remember that. We were down in Mayapore at the time. There was a lovely ball at the old Artillery Mess and we collected about four thousand rupees just from that.'

'Oh well, if you were down in Mayapore you probably didn't know, which isn't surprising anyway because I had to remind Millie how Mabel refused to give anything. It was very embarrassing for John. After all Mabel was rich in comparison with most of us. She got simply loads from her father, the Admiral, and quite a packet from her first husband, the Pankot Rifles chap who gave all that silver to the mess. And she simply wouldn't give a penny for Dyer.'

'But that means you're saying she was mean – '

'Only about Dyer. At the time we all thought he'd saved the poor old empire and ought to have been given a peerage not the sack. Of course since then people have blamed him for turning Gandhi against us. But the point is, and I was awfully embarrassed because I thought Millie must know if *I* knew, but it seems John never said a word to her, only to me. He told me in strictest confidence, or

372

rather it slippped out and he asked me not to say anything
to anybody, he told me Mabel sent money to the funds the
Indians raised for the widows and orphans of the people
Dyer shot. She *told* him she'd done so. I think she said she
sent it to that old Muslim, M.A.K.'s father, the man who
was on the Governor's Council down in Ranpur at the
same time as John's father. Sir Ahmed Kasim, wasn't it?
She told John she'd done it but had asked Sir Ahmed, if it
was Sir Ahmed, to pay it over anonymously because she
didn't want to harm John's career. John told me it was a
hundred pounds. In nineteen twenty that was a hell of a
lot of money.'

'It still is,' Nicky said. 'Do you think Sir Ahmed paid it
over?'

'Nicky!'

'Perhaps she gave it to his son M.A.K., to swell the
Congress Party Funds?'

Fenny said, 'But Sir Ahmed was pro-British. People
said he was awfully upset when his son joined the rebel
faction of Congress, as we used to think it.'

'Rebels run in the Kasim family,' Nicky said.

'Oh, I'd hardly say that,' Fenny objected. 'M.A.K.'s
own son, the young Kasim boy we met in Mirat at the guest
house, struck me as rather sweet for an Indian. And you
couldn't call him a rebel, working for an Indian prince. As a
matter of fact it was in Mirat I found out Millie didn't know
about Mabel giving money to the Jallianwallah Bagh
orphans and widows, because I asked her if I was right
thinking she'd sent it via the young Kasim boy's grandfather and she simply didn't know what I was talking about.
So I thought I'd better shut up. Mabel was still alive then.
But she remembered and asked me last week when she was
hot on the tail of these other donations.'

'I wasn't thinking about the Kasim boy you met in
Mirat,' Nicky said. 'I was thinking about the other one,
the one who got the King's commision and has been
captured fighting against us in the INA.'

'Really?' Fenny said. 'I didn't know about that.' She
looked doubtful as if Nicky had said something in bad

373

taste. 'All I know is what everybody else knows, that M.A.K. himself is ill and has been released to go and live with the Nawab on some sort of extended parole.'

'He's not ill,' Nicky said. 'He's being cosseted by Government and a fat lot of good it'll do. The Nawab's probably anti-government as well and M.A.K.'ll be the first to call his officer son a bloody hero. It's double standards all the time. It makes me sick. But that makes it easier bidding it all a fond farewell.'

There was silence. Even Fenny seemed prewarned of Nicky's inevitable announcement and to recognize that the moment for it had arrived.

'It's a salutary thought,' Nicky said after a while, 'that Bunny may have been killed by a one-time officer of his own regiment. After all why not? I've been checking up. A Lieutenant Sayed Kasim was commisioned into the Fifth Ranpurs. He was the first Indian the Ranpurs ever took. There were plenty of others but he was the first. Bunny always took immense pains with his own Indian officers. And I took pains with the wives. God knows it was sometimes a hard grind. And you wondered at the time whether it was worth it. It seems it wasn't. It's a bloody bore because you end up distrusting everybody. Sometimes I even look at old Fariqua and try to work out what it would take to make him do the dirty on me even though he's gone around red-eyed ever since I told him Bunny had bought it. Incidentally, Clara, Fariqua lives in a village outside Ranpur. If you do go down to your sister you might help find the old boy a job. He has so many spare wives around there he'll need the money and have to go on working until he drops.'

'Are you really going home, Nicky?' Clara asked when she could manage it.

'Yes.'

'Have you decided when and how?'

'The answer to when is as soon as I can. As to how, I'll do what Fenny says Mildred would have liked to. Scrounge a lift with the airforce even if it means being stuck in somewhere like Cairo for a bit. I'll auction

374

everything off and just send a trunk or two of odds and ends by sea. And if the boat's sunk it won't matter much. There's really nothing of value to take back with me.'

Clara said:

'I'll miss you dreadfully.'

For an instant Nicky seemed ready to crumple. But the iron will was not to be broken.

'Oh well, I'll be back in a year or two I expect. When the boys are off my hands. Do you know, there are loads of things I've never done out here? When Bunny was alive he always promised we'd go down to the Coromandel coast one winter, but we never managed it and we never got to Goa either. And then it would be nice to see the Taj again. Bunny thought it terribly overrated but I must say I thought it rather splendid. And of course I'd like to see Gulmarg again, and Ooty, and even dreary old Simla.'

Her friends said nothing. They nodded encouragingly but absentmindedly. The dispiriting fact had not escasped them. Already Nicky Paynton was talking like a tourist. It was this that drove home to them the terrible bleakness – thinness – that settled upon and somehow defined anyone whose connexion had been severed; and then as their glances mercifully fell from her one by one and turned upon the garden Fenny cried out:

'God, what's that?' She jerked out of her chair, startling them. 'What? (one of them shouted) What is it Fenny?' Her alarm was infectious. Her plump ringed fingers were crossed at her throat. She had become speechless and was staring, horrified, at a patch of petal-strewn grass, a corridor between long rectangular beds of rose-trees, bush and standard, vagrant-looking with green reversionary shoots pale and erectile, already sucking the life out of the roots. Along this path the creature crawled, slunk, to-wards them; a black spectre of famine worn to its hooped rib cage and the arched column of its backbone. A thin dribble of saliva hung from its open mouth.

'Millie!' Fenny called, and then turned and went into the house still calling her. The others stayed where they were, watching the apparition approach the verandah steps slowly, dragging one leg, pausing every few paces to rest, droop-headed, before struggling on, its eyes upturned and fixed on the objective, showing blood-shot whites.

'How can she?' Nicky exclaimed. 'How can Sarah have let it suffer like this? She ought to be ashamed.'

'But Nicky, it means it's getting better,' Maisie said. 'It's looking for her.' Even Maisie could not manage to say the animal's name. She went to the head of the steps cautiously and called down to it, 'Sarah? Where's Sarah, then? There's a brave old soldier. There's a brave old boy.' And got gingerly down on one knee and extended invitation through an outstretched arm and placating fingers which the animal observed from below, raising the iron weight of its neck a fraction of an inch and then lowering it again and standing there at the bottom of the steps as if unable to work out the complicated problem they presented.

Mildred was not on the telephone. Fenny thrust open the door of Mabel's room which she and her sister were sharing. Neither Mabel's old bed nor the charpoy she herself slept in was made up yet. Fenny thought this unforgivable of the servants but blamed Mildred for not controlling them better. However she held her tongue.

Mildred was sitting on the edge of Mabel's bed, topping her glass up from her private bottle.

'Millie, that dog's got loose and is crawling about the garden.'

Mildred put the bottle back on the bedside table.

'What did you say?'

'The dog. It's got loose. I can't bear to see it. It looks as if its come to die.'

The corners of Mildred's lips twitched and then curved down in the characteristic smile.

'Lucky dog,' she said.

'Oughtn't we to ring Sarah and get her back here quickly? She can't let it go on like this, Millie. I know she means well but it's not fair, it's not kind.'

'She'll be back any moment now.'

Fenny looked at her watch. It was barely twelve.

'But she never gets back from the daftar before one when she goes in on a Saturday and if the vet isn't rung before then we probably shan't get him until this evening.'

'I said she'll be back any moment.'

Mildred took a drink then looked at Fenny.

'Sarah passed out at the daftar. Only we're not supposed to know. Dicky Beauvais found her in what he calls a fainting condition in the map room. She got him to promise not to tell me. But apparently it's the second time this week and he thought I ought to know. He decided honour would be satisfied if he rang Kevin and left it to Kevin whether to tell me or not. He'll be back with her in about ten minutes I should think, with some story about the daftar being slack.'

Fenny sat heavily on the charpoy. 'There! Perhaps she'll listen now and stop being so silly. It's ridiculous her going into the daftar at all.'

'Is it?'

'Millie, you can't let her go on like this. She can't go round fainting all over the place. If you don't speak to her I will.'

'Haven't you spoken to her already?'

'What do you mean?'

'What should I mean?'

'I don't know but if you're not going to do anything I shall have to tackle her myself.'

Mildred got up and stood with her back to Fenny, arms folded but still holding her glass, looking out of the window which gave on to the verandah at the front of the house.

'Directly Dicky Beauvais has gone,' Fenny continued, 'I'll talk to her then. I suppose we'll have to deal with the business of the poor dog first, but one of us must talk to her.'

Mildred said nothing.

'I've been thinking, Millie,' Fenny said. She had always been a bit afraid of her sister. 'You don't honestly need me here much longer. And if Sarah doesn't get a holiday soon she'll crack up. Why don't I do what I suggested the other day, take her back with me to Calcutta, in say a couple of weeks' time? Minnie's perfectly competent with the baby and I can't see Susan being allowed home just yet. When she is we could all meet in Darjeeling for a few weeks and be together in Calcutta before Christmas. Even *for* Christmas. Let's face it Millie, Pankot's awfully dull for two young girls like Sarah and Su.'

'You used to say what a jolly little place it was.'

'Well it's not any more.'

'No,' Mildred said. 'And compared with Calcutta it's got nothing to offer, has it?'

'Very little.'

'No madly handsome young officers fresh from the jungle or about to go into it and ready to tear the place apart?'

Fenny laughed, relieved by what looked like Mildred's change of mood. She said, 'Oh, we have our share of those!'

'So I should imagine. Can you wait two weeks?'

'Oh, Millie. All I ask is for you to give it some serious thought. It would do Sarah the world of good.'

'You think so?'

Fenny hesitated before speaking her mind. 'I know it's been difficult for you without John all these years. Now don't misunderstand, Millie, but it's always seemed to me a great deal of the weight of *your* burden has fallen on Sarah's shoulders. It's in her nature, I know, to take on responsibilities, but it's not right, not for a young girl. And it begins to show and then it's difficult. I mean – with men. We don't want Sarah on the shelf, do we? I know she could have married several times, certainly once. There was Teddie wasn't there, before he switched to Su? But that's the point. If she isn't careful, a girl like Sarah begins to look sort of discarded or second-best choice. And she isn't. You should have seen her just in that very brief time she was with us. She looked stunning. The boys we had in certainly thought so. One in particular – '

Mildred swung round. 'Don't tell me any more, Fenny! I don't want to know. Just get on with it. Take her to Calcutta. The sooner the better, I imagine.'

'Well, you might sound more enthusiastic! Don't you want Sarah to have a good time?'

Mildred laughed. She picked up the bottle, sat on the bed, filled her glass again. And laughed. Then she clattered the bottle back on the table between the water jug and the table-lamp. She took a hefty swig. But the gin didn't compose her. Her eyes glittered under lids which were for once wide open.

'A good time?' she asked. 'She's *had* the good time, hasn't she?'

'Millie, what on earth's wrong with you?'

'Oh, stop putting on the act. It's very good but it's beginning to irritate me. I don't want to talk about it and I don't want to know any of the details. Not any of them. Now or ever. But you can stop treating me like a bloody fool because I know exactly what's going on.' She took another drink. 'I'm even grateful to you for trying to cope with it without my knowing, although it's the least you can do considering you're bloody well to blame. If you want Sarah to go on thinking she's fooled me that's up to you. But you're my little sister. You were always silly and it would be bad for my morale to let you imagine *you'd* fooled me.'

Fenny did not reply at once. She looked at the glass.

She said, 'You're drunk, Millie. That's all I know. So you must be right. If it's any consolation I'll admit I'm silly. Dense. I haven't the slightest idea what you're talking about.'

'Oh?' Mildred drank most of the rest of the gin in her glass but did not top it up. 'Let's forget it then. Let's pretend everything in the garden is lovely and just do what seems best for Sarah. Since you're so concerned about her why don't you ring Captain Travers or Colonel Beames and ask one of them to drop in after lunch to give her a check-up?'

'Well, yes, we could do that. Isn't it a bit out of

proportion though? They're both busy men and what can either of them say except what I say, that she's been overdoing it and needs a holiday?'

'But suppose she's really ill? I'm surprised you haven't thought of that, Fenny. I tell you what. I'll ring Travers now myself. I'll do it right away.'

'Well. If you think so.'

Mildred finished her drink. 'I think so,' she said. She waited for a moment as if challenging Fenny to stop her and then smiled and went into the hall, leaving the door open. Fenny heard the ping of the bell as the receiver was lifted and then several rapid pings as Mildred impatiently jerked the hook up and down to wake the dozy operator. Sighing, Fenny got up and went into the hall too.

Mildred was at the telephone but the receiver was back on the hook. She was not ringing anybody.

'You were really going to let me!' she exclaimed.

'But it was your idea. Why should I stop you?'

'Haven't you honestly the least idea what I'm getting at?'

'No, I haven't.'

'Then you'd better come in here.'

Fenny followed Mildred into Sarah's and Susan's bedroom. At the wall opposite the foot of the beds was a chest of drawers. Placed centrally on its top among neatly ordered lacquered boxes stood a photograph of Sarah's father. Fenny gazed at it fondly for a moment. Mildred went to the chest and opened the second of three long drawers.

'Look,' she said. She turned back piles of neatly laundered underwear. Fenny looked. There were two pudgy blue-wrapped packages, both unopened. Mildred covered them up again and shut the drawer. She went out of the room and after a few moments Fenny went too. She found Mildred back in their own room pouring herself another drink.

'Shut the door, Fenny,' Fenny did so. 'Do you want a gin too?' Fenny shook her head.

'The one thing I've always done for Sarah,' Mildred

began, 'and perhaps it's the only thing, is make sure she's got plenty of sannies when she's due, because like I used to be she's as regular as clockwork but has an absolutely ghastly time, worse even than I did before she was born. She was due a week after she came back from her visit to you in Calcutta. I gave her one of those packets then. She was due again last week and that's when I gave her the other.'

'Millie, what are you saying?'

'That according to the evidence in that chest of drawers she's missed twice and hasn't told me. I thought perhaps she'd told you. I thought she might have had to. To make you help her get hold of the bloody man you so kindly introduced her to, or get rid of the thing in Calcutta.'

Suddenly Millie rounded on her.

'And isn't that the truth, Fenny? Isn't that what your cosy little trip to Calcutta is all about? To fix things up with some snide little emergency officer or fix them up in a different way with a shady Calcutta doctor or pop her neatly into an expensive clinic as a Mrs Smith requiring a d and c?'

'No! No, Millie! Oh, no.'

'Well, that's what you're going to have to do. Get the bloody thing aborted. My God, I could murder you. You have charge of her for just twenty-four stinking hours and she's in the bloody club.'

Fenny sat down, with her hands at her cheeks, her eyes shut. Mildred sat too, facing her.

'What are you doing? Working out which one of you and Arthur's adoring and adorable panting bloody boys it was? Or isn't there any doubt in your mind? What a stupid woman you are. In Mirat you made that ridiculous fuss about her riding in broad daylight with the young Kasim boy. Was it wise – isn't that what you asked me? Wise! A pity you didn't ask yourself if it was wise before you chucked her into the arms of some randy little English officer from God knows where. What was he? All strong white teeth and bloody prick? Did you fancy him yourself? Did you get a kick out of handing him Sarah?

Because that's what you did and I never intend to forget it. Never. Just as I never intend to be told who the little cheapskate was. It hasn't happened. Look at me, Fenny. It hasn't happened. You'll take her to Calcutta and between the two of you *deal* with it. Get rid of it. I don't want to know how or where or how much it costs. You get the money from your husband because he's equally to blame. But *I* don't want to know anything more about it. And if anything goes wrong it's on your head, not mine. Because I can't stand any more. I can't and I won't.'

The sound of a car entering the drive arrested her. She got up.

'Now,' she said. 'Pull yourself together. When everybody's gone you can start worming it out of her. Pretend I don't know if you like. But *deal* with it. Do you understand?'

'Millie, you don't *know*. You're only guessing. You don't *know* anything.'

Mildred leaned over her, lowering her voice but speaking vehemently and distinctly. 'Two missed periods? Fainting at the office? For God's sake what more do you want? And today's not the first time I've wondered what was wrong with her. I *am* her mother. A bloody bad one, but I am *that*, and I *know*, *I know from the look on her face*.'

She went briskly to the door, opened it, and in her ordinary abrasively cheerful voice said, 'Dicky! What a nice surprise. Aren't you both rather early? Well, all the better. You'll stay for lunch, won't you Dicky? I'll tell Mahmoud. Sarah dear, you're looking exhausted. Why don't you freshen up and get out of that boring uniform? Dicky, use my bathroom, but go through the dining-room. My sister's in the bedroom powdering her nose. But literally.'

There were several kinds of footsteps going in different directions away from the hall and presently Fenny heard a man's in the adjoining bathroom and the click of the bolt on his side of the door. She heard Dicky beginning to urinate – a splash followed by a murmuring silence as

382

he considerately redirected the stream away from the water to the porcelain.

She got up. There was no one in the hall. Sarah's door was ajar. She tapped and went in. She could see the compact shape of his body, uniformed, and smell its assertive masculine odour. She wanted to hate him but could not. Dimly she had always seen that he represented the kind of force that would make the world safe for her and Arthur while laughing at them. For an instant she entertained the absurd idea that he might be forced to do the right thing. But he was gone, as such men always were – involved in apparently lighthearted but in fact complex affairs that had to do with the world as it really was. For him military status was merely part of a game of the compulsory kind. And in her heart she knew that Sarah had used him as he had used her. But had been less expert. Meanwhile there was the question of the dog. She could not remember the dog's name but now that it had come into her mind she could not get it out because it was a living thing whose destruction Sarah had opposed with a significant and dangerous passion. Oh God, she thought, let me be wrong, let Millie be wrong.

Just then through the half open doorway into the bathroom she caught sight of Sarah standing by the handbowl, grasping the side of it with one hand, reaching for the tap with the other. At the same instant in the little spare on the other side of the bathroom the child woke and cried and Minnie's voice came through quite clearly, speaking to him soothingly. Sarah raised her head, not to look towards the child's room but straight ahead of her into the mirror above the basin as if the source of the cry were there in her reflextion. Then she lowered her head again and twisted the tap on and watched the water running in and away.

Dicky Beauvais was kneeling on one leg by the dog's side stroking its head. The others watched from the safety of the verandah. The dog sat on its withered haunches. It swayed when Dicky stroked it.

'What do you think, Captain Beauvais?' Maisie Trehearne asked.

'I don't know. The poor old boy looks pretty much a goner.'

'But don't you think his coming out means he's feeling better?'

'Maybe. On the whole I'd say it's too late. It'll be rotten for Sarah.'

'It's suffering.' Nicky insisted. 'It's dying on its feet. I should have thought anyone could see that.'

Mildred alone was seated, holding her drink under her chin. When Fenny came out ten minutes later Mildred glanced up but Fenny did not look at her. She went to the head of the steps.

'Dicky, I've told Sarah about Panther. She leaves it to us.'

'Oh.' Again he stroked the dog's head. The neck was arched down, the jaws open. 'Poor old fellow.'

He stood up. 'I'd better ring the veterinary officer hadn't I, Mrs Layton?'

Mildred said nothing. He looked at Fenny.

'Isn't Sarah coming out to see for herself?'

'No.'

'Perhaps if I could get the dog round to the gharry it would be better for me to take him than bring the vet up here.'

'I shouldn't if I were you,' Mildred called. 'He could have a fit and you could end up driving over the khud and killing you both. Take him back to the mali's shed if you can. It's not the most elevating sight, is it? Or better still get Sarah to do it. After all she's responsible for keeping the wretched thing alive and for it ending up in this state. She oughtn't to be allowed just to opt out.'

'I'll get him into the shed, Mrs Layton.'

Dicky bent down again.

'Come on, old boy. Come along. You can make it.'

The servants had gathered at a safe distance. Dicky tried to direct the dog's attention to them.

Mildred spoke to Fenny who was watching Dicky.

'Have you persuaded Sarah to go to Calcutta with you?'

'Yes,' Fenny said, without looking.

'Come on Panther, old son,' Dicky said. 'Come on. Rabbit.'

Its tail moved once, a slow-motion scything movement across the grass and Maisie Trehearne exclaimed, 'He wagged his tail! I told you. He's feeling better. It's awful to talk about destroying him now, after all Sarah's done.'

Then she added, 'We owe so much to dogs,' and Mildred started laughing: a clear fluting laugh of genuine amusement that made everyone except Dicky down there on the grass turn to look at her in astonishment. Only Dicky noticed the effect that the sounds Mildred was making had on the dog. It lifted its head and snapped at the air or at Dicky's hand which he jerked out of reach. It began to tremble. It went on snapping as if the peals of Mildred's laughter were coming at it in some visible form: small predatory birds or maddening insects. Dicky backed away and shouted a warning to Mrs Layton but she did not hear. Her laughter seemed to have become uncontrollable and suddenly the dog twisted its body and began dragging itself round, still snapping at the air, making no sound but moving away from the steps and increasing the width of its circular chase until it was blundering through the nearest of the rose beds shaking the bushes and scattering petals.

The servants also scattered. Dicky stood, alarmed but on the defensive at the head of the steps with only his bare hands to fight off an attack if the dog took it into its head to go for any of them. But the impact with the rose-bushes had disorientated the animal. It no longer traced a circular pattern but a random one, staggering from bed to bed with a high-arched back and low slung head, wreaking havoc, putting distance between itself and the inhospitable verandah. Suddenly it emitted a stream of pale yellow excreta and then began to drag its hindquarters as though it were dying from that end up. It came to the path between the two rectangular beds and fell on its side. For a while it moved its forelegs, dreamily dog-paddling the air; then it twitched and was still; twitched again and was still again. The intervals between spasms became longer.

Fenny said, 'It isn't rabies, is it, Dicky?'

'No. I've seen rabies.'

They waited for a further spasm that didn't come.

'That's that,' Dicky said.

He went down the steps and called up to Fenny.

'Perhaps as I've handled him I oughtn't to come back into the house though. Would you phone the vet-johnnie, Mrs Grace? I'll get something to cover him with. I expect the servants have some sacking.'

He went off towards the servants' quarters.

A few minutes later he reappeared with a length of gunny, approached the dog's body from behind and then put the sacking over it.

'Dicky, what's all this about not coming into the house?'

Mildred's voice carried strongly. She came down into the garden. He waited for her. She joined him. The dog's body was between them. 'Of course you must come in. You're staying for lunch.'

'Mrs Grace is afraid it might have been something like rabies. It wasn't but I don't want to risk anything.'

'There isn't any risk. It was just a fit. But if you prefer to stay outside until the vet comes by all means do so. Fenny's been on to him and he's coming right away. And you must stay to lunch. I'll need you to cheer Sarah up. Kevin rang me, incidentally. I know about her not feeling well at the daftar. I'm grateful to you for tipping me off.'

'I felt pretty shabby because she'd made me promise not to mention it in case of worrying you. But I thought her health more important than my word.'

'Absolutely right.' She looked down at the heap of sacking. 'I expect this will be the last straw. But we've been cooking up a scheme for Fenny to take her down to Calcutta and get her out of it for a bit. I shall ring Dick Rankin this evening and tell him she oughtn't to go into the daftar between now and then. Come along, Dicky. Don't let's stand here. I'm not feeling so hot myself.'

She moved away. In a moment or two Dicky was walking at her side.

'There's something I've got to tell you, Mrs Layton. And something I want to ask you about. I was going to tell Sarah this morning, that's why I was looking for her and found her – like she was.'

Mildred had stopped. She smiled. She said, 'I hope it's nothing unpleasant.'

'Not unpleasant exactly. I mean – I've been posted. The order came this morning. I've got to report to the military secretary at Fourteenth Army.'

'When?'

'I must leave tonight. There's some transport going down to Ranpur. I'm flying from Ranagunj tomorrow morning.'

'To Comilla?'

'Yes.'

'Is it promotion?'

'I've no idea what's entailed. My guess is I'll be in Imphal inside a week.'

'I won't commiserate,' Mildred said. 'I expect you're glad. No young officer wants to be stuck in a place like this for long. But we're going to miss you. You've been an absolute brick. Like part of the family.'

Dicky blushed.

'You've been very kind to me,' he said.

'You had something to ask me about.'

'Yes. I'm sorry because it seems the wrong sort of time.'

'But it's the only time you have, isn't it?'

'I don't quite know how to put it. Probably you guess. I mean, you have a right to. I've taken up a great deal of your daughter's time – Sarah's *and* Susan's. What you said, about being part of the family, that's what it's been like for me. I was terrifically pleased being asked to be godfather to Susan's baby. The thing is, one day I'd like really to be part of it.'

Dicky's blush had deepened. But he kept his eyes manfully on hers.

'I know there can't be anything official,' he continued.

'I mean, in the circumstances. But I didn't want to leave without telling you what I feel and asking if you think there's a chance, and of course if you'd approve.'

'Are you saying you'd like to be John's and my son-in-law, Dicky?'

'Yes.'

Mildred put a hand on his arm.

'My dear chap. I can't actually think of anything nicer. That's all I *can* say. But you've already appreciated that. I'm sorry you have to go without being able to say anything to her, but perhaps it's as well. I made up my mind some time ago that all questions of this kind would have to wait until my husband comes home. But an understanding – not necessarily binding – but an understanding between the two of you would have been a different matter. You've thought hard about it, haven't you Dicky? It isn't just a case of feeling sorry for her?'

'Sorry? No, why should I feel sorry – ?'

'People exaggerate so. But it's only a temporary setback and she's getting better every day. She's had the most ghastly luck when you work it out. Later on she'll need someone like you, Dicky, but I wouldn't want you to take it all on unless you were absolutely sure. I must confess I was rather hoping for something like this to give her back a feeling of stability. I'm sure it's all she needs. That, and someone she can lean on, really depend on in the future. Personally, I couldn't be happier. I think the form is for me to talk to her, when that's possible, and to let you know what sort of reaction I get and then for you to start writing to tell her a bit of what you feel, but not too much. She needs time as well as reassurance.'

She tapped his arm. 'Now come along in and have a drink. I suggest we keep this entirely to ourselves, at least for the time being, but you and I will know what we're drinking to.'

'Mrs Layton – '

'What, Dicky?'

'I'm afraid I must have made the most awful mess of it – '

'Mess? What do you mean?'

'You were talking – you were talking about Susan.'

Mildred let go of his arm. She studied his face. The blush had gone. He looked quite pale, for Dicky.

'Weren't you?' she asked.

He shook his head. Briefly she touched her own, tracing the outline of her left eyebrow, and then put her hand to her throat, linking the little finger into the string of seed pearls. She smiled but her eyes showed no amusement nor for that matter embarrassment at having jumped to the wrong conclusion.

'I'm sorry. I'd no idea you felt like that about Sarah. Has she?'

'I hope, a bit. But I don't know. I was going to speak to her today.'

'Yes, I see. Of course there was a time when I wondered. But then when Teddie was killed I thought you realized it had been Susan all the time.'

She moved away from him, a pace or two; but stopped and said, 'It's up to you of course, but my advice would be to say nothing just yet.'

'Would you tell me why, Mrs Layton?'

The pearls had become twisted. But this was the only sign of agitation.

'I shouldn't want you to leave Pankot with your hopes completely dashed.'

'I'd risk that. And it might be otherwise, mightn't it?'

'Perhaps. But I don't think so. I don't get the impression she's fond of you like that. I must take your word for it that so far as you're concerned the scales have finally gone down in her favour. You *have* been thrown together more by Susan's illness. I should be surprised if she feels the same about you but – let's say I'm wrong. Then I'd have to tell you I have reservations about your coming to any kind of understanding. I'm sorry if that sounds unfair or illogical. But what could have been a good thing in Susan's case, a good thing for you both, wouldn't necessarily be in Sarah's and yours. With Susan there's the element of dependence, the question of the child, the need she has to feel wanted again, which is why I asked you whether you were sure, absolutely sure, about taking it all on. But Sarah's very independent. She's about and around, if you see what I mean. I'd hate you to go off to Burma or whatever, feeling chipper, and then get a letter saying she's met someone else.'

'Is there someone else, Mrs Layton?'

'Someone adored from a distance?' Mildred smiled. 'I simply can't say. Sarah's never taken me into her confidence. She's always been the quiet introspective type. But she's pretty determined and she can be impulsive. Susan's the one who feels the need to settle down to an ordinary kind of existence. I was never absolutely happy about her choice of Teddie and I'm pretty sure she ended up regretting it. But they both rushed into it and I think a lot of her trouble is that she's feeling guilty about him.'

'Guilty?'

'I believe that when you turned up she realized what a mistake she'd made. Perhaps she feels it showed in her letters to him.'

'Did she ever say anything to you, Mrs Layton?'

Mildred had folded her arms but still played with the necklace. The movements of her fingers were more assured.

'No, Dicky. And don't run away with any ideas. It's all much too complicated. You seem to have made your choice anyway and apparently it's not Susan. Let's go in. I'm dying for a drink and I'm sure you are. At least we can drink to your safe return. *That's* the important thing.'

The verandah was now unoccupied. Everyone had gone indoors to avoid the sight of the heap of sacking. Weeks later, sitting on an empty upturned ammunition box and resting his pad of paper on his knee, Dicky ended a letter to Sarah: 'There was a lot I wanted to talk about that last afternoon in Pankot but somehow everything conspired against it. My fondest love to you. And to Susan. And of course to my godson.'

She woke to the strong sweet smell of roses and did not need to open her eyes to know they were yellow. In any case if she opened her eyes the scent of the roses would almost certainly go away, dismal proof that she was only dreaming them. She turned her head and slowly let the white room come into focus. The scent was fainter but it had not gone and she guessed she was not alone.

She looked round into the massed pale yellow velvet petals of the flowers which Sarah had placed on the pillow and was holding there with her left hand.

'Hello, Barbie. Are you feeling better? I've brought these from the garden. I remembered the yellow were your favourite.'

Barbie smiled and nodded.

Her voice, of which she had been proud, had become a humiliation. It was weak on the consonants. It cracked on the vowels. When she spoke she could feel the vibrations in the tight drum of her chest.

'Thank you, Sarah.' She tried to whisper it but the first vowel betrayed her. One had to face it. 'My silly old voice,' she said in two registers at once. 'It seems to have packed up on me. Some will think it a blessing if it keeps me quiet.'

The roses trembled as the fractured sounds hit them.

'You've been here before, haven't you?'

'Once or twice. But you were very sleepy.'

'You were in uniform. You brought me a bottle of barley water. I still have some. Would you like a glass?'

'No, but I'll give you one.'

'It would oil the cogs.' She watched from the pillow-bower of roses while Sarah poured barley water. Helped into a drinking position she could feel her own backbone against Sarah's hand. Her wasted body filled her with revulsion; in the room it alone lacked the security of shape and form and definition. It was like something the bed had invented, got tired of and left half-finished to fend for itself.

'I shall be glad to get out of here,' she said when Sarah had resettled the pillows to support her in the half-upright position the nurses were always trying to keep her in, in an unequal struggle against the gravitational pull of the foot of the bed and the mattress under her bony buttocks. 'There is something about a hospital bedroom that drains one of self-confidence. One feels anonymous.'

'You have your name on the door.'

'Have I? That's handy. It minimizes error. Was I in this room when you came before?'

'No, in one with three other beds but only one was occupied. By a Mrs MacGregor whose husband was an engineer.'

'I remember curtains round the bed with sprigs of forget-me-nots and scarlet pimpernels. And a horrible thing like a bomb. But it was only the oxygen. Why have I been moved to a room of my own?'

'Captain Travers thought you'd like it. You've got a private balcony. When you're better you'll be able to sit out and not be bothered by people.'

'People have never bothered me. It's been the other way round. Was I very ill?'

'You had pneumonia.'

'I know. But Edwina had pneumonia. She wasn't in hospital more than three weeks. I've been that already.'

'A little over.'

'Shall I be here much longer?'

'A week or two I expect. You're much better to-day. You'll make strides now.'

'Was Clarissa very cross?'

'What could she have to be cross about?'

'Cross with me for being ill.'

'She visited you. She wouldn't visit you if she were cross, now would she?'

'I don't remember her visiting me. I only remember you.'

'I expect you were asleep.'

'Will she have me back?'

'Of course she will. There isn't any question.'

'I thought Dr Travers might be keeping me here because he knows Clarissa's *had* me.'

Sarah smiled. At the turn of phrase presumably. It was what soldiers said. I've had it. It was very expressive.

'And she knows the mission's had me too. I showed her the letter.'

'You mustn't worry about Clarissa.'

'Is my trunk still safe?'

Sarah nodded.

'Still in the mali's shed?'

'Yes, still there.'

'Does your mother know?'

Sarah shook her head.

Barbie looked at the roses. 'It was wrong of me getting you to hide it. But Clarissa would have drawn the line at the trunk. It had better go to Jalal-ud-din's. If we could move it one day when your mother's out.'

'Mother's unlikely to look in the mali's shed. Anyway it's doing no harm. Whenever you want it it's there. You only have to ask me or mali.'

'No. Your mother will get to know. And you'll be in trouble. There are some little toys in it. Things the children made for me. If I give you the key you could get them out. The baby could have them when he's older. The mali could keep the trunk. Everything else in it can be thrown away.'

'You said the trunk was your history.'

'Lying here one has no history. Just each hour of the day.' She grinned.

'Yes you do. And you needn't worry about the trunk or about Clarissa having you back. Just concentrate on getting well.'

'Is Susan getting well?'

Sarah nodded.

'And the baby is all right?'

'The baby's fine.'

393

'Is Susan quite near me?'

'You can see the nursing home from your balcony.'

'Then I'll sit out there and transmit prana to her.'

'What's prana?'

'The goodness in the air. You breathe it in. And out. Like smelling roses. Like blowing dandelions.'

'Like what?'

'Blowing dandelions.'

It was one of the more difficult words. It came out so distorted she doubted that Sarah would understand. Her eyelids felt heavy. She let them close just for a second or two.

When she opened them Sarah had gone, the roses were in a vase and the lights and shadows in the room had rearranged themselves as they did in theatres to denote the passage of time.

The red hospital blanket round her knees and chest reminded her of Christmas. Seated in the wheelchair at the open doorway between the room and balcony she might have been surrounded by shiny pink- and blue-wrapped parcels and by children waiting for their turn to climb on her knee and whisper secret longings and desires. She could smell pines. Through half-closed eyes she could transmute the gold of sunshine on the leaves of the trees into snow and ride the sleigh of the chair high above the roofs of the hospital and the carved balconies of the bazaar and the spire of St John's. Santa Barbie: leaving a lingering glittering frosty scent of her own magical intrusion.

We could go down to Ranpur she had said to do some Christmas shopping. Oh I shall never go to Ranpur again Mabel answered at least until I'm buried.

The reply had begun to trouble her with its vagueness, its curious subtlety. Its element of prophecy.

She opened her eyes fully and through the balcony rails she saw the girl walking in the afternoon sunshine along the tarmac pathway from the nursing home. Sarah with roses. The girl looked up. The red blanket had caught her eye. She waved and came on. It seemed a long time before Barbie heard the door open in the room behind her and the little Anglo-Indian nurse say, 'You have a visitor.'

'Hello, Sarah,' she croaked. 'You see. I'm on the mend except for this wretched voice. If you wheel me in we can see each other. There's only room for one on the balcony.'

Roses descended upon her lap and she felt the chair grasped and tip up as Sarah began to negotiate it back into the room. When they were settled, seated together at the window, Barbie said, 'You've been visiting Susan. How is she?'

'Much better. Captain Samuels thinks she can come out quite soon. And incidentally Captain Travers seems very pleased with *you*.'

'Have you seen him?'

'On the way in. He thinks about another week will do it. Perhaps two to be on the safe side.'

'Did he mention my voice?'

'No. Why are you worried about your voice?'

'That's what Doctor Travers says when I ask him. But listen to it. It gets no better.'

'It's only a bit hoarse. You'll be all right when you're on your feet and walking in the fresh air.'

'I hope so. It would be awful to lose one's voice. For me, like a painter to lose his sight, a musician his hearing. It was never a singing voice of course, but it carried in the schoolroom. Mr Cleghorn said it had a note of command which he advised me to develop because it was very important for a teacher. When I was a girl I took elocution. My mother paid for me to have the lessons to help me in later life and in her decline she often asked me to read to her. You put such expression into it, Barbie, she used to say. It was the best of times, it was the worst of times. She died half way through A Tale of Two Cities.'

She lifted the bunch of roses to smell them. Sarah took the opportunity to speak.

'Barbie, I shan't see you again for a while. I'm going back with Aunt Fenny to Calcutta to stay with her. We're going tomorrow. When Susan's okay she and Mother are going to join us so that we can all go to Darjeeling, probably some time in September.'

Barbie let the roses fall. Her body seemed to have reacted of its own accord in advance of the sense of dismay, of loss, which was slower, only just now taking hold of her.

She said, 'What about the baby?'

Sarah gathered some of the dropped petals from around the bunch on Barbie's lap.

'Well of course they'll bring ayah and the baby with them. Captain Samuels thinks it would be better for Susan not to go back to familiar surroundings right away, so tomorrow after we've gone Mother's going to close Rose Cottage and move into Flagstaff House until Susan's discharged. Then when Captain Samuels gives the word they'll come down to Calcutta.'

'Close Rose Cottage?'

'Only until we get back. Perhaps for Christmas. We're sending Mahmoud on leave but the mali and his wife will look after things.'

'Who is this Captain Samuels?'

Sarah paused. 'A very intelligent man,' she said.

'But the journey, Sarah, with a tiny baby.'

Sarah dropped the petals into a wastebin.

'I don't think the baby will come to any harm. He's quite a tough customer. And I think we can depend on Mother to travel in the maximum comfort and with every available amenity.'

'I'm sorry. It's none of my business. I was looking for objections. Because I don't want *you* to go.'

'I must be going in any case. I've promised Aunt Fenny.'

'I didn't know your Aunt Fenny was in Pankot.'

'She came up to help Mother. You know what some families are. In trouble they close the ranks and stick together.'

'Wouldn't it be better for her to wait? Until you can *all* go, with Susan?'

'She can't be away from Uncle Arthur any longer. Well.

That's one answer. But I'm the culprit really. They've decided I need a holiday.'

'Are you ill?'

'No, Barbie. Do I look ill?'

'No. No, you don't. You look tired but that's not surprising. Oh, I should be glad for you, shouldn't I? You liked Calcutta.'

Sarah nodded. She was looking at the roses, still touching them, making sure all the loose petals had been gathered.

Barbie observed the pale gold lights in the girl's hair. She felt possessive in her love. She moved a hand to make contact, but Sarah misunderstood. She must have thought the movement of her own fingers among the petals had begun to irritate the invalid. She took her hands away, folded them in under her arms but stayed bent forward in the chair, her knees almost touching the red blanket.

'Will you visit Captain Merrick when you're in Calcutta?' Barbie asked.

Sarah shook her head.

'He's probably gone anyway. To somewhere where they fit artificial limbs. I believe they get on to it quite quickly nowadays.'

'But he's only just had the amputation.'

'It's two months ago.'

'I've lost track of time,' Barbie said. 'What will happen to him?'

'I suppose they'll find him a job somewhere either in the police or the army. He wouldn't be the only officer around with a disability. Why?'

'I've been thinking about him.'

'Have you, Barbie?'

'Lying here one has little to do but think. I've been thinking about something you said after you'd been in Mirat. Do you remember? We were sitting under the pine tree and you said you thought Captain Merrick had got it all wrong about the men he arrested in Mayapore, the ones who were supposed to have attacked Miss

Manners. You said it would be terrible not just for them but for him, to have got it wrong but never see it, never believe it.'

'Yes, I did, didn't I? What made you think of that?'

At last Sarah looked up from her study of the roses. But her eyes were not lit by more than polite inquiry. Perhaps it hadn't been her interest in the question that made her look up but her arrival at the end of an earlier train of thought which enabled her to.

'I've been wondering whether *I* was wrong, about Mabel, about Mabel's wishes,' Barbie said. 'And if I were whether it will be more terrible knowing it than not knowing it. Wouldn't it be more terrible for Mr Merrick to *know* he'd got it wrong?'

'Perhaps, for a moment. But better in the end surely?'

'Better to know and to say, I got it wrong? But everything that happened as a result of him getting it wrong would be on his conscience forever wouldn't it? There's nothing he can do now to put it right, is there? Even if those men have been released from prison since.'

'Wouldn't that be better than having *no* conscience?' Sarah looked down at the roses again. 'Don't let's talk about Ronald Merrick. Let's talk about what's bothering you.'

'It's connected really,' Barbie said. She could observe the fair head again without disguising the depth of her feeling. 'Everything seems to be. Even spoons. I think it's this room. It addles my mind. The walls are so white and bare.' If she shut her eyes she could feel how everything depended now on the pumping of her old heart and the strange electrical impulses of her brain which switched from one picture of her life to another, encapsulating time and space, events, personalities. 'I saw her,' she said. 'I was very frightened because I heard her first and mistook her for Mabel. When she left I heard the car. It went towards West Hill.'

She had closed her eyes. Now she opened them and found Sarah watching her.

'People said it was a joke, didn't they? When her name

398

appeared in the book. They said it must be someone playing a joke in bad taste. But I saw her. It couldn't have been anyone else. The way she talked and stood, genuflected. You could see she had held a position of importance in public life. I wished I could have seen her face. But there was this veil and the old-fashioned topee with a wide brim. And she sat in front of me. When she looked to this side, that side, there was just a shadow of a face.'

'Who are you talking about, Barbie?'

'Miss Manners's aunt, Lady Manners. You met her in Srinagar. Your houseboat was moored close to hers. Everybody else was embarrassed, because of the child being there. But you – ' She stopped. Sarah was looking at her in the oddest manner. 'Have I only imagined it?'

'Imagined what, Barbie?'

'That you crossed the water and talked to her. And saw the child. Yes, I'm sorry. I remember now. It seemed to me the sort of thing you would have done, so I imagined you doing it. The picture was very vivid. All that hot sun and deep green water. Fronds of a kind of willow hanging above the roof of the houseboat. And the child crying. Motherless, fatherless child. But it had Krishna as well as Jesus. I think Miss Manners must have been rather a special person. She could have got rid of it. I mean before it was born. People would have praised her. And her aunt would not now live in obscurity. But – '

'But what?'

'Obscurity or not she was very proud. You could tell. Not of herself, of her niece. My father once said to me, Barbie, there is a conspiracy among us to make us *little*. He was tipsy at the time of course. There was a stage of his tipsiness between the initial release and the final moroseness and anger when he sang and talked and said things like that. My mother told a neighbour whom she wished to impress with our superiority, "My husband has a lot of the poet in him." After that I used to watch him hard. I imagined the poet in him as an unborn twin, one that could be cruel to him as well as kind. Like the demon spirit of a party. After he said that about there being a conspiracy among us to make us little I thought of the demon spirit or poet as a giant bottled up inside him and turned into a dwarf by a spell which only liquor could break.'

Still gazing down at the fair head, bent above the roses, she continued. 'My father's life was full of anomalies but so was my mother's. For instance she was a great church-goer. Her piety on Sundays inspired me as a little girl. It was through her local connexions that I got into the church school and stayed on as a pupil-teacher. But when I was grown and told her I wished to serve God in the foreign missions, the missions to India, she was very shocked. Oh, Barbie, she said, not among heathens! She made me feel my ambitions were wrong, almost sinful. Perhaps they were. Even when she was dead and I'd summoned the courage to apply I went to my first interview as if I knew I was doing something to be ashamed of. I huddled into myself. I walked through the streets hunched. I made myself small. To slip through the mesh of people's disapproval and not to be noticed. When I sailed for India I thought: Now I can be large again. But that has not been possible. One may carry the Word, yes, but the Word without the act is an abstraction. The Word gets through the mesh but the act doesn't. So God does not follow. Perhaps He is deaf. Why not? What use are Words to Him?'

Encouraged by Sarah's quietness she touched the girl's head, smoothed the soft helmet of hair. Almost indiscernibly, but unmistakably felt by the hand, the girl inclined her head briefly into the caress.

'I shall never see you again!' Barbie cried suddenly. 'Don't go to Calcutta!'

Sarah laughed: a girl embarrassed by a foolish and importunate elder. 'Oh, Barbie, I'm not going away for good!'

'No.'

There are these spoons, she wanted to say; and began to – but mercifully her voice gave out and she was saved the indignity of rambling on about such nonsense. Apostle spoons! She grinned and shook her head. Her voice came back. 'You'll write to me if you have time, won't you? And if you meet a Mister Studholme . . . but that's unlikely. Very unlikely. He's Mission. Although very important.'

'I don't think Aunt Fenny knows any mission people. I'll try to write though.'

Barbie began to tell her about the mission headquarters in Calcutta but as she did so she tuned out of her voice and into the soundless echo of the white room.

There is a letter in my handbag from Colonel Trehearne, the echo announced for her. The walls shone with an extra purity as if they had absorbed the simplicity of Colonel Trehearne's kindness and the clarity of Clarissa's eyes. There was a letter for you, Barbie, Clarissa had said standing by the bedside like a caryatid supporting the weight of a celestial esteem which might have weighed a lesser person down. I brought it with me. On the back of the envelope there was an engraving in shiny blue ink of the Pankot insignia. My Dear Miss Batchelor. Two huge epergnes floated across the room. Empty. Awaiting a cargo of apostles. 'There is your sou'-wester too,' Clarissa said, 'but I didn't bring it. Captain Coley found it in his driveway.' They were out,' Barbie whispered. 'They?' 'He and his servant.' Clarissa did not ask why Barbie should visit Captain Coley. Probably she knew from Colonel Trehearne. But spoons were not mentioned by either of them.

The spoons and the note to Captain Coley must still be in her room at the rectory bungalow locked in the drawer of the writing-table where she had put them after getting home soaked. 'It was kind of Captain Coley to return my hat,' she said. Clarissa said, 'Why should he not? Your name is in it.' Enclosed by white walls she was aware of risk: her own, not Coley's, not Mildred's. The return of the sou'-wester had been a master-stroke. She would never again be able to put it on her head without feeling the pressure of Mildred's contempt. They had seen the significance of the sou'-wester and coupled it with the mystery of the missing spoons. They must have known they had not been alone. Coley might care. Mildred did not.

'I must go now, Barbie,' Sarah was saying. 'Is there anything you want?' She shook her head, thinking: I want you to help me find Lady Manners so that I can give her the spoons as a present for the child. I want us to sit together in St John's and wait for her and for you to say, Lady Manners, this is my friend Barbara Batchelor, a holy woman from the missions. Or to go with me into the region of West Hill where the rich Indians from Ranpur have summer houses in which they live for a few months of the year without being bothered by us or with us and are seldom seen in the bazaar, having their own sources or sending servants into ours for the products of the West. We could go into West Hill (curiously named) and search and ask. But you are going to Calcutta. And in any case haven't met her after all, it seems. Or have you? This time you didn't comment.

'Good-bye, Barbie.'

'Good-bye, Sarah.'

The girl bent and kissed her. Barbie put up her arms. Sarah submitted to the embrace. Then she rearranged the blankets.

'Shall I wheel you back to the balcony?'

'Please. Then I can watch you go down the path.'

'I don't go that way, Barbie, I'm afraid.'

'Is Captain Beauvais waiting for you with a car?'

'No. I'm getting a tonga.'

'Oh, but I was forgetting. Clarissa told me Captain Beauvais has gone.'

'Yes, and now I must.'

She felt the girl's head close to her own again and breath coming against her cheek as though she were an old yellow candle being blown out very gently. Some time later she was surprised to see the girl on the tarmac pathway, having walked out of her way to wave, and waving, and then coming back towards the building to follow the path round to the front where a tonga would take her on the first stage of the long journey to Calcutta.

She looked at the familiar panorama and after a while pulled the blanket up to her throat and tucked her chin in. The sun dipped below the overhanging roof of the balcony and shone through her eyelids. The little Anglo-Indian nurse had never left her on the balcony so long. Perhaps she had forgotten her.

She pictured herself abandoned there, until dark, and beyond; for many days, through the changes of season, from one decade to another, while the building slowly crumbled round her, leaving her isolated, high up on a pillar of jagged but stubborn masonry, enthroned, wrapped in the scarlet blanket, with a clear view across the uninhabited valley to the ruins of the church of St John.

3

Isobel Rankin's generosity to Mildred in allowing her to move into Flagstaff House and close Rose Cottage did not escape criticism. Lucy Smalley, more or less indistinguishable nowadays from the potted palms and stained napery of Smith's Hotel, said it was a bit odd that a place could be closed, however temporarily, and yet escape the net of the accommodations officer who she swore slept with requisition orders under his pillow in the hope of being woken in the middle of the night by one of his spies and tipped off about a bungalow that had been left empty for a day or two, so that before daylight a notice could be tacked to the door denying entry to its rightful owners.

'I heard about Nicky Paynton's decision to go home within a few hours of her making it,' Lucy complained, 'and I rang him at once, because Tusker wouldn't, and he said he had a waiting list and had already made provisional allocations. He was barely civil.'

But Lucy Smalley's disappointment did not prevent her turning up several weeks later at Nicky Paynton's auction party, wandering from room to room in the place she had briefly visualized herself and Tusker moving into, and

403

wanly watching the auctioneer – Nicky Paynton herself – hammering down the familiar detritus of an Anglo-Indian career.

The most prized items were those which had practical use, scarcity value and a comparatively short life – a radiogram, a refrigerator, a portable wireless set, an electric iron and an ironing board, two electric fires, an electric fan. After these, for which the bidding was on a tense but modest level, Nicky had success in getting rid of crockery, cutlery, glasses, two alarm clocks, blankets, sheets and pillow-cases, a picnic basket, camp equipment, and assorted thermos flasks which were a godsend on the trains packed with ice or filled with decent drinking water. Lowest on the list of desirable things were the ornamental coffee tables, the Benares trays, numdah rugs, vases and ornaments which for most people who could find room for them would be replicas of those they already had.

Finally there was the stuff which in other circumstances might have ended its days in a modest house in Surrey, and still might, although not in the possession of Colonel and Mrs Paynton. The Payntons themselves had bought it at an auction in Rawalpindi. It had spent quite a number of years in storage, and on loan, during the periods when Nicky and Bunny were moving too frequently from one station to another for it to go with them. A mahogany sideboard, elegantly proportioned, a mahogany dining-table (with two leaves) and a dozen imitation Georgian chairs, plus two armed servers, were the chief items on this particular list. Supplementary to it were two wing chairs covered in rather murky but genuine tapestry – one man-size and the other woman-size. These chairs, Nicky announced, had belonged to the late General Sir Horace and Lady Hamilton-Wellesley-Gore and one of them had been sat in by the Prince of Wales when he toured India in 1921.

'They were snitched from under my nose at the 'Pindi auction,' Nicky explained, 'by a simply frightful chap with pots of money. He turned up next year at the same beano in Gwalior and without telling me Bunny played him for them at poker and the next thing I knew they arrived on the doorstep. So what am I bid? No reserve price. Going for a song.'

Maisie Trehearne called out a figure which her husband didn't hear. He called out a lower one and under the screen of the ensuing laughter Clara said to Nicky, 'I want the chairs.' She doubled Maisie's figure.

'You must be mad,' Nicky said. 'But I'm not saying no.'

The chairs were knocked down to Clara Fosdick. Her sister in Ranpur wouldn't be pleased – she already housed some of Clara's and Freddie's old furniture – but these were chairs Clara and Nicky had sat in, many a winter evening, over a pine-log fire listening to the news.

When the auction was over the dining-room furniture was still unsold, but Nicky's farewell party got under way merrily enough. In the next few days the stuff that had been auctioned off would be collected and removed, leaving the two women bereft of most of the things that made the bungalow into a home. But that was all to the good, they felt. Their departure from a place in which nothing belonged to either of them would come as a relief and with luck (from Clara's point of view) they would have a few days together in Ranpur, perhaps more because although five days was all the notice Nicky would get of a flight from Ranagunj she had to be prepared for postponements. Her final departure might be a relief as well. Already, at the height of the party, they were both on tenterhooks, and old Fariqua had obviously been at the rum bottle.

For the party he had put on the white trousers, tunic, Ranpur sash and head-dress that he used to wear to go in to mess when Bunny dined there, but the pugree was indifferently swathed and the fan of muslin which should have been as perky as a cock's comb had flopped over. As he got drunker he grew lugubriously into the role of skeleton at the feast, chief mourner at the wake for Bunny Paynton, the only one with a long face, sodden with the liquor that bouyed other people up.

'To look at Fariqua,' Lucy Smalley said, with what was

becoming after the years of her social frustration an unerring sense for saying the right thing at the wrong time, 'you'd think Nicky was going to invite bids for him as well.'

She was saved the rebuke that Maisie Trehearne might have administered by the arrival of the general's lady, Isobel Rankin, to whom all heads turned, like compass needles to a magnetic north. There was nothing unusual in this ritual observance, this metaphorical doffing of caps and bending of knees, but this morning a special intensity attached to it, because of certain rumours that had been taking shape and seriously disturbing the station's sense of balance and proportion and were now contributing a ground-swell of uneasiness to the determined light-heartedness of the occasion.

Nicky had announced her decision to go home in mid-July. Thereafter, slowly and quietly she had made her depositions, settled her affairs, transferred money to London, paid her debts, written to Dora Lowndes to warn her and advise her to say nothing to the boys until she got a cable from Clara Fosdick confirming her departure. She had also written to her friends in India and given them Dora Lowndes's address. By the middle of August she was ready to take the last step. The airforce liaison officer on Dick Rankin's staff told her he would start pulling strings the moment she said the word. For a week she did not say it and it began to look as if she might change her mind at the last moment. But it was during this week that the rumours were first heard and by the end of it there seemed little doubt that there was more than a grain of truth in them. If Nicky had been wavering her mind was now abruptly made up again. She rang Wing-Commander Pearson and asked him to pull the first string on the last day in August. She announced her auction and farewell party for that same day.

The rumours which had encouraged Nicky to stick to her decision to go home had begun at area headquarters as a result of the circulation of curiously worded documents from higher authorities about reallocation of areas of military responsibility; innocent enough on the surface and apparently without reference or application to the military hierarchy established at Pankot. This hierarchy was still in effect the old Ranpur Command whose authority, in spite of erosion here and there, extended over large stretches of the province's territory.

But between the lines of the documents' oblique phraseology casual references acquired dangerously direct meanings. Among the senior members of Dick Rankin's staff the junior officers detected signs of that alert fascination which people in high places cannot disguise when first glimpsing a future upheaval which they know they are personally too distinguished and secure to be adversely affected by.

What had emerged was an image of Pankot stripped of a proportion of its powers as a central seat of military control and administration. How large a proportion could only be guessed at but since it was human nature to adopt a pessimistic view of any rearrangement from above the guess was that for 'a proportion of' one had to read 'most of'. Once such a guess had been made the rumours proliferated, some of them disagreeably backed by mounting evidence that the guess was correct: rumours that the old Ranpur Command was to be hacked up into several areas and redistributed on a geographical rather than a viable military basis between Central and Eastern Commands, that Pankot would be separated from Ranpur and become a training and rest centre with a Brigadier as its area commander; that a new OTS was to be established, most of whose cadets would be Indian; that the old Governor's summer residence which dominated the height of East Hill and had been closed throughout most of the war, was to be reopened – not, as Isobel Rankin had often proposed, as a convalescent home for wounded British and Indian officers of all three services, but as a leave centre for American troops of non-commissioned rank. Only in the bazaar where the rumours were quick to penetrate was the latter news greeted with enthusiasm.

One or two ladies swore there had already been a rise in prices to prepare people for the new era of native prosperity.

'We shall all have to get used to walking,' one of them said, 'because the cost of a tonga up the hill to the club, should one manage to find one not already loaded with GI's, will be quite beyond *our* pockets.' But on second thoughts, she went on, one would probably stop going to the club because it would be crowded with American officers – those in charge of the leave centre – and perhaps with top-sergeants, whatever species *they* were. If the cinema was any guide even the sergeants in the American army seemed to get saluted and to call officers by their Christian names, so they would all be at the club with their hands in their pockets, their bottoms hanging out of their shiny trousers and cigars in their mouths, getting drunk, breaking the place up and bringing in Eurasian girls.

Moreover, she said, with Pankot's military role downgraded there would be fewer and fewer *young* British officers doing a stint on area headquarters staff between regimental and active appointments. From area headquarters as it now existed the top and junior levels would be creamed off and the men would be off to brighter places. Probably only men like Major Smalley could expect to survive from the old to the new regime, if such a thing could be called survival. And Flagstaff House would be occupied by some doddery dugout Brigadier. In Mildred's father's day, the Ranpur Command had carried a lieutenant-general's hat. It still carried a major-general's.

Which brought one to the Rankins. What glamorous appointment would fall into their laps? Already people had it on good authority that they were for Mountbatten's staff and the fleshpots of Ceylon; that they were for the India Office and home; for Washington on a military mission, for Moscow, for Cairo, for Persia; Simla at the very least. Two days before Nicky's party Dick Rankin had been driven down to Ranpur to be flown to Delhi. When he got back perhaps he would have fuller details of the station's fate and of his and Isobel's brighter prospects.

And here was Isobel, arriving too late for the auction, alight and vibrant with both power and discretion, giving nothing away which was only comforting if it could be assumed that she had nothing to give and was as ignorant of what was in store as the least among those present.

She embraced Nicky in the centre of the crowded living-room, apologized for being late in a voice that carried above the resumed conversation and then without lowering her voice said, 'Where can we have a word?' which caused a tremor of delicious apprehension, a pause in the flow of talk. Nicky led her into the dining-room where the unsold table, chairs and sideboard already appeared to have lost their sheen.

'Nicky, I'm late because I waited for Mildred to get back from visiting Susan, but she rang and asked me to come along on my own and to warn you that she's bringing Susan with her.'

'Oh.' The two women looked at each other straight. 'Is Susan allowed out then?'

'It will be the first time.'

'A noisy party? What an extraordinary choice.'

'She wanted to come. She asked this Captain Samuels chap and apparently he said it was a first-rate idea. He hopes it's all right if he looks in too. I think he'll take her back, to save Mildred doing it.'

'I must say that's a bit cool, isn't it? I don't know Captain Samuels and its a private farewell party not a therapy session. Is she really fit enough? I should hate a scene. That's why the trick-cyclist wallah insists on coming isn't it? To be on hand if Susan throws a fit or does something odd.'

'He says she's well enough. In fact he's letting her out in a day or two. She'll be coming up to the House, so I can only assume he knows what he's doing. He thinks a party would be a good icebreaker. Do you mind?'

'As long as its only ice. Does she know about Bunny?'

'Yes. And she knows you're going home. That's why she wants to come. It's very sweet really.'

'I hope she's not going to be condoling,' Nicky said. She looked feverish.

'The thing to do is tell everybody before she gets here and prepare them to look as if they're acting naturally. Did you sell this dining stuff?'

'No.'

'Mildred may want it. Try to persuade her. She has a lot of plans for the cottage. In any case she could store it. I'd have it myself but God knows how much longer we'll be here or where we'll be going. What about getting Jalal-ud-din's man along? He might sell it like a shot to one of his rich Indian clients.'

'I'll see.'

They went back to the living-room, separated and passed the word that Mildred was bringing Susan and that Captain Samuels would be looking in to take her back to the nursing home to save her mother going all that way herself when the party was over. Prepared for important general news this struck the guests as an anti-climax and it took a while for it to sink in and to be recognized as important too, important to the old Pankot if not to the one currently in a state of derangement of its own, which one had to hope would turn out to be as temporary as Susan Bingham's had proved. Curiosity and nostalgic affection began to flow out to her in advance of her arrival. Heads kept turning towards the door through which she would enter.

As she did, within ten minutes of the first warning, unannounced by any sound of tonga or car wheels that could have hushed the sound of talk and laughter; a step or so ahead of her mother, wearing a simple full-skirted dress of white with navy-blue polka dots; to all appearances unchanged, a pound or two heavier perhaps but as pretty as ever, prettier if anything, and with that familiar flush on her cheeks which suggested some special happiness anticipated or re-encountered.

To look at her, as she greeted Nicky and her mother's other friends, was to doubt the truth of the accounts of her bizarre behaviour and to guess that no explanation of it

410

would ever be had. It was as if it hadn't happened. No unhappy memory seemed to live behind her face. Her smile was not the smile of someone with a secret life. She was looking at the world as it was.

She said nothing, did nothing, that could be reckoned odd or interpreted as an indication that her mind was still clouded in any way by her illness and misfortunes. There were omissions, but were they significant? She did not mention the baby, but that could as easily be put down to a regard for other people's feelings as to anything sinister or threatening. She was punctilious in thanking Isobel Rankin for the invitation to Flagstaff House and said how much she was looking forward to it. Since the baby and the ayah were already installed there with Mildred one could surely assume that by 'looking forward' she meant glad to think she would see the baby again as well. In any case, Captain Samuels would not let her out if he had doubts about her attitude to the child.

She said she was also looking forward to the holiday in Darjeeling and Calcutta. She said she missed Sarah's visits but had had postcards and letters to make up for them. Out of Nicky's hearing she told Clara Fosdick how sorry she was about Brigadier Paynton, about Nicky's decision to go home and about Clara herself leaving Pankot to go to live in Ranpur. She said she hoped Mrs Fosdick would come up to spend holidays with them at Rose Cottage.

Her mother had briefed her well. She knew about the rumours of change and said it all sounded rather dreary. She asked Clarissa Peplow how Miss Batchelor was and seemed surprised to hear that although much better she was still in hospital. Clarissa assumed that in the case of Miss Batchelor's illness, Sarah – not Mildred – had been Susan's informant.

She did not mention the dog, Panther. Maisie found the opportunity to ask Mildred whether Susan knew the dog had died and Mildred said she had had Samuels's permission to tell her and had done so, without the gory details, and Susan had taken it well but not referred to it again. If there were any forbidden subjects they were the dog and

411

the baby. Was Dicky Beauvais a third? Apparently not. She said, 'I had a letter from Dicky the other day. He sounded a bit browned off. After all that rush he's still stuck in Comilla waiting for a posting. I must remember to tell Sarah because the letter was to us both.'

She moved gracefully, freely, perfectly at ease. She sipped her drink as if she intended to make it last and had accepted it only to be sociable. When Lucy Smalley suggested she should sit, not tire herself standing, she laughed in a friendly way and said she had sat enough in the last few weeks and needed exercise. She went from group to group, watched but not shadowed by Mildred who had shown only one sign of the strain she must have been under when at a first attempt to raise a full cocktail glass to her lips she spilt a few drops and waited (Clara Fosdick noticed) for at least a minute before raising it again.

'How relieved Mildred must be to have Susan her old self again,' Maisie Trehearne said.

'I wouldn't call it that,' Nicky replied, blowing smoke to one side, holding her glass high to minimize the risk of her elbow being jogged. 'Susan used to take up a position and let people swarm round her. I've never seen her mingle in my life. But that's what she's doing now. I'm half inclined to think the Jew-boy trick-cyclist is cleverer than Mildred gives him credit for.'

What Nicky had observed, perhaps because she was more alert to the shapes and patterns of her last party than any of her guests could be, was true. If a change in Susan were to be noted it would be this one: the freer-ranging movement and presentation of herself within the tableau. Before her illness she would have stood herself at its centre, receiving tribute. Her new mobility suggested that she was offering it, reaffirming her commitment to a society she had lived in since childhood and had now returned to, after a brief but inexplicable withdrawal.

Interest in the unknown Captain Samuels, the Jew-boy trick-cyclist, mounted. Apart from Mildred no one at the party had ever met him and no one had been inquisitive enough to investigate him since hearing his name in connexion with Susan. Mildred's attitude had summed up all one needed to know or feel about an RAMC analyst. The job was not one which could normally be taken seriously. No man who fitted the picture conjured by the name could be recalled from among the welter of new or itinerant faces at the club. Samuels probably kept himself to himself. Neither Beames nor Travers – who might have expressed professional if not personal opinions – had turned up. Both had been invited, but it was obviously a busy morning at the hospital.

Someone, perhaps its new owner, put a record on the radiogram: a selection from 'Chu Chin Chow'; but the record was so worn that only people close to the machine could make much of the tunes. Fariqua and the cook-boy Nazimuddin were bringing in plates of bridge sandwiches and canapés. Nicky called out, 'Food everybody. There'll be more in the dining-room in a minute so everyone just help themselves.' Several guests went through to relieve the crush in the living-room where there was a gradual rearrangement of groups which left Susan temporarily unattached. She took a sandwich from the plate offered none too steadily by the spectral Fariqua and went to stand a little apart by a window that gave her a view of the front verandah and compound.

In an instant her mother joined her and by chance or design interposed herself between her daughter and Lucy Smalley who had seen that Susan was alone and was approaching her. So even Lucy who was close to them was unable to say how Susan's cocktail glass fell out of her hand and splintered on the parquet floor. Later, considerably later, Lucy said she had always felt Susan dropped the glass deliberately. She couldn't say why she thought so but her intuition told her that this was what had happened. Mildred had been talking perfectly naturally to Susan, saying, 'Are you all right, darling? Not too tired?' and Susan had said also quite naturally but a bit testily, 'I'm fine.' And the next thing was the sudden sound of the breaking glass and a little cry from Mildred; no sound,

413

Lucy recalled, from Susan, but Mildred saying, 'Did I jog you?' And then the incident – if it could be called an incident – was over.

There was a stain down Mildred's skirt. Susan stooped and picked up the unbroken base of the glass and started to gather the fragments. She handed them to the cook-boy who came to help her and then stood up. 'My fault,' Mildred said, while Susan apologized to Nicky for the mess.

Susan declined the offer of another drink and went to talk to Mrs Stewart, Clarissa Peplow and Wing Commander Pearson, leaving her mother with Nicky who said, 'D'you want to sponge that skirt?'

'It won't stain.'

'Then come into the dining-room and see if you want this furniture.'

On their way past Susan Mildred spoke to her.

'I'm going into the next room for a moment. You'd better keep an eye open for Captain Samuels. I don't think he knows anybody.'

'Is this him now?' Clarissa asked. They turned to look.

Susan said, 'Oh yes. That's Sam.'

Nicky Paynton threaded her way back towards a door that stood open to the side of the verandah. 'Come in,' she shouted when still a few feet away. 'I'm Nicky Paynton, the one who's throwing this shindig.' She pushed her hand out at him and kept it there until he relieved her, as it were, of its weight. The noise in the room had begun to subside directly it became clear why Nicky was making her way towards this part of the room. Here was the stranger: the Jew-boy trick-cyclist. The noise diminished to such a degree that the sounds of merriment in the dining-room seemed to belong to a different party, almost a different world; one safe from such an intrusion. Astonishment more than curiosity caused the hush accentuated by the continuing drone of a male voice which, finding itself solo, ceased for a few seconds and then resumed, nudging the general conversation slowly back to life.

Captain Samuels was slender, fair-haired. He looked

down on Nicky from above average height. He did not smile. When she let go of his hand he did not let it fall but lowered it carefully. He did not attempt any of the opening gambits which a guest might have used in the special circumstances which had brought him to the party. He did not appear to have spoken at all. He gave the impression of being a man who had dispensed with casual physical responses as timewasting.

The image of the Jew-boy trick-cyclist was completely shattered. He was remote, patrician; in the opinion of most of the women present disturbingly, coldly handsome. It was a shock to see, on closer inspection, how young he must be. His youthfulness made the attention he instantly commanded seem, to those who were giving it, as disagreeable to them as a personal affront would be: the more so because he did not appear to be conscious of any obligation to conduct himself with that air of apology for *being* young which was usually considered part of a young man's charm when in the company of his elders.

Theoretically, Nicky might have been said to lead him into the room. In practice she went ahead to prepare a way for him to use. At the end of it stood Isobel Rankin. He took his time reaching her.

'May I introduce Captain Samuels?' Nicky said. 'Captain Samuels, Mrs Rankin, the wife of our area commander.'

They murmured how-do-you-do to one another.

'Are you related to friends of ours at home, Myra and Issy Samuels?' Isobel asked him, after he had declined the drink which Nazimuddin offered on a tray.

He observed her very closely.

'Sir Isaac Samuels?'

'Yes.'

'No. He is no relation.'

'But I gather you know him.'

'Professionally. I've met Lady Myra at Chester Square.'

'If you've met Issy professionally does that mean you're interested in tropical medicine too? If so you're in the right place. How long have you been in India?'

415

'Since the middle of May.'

'And in Pankot?'

'Since the end of May.'

'Really? As long as that!'

Listeners, hitherto fascinated by the social connexion through mutual friends of the general's lady and the young army-doctor, now recognized a rebuke. Captain Samuels had neither sent in his card nor signed Isobel Rankin's book outside Flagstaff House: an essential step for an officer to take if he wanted to be considered officially on-station. In the old days for an officer to have been on-station since May and not to have signed the book by the end of August would have been unthinkable. Nowadays, with so many people coming and going and holding temporary appointments the ritual was not so strictly observed, but for a man appointed to the staff of the hospital not to have observed it was still a serious omission, the result either of sheer ignorance or, which was worse and presumably the case here, indifference.

'I know absolutely nothing about psychological medicine,' Isobel continued when it was clear that Captain Samuels had no comment to make. 'I don't suppose Guy Charlton does either.' She referred to the chief medical officer, Beames's military counterpart, who was new on-station himself. 'So I imagine you pretty well run your own show. Are you a Freudian or a Jungian? Isn't that what one is supposed to ask?'

For the first time Captain Samuels allowed himself a flicker of emotion: it seemed to be amusement.

'People do,' he said. 'Personally I find Reich's ideas on the subject of considerable interest.'

'And what does or did Mr Reich say?'

'Any answer I could give would be an over-simplification.'

'That would be the only kind I would understand. So do tell us.'

Again he studied her. But Isobel Rankin had never yet been quelled by a look and wasn't now. He glanced at Nicky, at Colonel and Mrs Trehearne; briefly at Lucy and

Tusker Smalley who had joined the group; either sizing them up or politely including them in the conversation.

'One must draw a distinction between analysis and treatment. Whatever the cause of a neurosis the psychotherapist is concerned with a patient's ability to relax, physically. This is a simple extension of Reich's belief that the human orgasm is a major contributory factor to physical and mental health, but the corollary need not be that all neuroses are rooted in sexual repression.'

Several seconds went by before Tusker Smalley went red in the face and said, 'Good God!'

Isobel Rankin glanced at him as if to stop him from making an issue of an officer having dared mention such things in front of women. The smile on her face was perhaps a little set, but she directed it again at Captain Samuels.

'What particular branch of tropical medicine interests you?'

'The amoebic infection of the bowels known as amoebiasis.'

'Oh, yes. What interests you so much about it? Surely it's of relatively minor importance? It's easily cured I gather. Is it one of Issy's pet subjects?'

'I wouldn't say so. But then I've come to the conclusion that in general English physicians aren't as interested in it as perhaps they might be, considering how large a tropical empire we have. And I would disagree with you, Mrs Rankin, when you suggest it is easily cured. Since coming to India it's struck me that even diagnosis is a very hit and miss affair. I should say that quite a fair proportion of my psychiatric cases are suspect of chronic infection, but it is very difficult to arrange for a convincing check.'

'What are the symptoms, a permanent kind of gippy-tummy?'

He smiled. 'It's rather different from amoebic dysentery. Unfortunately it can be contracted and carried for years until it eats through the walls of the bowels and invades more vital organs. At least that is the theory a few

417

people have. Without a convincing check it tends to go undiagnosed and the symptoms aren't alarming. A general air of languor, as lassitude. A tendency to concentrate the mind rather obsessively in one direction.'

'Why is a convincing check so difficult?'

'I think I should not explain why. I shall get a reputation for indelicacy. I apologize if my earlier remarks caused any offence.'

He looked at his watch.

'Not at all, Captain Samuels. I asked a question and you answered it. I see you are pressed for time.'

'I have quite a full afternoon ahead.'

'Then I expect you want to ask Mrs Bingham if she's ready to leave. But you must come up to Flagstaff House one day and tell me about these theories of yours. I'm always interested to hear a young man talking on his subject. I'll ask Guy Charlton to bring you along.'

Samuels made no answer. A slight inclination of his head towards her was his sole acknowledgement of her invitation. Several people in the group round them were astonished that Isobel Rankin had made it.

But having made it she ended the conversation by moving away. The group dispersed. He took the opportunity to look around the room. He did not appear to be interested in meeting anyone else. Eyes were averted if he chanced to look into them. Hints of extraordinary behaviour were already reaching people who had not heard the conversation. As soon as he saw Susan he went through the crowd towards her.

'Hello, Sam. Is it time?'

'If you're ready.'

She said she was. She introduced him to Clarissa, Mrs Stewart and Wing-Commander Pearson.

'I must say good-bye to Mrs Paynton,' she said. 'Will you come with me, Sam?'

He put a hand on her shoulder. The gesture, although brief, struck those who saw it as unnecessarily possessive. Susan belonged in the room. Samuels did not. But he was taking her away. She was allowing it; at least, the girl in the polka-dot dress was allowing it and it now occurred to the watchers that in a subtly disagreeable way the girl was not the Susan they knew at all but a creation of Captain Samuels, or a joint creation of the two of them, a person who had emerged from a secret process of pressure, duress, insinuation, God knew what. And God knew what they talked about, or whom they talked about, when they were alone during sessions of analysis or whatever it was called. As Samuels followed her his glance fell here and there upon faces as if he were looking for evidence of mental and emotional disorders of the kind he had presumed to uncover in *her* but blamed *them* for. He bore himself like a man taking someone out of an area of contagion.

'Mrs Paynton,' Susan was saying, 'thank you for letting me come to your party. I'll only say *au revoir* if that's all right.'

Holding glass and cigarette in one hand Nicky used the other to give her the half embrace which had become part of her farewell party armour.

'*Au revoir* it is then, Susan. Probably true too. It could be ages before they pop me on to a plane.'

She nodded at Captain Samuels.

Mildred was waiting at the open doorway.

'Are you off now then, darling? Would you like me to come round this evening?'

'No, there's really no need. You must be bored stiff coming down every day, there's no reason to do it twice.'

That much was heard. Mildred went out with Susan and Captain Samuels. For a minute they stood talking on the verandah, then Samuels and Susan went down into the compound and climbed into the tonga that had been waiting. Mildred came back into the house, not through the doorway they had left by but through the main entrance. It was some time before she reappeared in the living-room and by then the party was beginning to break up.

When Isobel's car arrived to take her and Mildred back to Flagstaff House she said to Nicky, 'You and Clara come back with us. There's nothing as depressing as an afternoon surrounded by the remains. We could have a rubber or two and wind down.'

'Fair enough. I'll get rid of the late-stayers.'

She did so by announcing that she was shutting up shop. Within ten minutes the house and compound were clear. Lucy and Tusker Smalley were the last to leave. Their tonga, they said, was missing.

'What bad luck you do have,' Nicky said. 'Shall I send Nazimuddin for one?'

'We can pick one up on the road, I expect,' Tusker said. Lucy had her eye on the Rankin car but Tusker waved to Nicky and started off down the steps and presently Lucy followed.

'Pankot *must* be changing,' Nicky said, coming back in. 'Poor Lucy and Tusker failed to cadge a lift. I'm sorry really. It spoils the shape of my last Pankot party.'

A limousine such as could be hired in Ranpur to drive leave and summer parties up into the hills and down again was coming along Flagstaff road which turned and twisted and was not easy for two large cars to negotiate if they met head on. But for them to do so was rare. Only Flagstaff House traffic used the road. In any case the general's car always took precedence over local traffic. Assuming this the naik-driver taking Isobel and her guests home was prepared to glide on and up and give the minimum of room to the limousine which he expected to pull over and come almost to a halt.

On the limousine's roof there was a luggage rack, piled high and covered by a rainproof sheet. Perhaps this extra weight gave the limousine's civilian driver the strange idea that his vehicle was the more important of the two, even though the furled flag on the bonnet of the general's car proclaimed that this was not the case. If he saw this symbol of the car's status he ignored it. He came on. At the last moment the naik-driver called a warning to his passengers and slammed on the brakes. The limousine sailed past. The general's car quivered under the pressure.

'My God!' Isobel said. 'The raving bloody lunatic. Who was it, Clara? Did you see?'

Clara had the offside window seat in the back.

'There were blinds down at the windows, so I couldn't.'

'*Blinds*?'

The naik-driver had got out with squared shoulders and bunched fists. He thought the other driver would stop to apologize or argue. He looked forward to telling him off and earning a good mark in the Burra Memsahib's book who it was known liked men to be sharp on the draw. But the limousine sped on. It was already rounding the corner. He did not even have time to get its registration number.

'What do you mean, blinds, Clara? What was it? A damned hearse? What was it doing on Flagstaff road if it was?'

'Not a hearse. Just a car with blinds down.'

'Was there a crest.'

'I didn't see one.'

'The only people who drive with blinds down are Maharajahs.'

'Or their wives. Mostly their wives.'

'Well, if we've had a call from a spare maharajah and his harem he's got off on the wrong foot. Unless of course it was old Dippy Singh. *He's* as mad as a hatter. All right, Shafi. It wasn't your fault. Let's get on.'

At the end of the road the tarmac broadened, providing a turnround outside an imposing iron gateway. There was a sentry. The guard-commander was also present as if he had recently been disturbed.

'Shafi, stop at the gate and ask guard-commander about that car.'

He did so. The sentry was already presenting arms. He clattered. The guard-commander ran forward, came to attention and saluted.

Shafi spoke to him. Presently he said, 'He says the car stopped and a lady got out.'

'Yes, I heard.' She called over Shafi's shoulder in Urdu. 'What lady?'

'An English lady, memsahib. An old lady. She wore a topee. She came to sign the book, memsahib.'

'Thank you.'

She got out, went to the other sentry-box where the book was kept, on a shelf, chained. She was there for a few seconds and then came back and got in.

'Carry on, Shafi.'

As the car moved into the grounds she said, 'The first time wasn't a practical joke then. She's signed out. "Ethel Manners, *pour prendre congé*."'

There was silence. Then Nicky Paynton laughed.

'That,' she said between gusts, '*that* has made the day for me. *Pour prendre congé*!'

She was still laughing when the car stopped under the great portico in front of which, in the centre of an immaculate lawn, in a circular bed of white chippings, stood the tall white flag-post, moored to the ground by ropes, like the mast of a ship. From this eminence great stretches of the Pankot valley were visible. Early afternoon sunlight shone upon it. Before going inside Nicky Paynton stood for a moment, still shaken by spasms of laughter, and gazed. Then, turning her back on it, she opened her handbag, got out a handkerchief, dabbed at her lower lids and joined her friends for what might be their last game of bridge together.

It was. Nine days later, aching in every bone and deaf in both ears, she stepped out of a Dakota on to the tarmac of an RAF aerodrome and into the amazing unreality of the Wiltshire countryside.

4

When October came Barbie stopped taking the spoons to the church with her. The old lady must have gone. She packed the spoons up, wrote a letter and asked Clarissa if one of the servants could take them to Commandant's House. Clarissa agreed. She had become solicitous. The next day Barbie had by hand a letter of acknowledgment from Colonel Trehearne. He asked her if she would do him the honour of dining with him on Ladies' Night in November.

For a day or two she did not reply because she knew she would not accept but while the letter of apology and thanks remained unwritten she was able to enjoy the pleasure the invitation had given her. Ankle-length black velvet, she thought; a brooch, no other jewellery. A special cropping of the hair and a set to add lustre to the soft natural waves on the crown of her head and forehead. Black slippers and a glittering black evening bag. Perhaps a velvet rose – crimson or purple – instead of a brooch. No. The brooch would be more distinguished. A gossamer-thin black silk chiffon stole to warm but not to hide completely the marble of her arms and shoulders. For the journey there a cloak of the same black velvet as the dress but with a warm scarlet lining. Perhaps a gilt or silver chain for the clasp at the throat. Elbow-length gloves. White, these. Or black? White, if she wore the brooch. Black for the coloured velvet flower. And a fine lawn handkerchief sprinkled with cologne.

When her letter pleading unfitness had been sent she studied the reflection of her wasted bony body and the lank straight hair that needed cutting. In such a dress all you would see would be the wild untended head, the gaunt collar bone and corded wrinkled neck, the scarecrow arms, the tombstone teeth that were too big for her mouth. And hear what had once been a voice; a hoarse grating sound alternating between a crackling whisper and an uneven cry.

She put Colonel Trehearne's letter in the drawer of the portable writing-table where there already lay the letter from the bank and the letters and picture postcard from Sarah in Calcutta and Darjeeling. The letter from the mission which had arrived on the morning of the christening and the undelivered letter to Captain Coley she had destroyed. The picture postcard from Sarah showed the headquarters of the Bishop Barnard in Calcutta and was postmarked September 6 which was the day Mildred had left Pankot with Susan, the baby and the ayah, and the day before Captain Travers had let Barbie come back to the rectory bungalow.

'You'll recognize this,' Sarah had written on the back. 'I hope you're better. I'm better too, fit as they say for human consumption again. Love, Sarah.'

Like so much that had to do with Sarah the postcard was an enigma. Normally the only place you could buy the card was at the headquarters of the mission itself. But Sarah did not say whether she had been there.

Walking, she found it difficult to go further than St John's in one direction and Mr Maybrick's bungalow in the other. For the bazaar she sent out for a tonga and did not get down from it until it returned her to the rectory bungalow.

In the bazaar she had the wallah stop outside Jalal-ud-din's. The first time she did this a minute or two went by before a ragged little chokra came bare-foot in search of an errand and an anna. But nowadays she was met at the outskirts by a dozen or more who ran behind the tonga advertising their prowess, willingness and honesty.

At first her own little boy had joined the opposition but, reassured of her loyalty, now waited outside the store until she arrived. To reach her he had to fight his way through a thicket of limbs mostly sturdier than his own. She gave him a list and money and clear instructions. While she waited she distributed sweets to the others. If there was a list for more than one shop she gave him one list at a time. The other boys lost interest once they had had the sweets but her own little boy ran to and fro from shop to tonga, tonga to shop, rendering a meticulous accounting between each visit. The purchases were mainly Clarissa's. When there were a lot of packages the chokra rode back with her to the bungalow, sitting at the driver's side, and helped her to carry the packages up to the verandah. Out of her own money she gave him a percentage of the total expenditure. She hoped that he got commission from the shopkeepers. She did not always specify which shop he should go to and sometimes he was gone for quite a time. Invariably, then, he came back with a bargain. Clarissa was pleased.

They conversed in a mixture of Urdu, Pankot hill dialect and English.

His name, he said, was Ashok. His parents had died in Ranpur. He had come to Pankot to look for work. He had no relatives. He did odd jobs. He slept where he happened to be when finishing the last job of the day. He was eight years old. It was his ambition to work in the elephant stables of a maharajah.

'There are no elephants in Pankot.' Barbie pointed out.

No, he agreed. But in Pankot a boy could earn rupees. And then he could go to Rajputana. There were hundreds of maharajahs in Rajputana. Each one of them had a thousand elephants.

At home, Barbie said, most little English boys of his age intended to be engine drivers. He said to be an engine driver would be all right. Providing there were no elephants.

'Do you have to be a special caste to be a mahout or even to go near the elephants?'

He did not understand. He said his father had worked for the Ranpur municipality. Ashok did not say in what capacity. She decided he was a Harijan, a child of God, an untouchable. The elephants were his dream. Perhaps in Rajputana he would be allowed to clear away their droppings. But there was probably a caste for that too. She did not know. Hinduism, Mr Cleghorn had told her, is not a religion but a way of life. So, she replied, should Christianity be. He had given her an old-fashioned look.

'What am I?' she asked Ashok.

'You are Sahib-log.'

'No, I am a servant of the Lord Jesus.'

She sat on the verandah steps of the rectory bungalow and offered her hand. Ashok looked at her seriously.

'Come,' she said, 'I am your father and your mother.'

He came. She clasped his thin shoulders.

'You don't understand,' she said in English. He smelt musky. 'It is all too long ago and far away. The world you and I live in is corrupt. I clasp you to my breast but you conceive of this in terms of an authority unbending. I offer my love. You accept it as a sign of fortune smiling. Your heart beats with gratitude, excitement, expectation of rupees. And mine scarcely beats at all. It is very tired and old and far from home. Ashoka, Ashoka, Shokam, Shokarum, Shokis, Shokis.' Somewhere she had got that wrong.

He laughed. His eyes were luminous.

'*Chalo*,' she said.

She put a silver rupee into his tiny hand. He salaamed and ran. At the gate he turned. They waved to each other.

'*Tu es mon petit Hindou inconnu*,' she whispered. '*Et tu es un papillon brun. Moi, je suis blanche. Mais nous sommes les prisonniers du bon Dieu.*'

'It's uncertain how much longer I shall be able to visit you.' she told Mabel. She had begun to think of a grave as a closed entrance to a long tunnel, dark and tortuous, which you had to crawl through on your belly if you ever were to reach that area of radiance at its end. For a while, she supposed, you might kneel huddled against the blocked entrance getting up courage to begin the journey. There were days when she thought Mabel had gone and others when the sensation of her nearness was strong. Today she seemed very near. 'I'm sorry there are so few flowers. There aren't many in the rectory garden. I don't like to cut them without asking permission and don't like asking too often.'

When next she saw Ashok she asked him to buy flowers. He came back to the tonga with both hands full of stemless marigolds and jasmine. She scattered these on the grave. Thereafter he had flowers ready for her daily: some wild picked from hedges, others (she suspected) stolen from gardens. For such flowers he usually refused payment.

'Do you know what the flowers are for, Ashok?'

Yes, he knew, they were for puja. For worship.

'They are for my friend.'

Ashok looked troubled.

'I am your friend,' he said.

'Yes. I mean for my other friend.'

'Where is your other friend?'

'In Pankot.'

'Where in Pankot?'

'She is everywhere.'

Ashok looked round. Was she here now? Yes, Barbie said. Her other friend was watching them. His eyes swung this way and that.

'Is she my friend too?'

'Oh, yes. But you won't see her.'

'Can you see her?'

Barbie shook her head.

He accepted this.

From an edition of the *Onlooker* she cut out a picture of an elephant bearing a howdah-load of sportsmen. It was a small picture. She fitted it into the mica envelope in which she had kept her subscription library ticket and gave it to him.

'My friend asked me to give you this, Ashok.'

He stared at it for some time. Next to one of the sportsmen in the howdah there was a lady with a topee.

'Is that your friend?'

Barbie examined it. The face of the woman was out of focus. 'No,' she said, 'but it is like her.'

Pictures were important to a child.

'When are you going to Rajputana, Ashok?'

Ashok shrugged.

'When you have enough money?

He did not answer.

'Have you changed your mind?'

He nodded.

'But there are no elephants in Pankot. Why aren't you going to Rajputana?'

427

'I will go if you go,' he said.

That night, saying her prayers, she wept.

For quite a long time after Clarissa gave her the envelope with the mission's name on it and a Calcutta postmark she did not open it but sat on the edge of her bed observing how still the old eavesdroppers were.

She knew without reading it that the letter was from Mr Studholme and that the only reason he could have for writing to her was to offer her a place in one of the bungalows the mission kept in Darjeeling and Naini Tal. Someone had died and left a vacancy. She did not want to fill it. In such a place she would die herself, unwanted. She would have to go but it would take courage. She picked the letter up and considered the consequences of destroying it unopened. But she could not cheat Clarissa like that. Was it good news about accommodation – ? Clarissa would ask at lunch. And then she would have to lie.

She went into the bathroom and brushed the taste of the lie out of her teeth.

She returned to the little room of which she had become almost fond because Mabel knew she was in it and she had survived to come back to it; Clarissa had become amenable and the creeper outside the window had not entered. An extra tack kept the crucifix straight when she brushed past it. Each toenail she had discovered, was beautifully wrought. The old people behind the curtain were enemies but were kept at bay. After she had read the letter they would part the curtains, advance on her and smother her. An act of mercy.

She cut the envelope with a sandalwood paper-knife whose upper edge was carved in the shape of a string of tiny elephants. Mr Maybrick had given it to her to welcome her back to what he called the land of the living. He hated hospitals. Which was why he had not visited her. It was quite a long letter. It was signed by Mr Studholme.

My Dear Miss Batchelor,

First let me say that this unfortunately is not to give you news of a vacancy at Mountain View in Darjeeling or at The Homestead in Naini Tal. However rest assured that I have your situation well in mind.

I write to you for two reasons and must in fact apologize for not having written weeks ago when I was told that you had been rather unwell but were recovering nicely. We oldsters are not so easily laid low. After years in the country I think we develop a special resilience. (Lavinia Claythorpe, up in Naini Tal, is eighty-eight this month.)

My informant about your illness and recovery was a Miss Sarah Layton whom I had not had the pleasure of meeting before but who called one day while staying in Calcutta with relations. Well that is the first reason for writing, to say I hope you are now perfectly fit again. I heard how indefatigable you had been looking after the poor lady whose death left you in some uncertainty about a permanent home. The second reason I write is really to test the ground for asking a particular favour. I am encouraged to do so by your earlier offer of voluntary services.

You will appreciate that since the beginning of the war the flow of recruits to our mission has been severely curtailed. Young men and women at home have had to answer other calls. Increasingly we have been hard put to it to fill teaching posts effectively and there is one area in which for a variety of reasons this difficulty has become temporarily rather pressing.

I am sure you will remember Edwina Crane? She was superintendent of our schools in Mayapore district, amongst which is the little school on the outskirts of Dibrapur. Since the death both of the Indian teacher there and of Miss Crane the Dibrapur post is one we have found it not at all easy to fill.

Fortunately, six months ago, we were able to place a Miss Johnson, a Eurasian Christian, who has been very successful and whom we hope will continue as teacher in charge of Dibrapur for some time to come. However, Miss Johnson recently announced her engagement to be married and has asked for a month's leave from 12 December in order to solemnize the union and go down to Madras province with her husband. To this request, naturally, we have acceded. What has proved more difficult to arrange is a teacher to take her place while she is away. The Dibrapur school is an infants' and junior school, most of its pupils come from nearby villages not from the town. Unlike the senior schools in the towns it is normally closed for a few days only at Christmas. There is a bungalow nearby where the teacher in charge lives. Mayapore, I'm afraid, is seventy-five miles distant. One is rather cut off. The town of Dibrapur is not salubrious. But the troubles that affected that area are long since over.

The question is, would you consider filling in for Miss Johnson? We should be most grateful. A telegram saying one way or the other would settle the matter. If your answer is in the affirmative I will at once instruct Miss Jolley in Ranpur to arrange your transportation from Pankot to Mayapore on, I suggest, 5 December, which would enable you to reach Mayapore on the 6th or 7th and have a couple of days with Miss Johnson in Dibrapur before she departs. The superintendent in Mayapore is Mrs Lanscombe whom I do not think you know. She would undertake all the arrangements for your reception and transportation at the Mayapore end. If you are agreeable I will ask Miss Jolley to telephone you at the rectory bungalow as soon as she has effected all the necessary bookings so that she can give you the details. Meanwhile my sincere good wishes: Cyril B. Studholme, M A.

She read the letter twice before folding and returning it to its envelope. On the second reading she knew what Sarah had done. She had visited Mr Studholme to disabuse him of any idea he'd got hold of that the old warhorse was past it. She had done this subtly, so that he had not realized it and had even forgotten to write a letter of good wishes on

430

her recovery from her illness. With this gesture of Sarah's, practical, unobtrusive, Barbie felt that their relationship had been sealed in a way that touched her more deeply than any open declaration of esteem could have done.

She put the envelope in her handbag. Again, as at the time of Colonel Trehearne's unexpected invitation, she wanted to be enclosed in the world of her private happiness so that she could experience it fully, exist for a while at its tranquil centre which was not a fixed point in space but a moving one gliding across a flat landscape in the long straight line which, in her imagination, was the road to Dibrapur. She shut her eyes and in the dim room turned her face to the enormous white sky and the scorching oven-breath of the sun that baked the earth and the body to a holy exhaustion.

India, she thought. India. India.

India, she whispered.

She said aloud, 'India. India. India.'

The children laughed. Say it again, Barbie Mem, they chorused. India, she cried. The first syllable was inaudible and the second seemed to spring shrieking from her throat, hover, then fall like a bird struck dead in flight. She lowered her voice and spoke in the breathy tone adopted for talking to Arthur, Clarissa, Edgar Maybrick and little Ashok. I must conserve my real voice, she said. Conserve it for use in the schoolroom at Dibrapur.

But her real voice had gone. Would the warmth of the plains restore it to life and vibrancy or was it permanently damaged? Would a Pankot winter of cold nights complete its ruination? These questions were rhetorical. The damage to her voice in spite of Travers's assurances was a punishment whose sting she only truly felt this morning. If she accepted the mission's invitation she would be doing so under false pretences.

She could only pray and having prayed decline, because prayer had long since become a matter of form, of habit. She did not even bother to kneel. Oh, God, she said, give me back my voice.

* * *

431

When she reached the hall she said loudly, 'Clarissa!'

The bead curtains merely shivered. They should have opened.

With the letter from Mr Studholme firmly held in one hand she parted the beads with the other and clattered through into the sea-green incorruptible room. And stopped.

Captain Coley rose.

Clarissa said. 'There you are, Barbara. I was just going to send to see if you had a moment.'

'Oh, I have plenty of moments.'

The old crone, cracking jokes. There had been a night when she felt she could have toppled this man over merely by placing a finger on his chest. Was there hair on it? She knew nothing except the prone view from above. They were looking everywhere but at each other. Mostly they looked at Clarissa who gleamed under this concentration of light.

Clarissa spoke: an oracle with questions instead of answers. With Coley present Clarissa had reverted. She no longer looked solicitous. She spoke as she might to children from whom it was her duty to prise secrets.

'There is some mystery,' she said, 'about a trunk in the mali's shed at Rose Cottage.'

'No mystery,' Barbie replied. 'The trunk is mine. Is it required to be removed?'

Clarissa silently referred the question to Captain Coley. Apt Coley. Barbie turned to him. His face (that martyr's face) was red and, she could have sworn, stippled with sweat on the anguished forehead, although the daytime November warmth had not come into Clarissa's room with him.

'Be appreciated,' he said.

Clarissa explained. 'Captain Coley is keeping an eye on things while Mildred is away, you see.'

'Including the gardening implements?'

'Not exactly,' he said. 'Spot of bother. Between the mali fellow and old Mahmoud.'

'Is not Mahmoud on leave?'

432

'Came back. Going to Calcutta tomorrow to join Mildred. Mrs Layton.'

Apt Coley did not use many words. After a decade and more as adjutant of the depot words were probably meaningless to him. Since his routine did not vary from one week to the next, year after year, he must use the same ones every day of his life.

'What was this spot of bother between the mali and Mahmoud?' she asked him.

'Suspected theft.'

'Why on earth should Mahmoud suspect theft? My name is clearly printed.'

'Covered. Trunk covered.'

'But didn't mali explain it was mine and that he had it only to look after for me?'

'That's why I'm here. Check his story.'

'But you still want it removed.'

He looked round the room as if looking for a place where it might go.

'Be appreciated,' he said eventually.

'When? Today?'

'Heavens, no.' For a moment he was almost stung to articulacy. Perhaps he feared one thing as much as a posting he couldn't get out of. The word Urgent. 'They'll be home for Christmas. Twentieth actually. Loads of time. Month in fact.'

'But you'd like to tell Mahmoud before he goes to Calcutta tomorrow that he can forget the trunk because it will be gone?'

The telephone rang.

Clarissa got up. 'That will be Isobel about the prizes for their farewell dance. Are you going, Captain Coley?'

'On duty that night, I'm afraid.'

Barbie knew that by farewell dance Clarissa meant the first and most important. There would be several others, in descending order of priority, with smaller bands, ending with a quartet. The Rankins were not going until after Christmas. No one knew where. They pretended not to.

'What a pity,' Clarissa said. Passing Barbie she added, 'Captain Coley is such a lovely waltzer.'

When they were alone the tension between them soared to a peak and then quite simply and quietly died as if they had survived an act of God and found themselves stranded and non-combatant.

'I danced too as a gel,' Barbie heard herself croaking. The 'gel' interested her even as she said it. It was a pronunciation a man like Coley might feel happy with. 'Which may surprise you. We danced at a place called the Athenaeum. Not *the* Athenaeum, naturally. I think it's real name was the Athenaeum Temperance Assembly. Every year there was a church charity ball. I loved the mazurka. My father taught me to dance when I was a child. He hummed the music. Once he danced me all the way down Lucknow Road.'

'Lucknow?'

'Lucknow Road. Camberwell.'

'Oh.'

'When will it be convenient?'

'What?'

'For the trunk?'

'Oh, that. I'll send it down.'

'Don't trouble.'

'No trouble.'

'There wasn't room, you see. For the trunk. But it's different now.' She waved the mission's letter. 'I'm back in harness. Going to Dibrapur.' Coleyism was catching. 'Clarissa won't mind about the trunk because it's only a week or two before I go. After that, who knows? If I do well Mr Studholme will be pleased with me, won't he? And I can stay in Mayapore for a while afterwards. Edwina's buried there. My friend, Miss Crane. I expect you remember. And then I'll be quite content to go to Darjeeling or Naini Tal. With all my luggage. I can always *write* to Colonel Layton when the war's over. I can leave it to him to decide where Mabel should have been buried. But I should like to see Rose Cottage just once more, Captain Coley. Preferably after Mahmoud's gone to Calcutta.'

'Going first thing tomorrow. Got him on a convoy to Ranpur.'

'Then the second thing tomorrow would be fine. Say eleven A.M.?'

'On duty tomorrow, I'm afraid.'

'Oh but that doesn't matter. Just tell mali. There's no need for you to be there.'

Coley inclined his head. There was a childlike grace about him which she suddenly understood and found pleasant. She felt that somewhere in the background he kept a box of bricks. She went with him to the hall where Clarissa, smiling and talking to the telephone, raised her hand in august farewell.

On the steps of the verandah Barbie said:

'Thank you for sending back my sou'-wester, Captain Coley. That afternoon I tried to deliver the spoons there was no one there. I must have lost it running – running in the rain.'

His face reddened slightly but the martyred look had gone, briefly, as it might have done centuries ago if a man from the bishop's palace had galloped up to the place of execution waving a paper that quenched the fire before it could take hold. He offered his hand which she took.

'Thank *you*,' he said. He hesitated. She feared a more intense declaration.

'Regiment most grateful. For the spoons.'

He turned, and went down the steps putting on his cap, thrusting his little cane under his left arm, making for a battered old Austin 7 which they both knew had been in the locked corrugated shed on that particular day.

5

She told the tonga-wallah she required his services for the entire morning and made a bargain. He was an enclosed dilapidated man with a curved nose and predatory sleeping eyes, a starved bird with folded wings.

'Is your horse strong?' she asked. 'Strong in the bone?' The three of them had bones aplenty. The horse was strong he said. She told him to drive her in the direction of Pankot railway station.

At the crest of the hill where the road led out of the valley through the miniature mountain pass she ordered him to turn round and stop. She got down and stood for several minutes. She could not see the celestial range of sunlit peaks. There was cloud there to the north-east, cloud that brought snow to the mountains and sometimes if the winds could carry them so far cold rain to the valley. But the late November sun was strong and the valley clean, bright, sparkling.

She pictured Aziz, arm extended, offering Pankot to her. She put out her own arm in conscious imitation and ordered the tonga-wallah to drive her back to East Hill and when he got there up Club Road. He gave no indication of having heard but when she got back in set off. No doubt he thought her mad.

Twenty minutes later they were passing the milestone half way up Club Road. There was no body lying there. All the bodies were buried but the jackal packs had multiplied; men ran with them on all fours, ravenous for bones. The tonga-wallah sat hunched letting the horse make its own pace.

At the entrance to the club it began to turn in as if this were its nature. 'No,' she called. 'Further, further.' Horse and man struggled for supremacy. The tonga lurched back on to its route.

They continued on and up past the familiar entrances to the bungalows between the club and Rose Cottage. She felt no pang. All this had been in another life. It seemed strange that it still existed. Staring at the road below her feet she counted the horse's paces and then said. 'Stop!' and glanced round. The equipage was outside the gates which the mali had left open, presumably because Captain Coley had told him to expect her. She imagined that most of the time while Mildred was away the gates were closed and padlocked. She told the tonga-wallah to drive in.

The first thing she saw was the trunk. It was uncovered. It had been placed conveniently on the front verandah at the head of the steps. The main door behind was shut and barred. The mali must be in the servants' quarters. She thought it lax of him to leave the trunk unattended and the gates open. Anyone could have come in and removed it. But he may have thought it too large and heavy for a casual thief. She went up the steps and tested the padlock. It was intact.

The trunk certainly looked bigger than she remembered. She had imagined it roped easily in the back of the tonga and herself up front sharing the driver's seat for the return journey. She glanced at the stationary contraption, the droop-headed horse, the drooped old man. He would need help, persuasion probably.

'Wait,' she said. The man said nothing. He was already waiting.

She edged her way round the trunk to gain the front verandah. Again she felt no pang to be standing on familiar ground. The unkempt plants on the balustrade looked confused by some rearrangement that was not clear to them and to which they would never get used. There was an element in the atmosphere that was neither warm and friendly nor yet quite cold and hostile. The window through which she could have seen into her old room was shuttered. She paused in front of it and had an impulse which she restrained to rap on the wood and cry: Is anybody there? and then to put her ear to the crack between the shutters and to listen for the sounds of the years she had spent there scattering in panic at the stranger's voice. She moved on round to the side where her old french window used to be. It was still there but was also shuttered. Again came the impulse to knock and again it was restrained, just in time. Her hand was already a fist, the knuckles resting against the wood which her forehead was almost touching. She stood like this waiting for the impulse to go away. When it had gone she felt hollow with her history, so long unused. She uncurled her fist. There seemed to be webs of newgrown flesh between her fingers.

She moved from the door and then stopped, arrested by a conviction that she was not alone. She glanced towards the corner of the bungalow where the rear verandah began, the verandah on which Mabel had died. It was coming from there, the sense of the presence, of someone in possession and occupation, of something which made the air difficult to breathe. She put her hand to her throat and felt for the gold chain with its pendant cross and then walked forward, turned the corner and gasped – both at the sight of a man and at the noxious emanation that lay like an almost visible miasma around the plants along the balustrade which had grown dense and begun to trail tendrils. The man stood as she had once seen Mabel stand, staring at the garden as if struck by a thought about it but also beyond it to the hills and where the mountains lay behind the impenetrable formation of sunlit cloud: a lean tall Englishman, dressed in civilian clothes and a soft tweed hat, his right shoulder towards her, his right arm extended and hand flattened upon the rail, gazing as from a height, upon a world spread out before him.

Fighting the sickness she called out, 'I beg your pardon. But would you please explain what you're doing here?'

Some ten yards separated them. He heard her voice but probably not the poorly articulated words. His sharp glance in her direction was not accompanied by any movement of his trunk or limbs.

'You,' she called again. 'What are you doing? This is private property, not a public right of way.'

She went to confront him. He let go of the balustrade, clutched the tweed hat at its crumpled crown and began to raise it; and then the nausea and her apprehension faded, scorched out of her by this courteous gesture. She had a wild notion that the man was Colonel Layton, released and restored and come home to find his family absent.

But she had seen Colonel Layton and the hat was now fully off, revealing a head and an unshadowed face, one half of which, the left, was branded under a lashless and uncanopied blue eye with a pink and white spider web of puckered flesh. There, on that side of his head, the man had been burned.

He put the hat back on.

'I'm sorry,' he said – and the apology served a dual purpose. 'My name's Ronald Merrick. I came to see the Laytons but the mali tells me they're in Calcutta. He invited me to stay while he made me a cup of coffee.'

He had moved round to face her. His left arm hung unnaturally stiffly. His right hand was bare. The left was encased in a black leather glove, the fingers and thumb of which were moulded to hold something invisible and useless.

'Oh,' she said. 'I do apologize. Of course, Captain Merrick. My name's Barbara Batchelor. I was *Mabel* Layton's companion. I used to live here.'

She put out her hand and at once wished she had not; not because by doing so she broke one of the stuffier rules but because the arrangements he had to make to reciprocate were complicated. Taking his hat off again, revealing once more the raw geography of his face, he inserted the hat into the black leather glove, clamped its fingers and then put his own warm living hand in hers.

'How do you do? Miss Layton mentioned you to me when she visited me in hospital. It must have been in connexion with a Miss Crane. Is that correct?'

'How clever of you to remember.'

'Not really. Sarah told me her Aunt Mabel's companion had been in the missions and often talked about Miss Crane.'

'Edwina and I were old friends.'

'Were you in the same mission?'

'The very same. The Bishop Barnard schools.'

'They are highly thought of. Were you in Mayapore?'

'No. I was in many places but never there. When I retired in nineteen thirty-nine I was superintendent in Ranpur.'

'That must have been a responsible post.'

439

She realized that she was trying to look at the right side of his face and the right eye and ignore the left. His short stubby colourless hair was stippled with grey on the left side and looked patchy. Had he been handsome? It was difficult to tell. She would have liked to touch the scarred side of his face and she had an equally strange desire to touch the gloved artificial hand and feel up the arm inch by inch to discover where the wood or metal ended and the flesh began. She thought she remembered Sarah saying it had had to be cut off above the elbow.

And she recalled then that Sarah had never liked him. Loving Sarah and believing in her though she did, she could not let herself be prejudiced in advance. He had acted with great physical courage; perhaps with moral courage too. His voice was wonderfully distinct; every word clearly enunciated. A man's voice.

She turned to where the chairs should have been, intending to invite him to sit. The verandah furniture was gone. She had not noticed it consciously until now. 'Oh, dear, they've taken away the chairs. We sat out almost every day even in December and January when it can be quite chilly in the shade even at midday. I suppose the chairs are inside. Mildred and Susan have been away since early September, and Sarah longer than that. She went to Calcutta with her aunt. Did she come and see you?'

'I left the hospital there in mid-July.'

'When did you reach Pankot?'

'Yesterday.'

'Are you here for long, for a holiday?'

'No, only for a week. I'm at the hospital for tests and fittings. But it's a kind of holiday. I'm allowed a lot of freedom so long as I keep the appointments with the medicos.'

She glanced at the hand. Perhaps it was new and painful.

'How disappointing for you that the Laytons aren't here. And *they'll* be sorry to have missed you. Especially Susan. She was tremendously grateful to you, for what you tried to do to save Teddie.'

440

Her voice had hit a patch of special roughness but she had also been hit by the terrible consequences for Captain Merrick of his heroic act, hit as never before because she hadn't known the man or been able to imagine in detail the ruined face and the awful artificial arm.

'My voice,' she croaked, and hit her chest as if to dislodge an obstacle inside, and wished it were in her power to heal them both. 'I had a very bad cold a while ago and this is the result.'

A movement caught her eye.

'Mali!'

She went to meet the man who had appeared on the verandah carrying a tray of coffee. Directly he saw her he set the tray on the ground and salaamed and then took both her proffered hands. His boy came up behind.

'Are you well, mali?' she asked in Urdu. 'And your wife? And the chokra. Oh! I can see he is well.'

All were well, the mali said. 'But look, Memsahib – '

He led the way past the high-grown plants on the balustrade to the steps where the view was not interrupted. She looked. And did not believe it.

All the central beds of rose trees had been dug up and turfed over. Lines of string and limewash mapped the place where a tennis court was being prepared. The roses in the beds that were left had been pruned down to bleak little skeletal bushes.

'Tennish,' the mali said. There were tears in his eyes.

She turned from the sight of desecration and found Captain Merrick smiling at the mali's boy because the boy's eyes were fixed on the black-gloved hand. He looked up at her.

'Have there been changes?'

'It's unrecognizable.'

'I was thinking just before you came what a fine garden it is, but I could see some work was being done.'

'It was once a mass of roses.'

'It must have been beautiful.'

Beautiful was an unusual word for a man to use except about a woman. She was grateful to him for using it now.

Her father had used it in similar contexts. Because of the poet in him.

The boy had taken up the coffee tray and the mali was unpadlocking the louvred shutters in front of the french windows of the living-room. He swung the shutters back and then went round the side of the house to the kitchen entrance.

'Would you like to see inside the house, Captain Merrick?'

'Only if you would like to show it to me. I'm content in the fresh air.'

'Then let's stay here. He'll be bringing out the chairs.'

The french windows were being unbolted from inside. With a creak one swung open and then the other. The mali came out with a chair she did not recognize; a dining-room chair. He set it down, went back in and came out with another. On his last journey he brought a basket-work teapoy which, like the chairs, must have come from the grace and favour. The chokra put the coffee tray down on this.

'Thank you, mali. I don't recognize the chairs.'

The chairs were from Brigadier Paynton Memsahib's house. Brigadier Paynton Memsahib had flown home to bilaiti.

'Yes, I know. What happened to our old table and chairs?'

The old table and some of the chairs were in the hall. The old sideboard was in the main bathroom. The rest of the chairs were in the mali's shed taking up room. All the old stuff might be sold. It was because Mahmoud had put the chairs in the shed that he had found the trunk and caused trouble. All the living-room furniture was being re-covered. The verandah furniture was in the bazaar being repaired and relacquered. The Indian carpet in the living-room was to be put in the young memsahibs' bedroom and a fine new Persian carpet had been ordered from Bombay.

From his expression Barbie saw that the mali, loyal to the old order, was nevertheless impressed by the new. In

442

time he would be impressed by the tennis court. Perhaps he already was and had only been upset for her benefit. That was very Indian. The tears in his eyes had been genuine but that was part of being Indian too.

They settled in the strange but elegant chairs and she dealt with the coffee. None of it mattered. For her Rose Cottage had ended with Mabel's death. She could not see the future that Mildred apparently saw for it. A Persian carpet was a wild extravagance. Or perhaps it was simply an investment. The boy brought out another cup and saucer and a plate of rather soggy looking biscuits.

'Roses or tennis balls,' she said suddenly. 'Which would you choose, Captain Merrick?'

He did not reply but took the cup of coffee in the one hand capable of dealing with it and which might still hold a racquet.

'I'm sorry,' Barbie said, choosing forthrightness. 'Were you a good player?'

'Pretty fair. I shan't miss it though so long as I can ride. I'm teaching myself to get up on a horse from the wrong side. I'm hoping to get a mount tomorrow. You need an arm with feeling and control in it to get up, don't you, for the horse's sake as much as your own, but the rest's a question of one sensitive hand and a couple of strong knees. Once I've mastered that there's no reason why I shouldn't train myself to play pat-ball too.'

'I think that's very brave.'

'Not at all. One's scale of priorities and comparisons changes, that's all. Actually it's rather like being born again. Even drinking a cup of coffee presents unexpected problems.' He smiled. 'But it tastes better when you get it.'

He stuck the saucer between the black leather thumb and forefinger, clamped them, picked up the cup and drank.

Having drunk he set the cup back in the saucer, reached over, lifted the plate of biscuits and offered it to her. After she had declined he put the plate back on the tray, chose a biscuit, settled back and began to nibble at it. The cup and

443

saucer were retained in that rigid grip. She noticed that he had taken the opportunity at some time to dispose of his hat by folding and placing it neatly into the right-hand pocket of his misty Harris tweed jacket. His trousers were fawn cavalry twill; the shoes chestnut brown with the high glassy polish of old shoes originally expensive and since well cared for. His flannel shirt was open at the throat. He wore a green silk scarf inside it.

Her eyes, taking all this in, now met his. He did not seem in the least embarrassed to be the object of such close scrutiny but met it with what she thought of as manly composure. Nevertheless she was ashamed of herself. She had been examining him as though he were not real. He had finished the biscuit and now drained his coffee cup. She wondered, thinking of the liquid going down, what intimate problems he also had to resolve, and looked away, saddened rather than embarrassed, and uncertain whether to offer him another cup. She sipped her own coffee.

'How are the Laytons?' he asked.

'Fine, I'm glad to say. I hear from Sarah sometimes. They've been in Darjeeling with Mildred's sister.'

'Mrs Grace. I met her at the wedding. Was the baby born successfully?'

'Oh yes, didn't you know?'

'I saw Sarah in June but I've heard nothing since. The nurse who specialled me told me Mrs Grace rang once to inquire how I was. I believe she was coming up to Pankot and that was early in July if I remember right. The baby was due about then, wasn't it? I suppose Mrs Grace was coming up for that?'

'No, the baby was born prematurely. In June. A little boy.'

'A boy? Teddie would have been pleased. And Susan?'

'Susan was pleased too.'

'I meant was she all right?'

'She had a difficult time but she came through. She was very brave. She was here on the verandah and Mabel was working in the garden. I was out. There was no one else

444

here. Susan saw her die. She acted marvellously. Ringing for the doctor first and then her mother. But the shock brought the baby on.'

'Mrs Layton senior's death was very sudden then?'

'Very sudden.'

She looked at him. His good arm was bent, the elbow resting on the arm of the dining-chair – a carver's chair, she supposed; her own had no arms – the good hand supporting his chin, one finger resting on his right cheek.

'She died the day Sarah was in Calcutta.'

'Yes,' He moved the finger from his cheek to the corner of his mouth and then tucked it under the chin. 'Sister Prior saw the notice in the *Times of India*. She thought it might be Sarah's mother. She knew Sarah's name was Layton and that she'd come from Pankot to see me, and Sarah said she might come again after the operation but she never did. Sister Prior thought she'd had to rush back here. She kept it from me. I wasn't shown the *Times* notice for a couple of weeks. Of course I realized at once who it was who'd died. I meant to write. But never did.'

'Didn't Sister Prior see the notice of the baby's birth a few days later?'

'I think she only looks at the deaths and marriages.' He smiled. 'Is there another cup of coffee?'

'I'm so sorry. Of course. No – leave it there.' She stood, poured the coffee. The cup and saucer were at a slight angle. She was careful not to fill the cup too full. She helped him to milk and sugar, then sat down.

He said, 'You're probably wondering how I knew to come to Rose Cottage.'

'Why should I wonder that?'

'Because the last time I was in touch with Sarah they were still at the Pankot Rifles address.'

'Oh, I see. Well. I suppose someone at the Pankot hospital told you they'd moved.'

'No.' He glanced at the palm of his good hand. 'I've not talked to many people at the hospital yet. But Teddie mentioned Rose Cottage quite a lot, Susan usually wrote to him from here, didn't she? She used to put the Rose

Cottage address on the flaps of the envelopes. He liked that. He liked to think of her in this setting. He said her father would inherit it when her Aunt Mabel died. But I'd forgotten that until I got to Pankot yesterday. I meant to get in touch with them at the other address or look them up in the telephone book. But as soon as I arrived I remembered about Rose Cottage and wondered if they'd moved in.'

'So you came up to see.'

'No, I came up to the club to sign on as temporary member but the secretary was out. They said he'd be back about midday so I took a walk up the hill. As soon as I started passing bungalows with names like The Larches, Rhoda and Sandy Lodge I was pretty sure I'd come across Rose Cottage. I thought I was out of luck after I'd passed the last place. But suddenly here it was. So I came in. The mali was working at the front.'

'You were fortunate to choose today. Mali was expecting me. Otherwise you'd have found the gate shut and padlocked. I came to collect my trunk. I expect you saw it.'

'Yes, I noticed a trunk. Where are you living now?'

'At the rectory bungalow. You saw the church spire? Well, it's just behind there. You must visit us. And there will be lots of other people here who'll be anxious to meet you.'

'Thank you.' He looked at his black glove. 'Not too many, I hope.'

'I'm afraid so. You're famous. Not only because of what you tried to do to save Teddie but because of your connexion with the Manners case.'

He continued to regard her.

'She was here you know,' Barbie said.

'Here? Miss Manners?'

'No, no, the aunt. Lady Manners. She came to Pankot this summer.'

'Oh, yes. Sarah told me the name had appeared in the Flagstaff House book. She said no one had seen her though. I never met Lady Manners myself.'

446

'I saw her. In the church. I knew it was her. It couldn't have been anyone else. But she must have gone. I've never seen her again. Forgive me, perhaps you prefer not to talk about it. After all, if it hadn't been for that awful case you'd probably still be DSP in Mayapore or something even more important like a Deputy Inspector General.'

Chin back in hand he continued to regard her. Briefly she found the situation disturbingly familiar, as if they had sat like this before in another life. Now he removed the cup and saucer from the smooth black glove and replaced it on the tray. He took out his cigarette case.

'Why do you say that, Miss Batchelor?'

'Isn't it true? People have always said that your superior officers failed to stand by you.'

He offered her a cigarette. She declined but asked him to smoke if he wished. She glanced round. The mali's boy was watching from a corner of the bungalow. She told him to bring out an ashtray for Captain Merrick Sahib. Merrick had selected a cigarette, returned the case to his inside pocket and taken a gold lighter from another. The live-hand had great dexterity. He blew out smoke. The mali's boy came with a brass ashtray. Merrick looked at him gravely then pointed at the gloved artefact. With a frown of concentration the boy tried to place the ashtray in the palm. Merrick reached over to help him secure it between the finger and thumb. The boy stood back, arms behind him, prepared to watch.

'*Chalo*,' Barbie said. When the boy had gone Merrick smiled at her.

He said, 'The curiosity of children has a great therapeutic value.' He blew out smoke again. 'Reverting to that other subject. I ought to correct any impression people have that my department failed to stand by me. It was an impression we were quite willing that the Indians should get. Nothing takes the steam out of the opposition more effectively than appearing to remove the cause of the conflict or complaint. But I always imagined our own people understood that.'

447

'But weren't you sent to a rather unpleasant area?'

Merrick was regarding her again. The eyelid from which the lashes appeared to have been burnt looked fixed. She found herself watching it to see if it blinked.

'Only with my full approval,' he said, 'and on the understanding that the department wouldn't stand in my way, if I renewed my application for a temporary commission in the army. I applied originally in nineteen thirty-nine and they sat on it then. And subsequently.' He paused to take in another methodical lungful of smoke and then let it escape in puffs with each of his next words. 'Actually you could say the army was my reward for my handling of the Manners case.' The smoke had gone. 'But probably only my Inspector General appreciates that fully.'

He noticed how her glance fell on his ruined arm.

'I hope you don't interpret this elegant monstrosity as payment deferred for having made a tragic mistake.'

'Oh no.'

'They were guilty, you know. The IG agreed.'

When he put the cigarette to his lips this time she thought for an instant that his fingers trembled slightly but she must have been mistaken. The live-hand now hung free, unsupported except by the forearm on the arm of the chair, and the cigarette looked as steady as a rock.

He said, 'One in particular is guilty. The ringleader. He is guilty for the rest of them.'

He gazed at her through wreaths of smoke.

'His name is Kumar,' he continued. 'The worst kind of western-educated Indian. With all the conceit and arrogance of the Indian whose family owns or once owned land, plus the arrogance of the most boring and unprincipled but privileged English lad who believes the world belongs to him because he was taught at a public school to think he should rule it by divine right instead of by virtue of a superior intelligence. It's difficult to see why she fell for it, but of course he spoke and acted like an English boy of that type.' He blew more smoke. 'And he was extremely good-looking.' He had not stopped regarding her.

448

He said, 'Well, enough of that, I can see you find the subject painful. I do too. As a reasonably conscientious police officer it's rather gone against the grain to see six criminals comfortably put away as mere political detenus.'

'Painful yes. One must find it that. But that doesn't mean we should hide it away or pretend it never happened or that it's over.'

'Oh, it's over. The girl's dead.'

'The child's alive.'

He smiled. 'I mean the *case* died with the girl. I agree, the child's alive. His child, presumably. At least one presumes she imagined so.'

'You told Sarah you were fond of the girl yourself. And yet you sound so bitter. About her.'

He seemed quite undaunted. 'I *was* fond of her. I had to take that into consideration. But I think I stopped being fond of her when I realized which way she'd jumped. So it was never a serious impediment.'

She thought: What a curious word to use. Impediment. And – jumped. That's a curious word too. Sexual jealousy? Racial jealousy?

She found herself suddenly unwilling, unable, to consider the matter. She felt drained of imaginative energy. She stared at the embryo tennis court. It meant nothing. It was simply a place to pat a ball to and fro, to and fro.

Between their feet the woman in the white saree abased herself. Beseeching them. 'We are gods,' she thought, 'and this was our garden. Now we play tennis. It's easier to beseech against a background of roses.'

That flash of inspiration had come, unexplained, unattended. But there seemed no more to come. She looked at him. Again he was regarding her. His chin was in his hand. He had stubbed the cigarette. It lay dead, bent double, on the little brass tray that had come from Benares on the banks of the Ganges where bodies were burnt and the ashes cast to float, float on, float out to an unimaginable sea. Her old trunk of missionary relics with them. Bobbing, lazily twisting, under a copper-coloured sun. Immense crowds came to the festivals on the banks of the holy river. Greater crowds than came to any church. The air was heavy with the scent of jasmine, decayed fish, human and animal ordure. In the trunk Edwina's picture sailed to a far horizon.

She said, 'I am your mother and your father.'

'What?'

'Man-bap. It wasn't that for Edwina. It was despair. But I suppose Teddie felt it.' She realized that in an oblique way – in his remarks about Kumar and a certain type of Englishman – he had been referring to Teddie, to men like Teddie, but she could not fathom his deeper references. The arm he had lost for Teddie span away too – on the swift current of the holy river: garlanded.

She had slumped forward, knees apart, feet splayed, her skirt stretched, elbows on her knees, her hands clasped.

'Tell me about my friend, about Edwina Crane. Was there much left?'

There was a long pause. She did not look at him. She stayed in that ungainly position.

'Enough to identify.'

She nodded. And to bury. She had never thought of that before. Never thought of the possibility that the coffin was light with a few scorched bones shrouded in fragments of burnt saree. 'And the letter?' she asked. 'What did she say in the letter, the one that was never read out at the inquest?'

'I'm afraid I don't remember except that it satisfied the coroner.'

'And satisfied the police. You remembered the picture. You must remember the letter. The letter was much more important to a policeman.'

'Is it important to you?'

'It might be.'

She glanced up. His chin was still resting on the live-hand, but he was looking at the garden.

He said, 'Well, it was a sane letter. Personally I should have recorded a simple verdict of suicide.'

'What did it say?'

'Simply that she was resolved to take her own life.'

'There must have been more.'

'You mean something to support the verdict of suicide while the balance of the mind was disturbed?'

'Yes, was there?'

'Personally I don't think so.' He seemed in a way to regret that Edwina had gone to hallowed ground. He added, 'But she did end the letter with the kind of statement that satisfied people she was off her head. The kind it was thought better not to read out. I can't think why.'

'What was it?'

He turned his head towards her, using his hand as a pivot for his chin.

'"There is no God. Not even on the road from Dibrapur."'

An invisible lightning struck the verandah. The purity of its colourless fire etched shadows on his face. The cross glowed on her breast and then seemed to burn out.

'"Not even on the road from Dibrapur?"'

He nodded.

For a moment she felt herself drawn to him. He offered recompense. He looked desolated as if Edwina's discovery were a knowledge he had been born with and could not bear because he had been born as well with a tribal memory of a time when God leant His weight upon the world. He needed consolation.

She became agitated. She felt for the gold chain and found it but it seemed weightless.

He smiled. He said, 'How serious we've become.' He shot the sleeve of his good arm and looked at the dial of a watch which he wore with the face on the inner side of the wrist. 'And I ought to be getting back to see the club secretary.'

She got up. 'No, wait. I want to give you something.'

She bent down to retrieve her handbag from the ground near the leg of the unfamiliar chair.

'Come, you can help me. The locks may be stiff.'

She waited until he had got to his feet and then led the

way round the verandah to the front, walking several paces ahead of him. The tonga-wallah sat hunched, half-asleep, his head at the same angle as the horse's. She saw to her horror that the horse had deposited a neat pile of manure between the shafts on the sacrosanct gravel of the drive.

She edged round the trunk and knelt on the first step, then scrabbled in her handbag for the key. The padlock clicked open easily, so did the left-hand clasp. The right-hand one had always been a brute. But it gave. She flicked the hasps up.

'Now,' she said. She raised the Pandora-lid, stared and cried out. From rim to rim the trunk was filled with the creamy white butterfly lace.

'But this isn't mine!'

She snatched at the lace and pulled it out. Beneath it were her relics.

'How did it get in here?' she wanted to know. 'I never put it in here. I've not seen it since the day Mabel showed it to me.'

She held the lace in both hands and then looked up to appeal to Captain Merrick. But the lace was before his time. She had a desire to show it to him. 'Look,' she said, and threw one end. He caught it deftly. She drew her arm back. The lace hung between them. The butterflies trembled.

'Isn't it beautiful? The woman who made it was blind.' She stared at and through this lepidopterist's paradise-maze but could see no further than the old woman's fingers. 'Mabel wanted me to have it for a shawl.'

He offered back the end he had. She gathered the lace in and then flung it over her shoulders.

'Can I carry it?' she asked, laughing. The lace smelt of camphor, lavender and sandalwood. These were the scents of Mabel's and Aziz's gift. 'She must have given it to Aziz, and he to me. During that time he had the key to my trunk.'

She pulled the lace off her shoulders. 'I'm sorry, Captain Merrick. You haven't the least idea what I'm

452

talking about. No matter. I opened the trunk' – she picked up the picture – 'to give you this.'

She held it up to him. He made to take it.

'No,' she said. 'The other hand.'

She reached up and helped to insert the picture into the rigid glove.

'It's small but much bigger than an ashtray. Is it too heavy?'

'I don't think so.'

The black glove, his good hand and one of her hands held the picture. Slowly they each withdrew the support of their living flesh.

'There you can do it. You can *carry* it.'

There was perspiration on his mottled forehead. He gazed down at the awkwardly angled gift.

'Oh, this,' he said. 'Yes, I remember this. Are you giving it to me?'

'Of course.'

One eyebrow contracted in a frown. The other – vestigial – perhaps contracted too.

'Why?'

She thought about this.

'One should always share one's hopes,' she said. 'That represents one of the unfulfilled ones. Oh, not the gold and scarlet uniforms, not the pomp, not the obeisance. We've had all that and plenty. We've had everything in the picture except what got left out.'

'What was that, Miss Batchelor?'

She said, not wishing to use that emotive word, 'I call it the unknown Indian. He isn't *there*. So the picture isn't finished.'

A drop of sweat fell from his forehead on to the bottom left-hand corner of the glass that protected the picture.

'Let me relieve you of its weight, Captain Merrick. I'll ask mali to wrap it in some paper for you. Meanwhile' – she began closing and locking the trunk – 'would you be so kind as to ask my tonga-wallah there to put the trunk in the back of the tonga? I'll ask mali to help him and also for some rope to lash it in. But I think it will require a man to order him to take it.'

'The trunk? In the back of the tonga?'

'What else.'

'I should have said it's much too heavy.'

'Oh, nonsense. It only contains my years and they are light enough.'

She strode round the bungalow calling the mali.

The trunk was roped, upended like a coffin on its foot, one edge resting on the footboard of the passenger seat, the other within an inch of the canopy above. The shafts of the trap were at a high angle. The bony horse looked in danger of elevation. The morose tonga-wallah stood at the horse's head, keeping it down.

She placed the lace shawl over her head like a bridal veil. Captain Merrick was examining the lashings and knots with a man's expert and wary eye for such things. At her approach he said, 'I don't advise this. Have you far to send it?'

'Just down the hill. To the church.'

'It's very steep. I think the fellow is right.' He jerked his head at the tonga-wallah. 'It's too great a load.'

'But I shall pay him well. He's an old man. The competition is very severe nowadays. The young drivers dash hither and thither and getting all the custom. It's a kindness really.'

'How do you intend to get back yourself?'

'In the front, of course.'

Captain Merrick said nothing.

'Do you disapprove of that? Of my driving hip to hip with a smelly old native?'

'The weight will be impossible.'

'But *I* shall balance the trunk. You see? We shall tip forward on to a splendid even keel. Are you walking to the club?'

'It was my intention. Mali says it may rain. Don't you think – '

But she interrupted. 'Where will you be going when you leave Pankot, Captain Merrick?'

'Simla.'

'For a holiday?'

'No. On army business.'

'We must talk again. There are many things I should like to discuss. I'll ask Clarissa Peplow to ring you at the hospital. At the military wing, presumably.'

'That would be very kind.'

She turned to the mali. She gave him twenty rupees. She ruffled the head of the mali's boy.

'Can you understand what I say?' she asked the boy in Urdu. He nodded. She smiled. In Dibrapur it might be all right.

She offered her hand to Captain Merrick. The mali had the packed picture ready for him.

'You won't forget the picture, will you? Will you help me up?'

They moved to the tonga. The footplate was very high. She felt his good arm take some of her weight. He had been a strong man. As she arrived under the canopy she was enclosed by the sadness of that. She stared down at him.

'Does it hurt?'

After a moment he smiled. 'A little.'

'Poor boy,' she said. Suddenly he seemed like a boy. A boy without bricks. 'You were going to be decorated. Did it come through?'

'Yes.'

'An MC?'

'A DSO for some reason.'

'But that is very distinguished, congratulations. Have you been invested yet?'

'Not yet. Next month I gather.'

'Where? In Simla?'

He nodded. She smiled at him compassionately. Simla meant the Viceroy. She felt that this would please him particularly.

'I'm sorry you missed the Laytons,' she said again.

'There'll be other opportunities,' he said. 'Shall I tell the fellow to get up?'

'If you would.'

He went to the horse's head. The old man came round, mounted, untied the reins from the rail and picked his whip out of the stock.

'*Au revoir*, Captain Merrick.' She adjusted the lace veil and raised her hand.

The equipage moved slowly and creakily out of the compound of Rose Cottage. As it turned into Club Road she saw the valley lay under a thin blanket of cloud and felt the first spots of a chill November rain.

She had not even noticed the sun go in.

The tonga gathered momentum. The old man began to apply the brake. Once or twice the horse slipped. Barbie could feel the weight of the trunk at her back: her years pressing on her pushing her forward, pushing her downward. She pressed her feet hard against the curved footboard but her legs had little strength.

There is no God, not even on the road from Dibrapur. But then (she argued) I am taking the road *to* Dibrapur, not from it. The tonga-wallah shouted at the horse which had stumbled. 'You mustn't shout at him,' she said. 'he's doing his best.' For some reason she longed to have the picture back. The rain was coming down quite hard. As they passed the club there was a flurry of tongas coming up the hill and about to turn in there. The old man's hands were knotted in the reins. One of the other wallahs shouted an insult.

'Hold your tongue,' Barbie shouted back. In turning her head she became more fully aware of the lace. Her head was a nest of butterflies. They were caught in the lank grey hair. She shut her eyes. Twenty stairs, including the landing floor. She began to sing. 'I've seen a deal of gaiety throughout my noisy life.' She opened her eyes.

Behind the equipage a peculiar light glowed on and off; winter lightning. Something troubled her. The lightning brought it closer. It was Mildred's face, eyes hooded, mouth turned down, quirked at the corners; glass held under her chin in droop-wristed hands.

The horse slid, stumbled, righted itself. It raised its tail. There was a smell of stable. The horse stumbled again. The old man jerked the brake on harder. She thought she smelt burning. She glanced at him. His eyes at last were wide open. He looked at her for an instant before redirecting his own troubled gaze at the road ahead and at the trembling flanks of his old horse; and Mildred's face was there again just for the split second it took for it to dissolve and reform and become the face of the man who regarded her, chin in hand, thoughtful and patient, so purposeful in his desire for her soul that he had thrown away Edwina's.

She began to tremble. She pressed with all her strength against the footboard. Below, Pankot lay shrouded by the mist of the winter rain which had left its snow on the summits. They were passing the golf-course. People were running for cover under coloured umbrellas.

Sometimes, although very rarely, these cold showers – penetrating the warmth of a Pankot November day – troubled the atmosphere and produced an imbalance, a rogue element of electric mischief that shattered the silence like a child bursting a blow-up paper bag containing flashes of paper fire.

There was just such an explosion now, as the rickety old tonga entered the steepest part of Club Road. It blared across the valley, jerking alive the unliveliest members of the club, comfortably cushioned in upholstered wicker, and was accompanied by the brightest amalgam of blue and yellow light ever seen in the region: an alert such as even the combined rifles of Pankot and its tribal hills could not have achieved by sustained fusillade.

The horse screamed; its eyes rolled; it reared, thrashing the space between its hooves and the greasy tarmac and then achieved both gravity and momentum, dragging and rocking the high-wheeled trap with its load of missionary relics.

Why! It is my dream! Barbie thought, hanging on to the blessing of it. Her hair flew long and black and she was a child dancing spinning down Lucknow Road and racing up the stairs and holding the pincushion high to her mother who held her black bombasine sides laughing to hear her father sing it:

I've seen a deal of gaiety throughout my noisy life,
With all my grand accomplishments I ne'er could get a wife.
The thing I most excel in is the P R F G game, a noise all night,
In bed all day, and swimming in champagne.
For Champagne Charlie is my name,
Champagne Charlie is my name,
Good for any game at night my boys,
Good for any game at night my boys,
Champagne Charlie is my name
Champagne Charlie is my name
Good for any game at night boys,
Who'll come and join me in a spree.

On the long downhill sweep the equipage gathered speed, out of control of the crazed horse. The wheel spokes span counter to the rims. Sparks from the burning brake and spray from the wet surface formed bow-wave and wake.

She opened her eyes and saw the toy-like happy danger of human life on earth, which was an apotheosis of a kind, and she knew that God had shone his light on her at last by casting first the shadow of the prince of darkness across her feet.

Careless of the shawl of butterflies she reached for the reins to help the old man resist the gadarene pull of the four horses. He tore at the monstrous membrane that blinded him and which blinded Barbie too like a great light followed by a giant explosion, a display of pyrotechnics that put the old November Crystal Palace shows to shame.

Ah! she said, falling endlessly like Lucifer but without Lucifer's pride and not, she trusted, to his eventual

458

destination. My eyeballs melt, my shadow is as hot as a cinder – I have been through Hell and come out again by God's mercy. Now everything is cool again. The rain falls on the dead butterflies on my face. One does not casually let go. One keeps up if one can and cherishes those possessions which mark one's progress through this world of joy and sorrow.

I remember (Sarah said) Clarissa Peplow telling me how Barbie suddenly marched into the rectory bungalow co-vered in mud and blood but still on her feet and said, 'I'm afraid there's been some trouble at the junction. Perhaps someone would kindly deal with it. I have seen the Devil. Have you a spade?'

The driver survived too. But the horse had to be shot.

Coda
Lines from the Hospital of the Samaritan Mission
of the Sisters of Our Lady of Mercy
Ranpur. December 1944–August 1945

'Good morning, Edwina,' Sister Mary Thomas More said. She had bad teeth. She smelt of garlic and of galloping corruption. 'Or are we Barbie, today? What are we looking at?'

Miss Batchelor wrote on the pad: The birds.

'I see no birds, Edwina. Aren't we speaking today, either? Is it a day of silence?'

Miss Batchelor wrote: It is the same as all days.

'Not all days can be the same. There is the one which we all await and ought to fear.'

Miss Batchelor wrote: Bugger off. Or bring me a spade. Suit yourself.

After Sister Mary Thomas More had pursed her crypt-like lips, Miss Batchelor added a postscript: And bugger the Pope.

There was bread and water.

It was the only food she liked. It was clean.

* * *

Sarah said, 'Barbie? Barbie? Don't you know me?'

Miss Batchelor could not hold the pencil because she could not see it and both her hands had been severed. When Sarah had gone they took away her shoes because of the tramping sound.

'Good morning, Edwina. Or is it Barbie? You don't know me. My name is Eustacia de Souza. I'm new. I mean I visit. You're my first. You must tell me all about yourself otherwise I shan't know what to do to help, shall I, and Mother Superior will be upset.'

Miss Batchelor wrote: You may tell me about the birds.

Miss Batchelor liked the look of Eustacia de Souza. Eustacia de Souza was as black as your hat, several shades blacker than Sister Mary Thomas More. Eustacia de Souza was not a nun.

Miss Batchelor added to her note: My name is Barbara, not Edwina. I am under a vow of silence.

'I understand, dear. At least I understand that part. I'm not sure I understand about the birds. Which birds do you mean?'

Miss Batchelor pointed through the barred window. Eustacia put on her glasses and peered.

'I can't see any birds, dear, apart from a few crows. You can't mean crows, can you? India's full of bloody crows.'

Miss Batchelor drew a picture of the horizon and a middle distance. She sketched a point of reference. A minaret.

'Oh, a heathen thing.'

Miss Batchelor shook her head. She struck the minaret through with her pencil and then drew a line and a ring. And made angular strokes, playfully. Like birds flying.

'Just a moment, dear.'

Eustacia clung to the bars like a helpful monkey. She was very ugly. Her bottom stuck out of a print artificial silk dress. She had white shoes and high heels. She stank under the armpits but it was the stink of hope.

'I don't actually see any birds there, Barbara dear. Are you sure they're still there?'

Miss Batchelor looked. She wrote: No – but they often are.

Eustacia sat on the spare stool and smoked and talked. About peculiar things. 'We've got them in Mandalay, dear. We'll be in Rangoon like a streak of piss before May's out. Cast not a clout. Old Billy Slim could screw me any time he asked, dear. Better'n my husband. Small as he is I'd put the flags out for Billy any day.' Eustacia frowned. 'Have you ever thought about length, dear?'

She did not look as if she required an answer. She looked at Miss Batchelor who sat contained by her dignity and desire.

'Do you have the least bloody idea what I'm talking about, love? Do you know where this is, dear, I mean what town for gods-sake?'

Miss Batchelor wrote: Ranpur, looking west.

Eustacia de Souza smiled and nodded. Then frowned again. 'West?' she said. She looked. She nodded. She smiled very wide 'That's where it is,' she said. Miss Batchelor was reminded of a melon. She felt thirsty.

She wrote: You must go now. It is the dangerous hour.

Mrs de Souza's face turned a nasty purple. When she had gone Miss Batchelor broke the tea-cups and waited for the relief of cold-water and winding-sheet. She screamed and struggled because that was the way Sister Mary Thomas More liked it. At the end the nun's coif was limp.

The landscape had changed because the light had altered. It was very hot. She wrote: Calendar. They brought her one. It said 6 June. She destroyed it. Next day they brought her another because Father Patrick was visiting. It said 7 June 1945. She put it on her bedside table, and, when Father Patrick had gone, under her mattress. But they did not take it away.

'How are you Barbie?' the girl with the fair helmet of hair said.

The calendar said, 30 June 1945. She wrote: I am in good health.

'Is there anything you want?'

She wrote: Birds.

'Birds?'

She wrote at length:

From the window, beyond the minaret, there are birds. Smudges in the sky. Not necessarily now. But there are birds there often. You can hardly see them but they circle, as though there is a nest there. There is a hill. Trees, I think.

She watched the girl reading the note. She put out her hand to touch her. The girl looked momentarily startled. Miss Batchelor withdrew her hand not wishing to frighten her. But the girl then reached out and held her.

'It's all right, Barbie. Let's look at the birds.'

They went together to the barred window.

Miss Batchelor tried to articulate. Her throat rattled.

'It's all right, Barbie,' the girl with the fair helmet of hair said. 'I understand. Where now, beyond the minaret?'

Together they watched. Distantly where the land folded there was a haze. Above it, birds.

'Yes, I see. I don't know why they're there. I'll find out. They must be quite big birds, mustn't they?'

Miss Batchelor nodded. She was proud of her birds.

She wrote to the girl: Do you live in Ranpur?

The girl said, 'No, in Pankot, at Rose Cottage. I'm only in Ranpur for two days I'm going to Bombay to meet my father.'

Miss Batchelor held the girl's hand. She felt that she had to say something important but could not remember what.

The girl came the following morning. She said, 'The birds belong to the towers of silence. For the Ranpur Parsees.'

Then she wrote it down on Miss Batchelor's pad as if she thought Miss Batchelor might forget it.

Miss Batchelor wrote: Yes, I see. Vultures. Thank you.

She looked round the room. She shook her head. She wrote: I have nothing to give you in exchange. Not even a rose.

For some reason the girl put her arms round Miss Batchelor and cried.

'Oh, Barbie,' she said, 'don't you remember anything?'

She nodded. She remembered a great deal. But was unable to say what it was. The birds had picked the words clean.

Often now she was left alone. Sister Mary Thomas More had used the word incorrigible. She sat at the window watching through narrowed hungry eyes the birds that fed on the dead bodies of the Parsees. At night she blew dandelion clocks and continued to blow them long after they had become bereft, deprived. To blow them to the bone was the one sure way she now had of sleeping, sure in the Lord and the resurrection and the spade.

A young Madrassi nun, observing her thus, and thinking old Miss Batchelor's hour had come, ran out into the darkling intermittently lit medieval corridor and brought the stark night-sister, who, standing in the traditional pose, with shriven fingers on patient's pulse, and uncommitted eyes, merely firmed her lips in imitation of the daylight brides, and then made a high mark on the bed-bottom board that charted the old missionary's journey across the hilly country of exodus.

Asleep Barbie no longer dreamed. Her dreams were all in daylight. Do not pity her. She had had a good life. It had its comic elements. Its scattered relics had not been and now can never all be retrieved; but some of them were blessed by the good intentions that created them.

One day after such a dreamless sleep, she woke, rose, knelt, prayed, splashed water on her parchment face from the rose-patterned bowl that sat like one half of a gigantic egg in an ostrich-size hole in a crazy marble top, dressed, had breakfast and marked off the calendar of the fair-haired girl's absence.

It was 6 August 1945.

The date meant nothing to her. No date did. The calendar was a mathematical progression with arbitrary surprises.

She took her seat at the barred window. Today it was raining. She could not see the birds. But imagined their feathers sheened by emerald and indigo lights. She turned away and rose from the stool. And felt the final nausea enter the room.

She stood, swaying slightly, in the ragged heliotrope costume which was stained by egg and accidents with soup, and then holding her naked throat, padded slippered to the secure refuge of her bed and sat, leaning her shoulder casually against the iron head.

She strained at the rusted mechanism of her voice and heard its failing vibrations in her caved-in chest.

'I am not ill, Thou art not ill. He, She or It is not ill. We are not ill, You are not ill, They are all well. Therefore . . .'

She raised a questioning or admonitory finger, commanding just a short moment of silence for the tiny anticipated sound: the echo of her own life.

They found her thus, eternally alert, in sudden sunshine, her shadow burnt into the wall behind her as if by some distant but terrible fire.

Appendix

'I find myself uncertain which of two recent events – the election of a socialist government in London and the destruction of Hiroshima by a single atom bomb – will have the profounder effect on India's future.'

Extract from a letter dated in August 1945 from Mr Mohammed Ali Kasim to Mr Mohandas Karamchand Gandhi.